FYRE

Justice at Cottonwood Falls

J.V. JAMES

Classic Old West Tales

Copyright © 2019 by J.V. James

All rights reserved.

No part of this book may be reproduced in any form or by any electronic or mechanical means, including information storage and retrieval systems, without written permission from the author, except for the use of brief quotations in a book review.

for Bob, the best storyteller I ever knew

CONTENTS

1. Sparks — 1
2. "Some signs is better'n others..." — 8
3. Tough as Old Boots — 16
4. A Hootin' & Hollerin' Hellabaloo — 24
5. The Cunning of a Flannel-Mouthed Liar — 31
6. Hightailin' — 40
7. Telling Cass — 46
8. Scattergun — 54
9. "Helluva thing..." — 61
10. "Just Don't Start Singin' Lorena" — 69
11. The Dwarf & the Sheriff — 77
12. Letters Home — 87
13. Shootin' Lessons — 94
14. The Red Legs — 101
15. Morris's Ma — 108
16. Smiles All Round — 118
17. Some men is better'n others... — 125
18. The Great Iron Horse — 136
19. Old Pap and the Seven-Thousand — 144
20. Preacher Rob Brimstone — 152
21. Fyre! — 160
22. The Looting of Boonville — 167
23. The Battle of Glasgow — 176
24. Sure Glad I Ain't an Inch Taller... — 183
25. The Taming of Marshal Clem Jenkins — 192
26. Grief — 201
27. A Secret Agreement — 211
28. A Battle Both Lost and Won — 218
29. Deputy Billy Fyre, U.S. Marshals — 228

30. "She's no whore and you know it…"	237
31. On for Young and Old	242
32. Some spots is better'n others…	249
33. The Old Unrest	256
34. Friends Reunited	267
35. "Man at the pot!"	276
36. A Part-Your-Hair-From-The-Left Man	284
37. ROOMS ~ WHISKEY ~ GIRLS	293
38. Tiny Jones	299
39. "My friend's kinda simple…"	306
40. Sick as a Barber's Cat	312
41. The Chucklehead Act	320
42. A Sad Death	330
43. This Prideful Man Means to Kill Me	338
44. Ever Seen a Sheep Ride a Horse?	349
45. Remember the Alamo!	357
46. A Time to Die	366
47. "Lucky hat…"	372
48. A Daily Ritual	382
49. "You ain't my son…"	390
50. Harmony	395
51. A Lone Rider	402
52. "Listen, if this all goes catawampous…"	408
53. The Tunnel	416
54. Why Do They Always Wear Black?	421
55. "Why do people keep sayin' that?"	428
56. Half a Toe	435
57. "He's good that dwarf — real good"	443
58. "Breathe…"	448
59. Justice	455
60. Two Red Bandanas	461
61. Home Fires Burnin'	469

Also by J.V. James	478
Wolf Town	479

CHAPTER 1
SPARKS

North of Cottonwood Falls.
Tuesday, September 20, 1864.

It was a hell of a thing, the way Billy Ray's war began. He was not in attendance, and knew nothing about it for weeks. By the time Billy heard the beginnings of it, he was three-hundred miles away, and it broke his good heart.

What's more, Billy got lied to — and it would be seven long years before he found out the truth of it. And by then, his name would be Fyre.

But we had best start at the start, and it happened this way.

Billy Ray had a brother called Horace — he was the opposite to Billy in just about every sense that mattered —

and he surely did love to mistreat him. But we'll get back to that soon enough.

It was closing in on midnight, and there'd been just enough moon to ride by. Horace Ray and his only friend, Jasper Jenkins — both dressed all in black, and with mud smeared over their clean-shaven faces — crouched behind trees in the darkness. One out the front, one out the back, each within twenty yards of the house.

Young Horrie's pale blue eyes gleamed with a firebug's eagerness, as he reached out and lit up the torch. Then he put it straight to the rag in top of the bottle, enjoying the hissing sound it made when it caught. A cold smile tightened his long drooping face as he hurled that bottle onto the porch, right at Old Man MacPherson's rocking chair. That chair was thirty years old, and had worn its own grooves in the porch, well used as it was.

The flames kissed the dry old wood of that chair, and it caught right away with a crackle.

As MacPherson started awake in his bed, Horace lit the second bottle and lobbed that one too. Crash-tinkle it went, through the window into the parlor, and on its way through, the flames grabbed the curtains and leapt! So did Horace's heart — there wasn't much ever warmed his cold heart, but that boy always did love a fire.

The MacPhersons had no need of lamps now — they had firelight enough to see what they were up against, and their terrified calls were music to Horace's ears as he threw down his torch and scurried across to his rifle.

"Water, get water," cried Old Tom MacPherson from inside.

"Use the buttermilk," his much younger wife Lucy called.

"It's no use," yelled their only son, "We gotta get out now or we'll all burn alive!"

And then he came, Old Tom — a good man doin' what's right, protecting his family. He was everything Horace Ray wasn't.

Tom threw his front door open and charged right on out hell for leather, his wild eyes blazing, that shotgun of his raised up as he searched for a target — and a fearsome sight he was too, with the great orange glow of the flames all around and behind him. Like a halo for the righteous, those flames were.

But that good man never got off a shot, and he never went one step further.

Because Horace Ray had been waiting, had planned out this moment. He had his gun raised, at the ready. At twenty-three, he felt it was high time he killed a man — and worse, he hoped to enjoy it. He smiled cruelly from the edge of the darkness, and the moment Tom appeared in the doorway, Horace squeezed the trigger of his Spencer. He blew a hole right through the throat of his victim, who fell to the right of the doorway and crashed down onto the porch, his head busting the rocking chair to pieces. In less than a moment the fire, hungry for fuel, took a hold of his nightclothes. And the smell of burning hair filled the night.

Horace felt a vague disappointment then, for he'd done his job a little too well — he'd have liked to watch Tom burn alive, hear him cry out for mercy, see him running out into the night all afire, plead for someone to end all his pain. But he didn't last long enough to suffer — and before the fire was even searing his skin, tough old Tom MacPherson had gurgled his last.

The flames appeared to leap higher then, and the voices inside the clapboard cabin were growing ever more panicked.

"Who's out there? Why are you doin' this?"

Then a quieter, womanly voice said, "Quick, out the back way!"

Next came the great boom of Jasper's old Hawken, and the terrible sound a man makes when he's only half done for. Horace felt disappointed he wasn't around back to see it, for it was surely young Jimmy, and he'd never liked him.

Two pistol shots rang out, and Jimmy was finished. Then came the screams of a woman — the crackle and spit as the boards of the house began burning — the terrible yawn of the fire as it clawed its way onward and upward — the sparks fizzing and popping, floating this way and that way, curling and whirling up into the night on the waft of the heat and the smoke.

And then, the hacking voice of Lucy MacPherson, coughing her way through her pleading. "Please, please ... whoever you are, please don't..." Here the coughing took over. "Don't sh.... We're ..." She coughed and spluttered some more, then managed to force out some words. "We're c-c ... coming out the front door. P-please don't shoot us ... we're women."

Women? thought Horace. *There should only be one, for the sisters are surely in town. The woman must be confused.*

Lucy Macpherson stepped into the doorway, her hands

in the air, her head hunkered down into her shoulders as if that might save her from bullets.

"Come out," Horace called, his own voice strange to his ears. Somehow too excited. Too young, not enough like a *man*. And then deeper, "We won't shoot a woman."

"Horace Ray?" Lucy called out, almost dazed. "No. Is that really...?" Then she noticed her husband, dead and smoldering beside her, blood pooled on the boards near his throat, flames licking all round him, and she half-sobbed, half-screamed. But the noise she made died in her throat.

Because Jasper Jenkins stepped round the corner right then and, easy as if it was just some church social, said, "We don't shoot women. But we sure got some fun planned for you, Ma'am. I always did like the look a' you. What are you now, almost forty? Best we get started right away!"

That was when Annie MacPherson stepped through the door behind her mother, and commenced firing her father's old Colt — firstly in Jasper's general direction, then in Horace's, which sent both of them darting for cover.

Five shots later she was defenseless, and Jasper was on her. He tackled the girl to the ground, then laughed it up big as he threw her over his shoulder. He carried the girl away screaming, the relentless heat of the cabin behind them, and Horace did the same with her mother.

Annie beat on Jasper's back with her fists as she cursed up a storm — but Lucy, by now, had gone silent, but for one choking sob.

"You've damn well ruined everything, Annie," said Horace, as soon as the pair dropped the women to the ground, forty yards from the fire.

"*Me?*" she cried. "*Me?*" Then she coughed 'til her eyes almost popped, as her mother patted her back, and made gentle sounds.

"Yes, you," Horace growled, and he walked up and down, up and down, his fists curling, uncurling, and curling again with each step the whole time he spoke. "Aw, Annie, I had it all planned out for us, and now ... this!"

"Now what are we gonna do?" said Jasper, taking his hat off and throwing it down on the ground before kicking it across the dirt. His blond hair shone in the firelight as he yelled, "Annie won't marry ya now! I still get Cass though, right?"

"*Marry?*" cried Annie and Lucy together.

"Shut up, you fool," Horace yelled. "Oh, Annie, what are you doin' here? It's Wednesday, you're meant to be in town with your sister and that old biddy seamstress!"

"She's sick," said Lucy, her voice breaking. "She felt poorly, so I kept her home." Then Lucy MacPherson crawled quickly toward Horace Ray, reached out and grabbed hold of his leg where he stood, and looking up at him she pleaded. "Please, Horrie, please let us live. We won't say a word, I promise. We'll never tell who it was. We'll do anything you..."

"*I'm not marrying this murdering pig!*" cried Annie, and her voice was a rising crescendo of fury. "He *killed* Pa. He *killed* my little brother. He..."

"Shut your mouths!" Horace said, pulling out his revolver. "Shut 'em right now, or I'll blow both your damn heads off." Then he viciously kicked Lucy free of him, and wandered up and down, up and down again, rubbing at his long face with his left hand, waving his gun around with his right, as he muttered to himself all the while.

"Tell him you'll marry him," said Lucy quietly, urgently, to her eldest daughter. Then louder, "She'll do it, Horrie, I promise. I can talk her around. She's eighteen now, she *should* marry. Just let us live. I beg you. Please!"

"And Cass?" said Horace, spinning around and pointing his gun at the woman. "She'll marry Jasper?"

"But she's promised to your brother," said Lucy, and clearly, her tone judged him poorly, for the words had come tumbling out before she had time to think. Then quickly, but softer, she said, "I only meant, why would you—?"

"I ain't missin' out," yelled Jasper. "We had a *deal*, Horrie. We burns all they own, kills the men, enjoys the mother then kills her, and later we marries the sisters to save 'em from they's plight."

"Shut up you fool!" growled Horace, turning the gun on his friend now.

Then a strange look came over his face, and he smiled, just a little. He put that gun in its holster, walked over and picked up the screaming Annie and threw her over his shoulder. Then as calm as you like, he said, "Jasper, me and Annie's off to the barn. You take the mother here first, and then we'll swap over."

By the time they shot them three hours later, both men had had their fill of the terrified women. Then they dumped all four bodies inside the still burning house, and set about covering their tracks.

CHAPTER 2

"SOME SIGNS IS BETTER'N OTHERS..."

Wednesday, September 21, 1864

At the first soft light of the dawn, Billy Ray woke with a start. And though he knew right away there was no one nearby, he was filled with a grievous bad feeling. But Billy had no time for bad feelings — he had places to be, a cause he must fight for, a destiny to fulfill. He tried to wave that feeling away, to leave it behind like a dream.

I just slept bad is all.

The thought didn't help none. The feeling stayed well attached to him, so he got on up and got moving, to shake it away.

He couldn't think of no reason to feel bad. He was his own master, doing what he believed in. He was safe enough too, having chosen a good spot to sleep, in a nice little clearing by a stream, fifty yards off the trail, where no one passing by could possibly see him. No shortage of trees between his camp and the trail, and half a small mountain behind him. Well, it seemed like a mountain to Billy, being used to mostly flat land as he was.

Seemed like someplace special, when first he seen it. Not just by looks, but by feel. First night away he'd been fine — but second night, all dread and bad dreams. Sure wasn't usual, that. But the night was behind him now, and a new day was dawning.

Face the day, he decided. *Face it front on.*

It was something his Pa always said.

He pulled on his boots, sprang to his feet and he stretched. He prided himself on his stretching, young Billy Ray. He was a lean one alright, but stronger'n he looked. He kept himself supple too, and could move real quick when he wanted — but there wasn't no need for that now. So he walked over, slow like, and gave his horse a rub behind the ears. Told her how pretty she was too, then left her to go right on feeding. This particular morning she seemed to prefer her own company — well, Billy knew how that felt, so he left her to it.

Jenny was well used to camping strange places, as Billy loved sleeping outdoors, and seeing new sights. She was trained not to wander too far, and he never had to tie her.

She had never been broken, way other horses were. Billy had spoken to her softly, looked in her eyes, run his hands over her for weeks — then one day he'd put a rope on her, made her lie down on the ground, held her there though she didn't much like it. Played with her feet, her ears, mane and neck, refused her the chance to get up while he spoke to her softly. After that, he'd allowed her to stand, jumped right onto her back — no saddle — and rode her around the corral.

It was downright unnatural, his brother had told him. He should break her properly, he'd ruin her.

But Jenny wasn't ruined at all — she was the best horse they had. And wherever they slept, Billy always talked to her first thing in the morning, and sometimes, she seemed to talk back.

Not so much today.

Social niceties out of the way, Billy set to work, rekindling the fire he'd heated his beans on last night. But he still could not shake that feeling. It was a dark one alright.

Coffee, that's what I need. I ain't worth a damn 'til I've had it, Pa says, and he's usually right — well — he's right about most things. And while I make coffee, another read of the letter might help.

If coffee and Cass's fine words couldn't fix a bad feeling, well, Billy Ray figured nothin' much else could. And this sure was a pretty little spot for some reading and thinking. Cold yet, and would be for awhile — for no sun yet shone into the clearing, what with all the tall trees in front, and that big hill behind rising up from the stream. But he never was bothered by cold, running hot in his body way he did.

He fetched some water from the rocky edge of the gurgling stream, and he set the coffee to brewing. Then he rested his long, strong back against a tree, and pulled out the letter again. He unfolded it slowly, with care — it may have to last him a while, depending on how long the war went. Billy had learned his letters pretty well, had nice handwriting even, and could read without speaking out loud. Good thing too — for this made it possible to hear Cass's voice in his mind, instead of his own in his ears. Seemed almost as if she was there, reading her letter out to him.

A most precious thing, Cass's voice was.

My dear Billy, the letter began. And just like each other time he'd read those words, the thrill of them lifted his heart up into his throat, and this time even set his eyes to blinking. Musta got something in 'em, he decided.

She had given the pages to him Monday morning when he left her. Right before he'd gone home and told Pa he was goin' off to war.

Cass begged him to stay, cried and everything, and she made him promise to read the whole letter each time he stopped on his journey. He had faithfully done as he'd promised. She meant the world to him, after all. He read it first thing both mornings too — *after* speaking to Jenny, of course.

He wiped his eyes clean and started reading again.

My dear Billy. I do wish you'd change your mind. I believe your Pa spoke right each time you argued this out. This war of secession, or northern aggression is no different to other wars, no matter what anyone calls it. Good men on both sides will die all for nothing. That is the truth of it. I've considered your arguments Billy, but it isn't our fight.

Your Pa is right. If rich powerful men wish to fight, have them do it themselves, and stop sending good men onto battlefields to die in their place.

Your place is back here with me, darling Billy, and of course with your kind old Pa too. And even with that brother of yours, who I suppose must care for you, though he shows it most strangely. I guess he might not be so bad, as you still seem to love him.

But here's what's important. And you'd better think on it quick!

You made me a promise, Billy Ray, to come back and marry me soon. Why not right now? Please! Turn around Billy, come back to me. I will be 17 soon, and Pa says we can marry then. That can't happen if you get your fool handsome head shot off, can it?

Even if you survive, what if you're gone a hundred months, like the man in that Lorena song you spend half your life singing? I can't wait that long, Billy, I'll be an old maid!

Last night was most wonderful. Oh it was! If I had known how it would feel, we could have done it before. Turns out it's a beautiful thing rather than a painful one. I guess Ma lied about that. What a thing!

I can't wait to tell Annie the truth of it.

Billy, don't show no one this letter. Or tell no one I spoke of these things! Alright? I trust you.

Now listen, if you'll only turn round and come back, I have some interesting ideas of what might curl your toes even better. Things we might try. I lay awake thinking of them all night while you slept beside me, and it was hard not to wake you and do them. How could you sleep! Now I wish I had been braver. Why, I'm certain you would not have left once we tried them. I blush just from my thoughts now — but then, the Lord would never have made us how He did, if we weren't meant for such things.

I won't write the things down Billy. I would not be so wicked. But maybe you can imagine some too? Well go right on and imagine them, for I am all yours, now and always. And I do believe — once we have our own home and don't have to be quiet for fear of discovery — you might find me adventurous in ways entertaining and lovely.

Oh, how I love you Billy Ray!

You promised me you would come back. Please be true. Come back my one darling love.

With all my heart, and my body now too, I love you.

Come back to me Billy.

Your Cass. Always, no matter what, always.

"No wonder I can't shake this feelin', Jenny," Billy called out to his horse. "I got so worked up to go fight for what's right, then my darlin' sweet girl went and gave herself to me that way. How does a feller ever get such sights and sounds out of his head? And how it *felt!* Why, Jenny, you got no idea of the softness, and the ... well, never mind! I don't wish to set us both to blushin'. But you could at least *look* like you're interested."

That little mare looked up for a moment and stared at him, like she might just have something to say. And Billy figured a talking horse couldn't be any more strange or wonderful than what he'd done with Cass before he left. He felt eager to hear whatever that horse might say too, for she always did seem like a wise one — but Jenny only twitched an ear, shook her head at his foolishness, nickered a little in an amused sort of way, and went back to nibbling at the grass.

"Big help you are," he told the mare, carefully folding the letter and placing it in his pocket. He unfolded his long rawboned body from its spot against the tree, stood up to his full six feet two, sauntered across to the fire and poured himself coffee. "Maybe I'll try to climb to the top a'that hill there, look out over the whole world and think on it. I'm torn right down the middle, it seems, between my two duties and destinies. Ah, maybe Cass is right, Jen. Maybe I should just go back and..."

It was right then he heard something off in the distance, and he stood still as a big city statue while he listened. Sounded like a few high-spirited fellers, he reckoned, and the song that floated before them could not be mistaken — they were singing *Lorena*.

It's a sign, he decided.

Reading the letter had pushed that bad feeling away, and now he packed up all his doubts too. He blew on his coffee and gulped it down quick as he could. He loved Cass, but he had decided.

Love would just have to wait.

Of course, he ignored what come into his mind right

then, which was a saying his Pa always said, it having been passed down from his Grandpa — *"Be careful a' signs, as some signs is better'n others."*

Mostly, young fellers ignore the wisdom passed down from their fathers and grandfathers — takes young'uns awhile to learn what wisdom is. But a few good-sized mistakes of their own is the cure for that.

Billy hurried through the forest and out onto the trail to greet them fellers he'd heard. Singing Lorena as they were, he hoped they might be fellow soldiers, on their way to the war. He had read in the newspaper that soldiers particularly loved the song. And if they *were* on their way to the fighting, his plan was to join them.

The voices stopped singing when they saw him, and from only a hundred yards off now, the pair in front returned Billy's wave, and one called out good and loud, "Howdy, friend."

Then right from between that front grinning pair, the one coming behind squeezed the trigger of his rifle, and the bullet hit the tree just a foot to Billy's right, just around about throat height. And lickety split, that supple, fast-movin' young man dived sideways and backways and downways for cover, and went crashin' through the brush helter skelter in search of his rifle.

Well, like that old saying went — *"...some signs is better'n others."*

CHAPTER 3

TOUGH AS OLD BOOTS

It was mid-morning when ol' John Ray heard riders coming from the north. It wasn't just horses he heard, but hollerin' too. And not the gleeful kind.

Bad sign, he thought, and he thought of his father. *Some signs is better'n others.*

John was a bee's knee less than six foot, was wide as an axe handle across his back, and could still outwork most ordinary fellers, even at fifty, and missing an arm. His face was what some would call ruggedly handsome — though the rugged part was sure winning — and that face told a tale of sorrow mixed in with goodness. His light-brown hair had long since faded to gray, but he mostly still had it, and kept it clean tidy and combed.

As the sound of the riders came closer, he heard it clearer, narrowed down the possibilities.

Only two horses, I'd reckon. But we'll see soon enough.

He was not a man who went off half-cocked, or jumped to conclusions.

The sound of two horses was not at all what he'd hoped for. Three was the number he wanted. And not so soon neither.

It was only two days since he'd realized Billy had actually done what he threatened to — and gone off to fight in that damned foolish war. The boy had had a full day's head-start.

John had figured it all talk a'course, just like always — Billy was barely seventeen, all hands feet and ribs he was yet to grow into. A long streak of pumpwater who could never quite shoot straight, and didn't much even like hunting. Oh, he went along — knew how to stay quiet, keep downwind. He was cleverer, tracking-wise, than most of the men John had known, and he'd known some good ones.

But that boy's heart just wasn't in killing — not even hardly for food. He had a soft heart, and was happy enough to go hungry, rather than kill wild critters. Preferred food he'd growed himself in the ground. When Billy did kill something though, he always thanked it — and he used every bit of it too. Reckoned it disrespectful to let anything go to waste. It was surprising how he'd gotten all a'that from his mother, without ever having known her.

Wasn't all he got from her either. Unlike John and Horace, Billy was blessed with dark handsome looks. Skin the color of butterscotch candy and straight shiny black hair just for starters. And though his features were somehow noble, his face was as fresh as a child's, his eyes soft and honest as the day — he was a looker alright, lucky feller. Not that he knew it himself. Billy never really thought about such things, and put no stock in handsomeness anyway.

From when Billy was yet a small child, strangers would stop in the street just to stare at him, watch him go by — folks had stared at his mother before him, though it wasn't quite the same, and had on occasion led to trouble. Even though she had not lived to raise him, she had given him a lot — that much was abundantly clear.

Weighs about what she did too, John thought then with a laugh.

Billy might not yet weigh more than one-thirty, and even that in boots, ringin' wet, but that boy was smart as a whip, with no shortage of courage — and when he got some experience, and growed into those big hands and feet, he was destined to be some real sort of a man.

But for now, Billy Ray was still John's little boy — just a big-hearted, gangly, baby-faced kid who did not yet even shave. John had always hoped Billy's future would be something to do with books, words or numbers, rather than guns and hard men.

That sorta man can go far — his head full of ideas and his heart full of goodness, John thought. *Yessir, he's sure like his mother — may that wonderful woman rest in peace.*

The last time John Ray saw Billy he'd spoken in anger — told the boy not to come back if he went off to fight. "Damn your soul to hell if you go fight for rich men," he'd growled at his son. "You know what war's cost me already." And all other eyes in the room had gone to where John's right shirt sleeve hung empty, stitched shut a few inches below his shoulder.

When he found out the boy had actually gone, he could scarce believe it was true. But John was a man of quick actions, and right away he sent his other son, Horrie — and the Town Marshal's boy, Jasper — to retrieve him. Billy had a whole day's head start though, so he figured it'd take them awhile to catch up.

And there was a small chance they wouldn't — these were dangerous times.

Horrie and Jasper were known around town as the Strawhead Twins — half on account of being the only two yellow-haired men in these parts, and the other half on account of 'em seeming almost joined at the hip.

Well, at least Horrie had himself a friend — but it was dang frustratin' for John. The Strawheads seemed almost to go outta their way to make folks dislike them. He hoped Horrie might grow out of it someday, but there wasn't no sign of it yet.

"Do what you have to," he'd told them as they packed some provisions into their saddlebags. "Subdue him and tie him to his horse if he won't come back on his own." He'd seen Horrie's pale eyes gleam when he said it, and almost took it back — that boy didn't need no more encouragement to beat on his little brother. But fetching Billy home was what mattered, so he set those boys after him and gave them free rein.

John gripped the porch rail with his hand now, craned his neck to see the riders as they came into view.

As I thought. Just two riders. Horrie and Jasper.

His heart sank.

Why back so soon? What's happened to my boy?

"Won't be nothin'," he murmured to himself. "They might just be blowin' off steam, and Billy comin' behind. We'll see soon enough."

Then he started, just a little, when his housekeeper, Rosie, spoke behind him. "Yes. I'm sure it's nothing at all."

But when he turned to look at her, Rosie looked very small. She was only John's age, and still pretty, he noticed sometimes — though he'd never acted on that, a'course. But right now she looked somehow aged, and her face seemed pale and stricken.

The two young men galloped their mounts toward the homestead, dust lifting and trailing behind them, the hoofbeats ringing loud through the otherwise silent day.

Still riding hard now they're close — another bad sign.

These boys were both twenty-three, and could sometimes be fools, but they didn't punish horses without reason. At least not whenever John could see them.

My boy. Not my boy.

The dread ate at him now.

It crossed his mind, just for a moment, that he'd rather lose Horace than Billy, if he had to lose one. Guilt rode through his mind right behind it, and he banished the thought.

It wasn't that he didn't care for Horace — he did. But that boy made himself hard to love.

He's just like HIS mother too.

He'd always been sneaky and secretive, just as his mother had been, before she ran off and left them. But a good father always tries his best for his boys, regardless of their shortcomings — so John always did his best for Horrie, and hoped he'd come good in the end.

The riders leaped from their dusty, sweat-covered horses, and Horrie's spurs jingled as he bounded up the stairs to the porch. He curled his lips in a sort of a snarl, and with a wild-eyed look he cried out, "They're all dead, Pa, dead and burned."

And right away, Jasper lent his weight to the statement, saying, "Dead when we found 'em. Every one." Then the Town Marshal's son went back to hiding under his hat. He stood holding the reins of the exhausted, foam-flecked horses, and looked at the ground while he waited for it all to play out.

As poor Rosie dug panicked fingers into his shoulders, John Ray thought only of his younger boy. Billy was the most precious thing in John's life. Just like his mother had been — before she died within a day of giving birth to him.

He gripped that porch rail tighter now, and his face all went numb. But John Ray was tough as old boots, and he yet had strength he could call on. He bit down on his feelings, forced his mouth to move, squeezed out the words then, "Who else?"

"Annie was there too, unexpected," said Horace. "I'm sorry." And then quickly — too quickly maybe — he added, "I mean, not sorry, ain't our fault, we only found 'em is all." Then he turned and looked round at Jasper, and said, "Well, Jasper it was found 'em first, I only come along later."

"What?" said Jasper, raising his head real sharp. But he

looked back down quick, and no one seemed to have paid Horrie's statement no mind.

"Help me get her inside, Horrie," John said, putting his one strong arm around Rosie. "And Jasper, go look after those horses, they look almost done for."

They went inside and set the woman down in the parlor. "Watch her a minute," John said. Then he went and fetched a glass of water, and held it to her mouth while she sipped some. That done, he stood facing Horace, looked right into his eyes, and said, "Tell me what happened. How did he die?"

Horace Ray's eyes flickered some then, and it seemed that he shrank from the gaze of his father — but he covered it up right quick, and went into a coughing fit. "It's the smoke, Pa. It's all still smoldering, and it gets all the way in your lungs."

John gripped the boy by the shoulder. "Make sense, boy. Tell it straight now. How'd yer brother die? And what was Miss Annie doing there with him?"

Well, Horace Ray looked at his Pa then like he had a tail growing out of his forehead. "Billy ain't dead, Pa. Least not that I know of." He broke free of John's grip, sunk down into a chair, pulled his hat down to cover his face, and he groaned like a man who's been ruined. "It was awful. The smell, Pa, the smell! The MacPhersons, all except Cass, all burned up in their home."

A shudder of relief struck right through John Ray's body, and he touched a quivering hand to the shoulder of his son. He had a vague thought then, a feeling maybe, that the Lord might yet strike him down for feeling relieved when his neighbors — his friends — had died.

"Ohhh," Rosie moaned. "Them poor folk."

A few moments of silence then followed before John spoke again. "I thought I smelled smoke once during the night. Couldn't have been that though, wind was wrong. But he was no fool, Tom MacPherson — not the sort to burn in his bed. You think it was foul play?"

Horace stayed hunkered down under his hat, but looked up from under there a little. "I ... I can't say for certain, Pa, but I don't believe so. Bodies was pretty burned up. Roof beams and all came down, whole thing collapsed in a heap all on top of 'em. They was all in their beds when it happened, looks like to me."

"Alright. We'll see soon enough. But first thing, we'd best go tell the Marshal." John ran his hand up over his forehead, then back through his hair — he grabbed at the roots of it so hard, it seemed like the blood all drained from his face. And suddenly, good John Ray felt very tired. "And Cass," he said, almost inaudibly. Then louder, "We need to tell Cass."

CHAPTER 4

A HOOTIN' & HOLLERIN'
HELLABALOO

Billy Ray had never been shot at before, and it sure did set that long supple body of his into action. His body wasn't waitin' on instructions from his brain, that much was certain. Off'n runnin' his legs went, through the trees to where his horse and his gun was, even before those three men spurred their mounts on toward him.

At least he had chosen his campsite well for the previous night. Steep hills were in mighty short supply in these parts, and he'd really only camped here for the novelty of seeing it. Brought up some childhood memories, that hill. Without doubt, it was the biggest and steepest he'd seen since moving to Kansas as a child, and he'd looked at it in wonder when he saw it.

No time for wonderment now though.

Only time for savin' your skin.

Billy's boots seemed barely to touch the ground as he

came bursting into the clearing, and ol' Jenny sure looked uneasy.

"Steady, girl," he called quietly, as he picked up the long back scabbard that held his rifle and threw it over his shoulder. Billy knew he had a little time, as he'd had to dismount to lead the horse in here through the thick forest, and the three men wouldn't find things no easier.

"Come out here with your hands up and we'll let you live," one of 'em called out from the trail. They hadn't rushed in after him, at least — they knew to be wary.

No way Billy was going to answer before he got himself hidden — he was young, but he wasn't a complete fool. Then again, maybe he was, for there was only one way out of this clearing — the way he'd come in. And those three men most likely knew it.

"Come on, kid," came the voice again. "We just want your money is all. You can keep your horse and guns, honest."

When one of the other men laughed it up big about that, Billy knew he was in trouble. He needed a plan, real quick.

Shoulda made a plan when I got here last night, it occurred to him then. But he put that out of his head now, looked around and picked out where he'd make his stand from. Then he crossed the little stream, balancing from rock to rock, as silently as he could manage.

Turned out Billy had luck on his side. There was some good sized rocks up that hill, which couldn't be got to from nowhere else but this clearing. It was steep, real steep — but that body of his was a wonder, he reckoned, the way his long arms stretched rock to rock, tree to tree, and he just about floated up that gnarly hillside, even with that long rifle on his back, though it snagged on a branch once.

Pays off to do all that stretchin', he thought to himself as he climbed.

Took him no time at all to pull himself up to the boulders he'd chosen, and he was up there well before the wary men worked their way through the trees and came to the clearing.

First thing Billy done when he got there was break off some small branches — quiet as he could manage a'course — and set them up in the gap between them two boulders.

He laid his red bandana on a flat rock, and laid twenty-one of his rimfire cartridges out in three neat lines on the cloth — seven to a line, for easy loading if it came to it. Next, he poured a little water from his canteen to make some mud, then he rubbed some onto his face. He washed his hand clean and dried them, then he settled in and looked out through the leaves of the branches, watching over his little clearing.

He hadn't yet doused the fire, and it still smoldered away a few feet from the edge of the stream. Jen started a little, uneasy; she turned around, stamped a foot. So he knew roundabout where the men were, though he couldn't yet see them.

"Don't move, boys," Billy called. "I got a bead on ya there at the edge a'the clearing." But he sounded less than convincing, even to his own ears.

"That's funny," one called back. "Listen, we never knew you was just a kid. Thought you was a Injun, if you can believe it. Not now you spoke, a'course. So we don't wanna kill you, right boys?"

"No way," one called out, and the other said, "Course not."

"Then you better leave," Billy called, "so I don't have to kill *you*." That sounded better, he decided. But he hoped he would not have to shoot.

"I see you there across the creek," called the one who was clearly the leader. "But I won't shoot you. Come on down and we'll all have a talk. Maybe you'd like to join us. We could do with another good man."

That scared Billy a second or two, but then he realized something. If that feller really could see him, he woulda been shootin' already, not just jawin' on about it. He'd showed his intentions clear enough.

"Why'd you try to shoot me anyway?" called Billy then. "Come forward into the clearing, or so help me, I'll shoot you right where you stand."

"Kid, you ain't even got no gun, I reckon," that same feller called out, and he strode on forward into the clearing. His hands were wide out to the side, palms facing the sky, so Billy could see he didn't have his gun at the ready. That was some big scary scattergun he had hangin' from a makeshift shoulder holster though. Sawed off *real* short, and that thing looked like a cannon through Billy's young eyes. "Come on down, son," the man called. "If you don't, I'm takin' your horse, and you won't get far then."

Billy didn't answer. He needed to be sure where the others were, even though he felt confident they couldn't get up to where he was. And he knew they couldn't shoot him, long as he stayed behind these rocks. But he could not allow them to take Jenny — she was not just his horse, but his friend.

Soon enough, he got what he hoped for. All three men were now in the clearing. The last two stayed wary, he noticed, their rifles pointing this way and that as they searched all about.

It was clear that they still could not see him. All three were scanning the low part of the hill, and they clearly believed no man could have gotten up as high as he was, for they never once even glanced up there. Their eyes never rested on any one place either, as they walked all through his campsite.

Seemed like they was settling in, for one feller poured himself some coffee, stoked up the fire, and commenced to rummage through Billy's meagre supplies for something to cook.

But young Billy Ray figured the feller was just trying to draw him out of his hiding place, so he sat tight and waited.

Patience is a virtue, his Pa always told him. *And someday, it might save your life.*

So Billy sat stiller'n a mountain, and he watched all they did without comment.

Then one of 'em — the boss one — began to walk toward Jenny, and Billy didn't like that at all. He picked up his rifle — his Pa's rifle really — and poked it through the brush he was hid behind, and he hoped the man would stop. But he kept right on, so Billy decided to give him a scare.

If them fellers had known young Billy had that

beautiful Spencer Repeater he'd "borrowed" from his Pa when he left, they might not even have come into his camp. But *know it* they didn't, and *come in* they did, and now Billy was planning to scare 'em.

Thing was, Billy's Pa had been right all along regardin' his rifle skills — that boy looked after weapons real good, but he never had been much of a shot. And to be fair, it's hard to judge, shootin' downhill that way.

He aimed that rifle at the ground, about four feet in front of that feller as he walked toward Jenny.

Heart pounding fifteen to the dozen, Billy Ray took his time aiming, then he squeezed the trigger, real nice and slow. And that bullet hit, oh, about four feet from where he had aimed it — right through that boss feller's foot it went, and he sure started up with some highest quality squealin'.

If there was a market for squealin', and some way to bottle it, Billy coulda made a small fortune outta that feller.

A'course, all hell broke loose then, and for boys with no wish to shoot him, they sure started firing quick.

They was runnin' for cover, divin' this way and that, yippin' and hootin' and hollerin' all the while. And them fools kept on shootin' up the rocks and trees down below Billy as they went, which it seemed to him didn't make no sense at all.

So he just sat tight there and waited.

Thing was, they still hadn't worked out he was up higher, as he'd only fired one shot and they'd not seen the flash. They'd missed the smoke too, on account of 'em making so much of their own smoke so quick, with all of their firing.

There's a lesson right there, Billy thought. *If you don't know where a man is, always look for the gunsmoke. If you got time a'course.*

Them boys had rifles and pistols and revolvers and shotguns and all sorts, and it seemed like they'd been lookin' for any old reason to fire off them guns all at once.

What a hellabaloo.

And with it all happening so fast, and in all the excitement, Billy caught the fever as well, and figured he might as well hurry 'em along some. He still had six shots before he'd have to reload, so he shot off a few here and there — over their heads, or into the ground just behind 'em, that was his plan — after all, he was only intending to scare 'em, so they'd leave him alone.

But the more them boys made a ruckus, the more gunsmoke they made, and the faster they went hither and thither — the more confused Billy became.

And the more confused Billy became, and the harder he *tried* to shoot straight, the worse the young feller's aim got.

So that was how Billy Ray killed his first man — with a warning shot gone awry, right through the brain pan of a filthy, murderin' road agent.

CHAPTER 5

THE CUNNING OF A FLANNEL-MOUTHED LIAR

As they rode into town John Ray asked several questions of his elder son. And if Horace wasn't so cunning, he and Jasper would have been caught out right then.

But Horace had planned their whole story, and coached Jasper in it the whole time they were setting up the bodies back at the MacPherson place, and covering their tracks.

He answered his Pa's every question, and his story checked out.

The main part they had to convince him of, was what they were doing there at all — for they *should* have been two days ride away, still on Billy's trail. Horace explained that to his father as they let the horses walk awhile.

"When we arrived in Council Grove it was already dark, so we dropped off the horses at the livery right away. That new hostler there, Bryson, said Billy had been there alright, but only fed his horse then kept going. But we were done for, Pa, so we got ourselves a meal at Harper's Saloon. Then Jasper got drinkin' a little and decided he wanted to get a bed for the night. We argued some but he wouldn't give in, so I decided to rent a fresh horse and set out for Wilmington alone."

"I weren't feelin' well, Sir," called Jasper from behind them.

"Fair enough," John said. "It wasn't *your* brother you was chasin'." And he looked hard at Horace, who went on with his story.

"I got the rented horse and set out, figuring my only chance to catch Billy was to ride through the night. Whole day's head start, Pa! What chance did I have, even then? You know how Billy is!"

"Yes, I *do* know how Billy is. He doesn't ruin horses, he'd have kept it to twenty miles a day, and you'd have caught him soon enough by renting fresh horses."

"I done my best, Pa," said Horace, his fists bunching now. "I got that rented horse moving, and a real nice horse it was too, at least to begin with. But an hour's ride, and the damn thing went lame. Weren't nothin' I could do but to walk it on back to the Grove."

"What did Bryson have to say for himself?" John growled, for it was a bad business to rent a man a lame horse.

"Said he'd only just bought the horse, Pa," said Horace, ducking his head under a branch that hung over the trail. "I believe him too, so don't you make him no strife. He was fairer than fair — refunded my money, plus ten dollars besides for my trouble. He was most 'pologetic, and asked only that I don't spread what happened. But he didn't have another horse to offer me until the next day."

Horace felt mighty smug as he told his father the story. It wasn't the truth a'course, but an easy lie to remember. In fact, there had been no horse rented, and the money flowed the opposite way — it was Horace who'd given Bryson ten dollars, a bribe to tell that very story to anyone who asked. Easiest ten dollars Pete Bryson ever made, so he reckoned.

Truth of it was, even if Horrie *had* wanted to catch Billy, he'd have been in peril himself — for just two months back, he and Jasper had gone up to Wilmington, and got run out of town by the Sheriff, some feller called Brimstone. That's what happens in Wilmington, when young fellers pistol-whip an old drunk just for the "fun" of it. They gave that Sheriff false names, and said they was brothers, just looking around before going out West with their families, who were waiting out at Council Grove right now. "Waiting for more wagons to join the train," they'd told him.

That Sheriff took a real good look at their faces, and told them if they ever came back he'd lock 'em in the hoosegow for a week, and maybe whip 'em with pistols each night, just so they knew how it felt. Real angry, that Sheriff had been.

But Horace's Pa — and Jasper's too — didn't need to know about that.

"So you just gave up on your brother" John asked his son coldly, "on account of one horse going lame?"

"I did all I could, Pa, I'm sorry."

"Sorry ain't good enough!" John yelled, and he glared at

his son as they rode. "You know what I reckon, boy? I reckon you're *happy* he's gone, and you never even *tried* to retrieve him!"

Then Horace Ray raised his voice to his father in a way he had never done before, and the spittle flew from his mouth as he ground out the words. "It weren't my damn fault that fool *kid* disobeyed you and went off to have an adventure. He does whatever he wants, and you let him get away with it all! Why, he's like a wild thing, hardly comes home half the time, and you damn well know it. Folks say he's half Injun you know, and I reckon—"

"What folks?" growled John. "And who's business would that be anyway? Well?"

"Just folks," Horrie answered, a little quieter. But he was on the prod again soon enough, voice-wise anyway. "I don't know *who* said it, Pa, I heard it third hand. Well, is he Injun or not? He don't look like you and me, and he sure acts like one, wearin' them fool soft boots and no spurs, and sleepin' out on the ground, and runnin' off all the time how he does, while I'm doing every..."

John reached out, grabbed the bridle of Horace's horse as he pulled up his own, and he stared his son down a long moment. When his voice came, it was quiet yet deadly. "I won't have you speak that way of your brother. He never goes away more than one night. Does his own share a'the chores and more, always has done. I will crawl your hump, boy, you hear me? One arm's all I'll need, you just let me know when you're ready."

Horace only stared back though, cold and defiant, and

he maybe even smiled a little. But that smile wasn't friendly, not one bit, and he did not speak.

"Why are you steering away from the subject, boy?" said John then. "It was simple enough — I told you to go bring him back, whatever it took."

"It wasn't *possible,* Pa," Horace growled. "You *know* that horse a' his is the best we got for long distance. I wanted that horse, but you gave it to him, and now you're payin' the price!"

"Wanted it after Billy had trained it two years, is more how *I* recall it!"

But Horace ignored the interruption, and went on with his rantings. "By the time the night passed, I woulda bin almost *two* days behind him. Ain't *no* chance I'd ever have caught him and you *damn well* know it! So don't blame *me* for *his* tomfoolery, I jus' won't have it no more, all this playin' of favorites!"

And with that, Horace Ray put the spurs to his horse and was gone in a great cloud of dust.

"I'm sorry," John said, almost gently, when he caught him outside the Town Marshal's office four minutes later. He tied his horse to the rail right beside Horrie's, took his hat off and held it in front of him. "You're right son, it wasn't your fault. You did what you could, and I'm grateful. You can tell us the rest a' what happened, in front a' the Sheriff."

Horace did not say a word, did not even nod. He felt powerful now, like his whole life was unfolding just how he wanted it. He felt power, even over his father, who now seemed somehow broken with Billy gone.

Jasper arrived then and hitched his horse to the rail, and the three men strode inside together. There was no one locked up in the calaboose. Only Jasper's Pa, Clem, was inside, and when he looked up from his paperwork, he saw right away from their faces that they brought bad news.

"What's happened?" he asked. "Is it Billy?"

"We'd best all sit down, Clem," John told him. "It's not Billy. I reckon we just let the boys finish their story, and you'll know it all soon enough. You might wish to take notes."

Town Marshal Clem Jenkins set up a fresh sheet of paper, picked up his pencil, and said, "I'm all ears."

He was too — them big ears of Clem's made him look a bit like a circus elephant, especially now he'd gotten a bit rounded at his middle, from too much exercising of the table muscle.

Horace explained then how he'd taken a room for the night — two nights ago in Council Grove it was, he made clear to the Marshal — then he and Jasper had talked about things the next day. They agreed they'd never catch Billy now, he was long gone. Then the pair had somehow got caught up in a card game, and couldn't quit while they were winning — and before they knew it, it was night time again, and they'd won quite a pile.

"So this is last night then?" said the Marshal, looking up from his writing.

"Yessir," said Horace. "So we decided to get some girls with our winnings, and have a good time before riding on home."

"Frequentin' cathouses now?" said John, raising an eyebrow.

Horace sure was enjoying his own story, and here he told his biggest lie yet, and put on an expression to match it. "Truth is I felt bad, Pa, like I'd failed — losin' Billy's trail that way. I felt all eaten up inside, and I guess I just needed ... I needed to take out my ... frustrations. I guess that's the right word."

"Well, can't blame young bucks fer that," Clem said, and there was amusement and pride in his voice. "You forget that they's men now, John. These two boys both work hard on that place of yours, and don't get to a decent size town much."

"That's right, Pa," said Jasper. "I'm so sick a' the one here in town, and since the trouble last month, she refuses Horrie—"

"Forget that damn whore, Jasper," said Horace in a hurry. "This is serious business we're tellin' of."

"Hmmm," said John then. "We'll talk more about this other *trouble* later."

"It weren't nothin', Pa, honest."

"That's the truth, Mister Ray," Jasper said, wiping his hair from his eyes. "You know Horrie's honest as the day, and I'd go to hell and back with him. If he says he paid her, he paid her."

And right then, Horace Ray thanked his friend with a nod — and more or less stabbed him in the back with his very next words. Because Horace had a new plan, and here he changed the story he'd coached Jasper in earlier.

He was a practiced liar alright, young Horrie Ray, and

he looked that Marshal right in the eye as he spoke, with his own eyes wide open. "There was a mixup at the cathouse then, Marshal. See, we both went off to some rooms with some nice painted ladies — they got *such* good ones there. But when I was done, I still felt like I wanted some more — only the one I was with was run ragged, like a horse rode too fast and too far."

"Galloped that fast filly too far!" Jasper laughed, and the Marshal laughed too. But John Ray, he sat and said nothing.

"Now you hush and don't interrupt, Jasper, and let me tell the story straight and clear," Horace said. "So I went out from that room and paid extra for a new girl. They sent me to another sweet thing in a different room down the hall, all the way at the end. *Real* pretty that second one. Knew her way round a man too. But what happened, when Jasper was done, he went burstin' into my first one's room to collect me, and she told him I'd left. So Jasper done hurried on without me. And I has to admit it, I'd fell asleep in that pretty one's bed. Like I said, she knew her way round a man — and she weren't no easy ride, I tell you that now. Bucked like a bronc. By the time I found out Jasper was gone, he had almost an hour's head start. Right, Jasper?"

Now Jasper Jenkins had never been the sharpest arrow in the quiver. But he knew his friend Horrie was clever, and he'd always relied on that fact — and if Horrie had changed their story, it must be for good reason. So Jasper only said, "That's the size of it alright," and he clamped his mouth shut and looked at Horrie to go on.

"So that was it, Marshal. I was tryin' to catch him, so I

went along quick as I could risk it, but there wasn't much moon. But Jasper thought I was ahead, so he went along kinda quick too, thinkin' it was a race a' sorts. Then when Jasper come near the MacPhersons, he seen the glow a' the fire there, and went down to see what had happened. And they was all dead from the fire, Marshal."

"Dead? The MacPhersons? No...." He paused then, pencil in hand and looked up at Horrie.

"It's true, Marshal. And when I got there a half hour later, that's where I caught him up. He was just sittin' there, shocked at what he saw. Right Jasper?"

"That's the truth alright, Pa. Most terrible sight I ever saw, why I just about cried a tear when I seen it." And Jasper Jenkins hid his face in his hands, so his Pa couldn't see that he lied.

And in that moment, Horace Ray knew he had *done it* — he had ensured his own survival. Because even if they *had* left something undone, left some sort of evidence the MacPhersons had been murdered, well, the Marshal's own son had admitted to being alone there. And with Horace's testimony, it was Jasper who'd be convicted of the crime — and Marshal Clem Jenkins was not *so* interested in justice, that he'd choose to hang his own son.

CHAPTER 6

HIGHTAILIN'

It was a good half hour before Billy came down from his perch. Or rather, a bad half hour.

Even though he knew them fellers had wanted to murder him, he felt terrible about what he'd done. Felt powerful terrible. He did.

A man's life, snuffed out, just like that.

There he is, down there dead.

I did that.

And Billy Ray knew it right then, he was just a big kid, out of his depth in the great wide world on his ownsome — and he knew that he should have stayed home with his family, stayed and married his darling Cass.

"He's killed Red," the boss had yelled as he hopped for it, zigging and zagging across the clearing to safety. "Run for it Joey, the kid's a dead shot." But he needn't have said nothin' at all — that other feller, Joey, he was already hightailin' it for all he was worth.

"I'm a'runnin' already, August," Joey cried. "You get runnin' yourself!"

Well, that hightailer, he sure knew what he'd been given legs for. The sound he made crashin' through the brush! But he must have stopped and come back for his boss once he realized he'd reached safety, for Billy still heard them the next two or three minutes — a groan of agony here, a "Sorry boss" there, and once, an "It weren't my fault, who expects a kid to shoot like that?" — as they made their way to their horses, up near the trail.

There was even a "Watch out he ain't sneakin' up behind us," followed by a "Quiet ya fool," and then he didn't hear no more words.

Next thing they were galloping away, back in the direction they'd come from.

That was maybe all that stopped Billy from heading home right then and there. He thought about it alright, but them murderous fellers were back on that trail — somewhere between Billy and home — and they'd surely seek revenge if they seen him.

And young Billy Ray, he knew something important they didn't. He knew that he weren't no dead shot. It was plain old bad luck for Red, and good luck maybe for Billy — that was the truth of what happened down there in that clearing.

He knew now, too, that he'd been lucky to get away with it. And that he'd better smarten up quick if he hoped to survive.

After a half hour he packed up his ammo, put his rifle in its scabbard, and he climbed down and went straight to

Jenny. She'd run off when the shooting began, and he'd known she'd return once it quieted, but he knew it woulda scared her real bad.

"You was brave, Jen," he said. "I'm real sorry you had to see all that." And he stroked her neck awhile, and rubbed behind her ears how she liked it.

Billy knew no one would believe it, the way Jenny looked at him then. But it seemed like she understood how he felt — how it pained him to take a man's life, even though accidentally. She wasn't much of a one for displays of affection, but she even nuzzled him some as he held onto her — and somehow, that made him feel better.

"He *was* a bad feller," Billy told the mare. But she flicked her head then to get free of him and went back to grazing. Billy knew he wouldn't get no more sympathy from her, so he went off and looked at the dead man.

He didn't look at him too close. Never looked at the face at all. Top of the head was shot away some, and Billy surely did not wish to see it. He half looked away to the side as he covered the head with his kerchief. Then he carefully went through the man's pockets.

He had the makings and a pen knife in one pocket, and Billy wondered a moment why men bothered to smoke. Wasn't much of a pen knife, not near as good as Billy's, so he pushed it back into the pocket and moved to the next one.

That next pocket was a whole different story.

Seemed like business must have been good. He had ninety dollars in there, all wrapped up neat and tidy inside of a letter. Sure, it was only paper money, so worth less than half what the number on it claimed — but Billy liked how it looked, especially the twenty and the fives. Didn't like the tens though, not with that picture of Lincoln on them.

Billy put the money down on a rock, placed the letter on top of the bills, and smoothed out the creases as best he could. Then he picked up the letter, put a small stone on top of the money so it wouldn't blow around if some wind came, and held the page up in front of him.

It was written in a scrawly hand, and he found it none too easy to work out the words as he went. Spelling didn't help neither. But without even thinking whether he should or not, Billy slowly — haltingly — commenced to read it out loud.

Deer Bert. Yer do us prowd goin off ter fyt fer wots ryt son. This hunnerd doller wil by you gud meels n mebbe a reel gud gun afore you git to the fyten. I love you son. So do yer Pa tho he dont nevr say mutch on it. Ma.

He read it a second time, and it went faster, of course, now he'd worked out what the scrawly words meant. He didn't know anyone called Bert. And while Bert's Ma sure couldn't spell, she really did love him, that much was plain.

Made Billy wonder what having a Ma would have been like, exactly. He had Rosie, of course — she was warm and kind and wonderful. And Lucy MacPherson was always good to him, treated him special she did. And then, too, there was that *feeling* Billy got, whenever he spent the night alone, sleeping out somewhere strange — *that* somehow felt like a mother's love, at least the way he imagined it might. The stars, the moon, the whole sky all to himself — the way it filled him and wrapped all around him. The precious, life-giving *embrace* of it.

There's nothing can embrace a feller quite like the sky can. Somehow, not even Cass.

But reading this letter, he could not help being envious of Bert, at least just a little. For though it also made him feel a little that way, its love was meant only for Bert.

He decided to read it just one last time. But almost right away, Billy heard a noise from the trees behind him, and realized he'd stupidly offered his back to anyone who might have sneaked in from the trail.

Another lesson learned.

As he thought it, he spun around quick and reached for his rifle — he'd taken the scabbard off and laid it down against a nearby rock before starting to search the dead man. But there was no more noise after that one, so he figured it must have been Jen.

Them fellers ain't coming back here, not for a dead man.

That body was Billy's responsibility. Red was a corpse now, but he had been a real person, flesh and blood, and somewhere maybe, he had people who loved him. Maybe he was the Bert referred to in the letter — or maybe he'd killed that feller Bert. He sure wished he knew. But either way, something had to be done.

I might be just a kid, he decided, *but I gotta grow up real quick now. I can't just leave a man's body here dead, and never report it to no one.*

He took out his rifle and raised it in front of him, wary like — there had been that noise after all — and walked out through the trees toward the trail. And as he got closer he heard it. A horse calling out to him.

No, calling out to Jenny, most likely.

A smallish bay roan gelding he was, and not such a bad-lookin' feller, though only the same size as Jenny — and she wasn't even much big for a mare.

He wasn't what you'd call flashy, but a stout solid feller with something extra about him. Short strong legs and good feet he had, and a calm, dependable look in his eye. Like he was making a feller a promise he intended to keep. His feet were well cared for, but he clearly needed a drink. Bit of a rubdown wouldn't hurt neither.

Red's horse, he must be. Them other two fools musta figured I was nippin' at their heels, and they didn't have time to take him. Well, I'll load up the body on top of him, and deliver Red to the next town.

It's the least I can do. Outlaw or not, he looked after his horse well, and surely deserves a decent burial, if only for that.

CHAPTER 7
TELLING CASS

John Ray wished to go alone to tell Cass, and the Marshal agreed it was best. Never did like the sound of grieving women, Marshal Clem Jenkins. But he told John to hurry on back, as he wanted him along when he went to check out the MacPherson place.

"We'll all go out there," said John, looking hard at the Strawheads. "All four of us together. Just give me twenty minutes to tell Cass what happened and settle her. In the meantime, you boys go eat something, you must both be half-starved."

Cottonwood Falls wasn't much, as towns went. Just one long wide street, pretty much, that ran east to west. But the locals had some town pride, had pitched in and built a good boardwalk both sides, and the town had most things folks needed.

There was a dozen houses in town — even some farmers preferred to live in town for the safety of it, but that had never bothered John Ray much.

Never bothered Tom MacPherson neither. John winced at the thought, but kept walking.

Aside from the houses, the town had two stores, and a church that doubled as a schoolhouse. No livery, but a good blacksmith. A saloon of course — and wherever you find a saloon you'll soon enough be needing a lockup as well, so they built one a'those early on.

The Marshal mostly didn't have much to do though, so he also doubled as the Postal Officer. John didn't mind Clem so much, but they weren't really friends — Clem was a bit self-important was all. A bit vain, and without much to back it with.

He was no Seth Hays anyway — now *there* was a man John respected. Seth Hays had been the first white man to settle the area, back in forty-seven, up in Council Grove. Indian trader to begin with. Before long he was doing a roaring trade up there, it being the last chance to get supplies for wagon trains heading West on the Santa Fe Trail. In fifty-four Seth built up a cattle ranch here in the Falls. Good one too. Seth had a finger in a few pies — owned the fancy restaurant up in Council Grove for one thing. Hays House it was called. But there was no restaurant down here.

John Ray had brought his family to the Falls in fifty-five. One of the first white men to arrive. Chose his hundred-and-sixty acres two miles north of town, his eastern boundary being where Fox Creek finally twisted around and entered the Cottonwood River. Had another pretty bend of the Cottonwood as part of the boundary too. Still almost twenty miles from the Grove, but when John first looked at the land, he figured his place would be the best spot for the railroad, and that might make his boys rich someday if it came.

As it was, the trail to the Grove went right through his place, but John didn't mind that at all. Like having two places, he reckoned.

The MacPhersons arrived the same week, and were considering the one-sixty next to John's. John commended Tom on his choice, and mentioned his thoughts about the railroad. Said he hoped Horace would claim it when he turned twenty-one, if no one else had by then — although he was but yet fourteen.

"Y'know, now I think on it, I don't much like the stink of railroads," Tom had said. "Ain't no sense crowdin' each other neither. I've in mind another nice place, two or three miles back toward Council Grove. Reckon I'll go for that one instead. Whole thing backs onto Fox Creek, but it has good high ground as well. Might build right up on top a' the rise." And with that, the two men became fast friends.

It had been Cass's birthday the day the MacPhersons arrived, John recalled now. Billy and Cass had been eight, and shy around each other at first. And now she had lost her whole family.

How do I tell her? Ain't no easy thing to hear.

John clomped along on that boardwalk, heavy of heart and of foot, wondering how he could put it. The right words were not coming to him.

Course they're not, and they won't, he decided. *For there ain't no right words for such a thing.*

He wished that street had been longer — he came to

the old seamstress's place too soon. He stood out front a moment, thinking. It had been built to be a clothing store, with living quarters out back. But fate had changed things, as it does. The seamstress wasn't even a seamstress no more, not really.

But she still knew a whole lot about it, and was happy to pass on her teachings.

Her name was Mary Brown, and her fingers had all curled up and went gnarly long ago. Too many years of hard work. Her husband had been gone two years, and she must have been pushing eighty. But Mary was a fixture of the town, and everyone liked her.

She'd had three sons, but they'd all died young, years before she and her husband came here. She didn't like to talk about it much.

Lately she slept the days away in an overstuffed chair, in the far corner of that big front room. It was Annie and Cass who actually did all the work. They stayed with her every week, from Sunday night until they went home to their family on Thursday.

She paid them more than fair really, and mostly they just kept her company, while she taught them a trade.

Annie won't ever keep anyone company again, thought John sadly. He was a man who keenly felt each loss of life — but particular so when that life was a young one. He took a deep breath and knocked three times on the door.

It was Cass who opened it. "Mister Ray," she said happily, and she touched his one arm then. "Do come in and sit, I'll get coffee. Did Billy come home yet? He said he was really going this time. Please, tell me he's come home already!"

He shook his head sadly. "No coffee, Cass, I can't stay. But thanks for the offer." He kept his voice quiet out of habit, but it didn't really matter.

Old Mary Brown hadn't stirred from her slumber in the corner when he entered, nor when he spoke. Wouldn't matter how loud they got really, she was three parts deaf on a good day.

It must give her peace though, he thought, *she sleeps even longer these days.*

Cass and John sat down side by side at the sewing table, half turned so they faced each other some. His mind was so weighted down, he'd forgotten to take off his hat when he entered. So he took it off now, placed it down on the table, fidgeted some with the brim of it.

I'm sitting in Annie's chair, he thought. And that hurt him, it hurt real bad.

"Mister Ray, are you alright?" Cass asked.

He looked up, managed almost half a smile and said, "Now how many times do I need to tell you, Cass? You just call me John. If you're to be family — *and you are* — it just won't do, you bein' so formal."

She could see all the pain in his eyes, and knew for sure Billy wasn't back. She reached out, put a hand on his forearm. "Don't worry, Mister Ray. *John.* He'll come back soon, I'm certain." And she gave him a reassuring smile.

"I got some terrible news, Cass, and ... I'm sorry. I'm so *very* sorry."

"*Not Billy?*" she said, her doe eyes growing wide in her panic.

"No, girl, Billy's fine, far as I know. It's your family. I'm sorry, Cass, they're all gone."

Without thinking, he extended his arm toward her, preparing for the girl to pass out from the shock of the news. But she did not pass out, did not move. She just blinked, as if that might change things. Like it was a dream that could be blinked away.

"I'm so sorry," John Ray said again. "They're..."

She looked away a few moments, turned half toward the front door, as if someone might enter. Then she looked back at him, into his eyes, all the way in, as if searching for something inside them.

He did not look away when he spoke. "I'm so sorry, Cass. There was a fire. Smoke must have got 'em before they woke. I'm told they were still in their beds, so they wouldn't have suffered. I want you to know that."

"But ... but Pa was always so careful. *And Momma?*"

"I'm sorry."

"Jimmy? Surely not *Annie?* Oh no, Mister Ray, please not Annie." Tears welled in her eyes, but somehow Cass stayed calm. Somehow.

"I'm so sorry." It was breaking his heart just to see her. And not a thing he could do. "It's all four of 'em, Cass."

"But ... no. *Where's Billy?* I want Billy *now!* Oh, Mister Ray! Where's Billy now when I need him?" And still she did not scream, did not squeal. But she moved toward the kind man who she knew would look after her, and she buried her head in his chest. And even as she broke open, that girl cried so softly and quietly, the old seamstress still did not wake.

And John Ray, he felt suddenly old again. He had never had daughters, but he loved this girl like she was one, for she and Billy had been inseparable for years, almost from the first day her family had come here.

He still wasn't sure what to do, but she was firmly attached. So he awkwardly placed his huge rough hand on her back; then he smoothed her gold hair; then he patted her back as she cried.

Another hand might have helped, he thought.

Then after awhile she pushed away from him a little, and he moved his arm out of her way. Then Cassie Jo MacPherson looked away, rubbed at her eyes some, sniffled a little. She stood on wobbling legs, walked unsteadily to the end of the table, leaning on it as she went. Then, when the table could take her no further, she turned and said, "Can I see them?"

"No, darlin'," he said softly, and got to his feet. "I don't reckon so. Best remember 'em all how they were. I'm gonna go out there right now with the Marshal, start to take care of things. Then I'll make all the necessary arrangements. You're family, Cass, even though Billy's not here right now when we need him. But he'll come home and marry you soon, and we'll all get through this together. We're your family now, Cass, don't forget it. Hold tight to that now."

And it was clear from his tone that John Ray meant what he said, every word.

"What if Billy's killed too? In the war I mean? What then?" And she rushed to John, and she clung to him. The strength of her grip surprised him as she sobbed against his chest.

"Shhhh, child, he'll come home soon." He stroked her strawberry-blond hair then to soothe her. "We'll wait on Billy together. Your rightful place is with us now. I already told Rosie to prepare you a room. Stay here for now, and don't tell no one if you can help it — maybe just Mary when she wakes. I'll come collect you when me and the Marshal gets back. Don't worry, Cass darlin', it'll be okay in the end."

"But what if it's not okay?"

"If it's not okay — it's not the end. I promise you that."

Then John Ray put on his hat, and went off to do what he must.

CHAPTER 8

SCATTERGUN

By the time Billy watered that horse, gave him a good rub down, packed up, had a quick bite, and got to loading that dead feller across his own saddle, the sun was shining down into that clearing, and it surely made things less pleasant.

That Red feller, he was heavy!

Billy had never had to move a dead body before — not a human one — and it shocked him how awkward it was. Seemed to him to weigh double what a live feller did.

"Guess that's why they call it *dead weight*," he called out to Jenny. "Dead weight, ya get it, Jen?"

She seemed to appreciate that one, and gave a short whinny, then went right on back to feeding.

One laugh outta his mare was one better than expected, so he quit while he was ahead, and went back to tryin' to lift Red up onto that gelding.

In the end Billy got the job done, but by that time him and Red was on much less friendly terms — in fact, by then, as the sweat poured all outta him, Billy Ray wondered just *why* he'd gone to all that trouble for a stinking drygulching outlaw.

"Woulda been harder to bury him though, a'course," he told Jenny when they finally made it out to the trail, put his long left foot in a stirrup and stepped up into the saddle.

Now if Billy had known that local area better — or had more experience of outlaws — he might not have dillied and dallied so long as he had. He might have left ol' Red for the buzzards, jumped up on Jenny's back, and hightailed it for the next town, then told the lawman to go back and deal with Red's carcass.

Well, we each of us learn from our mistakes, and no reason Billy should be different.

Thing was, Red's outlaw friends — Joey and August was their names — were not about to let some kid best them.

Well, August wasn't, at least. Damn kid had shot him in the foot, just for one thing. Front corner of his boot was part missing, and his little toe too, he figured, and maybe some foot from behind it. Not that he wanted to look. There'd be time for that later, when he cleaned it. But for now, some good slugs of whiskey would just have to do.

And while August didn't care about Red, he did care about the ninety dollars Red had been holding. He wanted it back, and he wanted revenge for his foot. At least it had numbed now, but he wasn't nohow looking forward to later, for he knew he'd be feelin' lively when he finally took off his boot.

He'd had several other fellers in his little gang over the

years, and hadn't much cared when he'd lost all them fellers neither. And Red, he wasn't much good for nothin' except givin' out beatings. That's how he'd gotten that Bert feller's hundred dollars.

It was August who'd blown Bert's head off, once it was all over.

Way he himself saw it, August was the brains, and he figured all others replaceable — even Joey, who'd been with him three years. He'd made some mistakes to begin with, but he'd learned a trick or two along the way, for sure and for certain he had.

Like when they ran from Billy, for example — they could easily have taken Red's horse. August figured the horse too small anyway, but he knew from experience that if they made a great show of hightailin' it, and left that worthless horse behind, odds were good that the feller they ran from would take his time, load up the body and take it to town — hoping of course that there might be a bounty on the dead man.

That trick had worked once before. And while he might be a dead shot, he was just a fool kid, way August figured.

Thing was though, Billy never even *thought* about bounties — he was just shocked by what he'd done, and was trying to do what was right.

And mostly, that's the way a man *should* do things.

But not always — as Billy was just about to find out.

Now, when August and Joey hightailed it back west, they got 'emselves to a ridge where they could watch the road from — just to see if Billy got outta there in a hurry.

And of course, he did not.

They could not see into the clearing from back there, only straight down at the road — and figuring him a dead shot, they did not risk going back. No, they needed to fight that boy on their own terms, and more careful this time.

They knew which direction he was going, for they'd tracked him that morning. Back then they'd figured he'd be easy game, just being one feller, one horse.

So what they did now, was double around on a back-trail they knew of, went along quick as they could, and got 'emselves up in front of him. It was actually the more direct route, and had been the only route for a time. But whenever the creeks swelled it was no use, so now it was only used as a shortcut by locals — and by outlaws doubling back on folk, like these fellers now.

Once they got back to the right road again, they got 'emselves into position at the best ambush spot they could find, and they waited for Billy to show.

Then they waited some more.

And some more.

Then, the waitin' bein' hot work, and none too interesting, those two boys argued a little, and drank some.

Waited.

Argued.

Drank whiskey.

Waited some more as they argued, for they was increasingly angered by the sight of each other — each blaming the other for all that had been going wrong.

"Where *is* that damn kid?" August said once. "What could he possibly be doin' all this time?"

See, those boys never woulda figured that Billy would sit by himself a half hour just thinking. Not to mention another half hour taking proper care of Red's horse. They just weren't the sorta fellers who did such things, so it never occurred to 'em others might.

So the whole time they waited they argued — for Joey had finally realized that the brains of their operation had not much brains at all. He wasn't about to say that out loud though — not in so many words — for even though August wasn't much of a shot, he carried a sawed-off scattergun with him, so he didn't need to be.

No sense riling him too much.

Still, Joey did have a strong argument for leaving Billy alone, way he saw it. So he did keep niggling at August a *little,* to try changing his mind.

So they disagreed and disputed, they quarreled and they quibbled, they bickered but stopped short of brawlin' — then they waited some more. And it was mighty hot down there behind that big rock, the sun shining right on them, and the glare from the creek in their eyes was making their heads hurt — especially Joey's, for he'd lost his hat when he'd hightailed it earlier.

And by now, despite plenty of whiskey, ol' August's foot was really beginning to throb. His mood was almost as ornery as Joey had seen it. So Joey stopped with the arguing then, for August was prone to fits of temper when pushed just too far.

They had waited so long, in the end, August figured that maybe, that kid had outsmarted them — and gone back the way he had come from. But he wasn't about to admit it. He was the brains.

So he finally gave in to Joey by saying, "Alright, ya weak skunk, you win. Let's go back to the hideout and fix this damn foot of mine." But right when he said it, there came a sweet noise to his ears. It was Billy, singing *Lorena.*

"Listen! He's singin' our tune," said August. And he even forgot about his foot for the moment. "Now get ready, *Stoopid,* and don't go off half cocked like last time."

Now, Joey wasn't bad with a rifle — but he seemed to lack patience, and always tried for the long shot. Truth of it was, Joey Smythe was not really cut out for drygulching.

Oh, he could shoot straight while out hunting food — but shootin' at men, that was different. Men scared him, because men can shoot back. That was why he'd deserted, about a week into the war, along with August and a few others. And the two had been together since, while other fellers came and went from their gang.

Or rather, they came and joined up, then got 'emselves killed in service of August and his many fool plans.

They'd had four of the gang killed just this past month — just a run of bad luck, August reckoned, and he would have moved the gang on elsewhere if they didn't have the best hideout they'd ever found. Anyways, four dead in a month was how Joey had found himself promoted to drygulcher two weeks ago.

So Billy and Jenny come trotting down a slope toward a small bridge at the bottom, with Red's horse trailing behind them, calm as you ever could hope for. And they have no idea that behind a big rock by the creek, August and Joey are hiding, their guns at the ready.

But instead of waiting until the horses step onto the bridge like he's meant to, that poor scared wide-eyed fool Joey steps out into the open when Billy's still fifty yards off. Trouble for Joey that, though — for the sun and the water conspires against him, and a nasty reflection of the sunlight half blinds him and he screws his eyes up against it. He hurries off a wild shot anyway, and it whistles right past the target — misses by maybe six feet.

That's when August, with a great howl of whiskey-soaked rage, turns that scattergun on his only friend in the world — and from two feet away, blows poor Joey's hatless head right off of his shoulders.

CHAPTER 9
"HELLUVA THING..."

When the four men approached the charred ruin that had been the MacPherson place, the thing that near done John Ray in was the smell.

He knew it too well.

John had endured such smells before, and also the sights that went with them. Perhaps if he had explained such things to young Billy, the boy would not have idealized war how he had, and maybe he would have stayed at home.

But John Ray never spoke about war — at least not in specifics.

Even though he was missing an arm, John had never been one to shirk hard work or responsibility. He ran a good ranch, and he led his men by example. But confronted as he was by past memories, he hung back now, told the Marshal and the Strawheads he'd rather not see the bodies.

"Tom was my friend," he said, "and his wife and

children good people. I'd rather remember them just how they were. If that's okay with you, Clem."

"I can understand that," said Marshal Clem Jenkins, stepping down from his horse. "Don't much fancy lookin' myself, but it's my *job* to check it all out. A Marshal must do things other men can't or won't. You wait back here, John, with the horses. If I need your opinion I'll holler."

John noticed that Jasper didn't seem none too keen to go neither, but followed along out of duty, sort of skulking behind. But Horace, he led the way, and seemed almost eager to look.

You'd think he'd have seen enough already.

But there went the young man, pointing out the bodies to the Marshal, as they approached what was left of the cabin — and what was left of four good people.

Strawheads always was a strange pair. One tall and one short, but both with their shaggy blond hair like a pair of the sheepdogs the English folk favor.

But without the intelligent eyes or the happy demeanor, John thought as he turned away and looked around. *At least the barn's gone undamaged.*

The others had tied their horses to trees at the edge of the clearing, but John had not yet dismounted. His horse — and the others as well — seemed uneasy at being here. It wasn't surprising. There was something about such destruction that set horses — and people — on edge.

John dismounted now, rubbed the neck of his gelding awhile to soothe him, then once he was quiet, led him toward the barn. He tied the horse to the rail of the corral it adjoined, then walked over and opened the barn doors up wide, and wandered inside. It all looked regular enough.

Too regular maybe, he decided. *There's somethin' ... somethin' ... ain't right.*

Thing was, Tom MacPherson was a usual sort of a man in many respects — did all the things most fellers do, or at least most of the ones to do with hard work, and keeping his place neat — but he had one somewhat unusual trait. Tom MacPherson always did keep the cleanest, tidiest barn anyone ever saw.

Except, that was, for a strip down one side, underneath a big work bench — that one section of floor was always covered in old straw and dirt.

Thing is, a tidy barn ain't *that* unusual — but Tom, he had a most *particular* way of doing things.

In fact, John and Tom had a running joke between them about it.

Like a pair of kids we were sometimes, John remembered now fondly — *two old fools who should have known better. But I guess, wherever two old friends meet in private, they're more like two children come out to play.*

They never said nothin' about it in front of other folks, for it might have got taken wrongly if anyone thought they were serious. But when it was just the two of them, solvin' the problems of the world out in this very barn, John would pick up a broom and say, "I reckon this place needs a clean. Here, I'll give ya a lesson in how these things work, Tom." And he'd commence then to sweep up a storm, pushing that broom with his one arm, always toward the barn doors.

Tom would watch him do it, always saying, "Reckon

you should leave the sweepin' to fellers with arms enough to do it right."

But he'd always stand by and wait 'til John put aside the broom. Then Tom would take hold of that broom, and sweep the barn *crossways.*

And that was just what was wrong here — it was clean alright, clean as ever — except, of course, for the buildup under the bench. What was different than normal though, was that dirt floor had been swept from the back of the barn to the front — normal-ways instead of across-ways.

Somethin' ain't right, thought John Ray. But no matter how he looked about, he couldn't find anything else out of place. So he walked back outside, closed the doors, and as he checked on and watered the critters, John looked all around for some other clue that might tell some of what happened.

It all seems so regular. But it ain't, I can feel it, it ain't.

In fact, if he ignored the sweeping, and didn't look toward the house — and somehow managed to ignore the terrible smell — he might have thought *everything* normal.

He glanced quickly toward the remains of the house. It was partly still standing, one corner of the heavy frame — but the roof structure had all come down. The others were kneeling, looking at something in a corner, and a shudder went all the way through him.

He did not wish to think about it. He turned and wandered away, went looking for clues again to occupy his mind.

The bright sun cast no light on whatever had happened here. The whole place seemed all in order, aside from the house. But then John noticed something — it was an odd little thing, but what was he trying to find, if not something odd?

John stood and looked down at it. A patch of flattened grass, like might be left after cutting and branding a steer. But not quite so wide, and just about the length of a person. Worn extra at the middle, and at the bottom end of it. And at the top of it, a small patch of dirt, patted down flat, then covered some by dry grass.

He knelt down, threw away the dry grass and brushed at the dirt. It was loose and damp. Patted down with boots maybe, but loose enough once disturbed. Rang an odd note, but nothing he could quite put a finger on.

That was when Clem called him over. He gave that flat patch one more look, and wandered back toward the house.

Clem and the boys met him halfway. Jasper didn't look none too well, but he followed on behind the others. John realized something about Jasper then — he often looked like a dog who was wary of being kicked, but felt like he better stay within kickin' distance anyways.

Can't be easy bein' Horrie's friend, I guess, thought John. He felt a pang of guilt when he thought it, but he was used to that pang by now.

Horrie's hard to love sometimes is all. Like he's got somethin' missing inside him. I'm just grateful he has a friend.

John took out his hip flask — he'd figured before he left home it might come in handy — and said, "Are you alright there, Jasper? Here, come have a drink and sit down, it's a lot to take in. I'm just glad I didn't find 'em."

Jasper eagerly took the hip flask, flopped himself down on the ground and took himself a swig. "Thank you, Mister Ray."

"What's with all you young'uns? You ain't children no more. Call me John now, remember?"

Jasper nodded his thanks, and Horrie took the flask from him and took a swig too — more a pour. Then he wiped his lips and said, "They's sure all burned up, Pa."

"Near's I can tell," said the Marshal with a shake of his head, "they all burned right in their beds. Mostly can't even tell who was who. Helluva thing, but an accident. Someone musta fell asleep readin's my best guess, and knocked over the lamp without waking. Fire's smoldered, smoke's overcome 'em, then they've burned right up when the place caught. At least they never suffered." Then he took a flask from his own pocket, and drained about half in one go.

All this panicked John Ray more than he would have liked. "But you *did* work out who was who, right? For the funerals, I mean. *For the graves!*" He grabbed his own flask back from Horace, but found it was empty. He shot the boy a hard look.

"Hold your horses, John, and don't worry. Horrie knew whose bed was which. He'd been here before with his brother. And besides, we can tell by their heights, more or less. And Lucy was wearin' a ring, it's still there, more or less, in a pool."

"Alright then," John said. "Alright."

"That fire sure burned hot," said the Marshal. "Damn roof caved right in on top of two of the beds. Never seen folk so thoroughly burned. Only Jimmy I coulda recognized. Helluva thing."

"How'd you know it was Annie?" asked John then.

"By what bed she was in," said Jasper.

But Horace didn't say nothing. He turned his head away, looked back at the house.

"The two girls shared a bed," said John, his voice tight and pained. "How'd you boys know it was Annie, and not Cass, that was burned in it?"

Jasper didn't speak this time, he just looked to Horace, who turned around then, looked evenly at his father, and spoke clear as water from a cool rocky stream.

"Their Ma kept Annie home because she was sick — but Cass still went into town to work for the seamstress, like any other week."

John stared at him a few moments before saying, "But neither of you boys had been to town to have learned that. Last you went into town was on Saturday, and you both came home that night. So who told you all that about Annie?"

There was no hesitation from Horace at all. "Billy, a'course." And he got a puzzled look on his face as he stared at his father. "Before he left for the war, Pa. Remember? He'd been in town already that mornin', and said his goodbyes to Cass."

"I've no recollection of him saying Annie was ill," said John. "Only that he'd spoken to Cass." He could feel the pressure of it all, the whole thing bubbling inside him, the terrible wrongness of the deaths of all these fine people. And John Ray doubted himself then, something he wasn't accustomed to. "I don't ... are you sure? Are you certain, son?"

"Sure I am. Don't you remember him sayin' it, Pa? Aw, you was too busy fightin' with him about war stuff. Always that same fool argument from him, over and over and over. That dang young fool and his war!"

John Ray put his palm out in front of him, signaling Horace to stop. "Alright. Alright. I'm sorry, son. This ... this all gets to me, is all." Then he looked down at the ground, and he seemed to grow shorter. "Brings up all the ... brings up things I'd rather forget."

They all looked where John's other arm should have been — but that wasn't what he'd meant, not at all. It was *other men* John was remembering. Friends. And strangers as well. Men from the army he'd served, and the army he'd fought against too. All good men, more than likely. Shot men. Throat-cut men. Blowed all to pieces men. And *burned* men — somehow *that* seemed the worst in his memories.

And John Ray — who had never been much of one for the drink — said, "Anything left in that flask of yours, Clem? Mine's drained, and I could sure use a drop."

CHAPTER 10
"JUST DON'T START SINGIN' LORENA"

"Not again," Billy yelled when that bullet came whizzing past and into the trees back at the bend in the road well behind him.

Jenny didn't much like it either. She reared up then broke sideways away from the noise, while Billy struggled to get her back under control. Then not a moment after that rifle was fired, came the great booming sound of a scattergun.

Even from the distance, young Billy Ray saw the result of the shotgun blast, and he could scarce believe it had happened. Not only how the man's head had been part of him one moment, and nothing but red paint on the wind in the next — no, not just that — but also the fact that the man's friend and ally could have done such a thing to him. It did not seem possible. Still, there was no time to think on the whys and the wherefores of it all, he was stuck in the middle of this, and he had to act fast.

It was a bad situation, and Jenny was spooked

something awful. Billy couldn't get off that horse quick enough. He had been unfooted from his right stirrup for one thing, and almost been unseated completely. And he had dropped the rope he'd been leading Red's horse with as well. Luckily Jenny had gone to her left, to the trail edge, and at least this put them out of the remaining gunman's sight.

For the moment.

Billy jumped down off of the mare and spoke softly to soothe her, and she let him lead her into the trees.

As for that horse of Red's, he didn't much care either way about gunfire — it was all in a day's work for him, no matter where the bullets come from or went. And being led along with the dead weight of Red on his back, he had felt right at home, and gone back to his days as a pack horse. So when Billy dropped the rope, that calm little gelding just followed Jenny along anyway — for somethin' to do, more or less.

"Ya damn stupid kid," August yelled from back behind his rock. "Now ya killed *both* my friends."

"Aw, not you again," Billy answered, loud and strong as he could manage, as he tied off the horses. "And considerin' I ain't even fired yet, I don't reckon it was *me* who killed this one."

Then he took out his rifle, and looked all around him, trying to decide what to do, and his heart was sure pounding.

"It's *your* fault I blew his damn head off," came August's hysterical yelling. "Joey was the best friend I ever had."

"Seems like when the Good Lord was makin' you," Billy called, "he left out the good sense to quit when you ain't got no chance."

Billy couldn't see August from here, but he knew he needed a plan. This crazed outlaw sure was persistent.

"Oh I won't be quittin'," August yelled back. "Now come out and face me like a man."

Billy knew he'd have to do something quick.

His Pa had always told him, *Man who loses his temper loses the fight. Always keep calm and rational, and remember to breathe.*

That had helped him when wrestling Horrie, and lately he'd more than held his own against his heavier brother.

So he took a deep breath and felt better, and he rubbed Jenny's neck now to quiet her. Then he took a couple more of those breaths, while he thought the problem through.

That loco feller had killed his own friend. But if August calmed down some and got to thinking straight, he'd come sneaking up on Billy and shoot him right here where he was.

Then again, I did shoot him in the foot before, so maybe he ain't up to sneaking far. But I need a better vantage point, and I need to keep him unhinged.

"What sorta skunk murders his own friend anyway?" Billy called. "Ol' Joey ain't gonna be happy when you meet up in Hell a minute from now. Weak as squirrel piss you are, I reckon."

"*Squirrel piss?*" August screamed. "Why, I'll give you ... *damn kid!*"

By then Billy had decided on which way to go. He

needed a clear shot at this angry outlaw, and he reckoned he knew where he'd get one. Long as the skunk didn't move.

He remembered how out of shape he'd gotten when Jenny reared — so he checked the weight of his canvas bag, and took a quick look inside it. Seemed about right, and Billy was satisfied he hadn't spilled any cartridges in all the kerfuffle.

"Wait here, Jen," he said quietly, giving her one last reassuring pat before leaving her. "And whatever you do, don't start singin' *Lorena!* Seems like every time someone sings them words we get shot at."

Then he began picking his way quietly through the trees, hoping to get a view behind the rock where August was hiding.

As he crept along, carefully choosing each footfall, he remembered what his Pa had once told him — *"You can't shoot worth a damn yet, but you can sneak around quiet as any Indian. Keep workin' on that, son, it might just save your life someday."*

He was glad now he'd listened to his Pa about that. Seemed like the more he run into these outlaws, the more of his Pa's wise words seemed to come help him out.

As for Billy's steps always being so quiet, his choice of footwear sure didn't hurt. He had never liked ordinary boots, and had worn only moccasins for years. First pair he'd got was a gift from an old Indian feller he met, just a few miles from home. Not Cottonwood Falls — that other home was in Texas, before they came up to Kansas.

His Pa's eyes had near popped out when he first seen

them moccasins on him. They was real fancy too. Billy was maybe just six then, and had never much liked wearing shoes.

Next day after that, Billy's Pa went out with him to where he'd met the Indian feller. They'd had some words together, and it was the one time Billy ever saw his Pa smoke a pipe.

Sometimes that whole part of Billy's life seemed more like a dream.

After that, for awhile, Billy still saw that Indian every so often, and his Pa seemed to allow it, long as he didn't tell no one else. Feller never came to their house though. He taught Billy to track some, now he got to rememberin' about it. But mostly, they just seemed to walk about together, the old man telling Billy what seemed like crazy stories of the sun and the moon and the stars, and a few about water and fire, and some about critters.

Then the Indian feller told Billy it was his time to move on, and he would see him one day in the sky. Awhile after that, the Rays moved to Kansas, where Billy had the old seamstress Mary Brown make up his moccasins. Billy's Pa made him get 'em real plain, no fancy adornment. Still, he always liked 'em a lot.

Comfortable *and* quiet they were. Better still, Cass had made this last pair with her very own hands. And they sure was helping him now, as he quietly went sneaking.

That crazed fool August kept up his yelling, and that made Billy's life easier, for he could tell that the outlaw wasn't moving. He didn't answer, of course, just moved along through the trees there, as quiet as he could, as fast as he dared — and all the while, August ranted and taunted and threatened, but he stayed right there where he was. Some of them tortures he had in mind, Billy hadn't ever even heard of — and some of the others did not even sound nearly possible.

That outlaw's loco alright. And his foot must be too bad to move much.

And then Billy found himself right where he wanted to be. Upstream, behind August, about fifty yards off, a clear straight line along the creek bed. He raised up his rifle and took aim, as careful as he could. Had him right in his sights.

But Billy Ray could not squeeze that trigger, no more than he could have cut off his own feet and cooked 'em for supper.

Even after all this feller had done, Billy *couldn't* shoot a man in the back — even *if* he could manage to shoot straight.

So instead of squeezing that trigger, Billy called out, "Throw down your gun or I'll fill you with lead."

Well, August mighta been loco, but he had no quit in him at all — just as Billy had observed a few minutes earlier. The crazed outlaw spun and fired wildly, the bullet not even coming anywhere close, then he limped and hopped for his life — and before Billy could fire a shot, August had put rock between them again, and all Billy's planning and sneaking along hadn't made much difference at all.

But he waited, gun at the ready, for August to show his face again. *And this time,* Billy decided, *I'm going to shoot him. Well, maybe ... if I have to.*

"Come on out, August," he called. "I won't shoot you if you'll just give up."

"Who's August?" came the answer from down behind that boulder by the creek. "I's Dan'l Boone, and you best prepare to die! *Squirrel piss, am I?*"

Then August commenced popping his head and his rifle — it was Joey's rifle in fact — up over the rim of that rock. Each time he poked his head up he fired, and each bullet came closer to Billy, and they were getting too dang close for comfort. That outlaw was a quick loader too, and had got off five shots in a minute.

At least he ain't got a Spencer — if he did I'd be in trouble.

That was around about when Billy remembered that he himself *did* have a Spencer. And that it could be used to advantage.

Billy had spaced all his shots out 'til now, and August had not seen the Spencer — so even if the outlaw *did* know about repeaters, he could not know Billy had one.

Next time he's almost due to pop his head up, I'll fire one off then get the next round ready quick. He won't expect me to have another shot ready so soon, and he might come out from cover longer, take time with his aim.

So Billy fired one off, and it hit the rock the outlaw was behind. The bullet hit maybe two feet too low, and ricocheted off with an echoing ping — then somehow Billy managed a smooth cycling, and his timing was perfect.

He squeezed off another round, right when August's head came up again — and that outlaw never even get his shot off. But he sure made a helluva noise.

To Billy's surprise, that bullet *almost* found its mark.

But it *didn't* go through August's head.

No.

What that big bullet *did* do, was to hit that huge boulder right at the top, and shatter the rim of it into pieces — shards even, that was the worst of it.

That loco outlaw had his kerchief over his mouth, but his eyes were completely unprotected — and some of them shards of rock made it into his eyes, and with quite some force.

And if the noise he'd made earlier, when he got his foot shot, was screaming — well, it had nothin' on the noise he made now.

Squirrel piss, was what Billy thought when he heard it.

But once he came closer, he didn't think so poorly of that miscreant's toughness. Because it became clear then, that ol' August's outlawing days were over — for he wouldn't be getting his sight back, nohow not ever.

CHAPTER 11

THE DWARF & THE SHERIFF

Four hours later, when Billy rode into Wilmington, there was no shortage of staring and muttering. He was leading a string of three horses — two with dead men over the saddles, and one with a live man all tied onto his. And that live feller had a blood-soaked bandana wrapped round his head, completely covering his eyes.

It made for a strange sight alright.

"Sheriff's office a hundred yards on your left, kid," an oldtimer out front of the barber's told Billy, with a disbelieving shake of his head.

No one else spoke to him directly, but he could feel something almost alive — an excitement that coursed through the town, like hot blood courses through a man's veins just before a big fight.

A real short stocky feller — as in four feet and nothin' much else — rushed across the street on bandy legs and burst on into the Sheriff's Office. A few moments later the Sheriff walked outside to greet Billy as he dismounted. And that short big-headed feller trailed right behind the Sheriff, and he looked real curious.

"Looks like you got a story to tell, son," said the Sheriff to Billy.

"I need a doctor," cried August then. "I need one right now."

"He does," Billy said. "Needs one bad. His eyes are all busted up from a rock I hit firin' at him."

"Go bring the Doc," said the Sheriff to the short feller. Well, that feller didn't answer, he just took off runnin' on them strong little legs of his faster'n Billy thought possible. Looked a bit comical to Billy, and after all that had happened, he coulda used a good laugh — but no one else laughed, not one lick, so he didn't either.

After watching the fast feller go, the Sheriff stepped down from the boardwalk to look at the dead men. He cringed just a little when he pulled back the blanket and saw one was missing his head. Then he came back and said, "Well, we best untie the blindman and get him inside. Doc Miller can look at him here in the calaboose, but he ain't going anywhere else. What's your name, feller?"

"Dan'l Boone," August said bitterly.

But the Sheriff said, "Wasn't asking *you*. I *know* who *you* are from your horse and that damn cannon you been murderin' innocent folk with. And the only thing I *don't* like about all this, is that *you* won't be suffering long. We'll be hanging you in the morning, August Greene. After a fair trial, of course."

"I didn't do nothin'," screamed August.

But the Sheriff only turned back to Billy, shook his

head slowly and asked him, "Now, how the livin' *persnickety* did you capture all these boys, young feller? You can help me gather up all these guns while you start to explain it."

Billy helped to collect the guns that belonged to the outlaws — but instead of answering the question, he politely asked the Sheriff if he could go to a livery and have all the horses attended to.

By then, that short feller was already runnin' hell for leather back up the street, calling that the Doc was on his way. His voice sure shocked Billy some — for such a small feller, he had the smoothest, pleasantest voice he ever did hear.

Mellifluous, that's what Rosie'd call it.

The Sheriff told Billy not to worry about the horses, he was not in the practice of allowing good animals to suffer anything they didn't have to. Then he told that fast feller, "Drop off the two dead men to the undertaker, then get the horses to Frank's livery to be properly cared for. And tell Frank it's me paying."

The short feller nodded, then moved toward Jenny so quick he scared her, which kinda startled him too. They sure made a sight, scaring each other that way.

"It's alright, Jenny," Billy told her. "He's gonna take care of you good."

"Settle down some, Morris," said the Sheriff to the small feller. "Half speed'll do just fine for now." Then as Morris led the horses away — roundabout three-quarter speed — the Sheriff confided, "He's my nephew, and a deputy too, but I keep him unarmed and in town, much as I can. Moves like that most the time. Reckon he's tryin' to make up for the lack of leg underneath him."

"Seems to *more* than make up for it," said Billy.

"Yessir," said the Sheriff. "He's a real good boy. Roundabout your age, I'd reckon. I guess you were wondering about that, what with his height. It's okay to wonder — most do. Just don't tease him about it and we'll all get on fine."

"Wasn't planning on it, Sheriff," Billy answered.

By the time they got August untied and inside, the Doc had arrived, and he said there wasn't much he could do besides wash out the eyes good and proper. Seemed to Billy the Doc mighta gone gentler on August. Even told him he didn't have no laudanum, and never budged from it. Allowed him a little whiskey though — but even that not until *after* he'd had a good dig at the eyes with his fingers.

Turned out August had robbed and killed one of the Doc's very best friends — a man who the Doc and the newspaperman and the lawyer used to play whist with. Not only was a good man dead, but they were now one player short.

"Don't suppose you play whist?" asked the doctor, as Billy helped the Sheriff lock up all the guns in one of the cells — Billy's Spencer repeater included.

"Sorry, Doc, never learned," Billy answered.

But he surely was learning a lot of good lessons — this one was *Be nice to doctors, and also their friends. A doctor might well end up with a whole lot of power over your comfort. Or your lack of comfort.*

As the Doc worked, August screamed up a storm, and

the air was near blue with his cursing. The Sheriff couldn't even hear what Billy was saying. So he had him stop talking, went to his desk drawer and took out some papers, then went through the stack 'til he found which ones he was searching for.

Then he cast his eyes over Billy's long thin body and said, "You look like you could do with a decent feed, young feller. From one Spencer owner to another, how's about you allow me to buy you a steak? Early supper, we'll call it. And while we eat you can tell me that story, every detail." He grabbed his hat off the peg, threw open the door, and headed off down the street, with Billy having almost to run so as he could catch up.

Seems like it ain't only that short feller moves fast round here. Must run in the family.

Once they sat down in Catrina's Family Restaurant and ordered, Billy told the Sheriff who he was and where he come from, and they took things from there.

He liked details, that Sheriff, and it took Billy quite awhile to explain all that had happened. By then their bellies were more than full, having filled them with steak and potatoes and beans — then overfilled them with a pretty good apple pie. Two pieces each.

"Don't know where you're putting it all," said Sheriff Mike Brimstone. But he said it with a big smile.

Once they were done eating, the Sheriff sat back in his chair and loosened his belt some. Billy would have done too, but he didn't have a belt, so he just sat back and looked around.

"By the way, Sheriff," said Billy, taking out Bert's letter

with the ninety dollars wrapped in it and handing it over, "I guess I should give this to you. I forgot to tell you, it was on that first feller, the one I shot accidental."

"Oh, no," he said when he looked at it. "I doubt that the Harrisons will be happy to see this ninety dollars back. He was a good boy, Bert Harrison. Just a young'un too, like yourself." And that Sheriff looked mighty sad.

Billy had noticed by then that no one in this town — aside from the Sheriff — wore a gun, so to change the subject away from poor Bert he asked about that.

"Keeps things more peaceable," said Sheriff Brimstone. "There's a lot of ill feeling these days. Some of it to do with the war, people taking different sides, as it were. But some folks just use the war as an excuse, and are out to settle old scores. So this past three months now, I make everyone disarm as soon as they come into town. You must have missed the sign, I suppose."

"I'm sorry, Sheriff, I must have."

"Had your hands full, I guess, but you'll know for next time."

"What if they don't want to disarm?" Billy asked, eyebrows raised.

"Then I assume they're outlaws, and shoot them. The rules are quite clear. And it's not only me to enforce it, I have another deputy too, not only young Morris. Dangerous to outlaws, that other deputy can be — he's killed several just lately. And speaking of August's gang," he added, pulling out the papers he'd taken from his desk drawer. "The three fellers you brought to town were all wanted men."

"Glad to be of help, Sheriff," said Billy, rubbing his belly then belching a little. Then he looked around, embarrassed, and said, "Sorry. Ate too much I guess."

Sheriff Mike Brimstone only laughed though, and spread the three papers out where Billy could read them for himself. "Rewards for all three," he said. "Unfortunately for you, only August and Joey were wanted dead or alive. Samuel "Red" Wilkins hadn't been with 'em long. Hadn't killed anyone that we're sure of — so you'd have had to bring him in alive to collect. Still, the others are worth five-hundred Lincolns between them."

"By gum," said Billy. "And I get some share of that with you?"

Mike laughed then and said, "Just how young are you anyway, kid? You're a tall streak alright, but you sure are wet behind the ears. Still, you did a man's job, Billy, and that whole bounty's all yours, you earned it."

"Double gum," Billy said happily. Then his eyes narrowed some, and an uppity look came over his face. "But I'm no kid, Sheriff. I turned seventeen a whole month ago, and I'm headin' off to the war."

"Quiet, son," warned Sheriff Brimstone, looking around to see who might have heard. "There's folks round here will wish to enquire which side you're planning to fight for — and if they don't like what they hear, you might not make it far out of town."

"I didn't really think about that," Billy said. "Seems clear enough to me which side's right, from talking with my brother about it, and reading some newspapers he gave me."

"You're honest, son, and that's admirable," Mike Brimstone said quietly. "And I know your heart's in the right place — most folk would have just kept that ninety dollars, and thrown Bert's letter away. You're a fine young man, but too trusting. You shouldn't believe all you read. Folks who own newspapers don't always report exact truth."

"It's funny you say that," said Billy, cocking his head sideways, how dogs sometimes do. "That's just what my Pa always said, almost down to the word."

That was when Sheriff Mike Brimstone said, "Billy, I don't know your Pa, never heard of him. But I reckon he'd appreciate me being straight with you now."

"You can't steer me back," Billy said. "I'm goin' to war."

"I know it," the older man answered. "I can't stop you from going. and won't waste words trying. But from all you've told me, you're gonna need some help and some guidance, even to *get* to where the fighting is. There's bad men all over these parts now — some are just murderers, others play at recruitment, but really, they're mostly the same. All have their own interests at heart, and it ain't safe to travel how you are."

"But surely—"

"No, listen, son," the Sheriff said firmly, as he put a hand up for Billy to stop talking and listen. "You need rest before you continue, and so do your horses."

"Only got one horse," Billy said.

"No, you got two now. That's one of the things that's important — you'll be needing a pack horse. Now you can't take August's horse, he stole that from someone he murdered, a friend of mine's brother. That one goes back to the man's wife. But you can choose either of the others, and most welcome to it."

"I ... I guess you're right, Sheriff. I'm maybe traveling too light, but it's still a bit much just for Jenny to travel so far with, even keeping it down to twenty miles a day, way my Pa always taught me."

Mike Brimstone studied him hard, and rubbed at his chin some. "You ran off without allowing your Pa to help outfit you, didn't you?"

"I..." Billy looked down at the tablecloth, picked up a speck of potato, put it onto the plate.

"As I thought. Well, tonight you'll stay at my house here in town. In the morning my wife will fix you a good breakfast." Then, leaning toward Billy, he whispered, "Not as good as this meal we just ate, but don't you tell her I said it — she likes to believe she can cook, so we all pretend to enjoy it. Even so, maybe you'll stay tomorrow night as well. By then, we'll have you outfitted properly. And I'll make you a map for where you want to go, and teach you what I can in the meantime. Deal?"

"But I haven't even told you which side I'm plannin' to fight for," said Billy. Then he tapped the side of his nose some, pointed at Mike Brimstone and said, "Ah, now I see. You already know which side — for you *know* which side's in the right."

"They're both right, Billy. And both wrong. And I don't care *which* side you fight for, and that's the whole truth. I have two brothers — both fools, I guess — fighting one for each side. I just hope they don't have to shoot each other."

"Wouldn't happen with my brother," said Billy. "He knows which side's right, and woulda come himself, only he's the eldest son. He'll have to run the ranch if something happens to Pa, so he never argued the war with him, way I did. Still, I can't imagine ever shooting at Horrie. I just couldn't — I'd have to let him shoot me."

"Well, that's just one more thing war does to families. Both sides ruin lives just the same. Anyway, that's why young Morris is here with me now. I just hope it won't be forever." And he sure did look sad.

"You really *don't* care which side I fight for, do you?" Billy asked, slowly shaking his head.

"I'd rather you don't fight at all. Much prefer you went home to your Pa, and lived a long healthy life. But if you're still fixed on going to war two mornings from now, I'll see that you leave here with at least a small chance at survival. Deal?"

Billy thought then of how much this Sheriff was just like his Pa, at least in most ways that mattered. And because of that, he would have said yes anyway — even if he wasn't so suddenly tired that he needed the two days of rest.

"Deal," he said with a solemn nod, and he held out his hand and they shook on it.

And that's how William Ray became friends with Sheriff Michael John Brimstone.

CHAPTER 12
LETTERS HOME

Billy didn't go along to watch August hanged. Just wasn't something he wanted to see. Mike could tell Billy had mixed feelings about it all, and he gave him a good talking to — set his mind straight on it in the end. August hadn't just *tried* to kill Billy, he had *succeeded* at killing several other fellers.

The Doc said there was no chance the outlaw would ever see again, so Billy argued that August wasn't much likely to kill again. But Sheriff Mike explained that hanging men like August Greene served *two* purposes — it stopped them from killing any more people for one thing, but it also served as a strong deterrent for other men with bad leanings.

And that second one was reason enough on its own.

"Besides," Mike said then. "Imagine the ways a blind man would suffer in prison. No, too horrific, don't even think about it. Or if we just released him here now, with everyone for miles around knowing he's killed folks they cared about. Either way, he'll die even more horribly, if we don't do what's right and hang him. It's a quick death, and I'll make sure it's done right."

Billy looked up at Mike. "Have you ever done it be—"

"Four times, Billy," he said. "Prefer I'd never had to. But better me doin' it right than some lynch mob messing it up. His suffering will be over in an instant."

So in the end Billy reconciled himself to it, but he still didn't go along to watch.

Mike changed the subject then, and said he would write to his sister in Boonville, and arrange for Billy to go there and wait for recruitment. Sheriff Mike didn't give away much, only insisted that this was the best place to go, and that Mike's Confederate brother would soon meet up with him there.

"Whatever else happens," Mike told him, "don't let anyone else recruit you. There's a lot of thieves and liars about."

"But what if some Union feller tries?" Billy asked him. "Can't very well tell 'em I'm on my way to go wear the gray, can I?"

"Any Union soldier questions you, you tell him you're on your way to fight for your Uncle, Devil Joe Brimstone, a Colonel who proudly wears blue. Say your name's Morris P. Brimstone. I'll give you a slip of paper with where to say you're going, every detail you'll need. Memorize it, and keep it to hand, just in case you need some sorta proof."

Billy pushed his fingers through his hair. "That'll be right hard to say. And what if they ask Devil Joe?"

"I've already written to Joe. He might fight for the

Union, but us Brimstones are Brimstones first, soldiers second. He'll verify the story, and they'll let you go on unmolested."

"Alright then," said Billy. "Not sure how well I can lie, but I will if I have to."

"You go to Boonville," said Mike, "wait with my sister, and when Preacher Rob gets there he'll see you're placed with experienced men. You might yet even survive the war, if you listen to just what he tells you. Rob is Morris's father."

"Preacher Rob, Devil Joe," Billy said, shaking his head. "In my family, we just call each other Billy, Horrie and Pa. We ain't even got middle names, let alone extras."

He also insisted Billy send home a letter, so his Pa and Cass would know they could write to him in Boonville.

Billy told Sheriff Mike what his Pa had said about not coming back if he went off to fight for rich men — but Mike told him to take no notice.

"I promise you, Billy," he said, "your Pa loves you, and only said that to keep you home safe. You *should* go back home, of course. But as you refuse to, you must write him, so he knows where you'll be. At least then he can write you back, and tell you how he *really* feels."

So while Sheriff Mike was off hanging August, Billy stayed at the house, wrote letters to Cass and his Pa then instead.

He found it strange, writing them. It was almost as if he'd become someone else, someone different already.

Perhaps he had, he decided.

I killed a man, just for one thing. There's no taking that back.

It took him four tries to get started on her letter, but each time he began to tell Cass what had happened, he stopped, crumpled the paper, threw it away.

The letter he sent, in the end, told little of what happened at all.

Dearest Cass. I do love you and always will. You are a wonder, my darling girl. Your precious letter sustains me through the difficulties I face.

I know my right place is with you. And yet I feel I must keep to the path I am on.

I WILL survive this war, and I WILL come home then and marry you, I promise it. Until then, you have your loving family, and my father and brother are your family as well.

Because, way I see things, we are already married. I will be true to you as long as we both shall live.

Forever your loving Billy.

P.S. For now, you can write me c/o the Postal Office at Boonville, M.O.

The letter Billy wrote to his father was easier in some ways, but harder in others.

Dear Pa. I am very sorry about some things. I should not have taken your Spencer, for one. But I figured you'd want me to have the best chance of coming home alive, so I took it. I had already packed before we argued. By the time I thought all about it, I was too far away to bring it back.

I am also sorry that I never listen. Truth is, I don't really know why I am doing this. Just seems like I have to, even now. I wish it was different, but it is how it is.

I got in two bad scrapes already, and those even before getting to the fighting. The Spencer helped some, so did Jenny. But mostly it was your words.

Wisdom, I now know them words to be.

All the things you told me over the years — things I never even knew I was listening to.

Like remembering to breathe. You would think any man would know that one already, but no. I forgot to breathe right when I needed to, but then your words come and saved me. Also about being patient — you were right Pa, that did save my life. And some other ones you said that I cannot remember right now.

Funny thing though. They all seem to come to me right when I need them, those words of yours.

Also, don't worry. I can sneak real quiet now.

Also, a real nice feller I met — just about full growed at four feet tall he is, you'd scarce believe it if you saw for yourself. Anyway, short or tall, he reckons anyone can learn to shoot straight, and he can teach me. If you can believe it. I hardly can believe it myself, but it's worth a try. They reckon he hits small targets 9 from 10 from a hundred yards out. I guess we'll see.

Also that short feller's uncle is a sheriff and he plans to outfit me the way he reckons you would have. If you had let me go to war, that is. Sorry again Pa. I guess I'm a bad son. At least Horrie is good, more or less. I'm glad you still have him at home.

That sheriff asked me if I was Indian, on account of my looks and my boots. Told me if I won't change to normal boots I should wear my trouser legs over these ones. Wide world sure is strange, what some folks looks down on others for. Sheriff warned me on that. Said to keep my hair cut short too.

They got some good cooks where I am now, but no one half so good as Rosie. They's nice ladies too, but Rosie wins on that score as well. She's a wonder, our Rosie. I miss her more than I can say. Tell her so, please, Pa — but make me sound less like a kid when you tell it.

Say howdy to Horrie and thank him for helping me get my thinking sorted all about the war. Thank him also for all them thrashings he gave me before I got too big for him. I see now he was teaching me never to give up the sponge, no matter how much something hurts.

I will come back after the war. But if you still want me not to I will only come back to get Cass then take her away. But I hope you changed your mind about that. I hope for that every night before I sleep, and am still hoping it when I wake every morning. It makes for strange dreams, I can tell you that much.

If you did changed your mind you can write me c/o the Postal Office at, Boonville, M.O.

Boonville is where I'm to join up with a real good outfit. Not sure what outfit yet, it's some sort of a secret.

I love you a lot Pa.

— Mister William Ray — (*I don't know why I wrote it official like that, I'm still just Billy really.*)

P.S. Please look out for Cass while I'm gone. She's just a kid really. I only found that out when I had to grow up so quick this long few days away from you both.

CHAPTER 13
SHOOTIN' LESSONS

Billy Ray ended up staying ten days in Wilmington. Ten days in which many lessons were learned — ten days in which several men died.

He and the Sheriff became good friends, and called each other Billy and Mike. But he made another, even better friend. Although you wouldn't be sure they were friends, if you went by the names those two called each other.

Once those two were sure of their friendship, they addressed each other in ways such as, "Howdy, ya Tall Streak a' Skunk-Stink" and "Howdy right back, ya Bow-Legged Big-Headed Flashy-Movin' Deringer."

I guess you can work out which was which.

At first Billy figured that short feller Morris might not be too smart, on account of him looking so different. But Morris was smart as a whip, as things turned out. And not just with words and numbers, but all sorts of practicalities too.

Third day Billy was there, Sheriff Mike told Morris to go coach Billy in how to fire and load his Spencer more smoothly and quicker. "Do whatever Morris says, it might just save your life," he told Billy.

Now, despite what Mike had told him about Morris's target shooting, Billy didn't think no four foot tall, bandy-legged kid had anything much to teach him.

Well, they was the same age, seventeen — but Morris just *seemed* like a kid, on account of his shortness. But Billy was a guest here after all, and Morris seemed like a nice feller. It woulda been rude to voice his true thoughts on the matter, so Billy didn't say nothin' much about that.

This was before the two of 'em had started up with all that fancy name-calling. But they *were* becoming friends already — and Billy didn't want to insult him, so he just went along with it. He could use some practice anyway, he reckoned, and Morris's company was pleasant.

Perhaps I'll be the one to teach him to shoot better instead. I did just bring in three outlaws.

Billy hadn't seen Morris ride yet, and he expected that such a short feller might ride a small pony. But his horse turned out to be a nice chestnut mare, just a little smaller than Jenny. Not much size, but flashy in how she moved, a quick stepper much like her owner.

The pair rode out of town to the north, around about three miles, then went left down a little side trail. Crossed the creek then at a point wide and shallow, rode through some trees, and came out into a large clearing.

Flat as an old drunk's singin' voice that clearing was, but a real pretty place just the same. Sky seemed somehow tall and steep here, with a few fluffed up clouds slowly drifting along — seemed like them clouds had someplace to be later, but they weren't in no hurry to arrive. That clearing was maybe 300 yards on each side, in sort of an oval shape.

They turned to their right and rode on a short ways before Morris stepped down and said, "We can let the horses graze while we practice. See the targets?"

Sure enough, there was round white circles, different sized targets, painted on some of the trees. Each was numbered as well, right above the target.

"Sometimes we shoot at the numbers instead," Morris told him. "The numbers are their heads, and the circles their chest."

True enough, they were numbered from one to fifteen. Numbers were hard to read on some though. Been shot up plenty since last painted on.

Someone sure enjoys shootin' at heads.

From where they was standing, and because of the angle they were at, some targets were about eighty yards off, but others a lot further away.

They tied their horses' reins to the nubbins so they wouldn't trip over them while they was feeding, and Billy said, "We can't hit but two of them targets from here."

But Morris only smiled and said, "Well, we'll see about that soon enough. With his Spencer, Uncle Mike hits targets past three-hundred yards."

"Believe *that* when I see it," said Billy.

"One thing at a time, my Pa always told me," said

Morris. "Now show me that rifle a'yours, ya Tall Streak a' Not Much."

That's where the name-calling began, but Morris'd smiled when he said it — not an unfriendly smile though; it was a real one.

Billy took out the Spencer and held it out in front of him, thinking Morris was going to take it. But he didn't want it.

"That's a pretty gun alright," Morris said. "Nice and clean too."

"I clean and oil it proper, each time I use it. Except when I was bringin' in the outlaws. Then cleanin' it had to wait."

"Fair enough too. Now shoot three into that nearest target — *Number Seven* — so's I can watch how you do. Quick as you can this first time. Pretend that *Number Seven* tree's one of them Union fellers, shootin' to kill you."

Billy did what Morris said. Not too quick though — he took his time aiming. Missed all three times, but at least the last shot hit the tree — a little too low though.

"That's one Union feller won't be having no children," said Morris, and the both of them laughed. "Too slow though, Billy. I reckon he mighta killed you first."

"But I got three shots off with this repeater in the time he got one. He'd have to make that first one count. Otherwise I just shot his jewels off while he was reloading."

"Alright then," said Morris. "Let's say *Number Seven's* run off then, lookin' for whatever fell out the holes you just shot through his sack."

"His ammo sack, you mean?"

"I mean what I mean," Morris replied with half a sly wink.

"That's ... not the nicest of thoughts." It sure made Billy squirm.

"That's war, Billy. Could happen to you. That's why we're doing all this. Now fire your remainin' four bullets at the next feller — *Number Six* — then reload from scratch, quick as you can."

Billy missed with all four, although one hit a branch, and Morris shouted, "Took off an arm, well done Billy, reload quick now!"

But when Billy reloaded, it was clear to the both of them, he was slower than a long rainy week. One with two extra Thursdays.

Thing is, the Spencer is different and strange compared to other rifles. They loaded strange too, through a tube that went up through the butt of it. And while Billy had used it some, he'd never worked at loading or shooting it quick. Seven shots had always been more than he'd needed.

"Wonder of engineering though, as my Pa puts it," Billy said. "Best rifle ever."

Morris half agreed. "It's a wonder alright, and a real good rifle — second best ever, maybe."

Billy wanted to argue that point, but Morris was focused on the job at hand — which was to get Billy quicker and smoother. He said they could argue about all that later, then he explained just *how* he moved so dang fast when he had to — which was to do things to the music in his head.

"Think I understand," said Billy. "How 'bout I try it to Lorena?"

"Nice tune, but too slow. Something lively instead. Just make a tune up, that's what I do. Then he took the Spencer and demonstrated just what he meant. It wasn't no proper tune, even Billy knew that, but it served the purpose. He could not believe how fast Morris loaded that rifle.

He was in a rhythm alright, and he sang words the whole time he went!

"Across-the-body, spin-the-tube-catch, pull-out-the-tube, get-a-handful."

"Drop-in-rounds, one-two-three, four-five-six, se-ven-re-place-tube-close-catch."

But that fast-mover didn't stop there, he started up shootin' then, while still singing his rhythmical song, although the song was much slower now.

"Cock-lever-aim-BOOM, cock-lever-aim-BOOM, cock-lever-aim-BOOM, cock-lever-aim-BOOM, cock-lever-aim-BOOM, cock-lever-aim-BOOM, cock-lever-aim-BOOM."

"Across-the-body, spin-the-tube-catch, pull-out-the-tube, get-a-handful."

Then he stopped, handed the Spencer to Billy, waved away some of the gunsmoke, and said, "Your turn."

To be clear on what *was* said and *wasn't*, Morris hadn't said the word "BOOM." That was just the noise the Spencer made, more or less. What he'd been saying then was "shoot." But of course, Billy never heard that, on account of the BOOM.

They concentrated then just on loading awhile, and not shooting. Slow at first, then quicker and quicker, Morris saying the words, making Billy say them along with him, as he went through the actions. He was getting quicker and smoother at it too.

Then Morris said, "Ready for that shootin' contest now, ya Long Streak Of Cowdung?" The words themselves had been mean ones — but again, there was a genuine smile came with 'em.

"Now what's that sorta talk for?" said Billy with a smile of his own. "Pick up your gun then, Shorty."

"Shorty's the best you can do?" Morris answered, slowly shaking his head as he picked up his rifle. "Why, I've seen bluebirds with more meat on 'em than you. You shoot *Number Seven* again — they don't quit them Union fellers, he's found his missin' stones'n come back — and I'll shoot *Number Eight* his other side. Ready?"

Billy hadn't noticed Morris's rifle until now. It was a lot more full-sized than his horse was.

"Can't just about shoot for tryin' not to laugh," Billy said, not even trying to keep a straight face. "That gun's taller'n you are, Bandy-Legs."

It was just about true too — if you stood 'em up side by side, Morris only woulda had three or four inches on his rifle. And to Billy, it looked a mite comical.

But what happened next wasn't comical.

A voice back behind 'em shouted, "Lookee what we got here, boys, two fellers playin' at shootin'. Why, look how pretty they's targets is painted. Hand over them guns, boys, and we just might let you live. Whose side a'the war you on anyways?"

CHAPTER 14
THE RED LEGS

There was four of them fellers approaching, dirty and mean-lookin' too, all of 'em on foot. Dressed in rags mostly, except for the one who was talking — he had a new jacket and britches, and a pretty nice rifle.

Still, they looked like they'd just walked a thousand miles to someplace, then another thousand back, but forgot to have a rest in between. Then Billy heard one of their horses nicker a little — away some, maybe down by the creek.

Shoulda kept an ear out. Another lesson I guess.

"We're not in any war here, friend," called Morris. He was just sort of cradling his rifle, same as Billy, as he half faced the men. Their rifles three-quarter faced the men though, that was the main thing. And both rifles were loaded and ready. Difference between them was, Morris didn't look nervy, the way Billy felt.

Caught out in the open, what a thing.

"War's everywhere, my little friend," that same feller called out, and the other three raised their left fists and shouted agreement. Two of the four had rifles, and the other two pistols, all in their right hands. All four looked like they'd be happy to use them, but they weren't pointing them yet. "Everyone needs to pick a side, boys. Everyone."

Them fellers were still fifty yards off, but slowly coming closer, spreading out some as they did.

Me and Morris are too close together, Billy realized then. But it was too late to change it. At least none of them had scatterguns.

"We got no money, if that's what you're after," Morris said. Then very quietly, without hardly moving his lips, he told Billy, "When it's time, you shoot the tall one on the left."

The feller leading the way stopped about thirty yards off and said, "Why, they're both nothin' but children, even the tall one! Whatever they's folks has been feedin' em, they's doin' it wrong. Never clapped peepers on such an odd pair." Then he shook his head and laughed before saying, "Show 'em your red legs, Tom, so they knows who they's dealin' with, and don't consider to make us no trouble."

We shoulda pointed our rifles at 'em sooner, while their pistols was not yet in range.

That tall one on the left did as his boss told him to — he put his pistol through his belt, and bent down to pull up his britches to show off his ankles. Lifted one foot up into the air — out to the side, like, and twirled it — then swapped over and put up the other foot. Like a strange little dance, it was.

His stockings were red as promised, or they had been at some time anyway. The half of 'em that still existed had faded to a light sort of pink — the other half was just his dirty skin showing through all the holes.

"Should that mean something to us, Sir?" Morris asked, like as if he was soft in the head, and never been educated on Red Legs.

"Oh I think you know what it means," said the leader, as the tall feller pushed his britches back down and took out his pistol again. But he still never cocked it — seemed like none of 'em had. Seemed they was none too worried by what they thought of as children.

"No Sir, honest," said Morris, sounding even more simple than before. "My own stockings is white, does that mean somethin' too?"

"Well, don't matter nohow," said the bossman. "Because I reckon you young fellers are on our side, and would want us to take them nice rifles to help out the cause. So you can just put 'em on the ground and step away from 'em now."

"Sir," Morris said, as if he was ten, and the other feller was his schoolmaster. "I guess you're just passing through, and not familiar with Wilmington yet. You see, there's a Sheriff and two Deputies there, who don't take kindly to what you're doing."

That filthy boss feller laughed it up big at that one.

"Don't take kindly," he said in a childish mimicking voice, that was meant to sound like Morris but didn't.

"Boys, this little kid says they ... *'don't take kindly'* ... to fellers like us down the road apiece." He paused a few moments so his friends could all laugh it up, before adding, "Well, little feller, it's a damn shame that ol' Sheriff and his fool Deputies ain't here to protect ya now, ain't it?"

"Oh, but that's where you're wrong," Morris said, cool as a well-shaded stone in a stream. "You see, Sir, I'm one of them deputies, and *you* are under arrest."

Morris had raised up his rifle as he said it, and trained it right on that boss feller.

"One thing strange," the boss feller said then, and he didn't seem none too concerned about the gun pointed at him. "How come you're so little, but your voice sounds like that of a man all growed up? And your head's so big too — too big for the rest of ya anyways."

"I'm a dwarf." Morris's voice stayed stone cold, and Billy would like to have looked at him then, but he didn't risk it.

"Da-warf anything like a midget?" that boss man said mockingly. "Heard'a midgets, never seen one."

"Same thing," said Morris.

"So you ain't a kid at all. You're just half a man."

"Enough talk," said Morris. "You put your gun down right now" — *and here, he lowered his weapon to point it at the filthy feller's jewels* — "or I'll squeeze this trigger, and there won't be but half a man of *you* left. If you get what I'm sayin'."

"That's real funny," the man said.

"Not for you," Morris answered abruptly. "Mister. It was Red Legs killed my mother, two years tomorrow. My

Pa was staying right out of the fight before that. But now he fights for Robert E. Lee. And I stayed here to kill men like you. So any time you wanna become half a man — maybe less — just go for that gun and we'll see."

For a moment, that filthy feller looked like he was going to laugh.

But he didn't laugh, not at all — not so much as a chuckle. Instead, he yelled, "Kill 'em, boys!"

But as that filthy skunk raised his rifle, Morris's first bullet went not through his jewels, but clean through that feller's dark heart. He went backways and sideways, tripped on his own feet and ate dirt, went face first hard into the ground. He never got a shot off at all, on account of him being so dead.

There was other shots fired too, but it happened so fast that Billy wasn't sure who had fired — or even if he himself had got any shots off. His hands sure were vibrating, and his ears rang.

It was the fastest thing he'd ever known, and maybe the loudest.

What he heard was something that sounded like "Lever-BOOM-lever-BOOM-lever-BOOM-lever-BOOM-lever-BOOM-BOOM-BOOM-echo-echo.

Then through the clearing gunsmoke, one by one he saw them four fellers was all laid out on the ground — three of them stiller than still, and deader than dead. The remaining one's hand stood up toward the sky from his elbow, and that hand moved just a little, keeping time with his moaning, as he gurgled his life away — one desperate gasp at a time.

"Nice shooting," said Morris, his gleaming eyes wide as saucers. He reached up and squeezed Billy's shoulder — half gentle, half firm — and stood there like that a few moments. Then he pulled Billy's hat down over his eyes, and said, "Yessir, not bad at all ... for a two-legged long-eared giraffe."

Billy just pulled his hat back up and, motionless, stared at his friend. Struck dumb for the moment he was.

Morris squeezed Billy's shoulder again before walking over to the last surviving feller. He kicked the man's pistol away, and stood over him, looking down.

"You look real tall from here," gasped the feller.

"That ain't no compliment," Morris said, "if it's what you were tryin' for. I guess you're under arrest, Sir. What's your name? And the names of all your dead friends?"

"Ain't sayin'," he said, and coughed weakly. Then he went back to gasping and gurgling.

"You'd better tell me," said Morris, "if you want your grave marked. Otherwise we'll just call you all *Unknown Outlaw*. Maybe even pile you all in together, save us diggin' so many graves."

"You can't—"

"Oh, we can," Morris said. *"Four Stinkin' Unknown Outlaws* — now there's a nice grave marker. Got a ring to it, ain't it? If you want a proper Christian burial, you tell me your name, and be quick. I reckon you ain't got two minutes of life left, so you'd best decide in a hurry."

Well that surely got the feller talking. Turned out he had a last request too — asked Morris to write to his sister in Omaha. "Tell her to let my boy know where I's buried," he gasped through his coughing and gurgling. "Tell her to raise him not to be like his Pa. He should be like his Ma was instead. Oh, how kind and lovely she was."

And his eyes gentled then.

And then that feller — Wallace Teller he was called — gurgled one last time, and the light all went from his eyes. And nothing was left but his body — and the words to his family, of course.

Words that had yet to be written, but might yet make a difference to his son.

CHAPTER 15
MORRIS'S MA

Turned out there had been seven shots fired — one each by three of the Red Legs, each of them missing their targets — one by Billy, which smashed that tall feller's left eyebrow all through his brain — and three by Morris, two of which passed through hearts and the other through the lung of Wallace Teller.

"That was nice shooting, Billy," Morris told him, as he gathered up the guns of the Red Legs.

"I was aiming for his chest," Billy said. It seemed like it shocked him more than the last time he shot outlaws.

"Still good shooting," Morris said. "You *can* shoot straight when you hurry. We can work with that. Well, I guess that's enough practice for now, we'd best get back to town."

And Morris walked off toward his mare.

"What about all these dead men?" Billy asked, looking down at the one he'd killed again.

"We'll get the undertaker to collect 'em up with his

buckboard. We'll have to come back, show Uncle Mike exactly what happened. There'll be paperwork for him to do. But he'll be happy, more or less. Mostly.

They called their mares over and rode on out of there then. Billy took one last look back at the bodies before Jenny went into the trees.

He didn't say anything else, just followed Morris along, until they crossed the creek. They found the Red Legs fellers' horses there. They were in poor condition alright, and had been hitched to the trees so they couldn't feed much.

"We'll leave 'em here," Morris said, "but loose so they can feed. Poor things are half starved, I reckon they'll stay right here with all this nice grass by the creek, rather than follow us down a dirt trail."

They dismounted, unsaddled the horses and untied them. They watched as all four went to the creek for a drink. Then Billy looked down at Morris and said, "That true about Red Legs killing your Ma?"

"What do you think?" he answered. And he didn't seem nearly so self assured as he had back there in the clearing.

"I'm sorry," Billy said.

"Me too," Morris answered. Then he climbed up onto his horse, turned and looked into Billy's eyes a second as if deciding whether to go on. Then the words began to come out of him, real quick-like.

"I seen it happen, you know. I was fifteen, even smaller then. Heard gunshots from out in the field, they was all laughing, and Ma was there — she was tryin' to run. I picked up my rifle and started runnin' too. One of 'em caught her, tackled her to the ground and threw her skirts up over her face, while the others all watched, all a'hollerin' about who'd be next."

He stopped then, and Billy said, "It's alright, you don't have to tell me." And he climbed up on Jenny.

But Morris wasn't ready to leave yet, and went right on talking. Slower now though.

"Naw, I reckon I do need to speak of it now for some reason. To you. Ain't spoke of it since I told Pa that same day. I guess I need someone I trust to listen. Someone my own age maybe."

"Alright," said Billy, but he was careful not to look at Morris then, as he'd seen the tears starting to form. "I'm ready to hear it."

"I was still quite a ways off, but I seen the flash of the blade in the sun. She'd took the kitchen knife with her. She stuck that feller with it, stuck him good too, in his side. That stopped 'em all laughing. Then he went, 'Bitch,' and shot her with his pistol. Right up through her chin. I should never have looked at her face after. What was left. Still fixed in my head, even now."

"I'm sorry."

"Me too. And so was the feller who done it — I shot him a few seconds after, from about fifty yards, with my rifle. They was just laughin' at me 'til then, and just let me shoot. It wasn't this Henry I shot him with. I just had a single shot then. Shot him on the run I did, shot him right through the side of his head."

Morris went quiet some then. Wiped his eyes. Sort of

grunted.

"But they didn't kill you," said Billy.

"No. Not sure why. I'd shot my one shot, then I throwed that rifle away and run to my Ma. I was cryin' I guess. I heard one of 'em say, 'Poor fool gump of a kid,' and I never forgot that. Crashin' sound come to my head and I figured I was shot dead — welcomed the blackness, I did — next thing I woke up, just layin' there next to my Ma and that feller I killed. Pistol whipped I was, not shot at all. Don't know if they meant it to kill me or decided to spare me. Maybe didn't care which I guess. We buried Ma in town the next day. Pa couldn't find them damn Red Legs, but two weeks later he went off to war. I been with Uncle Mike ever since."

"You can come fight with me, if you want," Billy said. It sounded kinda silly to him when he said it. He felt like a kid, offering to help out a man. He had underestimated Morris all along, because of his size.

Another good lesson.

"No, Billy, but thanks for the offer. I won't go to war. My Pa's wrong to have done so, I reckon. I love him, but even the best and smartest man will always be wrong about some things. You can stay here with me if you want. We'd make a good team."

"Can't do it," said Billy, sadly shaking his head.

"Alright." Then Morris told his horse to get going, and away they all went again.

They were almost to town when Billy next spoke. "Morris. How'd you shoot all them men so dang quick?"

"It's the Henry," he answered, patting it like it was a

favorite horse. "Better repeater even than the Spencer." He seemed cheered up again now.

"My Pa says the Henry's no good. Not that he's ever seen one. Says the Henry's built flimsy, and will fail you first time it gets dirty."

"Your Pa's maybe half right," said Morris. "Uncle Mike says those same things — that's why he chose the Spencer. Him and Pa always argued about it — Pa uses the Henry. Only two things. If the Henry gets mud in the spring it won't work — it's on the outside, see?"

"What's the second thing?"

"Not so powerful," Morris admitted. "Spencer shoots maybe 500 yards, the Henry not nearly half that."

"Then how's it better? Think I'll stick with my Spencer."

"You blind? You just seen how it's better, Billy. I got my third shot off just after you fired your first — I could have got all sixteen off before you got five. Might have just saved us, this Henry." He cocked his head a little and raised his eyebrows before adding, "Something to think about. Maybe you can try it tomorrow. See what you think."

Well, as it went, Billy did try the Henry next day, and he could not believe it. It was a wonder, that Henry. And Billy decided then that his Pa was wrong about two things — the war, and what the best rifle was.

Best thing of all, the gunsmith had one in back of his store — some feller had ordered it, but gone off to war before it arrived, and a letter had come to that poor feller's family, saying he had been a brave soldier, but he weren't comin' back.

Gunsmith had a whole lot of the rimfire cartridges too, as that feller had ordered a heap to take with him, as well as Morris having ordered a whole lot for himself too. It had sat there two years now, that Henry — half because it was expensive, but mostly because Morris told the gunsmith he'd keep working on the Sheriff to buy it.

But Billy had money from the bounties, and was glad to spend it on something so good. And the gunsmith, he was just relieved to finally get back his money on it without disappointing Morris. The gunsmith liked Morris a lot.

That $500 in bounties Billy had, it sure made a great whack of difference. He bought up big, best of everything he could get, and a top notch packhorse to carry it all. Even if he'd took nothing else, he'd have needed a packhorse to carry the weight of all them rimfire cartridges he bought.

"Not like you can buy 'em any old place," the gunsmith said. "But I hear tell a few Union regiments has Henrys — so if you find these rimfires on a dead man, don't leave 'em behind."

One more advantage of the Henry, the cartridges were a bit smaller and lighter than the Spencer's. So he could take more of them in the same space. And just like the Spencer, the cartridges were copper, so they'd survive most anything, including being wet — not like the paper ones most rifles used.

Billy had known all along that Red's horse was too good to just be a pack horse. He'd decided to name that horse Percy, on account of him being so short in the legs — because Percy was Morris's middle name.

He told Morris he *woulda* called the horse Bandy Big-

Head Sawed-Off Stink-Fart — only it was too much name for such a small horse.

So he just called him Percy instead.

He figured Percy and Jenny could share the duties between riding and carrying.

Well, that plan went awry before long. Two days after the Red Legs incident, Billy and Mike and both deputies went back to that clearing and practiced some rapid shooting together — and they all of 'em realized Jenny might not ever quite get used to a whole lot of gunfire.

She was fine with the occasional shot from who she was with — even when Billy shot rounds from her back — but that pretty little mare was clever enough to know that *other* gunfire might hurt her.

And Billy respected that.

It wasn't easy to do, but he decided to leave Jenny where she'd be safe. He knew Morris would look after her properly — why, that short-legged feller seemed to love her almost like Billy himself did.

She'd be safe here in Wilmington, not getting shot at, he decided.

And that little gelding Percy, why, he was a wonder!

He didn't seem like he could even *hear* gunfire. He might just be the horse to go to war on, Mike reckoned, if you *really* had your heart set on going.

And still, Billy did.

Two other things Billy learned that day out in the clearing. Both to do with the Henry.

First thing, the sight on that rifle was a whole lot easier to use than the one on the Spencer. After using the Henry, he felt like his eyes had gone bad when he tried to shoot with the Spencer again.

Second thing, it seemed that slow careful aiming just gave Billy too much time to think — Morris had him just snap a few shots off at the targets in a hurry without thinking.

And it turned out, after all, that Billy *could* shoot straight.

"That's how you shot that tall Red Legs feller when it mattered," Morris said.

"But I shot him too high," Billy reminded him.

"You couldn't have shot him no deader," Morris said. Billy had no argument for that.

So whenever he took time to aim, Mike and Morris kept reminding him, "No thinking, Billy, just shoot."

So that's what he did now. And anywhere within a hundred or so yards, he shot those targets nine out of ten, just as good as Morris, and almost as fast — though he wasn't quite so good from out further.

"Don't worry, you'll keep getting better with practice," Morris told him. And he knew it was true.

It took some getting used to, the way that Henry spat the spent cartridges way up high out the top of it, right into Billy's field of vision — but it was a blessing as well. He didn't have to jerk it between shots, way he'd done with the Spencer to get rid of the cartridges. That had been costing him time —*and* he'd had to keep taking aim fresh again for every shot.

With the Henry, he hardly needed to ever refocus his

eye. Shot after shot hit the target, and if *one* missed, the next one sure didn't.

And even though that open top made it vulnerable to snow and dirt dropping inside it, that rifle was so quick and simple to use, it more than made up for it, shooting sixteen rounds off in just about that many seconds. Best he could get with the Spencer was a shot about every three seconds, and sometimes he had to rifle it twice before it'd shoot.

No, he'd decided quite quickly, *Morris is right. The Spencer's second best after all.*

Even Sheriff Mike stopped arguing for Billy to keep the Spencer once he watched how quick Billy improved with the Henry. "Just keep that thing out of the mud," was all he said now. "And treat it gentle. It's made of poor materials, compared to the *best* rifle money can buy."

Mike made him buy an Army Colt too, even though Billy had never been any good at all with pistols. "You *have* to have one," he explained. "You never know what might happen. It's six more rounds to hand whenever you need it — and at some point, believe me, you *will* need it."

It was not Morris, but Mike, who taught him to use the Colt. Or rather, Sheriff Mike gave both of them lessons together. They was both right handed, but he made them wear the holster low on the front of their left thigh, for easier drawing while riding a horse.

When they argued, he made 'em try it both ways. Then after, he didn't even say, "Told ya so."

They mostly just did whatever he said after that.

Again, with the six-shooter, as long as Billy didn't *think* about aiming, and just fired it quick, he wasn't too bad at all. Not so good as he'd got with the rifle, but a dang site better than ever before.

But that Morris, he was a wonder. Up to fifty yards, he was as good with the Colt as Billy was with his Henry — and by the time Billy left for Boonville, Morris had even started doing fancy tricks with it, gunfighter style he called it.

Didn't impress his Uncle Mike much — he reckoned tricks was for fancyboys, and a real shooter keeps things all simple. Made for some fun conversations, and the Sheriff gave Morris as good as he took in the battle of name-callin'.

As for his Pa's Spencer, Billy left it there with the Sheriff. Asked him to use it sometimes, make sure it remembered how to sing. Said he'd pick it up on his way home, once the war was all finished.

"Make sure you do," said Mike then. "Your Pa will be happy to see it, but not half so happy as he will to see you."

Billy liked it that the Sheriff preferred the very same gun as his Pa — but he liked the reminder, too, of what Morris had said about even the smartest and best of men being wrong sometimes.

That's a lesson to remember, he thought. *It's not disrespectful of Pa to choose different to him. But also, I'll be wrong myself about some things, and I can still respect myself when I make a poor choice here and there. Just hope I keep making my share of good choices.*

But after ten days in Wilmington — plenty of time to see his *bad* choice for what it was — Billy Ray still went off to Boonville to fight in the war.

CHAPTER 16
SMILES ALL ROUND

While Billy was being educated on all things gun, dwarf, and Brimstone in Wilmington, his father and Cass received the letters he'd written.

Cass had done as John told her to, and come to live in the ranch house with him and Horace and Rosie — but she didn't stay in the spare room that Rosie made up for her.

Heartbroken and lost as she was after losing her family, Cass needed Billy's comfort — but as he wasn't home, the nearest possible thing was to sleep in his room. In his bed. The smell of him was around her, and that was some small comfort at least.

Wasn't much, but sometimes a small thing makes a big difference.

Horace sure surprised her. Surprised John too. He was more considerate of Cass than he'd ever been of anyone before. Seemed to John that the boy might finally be coming good.

About time, he reckoned.

Both John and the old seamstress Mary agreed that it would be best for Cass to stick to her usual routine. Much as that could be done anyways. Of course, the big change was staying at the Ray place instead of going home to her family.

If Billy had been there, she might almost have been able to imagine her family weren't gone. To imagine she and Billy were married, and living in the house with his family 'til they built their own place.

That's the way she tried to imagine things when she hid under the covers in Billy's bed. Didn't much work.

It was a horror, losing your family that way. And as kind as folks were at the burial and after, it did not take away how big the hole inside Cass was. Just about filled her, that hole.

She felt like only Billy could go any ways to making her feel any way real again.

Before this, John never usually went to town much, but after what happened to her family, Cass was understandably clingy. And John still felt like something was wrong about the fire.

Something.

Aside from his gut feeling, a few strokes of a broom and a strange bit of dirt was all he had to go on, and it wasn't nearly enough. There was *something* not right, he was certain — but he couldn't nail it down.

Still, he felt uneasy. And he knew Cass had never really felt comfortable around Horrie, so to begin with at least — even though Horrie offered — it was John who escorted Cass to town to go to church every Sunday, then went in and brought her back home every Thursday as well. He made excuses to ride in and check on her other days too.

Mostly he kept Horrie busy those days with extra jobs on the ranch. Sometimes he sent the boy to Council Grove for things — he knew the boy liked to go there, and for certain was going to the cathouse. But it mattered more that Cass grew comfortable with him slowly. As nice as Horrie was acting, it might take awhile.

And so it was, that when Billy's letters arrived, it was John who received them. It was Thursday, he was on his way in to collect Cass, and stopped by the Marshal's office to check just in case.

Sure enough Marshal Clem Jenkins had just got the mail.

"One for you, one for Cass," he told John.

"Thanks, Marshal," he replied. "Or should that be Postmaster? Man like you wears two hats, I guess you should use both titles at appropriate times."

"Marshal's fine," said Jenkins, a small hint of annoyance in his voice. Then, friendlier, he asked, "From Billy, them letters, I suppose?"

"Looks like his neat hand," said John, waving them out front to fan himself.

"Well, come on then, open it up and see what trouble he's found, John."

That Marshal looked mighty eager to hear just what Billy was up to, but John was a private man when it suited him, and not easily pushed into doing what others expected.

"I'll be sure to let you know, Clem. But not right now. Figure it's only fair to Cass that we open and read 'em together. She has as much claim on him as I do by now — maybe more. Thank you kindly, Postmaster. Maybe I'll see you later."

John Ray nodded at the Marshal and turned on his heel and walked back outside. Instead of just leaving his horse hitched to the rail there, he mounted him and rode up the street to the seamstress's place, then tied the gelding up again there.

He stood out front a moment with those letters in his hand, and John felt as nervous as the day he asked Billy's Ma to marry him.

What a thing, he thought.

He took a deep breath, the way a man must, then he strode up the steps and he knocked three times on the door.

It was Cass who opened it. "John," she said, and she managed a thin smile and touched his one arm then. "I'm not yet ready, you're early. Mary's asleep of course, and ... *oh, John, is that letters from Billy?*"

That girl got more excited than John had seen since ... well, she got real excited. Did a sort of a dance on the spot, so he handed her the letter with her name on it.

"Mail just came in now. Thought we should maybe be together when we read 'em. If that's okay with you."

"Of course, Mister ... of course, John." She still slipped up and called him by *Mister Ray* sometimes. She squeezed his wrist, a sign of affection she exercised with only a select few. "Thank you for being so considerate, I know you must be busting to read it. Shall we sit?"

With the peaceful, rhythmic breathing of the sleeping Mary for their music, the pair sat at the sewing table then — Cass in her own chair, John in the chair he would always think of as Annie's — and with trembling fingers, Cass opened her letter. But she closed her eyes before looking, and said, "You too, please. I can't do it on my own. Just in case."

"I know," he said. "I feel the same, more or less."

Then he opened his too, and the girl said, "Okay, let's begin."

He hadn't got one single line read when Cass went, "Oh. Oh. Oh, that's beautiful."

And he looked up and saw she was smiling, the first real smile he'd seen on her in a while. Then he read the start of his own letter — he was a man who read well, but still mouthed the words as he read them — but after getting only as far as, *"Dear Pa. I am very sorry about some things. I should not have taken your Spencer..."* he skipped to the end of the letter and read the last lines.

Somehow he dreaded dire news. And while it was already clear the boy wasn't coming back soon, there was no other terrible news — and John Ray breathed a sigh of relief.

Back to the start of the letter he went then, and commenced to read it right through. When he got about halfway he looked up at Cass, and the dear girl had *such* a look on her sweet youthful face. Her hands were clenched on that letter, her mouth all a'wobble, there were tears by the bucket streaming over her cheeks and all down onto her dress — but the joy and relief on her face, it warmed up John's heart in a way his old ticker really needed.

It was clear that Cass was reading her letter over and over. Hers was a single page, considerably shorter than John's. He thought of letting her read his too, but he knew she would worry more if she did so.

So when he finished he carefully folded it and put it away in his pocket.

For a moment she looked disappointed, but she covered up quick. "Your letter was longer," she said, searching his eyes for the truth. "Any bad news?"

"No, Cass, all good. Except for him not coming back yet, of course, but I'm sure he told you that too." He fiddled with the brim of his hat where it lay before him on the table. "It was mostly him saying sorry for taking my good rifle. Must have said sorry four times. For such a smart boy, he still doesn't get that I really bought that rifle for him. What the dickens does he think a one armed man's gonna do with a repeatin' rifle anyway? I'd have bought the Henry for myself, if any repeater. Once it's cocked, one arm'd pretty much get the job done, repeatin' wise."

"So why didn't you just tell him the Spencer was his, John?" She looked confused, but that smile was still all over her face along with it.

"Horrie, a'course," he said with a sigh. "Always complaining how Billy received unfair treatment. I bought Horrie the same repeater, same day. But he'd have found a way to complain. So I said the other one was for me, and gave Billy my old Hawken."

Cass laughed so brightly then, it seemed almost just like old times. "That Hawken," she cried. "The noise of it! And the *smoke!* It scared Jenny a little, that's why he started borrowing the Spencer. What else did his letter say, John? If you don't mind me asking."

"Course I don't mind," he said. "Mostly he just said to look after you and Horrie. And he talked about that little horse of his, like always. You know how he is."

"I think he loves that horse more than he loves me sometimes," she said. And if she was still dissatisfied at not seeing John's letter, she made a fine job of hiding it, for her face fairly beamed now. "Or maybe he loves us both equal, which is good enough for me. Oh, he'll come home soon, John, I know it. The silly war won't last long, I read it in Mary's newspaper."

"Reckon you're right," said John.

"I'm going to write him back, this very minute," Cass said, pushing back her chair and jumping to her feet to go get some paper. "Or...?"

"Maybe take your time, choose your words," John answered. "Who knows? Right words, maybe he'll change his mind and come runnin' right back. Worth a try, don't you think? Mail don't go out 'til Monday now anyway."

"Perhaps you're right," Cass said with a smile. "I'll write a note for Mary and go get my things."

If they'd written to Billy right then, and rode straight to Council Grove to send it, well, perhaps things might have gone different.

But they didn't do it that way, and things went how they went.

CHAPTER 17
SOME MEN IS BETTER'N OTHERS...

That night, over supper at the Ray ranch, things were happier than they'd been in some time. Rosie was so joyful she cracked open a jar of preserves and made Billy's favorite — blackberry pie — even though he wasn't there to enjoy it.

"You'll be married before you know it, young Cass," Rosie said happily, "so you'd best learn how to make this while he's away."

Horace put on a happy face, and did a fine job of seeming happy his brother had written. He was pleased about it alright, but not for the same reason as the others. He asked a few questions about what the letters said, but John avoided straight answers about it whenever he asked. In fact he didn't say a whole lot to Horrie, until later when they were alone.

Soon as they'd all finished their pie, Cass said how wonderfully tasty it was, and offered to help Rosie with the dishes. The older woman only laughed and said, "Get out with you, girl. You go and get writing to Billy now, you know I don't need you under my feet. Well, go on, run along."

Then Cass said goodnight to everyone, and Rosie did too — for she planned on writing a letter to Billy as well, soon as she got the dishes done.

Once the ladies were gone, John had a few questions of his own. With a sideways nod of his head, he motioned for Horace to follow him out to the porch, so they'd be away from where the women might hear them.

"Horrie," he said once they got there, "you've been good to Cass since what happened, and I wanted to say that up front."

"Alright, Pa," his son answered. "Anyone woulda treated her the same, poor sweet girl. Such a terrible thing. But I don't understand what you mean — up front of what?"

John lit the lamp that hung over the porch, made Horrie wait a bit before he went on. "Billy said some things in his letter. Things about you."

"Aw, Pa, what's he said? I ain't done nothin' at all! And if he says I have he's a liar, and I ain't gonna put up with—"

"Enough," John growled, putting up his hand. "Listen to me now, boy. You'll have time to speak when I'm done."

Horrie walked away a few steps, clenching and unclenching his fists with each step he took. But he stopped, ran the fingers of both hands through his hair, then he turned around towards the lamplight and came back.

Most of the edge was gone from his voice as he said, "Alright, Pa, I'm sorry. What is it?"

"He mentioned all the hidings you gave him when he was smaller, but—"

"We was just playin', Pa, you know that!"

"Your notion of what constitutes *playing* bears close examination. But he actually thanked you for that."

"He did? He put that in the letter?" Horace smiled some then.

"Said he knows you were teaching him persistence."

"Per-what-ence?"

John turned away a moment and shook his head, before facing his son again. "Well, it's not the word he used. He said you taught him never to give up the sponge."

"Why didn't you just say so, Pa? Can I see it? The letter? I'd really like to see it." His voice went from excited to emotional then, and he looked at John's eyes when he spoke now. "He's my brother, only one I got — even if he is a proper spooney, headin' off to that dang fool war like he did."

"Hmmm. Funny you should say that," said John, and he took the letter from his pocket. But instead of placing it in Horrie's outstretched hand, he unfolded it and stepped back under the lamp so he could read out loud from it. "Perhaps you'd like to explain this, Horace." And here, John made a pretty good fist of mimicking Billy's voice. *"Say howdy to Horrie and thank him for helping me get my thinking sorted all about the war."*

The words had been unexpected alright. And Horrie

knew he had to act quick. What else had that damn Billy said? There might be a way out of this yet.

"That don't make no sense, Pa," he said. "There must be other words he wrote with it. Show me the letter, alright?"

For half a year now — ever since Horace had come up with his plan — Billy had kept their secret agreement perfectly well. He had always kept Horrie's name out of his arguments with Pa about the war.

That had been their deal — Horrie brings Billy the *"honest"* newspapers, and helps him work out their *"true meaning"* — and in turn, Billy never mentions his part in it.

John had walked away, stood against the porch rail, and was staring out into the dark. Seemed like he was taking his time to decide whether to show Billy's letter to Horace.

"Please, Pa," Horace said then in the most pitiful voice he could manage. "He's my brother, can't I see his words too?"

John waited a moment before turning and saying, "Of course you can. But I want an explanation once you've read it."

He handed Horrie the letter then, and the boy took it under the light and read the whole thing.

"He sure does write a pretty letter," he said when he finished. "He surely misses us all, and I reckon he'll head back soon." And he handed the letter back to his father.

"That doesn't any way answer my question," said John then, as he folded the letter and put it back in his pocket.

"Ain't completely sure, Pa. We talked some about it a

few days afore he took off. I think maybe he got the wrong end of the stick as to what I was saying."

"And what *was* you saying, exactly?"

"Well, one minute he was on about the war — which usually, I never let him talk about with me, but he still always tries — then he started talkin' about marryin' Cass."

"Go on," said John, and he plonked himself down in his chair then.

Horace stayed on his feet though, back out of the light, and he said, "Seemed his talk was all about providing for her and protecting her. How a real man should build his wife a home, not just bring her to live with his family. And I guess I agreed with him on that, and said something about a real man doin' what's right. That's all I said, I reckon. Then he went back to banging on about the war, and how doin' what's right meant fightin' against Northern aggression."

John made a thoughtful sort of a *"Hmmm"* sound then, but he didn't say anything else yet in actual words.

Horrie figured he was on the right track, so he built some more on the same story. "I told him the best thing he could do was to stay here to keep her safe. Told him he could get killed there, then who'd look after Cass? And he said, 'You and Pa would a'course.' Well, I had to agree that we would, as it's true. But that it was best he stayed home and did so himself."

"Anything else?"

"Just one more thing, Pa. Now I'm talking it through, I remember what he said that was odd. He did thank me, sort of. Said I'd helped clear his thoughts all about what's important. Said that a man needs to do what's right by the people he loves, even if it ain't the best thing for himself. I figured that meant he'd decided to stay home — but maybe he'd took it somehow opposite. You know how he gets about the war — he goes this way and that, speaks too fast, and it's hard to tell quite what he's thinking when he gets all worked up. But there was a calmness to him this time, and I took that as a good sign."

"Well," said John with a sigh, "some signs is better'n others, I guess. I think I'll retire, son, and write Billy a letter, so's I can send it off with Cass's and Rosie's tomorrow." And when he got to his feet, he seemed like a man with the weight of the whole dang world on his shoulders.

"Goodnight, Pa," Horrie said. "I might go write him too."

"Appreciate that, son," John said with a nod. "More of us begs him to come home the better. Goodnight, Horrie. I'll see you at breakfast."

The scratching out of letters that night at the Ray place was mighty heartfelt, for the most part. All four of them writing at once, was how it turned out.

But only one of those letters would make it to Boonville — Horace Ray would make certain of that.

He had a plan that woulda made his Pa's hair stand on end, if ever he was to learn of it.

Once everyone else was asleep, Horace went out to the bunkhouse. It was small, but of solid log construction like the house, and each of the four beds was in its own corner.

Right now there was only Jasper and two other

cowhands — though if Billy didn't hurry on back they'd be needing another quite soon.

Horrie snuck in quiet-like, sneaked up on Jasper and clapped a hand over his mouth. "Wake up," he whispered.

Lucky thing Jasper wasn't an Indian, he would have slept through a buffalo stampede — just went right on sleeping he did.

Horace kept one hand over his mouth and pinched his nose shut with the other. That did the trick soon enough.

Jasper made a strange noise like as if he was choking and jerked awake. Horace wasted no time telling him to shoosh.

"What is it, Horrie?" Jasper loud-whispered. "I was sleepin', dammit. What time is it anyway?"

"Come outside, it's important. Five minutes you can go back to sleep. Come on, move it, you useless lump."

Like always, Jasper did what Horrie told him, whether he liked it or not. Once outside, they walked away into the darkness where no one could hear them, and Horrie told Jasper what he wanted him to say the next morning — then he made him repeat it all back to him.

Then they both went on back to their beds.

Next morning over breakfast, they were all quieter, more subdued than they'd been the night before. The excitement of receiving Billy's letters had got them all worked up, but having written back to him, the truth of the situation was clear and stark in everyone's minds — Billy was all the way off in Boonville, recruiting for a war in which he would likely be killed.

No matter how much they loved him, how much they

begged him, how much they prayed for him to come home to them, the headstrong Billy Ray was gone off to fight.

John considered traveling to Boonville to try to drag the boy home. Of course he did — it was the first thought he'd had when he saw where Billy was going. Considered sending Horrie after him too.

But John knew how these things worked — once the army had him signed on, they wouldn't release him, not even if Billy agreed. And he would *not* agree — that boy was stubborn as his mother.

It was no use sending Horrie and Jasper, no use going himself. And besides, they were one man short already with Billy gone. There weren't men enough around to replace them, and it would be the best part of three weeks there and back.

The best they could do was get their letters there fast.

So it seemed mighty fortuitous when Jasper came to the door as they sat eating breakfast, and said, "Horrie, can you come to Council Grove with me? I gotta go right away for Pa, important like. Asked me to last night. I don't wanna go up there alone, just in case them two big fellers ain't moved on yet. You remember what they said."

Horrie answered, "They ain't nothin' but talk, most likely. But you're right, I'd best go with you, just in case. Give me two minutes to eat, then we'll go. We can look for them six missing beeves on the way back." And he started shoveling eggs and bacon into his mouth in a way that usually saw him reprimanded by Rosie.

"What's all this about?" said John.

Horrie's mouth was too full to speak — he had done it

deliberately, for he wanted Jasper to tell it, so it all sounded natural, and didn't make John suspicious.

Jasper said, "Thought Horrie woulda told you, Mister Ray. Six missing from the herd when we checked yesterday. They won't be gone far—"

"Not the cattle, Jasper," said John. "The—"

Horace spoke between bites then, saying, "Nothin' much, Pa, it was just some fellers we were beatin' at cards. All but accused us of—"

"Not that either," said John. "This important business for Jasper's father. He didn't mention anything to me yesterday."

"He didn't yet know, I expect," Jasper said, nodding his thanks to Rosie for the cup of coffee she handed him.

"Well," John said thoughtfully, "None of my business, I guess."

"Ain't that, Mister Ray. Pa said he only realized later. Mail feller had made a mistake, left somethin' that shoulda come to Pa up in Council Grove. Wanted Posters and such is my guess — all he told me was *'Important Town Marshal business.'* He keeps such details secret from me, like I'm some sorta stranger. Wants it done right away though, so my guess is Wanted posters."

"Strange he's not going himself is all," said John.

"He don't trust them new fellers halfway between here and Emporia," Jasper replied. "The Emporia Town Marshal asked Pa to meet him out there today. Sheeps has been goin' missing, more and more every week." Then he handed the empty coffee cup back with a, "Thanks, Rosie, your coffee's the best."

"He can't be in two places at once, Pa, no matter how good he is," Horace said, as he stood up and took some folded pages out of his pocket. Then he waved the pages around in front of him and added, "Suits me anyway. I want my letter to get to Boonville before Billy leaves there. Sooner I post it the better. Up to you if you want yours sent or not."

"Oh yes," said Cass, who'd been silent all this time. She still didn't usually speak much round the Strawheads. "That's a wonderful idea, Horace. I'll go get my letter too, if you don't mind."

"Course I don't," Horace said. "Did you write him too, Rosie and Pa? Up to you, but we could send 'em all off together. I'm sure he'll be thrilled to hear from us all the same day. Might change his mind even, all of us askin' him home all at once."

Rosie and Cass had already rushed off to retrieve their letters, and John took his from his pocket and handed it to Horrie. "Send 'em all separate," he said. "That way, even if one or two get lost, he'll still receive something."

"Still don't trust the mail, do you Pa?" Horace said.

"Used to trust only my own two hands," John answered, then held his one hand out in front of him, as if to admire it. "Now I trust only half as many things as I used to."

If John Ray had stuck completely to what he trusted, and took the letters to Council Grove himself, again, things would have gone different.

But he didn't.

So when Billy Ray received news from home, it was

only the letter that his brother wrote — which was all part of Horace's plan.

And that plan, it was eviler and meaner than a dying outlaw with two shotguns — a dying outlaw who's been cornered by the feller he hates the most. A dying outlaw with nothin' left to lose.

CHAPTER 18
THE GREAT IRON HORSE

It had almost been a tearful goodbye back in Wilmington. Billy had become mighty close to Morris, and felt more of a kinship with him than he'd ever felt with Horace.

It was a strange feeling, alright.

He promised the Brimstones he'd come back in one piece, and that he would return for Jenny and the Spencer as soon as he'd helped win the war.

Sheriff Mike had told him enough times that the South couldn't possibly win now, so he didn't tell him again then. He just said, "You come back, Billy. You'll always have a bed with us here, whatever else happens. I mean that."

Then Billy had waved at them one more time in a hurry, and quickly turned and rode away so they didn't see his eyes getting steamy.

The trip to Boonville wasn't completely uneventful. He had to draw his gun twice — the first time he didn't have to fire it, but the second time, he had to chase a few fellers away by shooting nine or ten shots of the Henry at their heels. They must have thought he looked like an easy target, but the rapid firing of that Henry sure changed their minds about robbing him.

And at least now, he didn't shoot anyone by accident, like he had done when he killed Red.

As for Percy, that horse didn't care who Billy shot at, and neither did the pack horse, a bay gelding whose name was Jack. He allowed them to share the duties, which they both seemed to like — and while Percy was also a fine pack horse, ol' Jack wasn't much of a mount. Still, it seemed like swapping sometimes made Jack feel more included in things, and he went at his work all the better once he carried the gear again.

Billy sure grew to like both them horses while he made the trip, but they weren't like Jenny — at least as far as being his friend.

Jenny's a bit like Cass in a way, he decided. *There'll only ever be one Jenny, just as there can only ever be one Cass.*

Instead of taking a direct route to Boonville, he went north-east instead, north even of the City of Kansas. It was a good many miles out of his way, but Sheriff Mike knew a thing or two about travel — including where was safe to go, and where wasn't. Billy trusted Mike and his maps, and four days later, he arrived in Easton, Missouri, all in one piece, having skirted around Saint Joseph, which was under Martial Law, and crawling with Union soldiers.

When he arrived in Easton, the train was due in two hours. There was a few Union soldiers about, but they ignored Billy completely. He was just a skinny kid after all, and his guns were well hidden away, just as Sheriff Mike had told him to do for this part of the trip.

He bought tickets for himself and his horses, and they all ate good meals while they waited. He was nervous about the train ride, a'course, as he'd never seen trains before.

But wasn't it a wonder, that train!

Once it got moving, Billy wasn't sure whether he felt sick or excited or both. That wonderful contraption moved and swayed a bit like a horse — but it sure made a terrible ruckus, and it seemed a whole lot less trustworthy than even a bad horse.

Oh, how it sways. Like a gigantic horse who's been slurpin' up whiskey, maybe.

Might have helped his comfort some if he went and sat in the seats like regular folk — but there was no way Billy was leaving his horses and all his belongings. Sheriff Mike had warned him about that. So he rode along with the horses, with his eyes closed and his back to a wall for awhile. But once his courage got up a bit, he looked out through the wooden slats at the scenery as it rushed by.

As for Percy and Jack, you woulda thought trains was a thing they rode on every day of their lives — Percy even lowered his eyes some when he saw how uncertain Billy was acting, then shook his handsome head at him. Seemed almost like he was a little ashamed at Billy's lack of courage.

"Sorry, Percy," Billy told him. "I guess you seen The Great Iron Horse before, but it's all new to me. It just don't seem natural is all."

That first train trip he took was 115 miles. Eleven stops in all. By the time Billy walked his horses down the ramp onto solid ground in Hudson, he had passed through a whole lot of places he'd never even heard of. And he wasn't done with trains yet.

Had to wait there in Hudson until the next morning, before the train from the branch line arrived. He sure wasn't complaining though — he had never so much appreciated having solid ground under his feet. Even walked around some to enjoy it — and he marveled at what a busy place it was. There was a whole boodle of folks there, just at the railway station. Figured every person in town must be there. But once he walked about, he realized that weren't even the quarter of 'em. Musta been a thousand people just in that one town, he reckoned.

Nearly got himself run over crossing the street, what with wagons and horses and people going every which way. Just lucky trains stayed on tracks, so as not to add to the problem.

Only good thing about trains, he decided, was they got you places in a hurry, and probably didn't wear your horses out. Maybe. He felt half worn out himself, but the horses seemed fine.

Then it was morning. He walked his horses back up another ramp, and after awhile they were moving again.

Forty miles this trip.

He used the time to do some of his stretches, and practice his quick draw with his revolver, as there was no one but his horses to see it — and they didn't care how slow his quick draw was. Although Percy looked like he might laugh once — just for a second.

Might have imagined it.

He decided Percy wasn't *really* laughing at him, and tried one of them fancy gunfighter tricks of Morris's a few times. But he kept on dropping the Colt, so he decided to give up on that.

Percy just looked the other way, first time he dropped it.

Sheriff Mike could have sent him on a more direct route, at risk of a little more danger. But in the end he sent Billy the long way, because he wanted him to ride on the train. For the experience of it, he reckoned.

"Every man should ride The Great Iron Horse at least once," he'd said. He hadn't added anything about how, maybe, Billy's life could end soon, so he'd best enjoy himself while he could. But anyway, it didn't need saying, they all knew the truth of it.

Billy thought about that for awhile, then the train ride was over.

He was at Sturgeon. Only forty miles to Boonville.

That was when he decided trains weren't so bad after all.

He walked his horses down the ramp, past the stock yards and into the street. He looked at his map, got his bearings, and bought a little food for the trip. There was a butcher in town, and he bought some cooked *mysteries* from him, of all things. He was looking forward to those, though he'd heard they weren't *usually* a good risk.

"These ain't no ordinary sausages, Friend," the butcher

had told him. "Prime beef minced together with pig fat, and syrup of maple to sweeten 'em up. Tell your friends all about 'em — they'll be famous one day, these here mysteries."

Turned out that butcher was right. Best mysteries Billy ever ate. He hoped that butcher did get famous — feller surely deserved it.

Billy headed south for Boonville from there. Made good time too, and was almost halfway by dusk. Paid two dollars to stay in a comfortable bed in a barn in a place called Thralls Prairie.

In the morning, he thanked them folks very much and set out on the final leg of the journey. He figured he had all day to do not much more than twenty miles, so he didn't push the horses too hard.

And in the late afternoon of the 10th of October, Billy Ray finally made it to Boonville.

He followed Sheriff Mike's final map, right through the town proper, and a bit further south to where folks lived on blocks a half acre in size.

He was some top notch sort of a mapmaker, Sheriff Mike Brimstone. His maps were in no way fancy, but he knew what was what, where was where, and never once had Billy gotten conflusterated about where he was. And right where he figured it should be, as he approached it, was Mike's sister's house, looking exactly as he had described it.

She was standing out front speaking to her neighbor when Billy rode up, and he saw the resemblance right off. Somehow she looked a lot like the Sheriff, but there wasn't one thing manly about her. And Sheriff Mike was a most manly lookin' sort of a man.

Made Billy feel strange, it did, Mike's sister looking so much like him, and yet being pretty. He didn't feel *too* strange, just a bit topsy-turvied — sorta sixed-and-sevened, more like.

Anyway, if he put the Brimstone resemblance out of his mind, he could allow that she was a real handsome woman — not so beautiful as Cass though, a'course. She was old too, perhaps even thirty.

Now, just to be doubly clear, it was Mike's sister who was the handsome one, not the neighbor. Why, that neighbor, she could *never* have been accused of prettiness or handsomeness or downright averageness even. She was something else alright — although Billy would have been too polite to put whatever that *something* was into words. To call that woman *Not Very Handsome* would have been a great compliment to her — she looked like someone had dug her up fresh from a boneyard, brushed off the dirt and then dressed her in someone's old clothes. She was missing great clumps of her hair too, and had just about as many warts on her face as some folks has freckles on theirs. There was even warts on the warts, and it took all Billy's resolve not to stare at the woman.

"Howdy, Ma'ams," he said from up on Percy's back after taking his hat off. "My name's William Ray. Would one a'you nice ladies be Mrs Thomas A. Hind?"

"You're Billy," said the younger, more handsome one. "I'm Daisy Hind. There's stables out back. Take your horses straight down the side here, I'll be with you in just a few moments. There's food for them too. And Billy Ray, this is my lovely neighbor, Mrs Ward."

That's one name I won't be forgetting. Mrs Wart. Ward. Mrs Ward.

Billy thanked Mrs Daisy Hind as he dismounted, and nodded a howdy-goodbye at the warts — the lady with the warts, rather — and managed not to stare at 'em much. Not too much. A bit. Seemed like she mighta caught him staring, though he wasn't quite certain of it, looking away again so quick like he did. Felt pretty sure she'd caught him though.

He almost said sorry for it, but that woulda made it worse, so he just pretended he was looking close at Jack's pack saddle, then he nodded and mumbled some before lowering his head and leading the horses away.

Didn't look back.

Didn't look back at all. Much as he felt like he needed to.

His face sure was heated by then though, and he hoped they hadn't noticed how red he went.

"First impressions is important," Billy's Pa had always told him. *"If you're gonna be a fool, wait 'til you're friends with folk first. That way they know you got good points as well, and it might average out in your favor."*

He hadn't *said* much. Not enough even. Just stared at that old lady like he'd never seen a wart before, then muttered and mumbled like some sorta chucklehead.

Too late for good impressions now I guess.

He shook his head at his foolishness and led the horses into the stables.

CHAPTER 19

OLD PAP AND THE SEVEN-
THOUSAND

※

It was a nice barn alright — solidly built from good sawn lumber, with separate stables for four horses. Fancy and town-like, somehow. No other horses in there, but there was good fresh hay and straw.

By the time Billy attended to the horses and had them put away, the lady of the house had come out to the stables.

"My brother Mike thinks highly of you, Billy," she said. "Even if you don't have the sense to stay out of the war."

"I bet I think higher of him, Ma'am," he answered, taking his hat off and holding it in front of him, politely as he could. "It's very kind of you to allow me to stay."

"I'm twenty-nine years of age, Billy," she said as she leaned in the doorway and watched him squirm under her gaze. "Being called *Ma'am* makes me feel like I'm sixty at least. While you're here, please call me Daisy."

"Are you sure, Ma'am? I wouldn't want to upset your husband or any—"

"My husband's not here, Billy," she said, coming

forward to brush a piece of straw off his shoulder, which made him flinch at her touch. "He's one more fool who's gone off to fight. Went with Joe, another of my brothers. Those two are off in Atlanta now. Fighting for the Union, if you wondered. Got all fired up and went right at the beginning — 18th Missouri Volunteer Infantry. Under General Sherman *now,* but they've been all over."

"But ... but ... you do know I'm here to—"

"I know, Billy, and don't worry — just because my husband and one of my brothers is fighting for the other side, doesn't change things with you staying here. Mike sent you to wait here for Rob — that's all that matters. Rob's a fool too — fights for a different side is all. And you've chosen to become a fool also. Well, pick up your things, come inside and I'll show you to your room. Then you can get yourself cleaned up before we eat."

"I ... yes, Ma'am, I—"

"Bill-eee." She waggled a finger at him when she said it, and it sounded like quite the warning — but she smiled along with it, sort of. "If you call me Ma'am one more time — or Mrs Hind, or Missus, or anything else but Daisy — I'll put something unpleasant in your food, do you hear me? And if I do that, you'll spend all your days here in the outhouse! You call me Daisy ... alright?"

"Yes, Ma'a—" He *almost* slipped up and said it, but saved himself from completing the word just in time, as the woman's eyes widened. And quickly, with a deliberate nod, he added, "Yes, Daisy."

"That's better," she said happily, and she led the way into the house.

Daisy sent him to clean himself up while she heated some stew, and when he came out, Billy felt much better.

He sat at the table where she said to, and she asked him all about how Mike and Morris was doing. That woman seemed about half fascinated and half terrified when she heard about Morris shooting all the Red Legs.

"Goodness," she said, shaking her head disbelievingly. "He was such a *sweet* little boy, last I saw him. Before his dear mother was killed though, that was," and she sighed. "I expect that's what changed him for the worse."

"Oh no, Daisy, I think you got the wrong end a' the stick from how I told the story," said Billy, and he put down his spoon and took on a most earnest expression. "He's still a *real* nice feller, I promise. You can rest well assured on Morris's niceness, I'd put him above *anyone* on it. To tell truth, I never met a feller I liked so much, and we became sorta like brothers. He's so decent and gentle and kind the rest of the time, I got a most terrible shock when he killed those bad fellers. I couldn't barely look at him for a moment. But he just pulled my hat down over my eyes, and went back to bein' his usual self right away."

"So not *always* a murderous young man then?" she said, with her eyebrows raised up.

Billy wasn't quite sure if she was joking or not, so he explained a bit more. "It was *them* gonna kill *us*, you see? He didn't wanna shoot 'em. Me neither — but I had to kill one as well. Way they forced things, it was either us or them had to die. I tell you though, if it wasn't for Morris, I wouldn't be here now, that's certain."

"Well, I'm glad he's with Mike and Judith. Seems like

Mike's the only one clever enough to keep out of the war, and he's passed that on to Morris. He always was the wise one, dear Mike. Is he well? Is Morris any taller? Would you like some more stew?"

It was a lot of questions at once, but Billy never had to figure out which one to answer first — because right then, they heard the beginnings of a grand commotion outside. Not close by, but at a distance. Sounded like a marching band, with music and everything, and a few people cheering like nobody's business.

Daisy whole expression changed, her eyes seeming almost to have lights set afire inside them. She looked to Billy and said, "They're here!"

"Who, Daisy?"

She had jumped to her feet by then, the stew and the plates and all sense of decorum forgotten, and she laughed a great hearty laugh.

Most unlike the way most pretty ladies sound, Billy thought.

"The Confederate Army, of course," she said. "And my dear brother Rob, who you're here to meet up with! You only just made it in time, Billy Ray! Well, come on, let's hurry along!"

And before Billy knew it, he was being dragged out the door by this enthusiastic lady, and they were out in the street, all caught up in a cheering mass of people. For the townsfolk of Boonville were all out lining the street to welcome the army.

A town full of people who surely know whose side to be on.

He was dumbstruck when he saw the army, of course — for Billy Ray was not used to seeing large numbers of people. He'd thought Hudson truly amazing, with so many folks going hither and thither, a bustling place he thought he might never see the likes of again.

But this — *this* — this was something altogether different. Into Boonville now came a swarming mass of humanity, riding and marching toward him behind a proud flag.

He saw hundreds of them at first, but still they kept coming round the bend — and it turned into thousands, the lines never seeming to end, and more and more flags here and there. And still Daisy gripped tight his hand, her cheeks rosy, her eyes bright and shining as she searched the approaching faces for one she had loved her whole life. Her brother — Morris's father — Rob *"Preacher"* Brimstone.

"Rob's the eldest," Daisy explained, never ceasing to search for him. "But my big brother's surely no Preacher. Name got stuck to him when he was young, and he never really minded. So it's still stuck, now he's thirty-five."

Mrs Ward came out too then, and looked less impressed than if the whole army had trampled her flowers and used her yard for an outhouse.

Billy nodded politely at her and said, "Mrs Wart-d." The *d* sound he put at the end didn't go no way at all toward fixing what he'd just said. That little *d* on the end sounded like a low popping noise that he'd added to make it all worse — and he felt his whole face burn with color as the old woman scowled at him. "I got a sort of speech problem sometimes," he added.

It didn't seem to help.

He had no hat to hide under either, for Daisy had dragged him out in such a hurry he didn't have time to grab it from his room — so he just tried to look as if he was engrossed in the parade.

Mrs Ward, he thought. *With a d. Mrs Ward.*

And he looked in a different direction and silently mouthed it several times for practice.

"Old Pap's Army," Billy heard someone call then, and the sound of that one voice became like a spark that was thrown in tinder, as the cheer was raised by the townsfolk of Boonville. They echoed it over and over, as people back in the town proper rushed into the street and took up the cry.

But soon it just changed to, "Old Pap!"

And sure enough, coming past Billy right now at the head of those 7000 men, a giant black horse bore a man of such stately bearing it could only be he — Old Pap himself, Major General Sterling Price, the former Governor of Missouri, and perhaps the greatest hero of the Mexican War. A true leader of men, who Billy had read about many times.

To think of it, right here in front of me, the flesh and blood of him, almost close enough for Billy Ray of Cottonwood Falls to touch.

And I swear he was lookin' right at me as he went by!

Then Price was gone too far to see, and his whole great army was filing past and moving toward the town proper. Mostly men on horseback, but some marching too, and their heads were held high, every one.

"Keep an eye out, Billy," said Daisy excitedly, and she gripped his hand so tightly it hurt. "He looks just like Mike, though his hair is much lighter. Except — oh no — he might be wearing a beard now."

Billy looked at Daisy as if she had grown two extra legs — one out of each ear — for surely, Morris's father would be easy to recognize, bearded or not.

And then, for the very first time — it dawned on him sudden-like — Billy realized that Morris's father might not be a dwarf. For some reason, he had always assumed it. And he realized now he was almost certainly wrong.

Luckily, Daisy had been too busy searching the faces to notice the way he had looked at her. He went back to helping her search.

It was true, what she'd said — there were so many bearded men, and most wearing hats, that recognizing the exact one you searched for would be like finding an honest banker in a big city.

But who knows, perhaps even honest bankers exist — for, at least in this case, the needle in the haystack they searched for *was indeed* duly recognized. And not only was he clean shaven, but with his hat on, he looked to Billy *exactly* like Sheriff Mike Brimstone.

Including his height of six feet.

Rob Brimstone and his sister Daisy had found each other in the very same moment. He broke ranks right away, then dismounted and embraced her almost in one fluid movement.

It was a happy reunion alright. Even Mrs Ward smiled

to see it — indeed, her smile even stayed when she looked at Billy, and he smiled right back at her.

By now, Daisy Hind had forgotten that Billy was there. As she led the way down the side of the house to the stable, talking fifteen to the dozen to her brother as she went, Billy wasn't sure whether to follow or stay where he was.

He looked after them uncertainly a moment.

Then Mrs Ward nudged his ribs and in a slow, high, thin voice said, "He's probably tired, don't you think? Perhaps he'd appreciate a hand with unsaddling his horse, and carrying his things inside."

Billy looked at the old lady, who was smiling — just a little — and said, "Thank you, Mrs Ward."

And with a little laugh she said, "That impediment in your speech comes and goes, I expect?"

And she laughed up a storm as she turned around and moseyed on back to her house.

CHAPTER 20
PREACHER ROB BRIMSTONE

He was different, "Preacher" Rob Brimstone. Different to what Billy expected. Different to his brother Mike. Different to his son Morris.

And different to how his sister Daisy remembered him. For Rob Brimstone was changed now by war.

He had seen too many die — the old, the young, and every age in between. It had not broken him, of course — Brimstones were too strong for that. But he was changed by the experience, and would never be the same man again as he had been before.

When Daisy accused him of it that night, as the three of them sat by the fire, Rob did not argue. Indeed, he agreed.

Said there was no point in denying it. For the truth is always the truth, no matter how painful.

He turned then to Billy, put down his coffee cup and said, "I know without doubt you're a good friend to Morris, and to Mike. Such friends are not easy to come by, and are of high value. There's more need of such folk than of soldiers, by my own reckoning." He went quiet a moment, and reflective, looking into the fire.

Billy said nothing, just waited, and so did Daisy.

Then Rob looked back at Billy with a great earnestness in his eyes. "I'd have you go home, Billy, rather than join up to fight. Please reconsider — go home, be a friend and a husband and father instead of becoming what I am, or worse. War is no place for men — it ruins us, and there's no going back from it, ever."

There was a world-weariness to his eyes that said even more than his words could — and it sent a chill through Billy, the way those eyes looked through him now.

That moment right there was the closest Billy Ray came to giving up on becoming a soldier. He saw, in some measure, the truth of it. The loss and the pain, and something else too. And if Billy had known what that *something else* was, he might yet have changed his mind and gone home — for the *something else* was the meaningless of it. The utter meaningless of war — of good men killing other good men, for mostly bad reasons.

But Billy was young and not wise yet. Respectfully, he declined the advice of Rob Brimstone. "I want to fight for what's right," he said. "And if you won't take me with you, Preacher Rob, someone else surely will."

"Alright then," he said. "But remember, I did my best. You'll join us, and I'll keep you close, teach you whatever I can. Mike's charged me with your protection, and that makes you family. We'll fight together, Billy Ray. We'll join you up in the morning. For now, get a good night's sleep. It may be the last you ever have."

And with that, they all said goodnight and went off to their beds.

Next morning Billy woke early. He had slept fitfully, and now he lay in that comfortable bed, waiting for the others to rise.

He still had time to back out — and he knew no one here would think any less of him for it. But he still believed in the rightness of what he was doing.

So when he heard the others stir, he went out for breakfast as keen as could be, to greet the new day, to enlist. To nobly fight against The Northern Aggression — that's how Billy Ray saw it.

"This is the best meal I've eaten in two years, Sis," Preacher Rob said to Daisy. "Enjoy it, Billy. Half the time we got nothin' but sloosh. We eat a lot of that."

"Whatever is sloosh?" asked Daisy with a laugh. "Sounds like mud and snake soup."

"Snake soup'd be a blessing next to sloosh," he said, lifting his plate to take a deep sniff of the flapjacks Daisy had made as just part of their breakfast. "Even if it did have mud in it, it'd be better than sloosh. If we're not in a town, all they give us is bacon and cornmeal. Once the bacon's cooked, you take the cornmeal and swirl it into the grease until it's a dough. Keep swirling that 'til you make a snake of it."

"It *is* snake!" laughed Daisy, as she poured Rob more coffee.

"Then you curl the dough-snake round a ramrod and

cook that on the campfire. That's sloosh. Tastes alright I guess. But after the first hundred times ... well, let's just say if I never have to eat it again I'll die mighty happy."

"How long 'til we'll leave Boonville?" Billy asked.

"Price hopes to recruit well here, so maybe a day or two," Rob replied. Then he blew on his coffee to cool it before taking a long careful slurp. "Ahh, real coffee! Half the time all we got's peanuts or chicory to make it instead. And don't get me started on the *nockum-stiff*."

"I'm almost afraid to ask," laughed Daisy. She was clearly joyful at seeing her dear brother after so long, and it warmed Billy's heart just to witness it.

"Nockum-stiff's what they drink when there's no whiskey. Some call it *Oh-Be-Joyful,* but it's the same poison, more or less. Any joy it provides would be paid for at least double later. Terrible stuff, whichever name they give it — don't you *ever* drink it, Billy, not unless you're dying already. That stuff'll kill you. Bark juice, tar water, turpentine, lamp oil, alcohol and sugar."

"Oh, goodness," Daisy said, screwing her face up in horror. "I hope you don't—"

"No, Sis, I still imbibe only rarely — and only when there's proper top shelf whiskey. Though there's times ... well, I'll spare you the details." His face went dark when he said it, but he quickly moved on. "I mean it, Billy, don't drink it. They put raw meat in it too, and ferment it up to a month. No wonder so many fellers die of the dysentery."

Billy screwed his face up some, then steered things right off that subject. "I forgot to tell you, Preacher Rob. Morris and Mike had me bring you a whole heap of rimfire cartridges for your Henry — I have the same rifle now too, since Morris persuaded me to switch from the Spencer."

"Good news, that. I was low, and we'll be needing all we can get these next weeks. It's a big push the old boy's got planned, and mighty ambitious. But he's the General. Well, Billy Ray, if you really wish to enlist, we'd best get a move on. Old Pap told Clark we'd be enlisting here maybe a day or two — but if the Union is foolish enough to attack us, it's best you're already signed on. At least then you might get your pay. If you live long enough."

"I'm coming too," Daisy said. "Every minute we get together's a blessing, and you won't leave me home now, dear brother."

"Hurry then," Rob said as she went off to get her coat, for the weather was icy.

When she returned, she said, "In all the excitement last night I completely forgot. Letters! One for you, Billy, and two for big brother. Hope you don't mind, Billy, but I asked for yours at the Postal Office, once Mike told me there might be some."

They both thanked her, and she handed the letters over as the three of them walked out the door.

They'd decided to walk into town, for there were horses and people *everywhere*. Indeed, the town of Boonville was swelled more than bursting, even here at the edge of it.

Rob and Billy both checked to see who the letters were from — but as much as they wanted to read them, it wasn't possible to do so while walking, without being run down by a horse. So reluctantly, both put their letters away to read when they next got a chance.

Billy was a little disappointed when he saw his was from Horace — not Cass or his Pa — and the truth was, the worry of it ate at him as they walked into town. But he wasn't about to act like some fool kid in front of Preacher Rob Brimstone — not over such a small thing as a *letter*.

The whole place was loco alright. Aside from the 1500-odd folks who lived in and around it all being there, many young men had flocked from neighboring towns to join Price's army. Add all that to over 7000 soldiers, and it made for 10,000 souls, all crammed into quite a small area.

The stores were doing a roaring trade. Too much trade in fact — already, food and supplies were dwindling, and it was clear even to Billy that Price's army could not stay here long.

"It's a good thing I knew you were coming, Rob," Daisy said quietly. "I've been stocking up for weeks."

They battled their way through the crowds. At one point there was some jostling, and a drunken soldier tried to challenge Billy to fight him — but one dark look from Preacher Rob Brimstone, and that man disappeared into the crowd with a hurried, "So sorry, Sir."

Rob questioned a couple of men, and it wasn't long before he found his commanding officer. Billy hung back with Daisy as Preacher Rob approached and briefly spoke to his commander, Brigadier General John Bullock Clark, Jr.

They kept their voices low.

John Clark was much younger than Billy expected, perhaps not even much over thirty. It was clear that the handsome young man was not happy, his annoyance plain even with half his face hidden by his giant mustaches. His look became one of consternation when he glanced across at Billy.

Preacher Rob appeared to be making a case for something — then after almost a minute, the Brigadier General threw his hands in the air, then stabbed a finger toward Rob several times, clearly laying down the law about something.

Then that man of noble bearing turned toward Billy, and in a great resonant voice commanded, "Come, boy."

'Sir," said Billy, with a respectful nod when he got there. The man was intimidating alright, perhaps more so even than General Price had seemed at the head of his Army, if it was possible.

"Captain Brimstone insists he is charged with your care, and bound by honor to protect you. Tells me you are *family*. And as such, he argues you should be admitted to what is, quite frankly, a brigade of experienced fighting men who will not like your presence at all! Will you listen and learn, do as you're told, put the lives of all fellow brigade members above even your own?"

Billy was terrified by the man's bearing, but he had been taking deep breaths, and somehow managed a, "Yes, Sir. I promise I will." And his voice didn't even sound weak.

"Brimstone tells me you have a good horse, your own kit, and a Henry with much ammunition. And that you know how to use and look after it all."

"Yes, Sir, that's all very true, Sir." He shook some inside, but his voice kept up strong.

"Alright then," the Brigadier General said to Billy with an air of finality. Then turning to Rob, he added, "It's on your shoulders, Brimstone. I'll trust you, as I have before. Sign him up with our man over there." And he pointed a deliberate finger at a recruitment table under an awning on the other side of the street.

CHAPTER 21
FYRE!

Preacher Rob thanked his commanding officer, and grabbed Billy's arm as he turned and walked away. "Not just anyone gets to join Clark's Brigade, son. No one who's not proved their worth before, anyway. Look how short the line is compared to all others. I still can't believe he agreed to it."

They crossed the busy street, almost getting bowled over by two fools, one chasing the other while drunkenly yelling something about him cheating at poker.

Billy felt relieved to be accepted, and again, he realized how lucky he'd been to have met Sheriff Mike back in Wilmington — anyone else would have been rejected, and it was almost a miracle, him being allowed into an experienced outfit like Brigadier General Clark's.

"One last chance to back out, Billy Ray," said Rob as they stepped up onto the boardwalk, and stood at the end of the line. Each man in line before him was a grizzled veteran, rather than the young men in most other lines.

"No," Billy answered, taking his hat off and running his hand through his hair. "I won't back out. Not even if the men won't accept me at first. I'll *earn* their trust."

"You'll have to," Rob told him. "But I have a good feeling about you. If Mike sent you, he had good reason. And you're Morris's friend. That makes you family to me. Now if you don't mind, I'll leave you a moment, go sit down with Daisy somewhere, and read my two letters. Morris's first, and then Mike's, I think."

The mention of the letters jerked Billy back to reality. "Thank you, Preacher Rob," he said, and took his own letters from his pocket. He had put the new one from Horace in with the one Cass gave him before he left.

He put Cass's letter safely away, then opened Horace's, unfolded it and began reading — being shuffled along as the line moved.

Billy. It is your brother Horrie writeing.

I am sure you will make a fine soldier. There is nothing so nobel as what you are doing. I only wish I came with you. Things are terrible bad here now. But as oldest I am air of the family so must stay for the ranch. I wish I was free to fight and maybe die a true and nobel brave man just as you are.

I am proud of you Billy.

I wish I could say the same about Pa.

He aint proud at all.

He hates you so much.

I never knew Pa could hate this way. I tryed to talk to

him, but each time he sayd he will crawl my hump if I mention you ever again.

You know how stubbern he can be. Once he decides a thing that is how it stays for ever.

Last time I sayd your name he did hit me. A bad one. It hurt a lot. Not the hitting itself was what hurt so much. More that he hates me for still loveing you.

Pa told Jaspers Pa that you are dead to him. Sayd he has only one son now. Jasper told me all that. I guess the whole town knows. I beat George Randall senseless for spredding it. But they all know I reckon.

It shames me some.

Pa will allways hate you Billy. I am sorry for you but cant change how he is. He told you cleer enuff he sayd.

Dont never come back Billy. He would kill you for sure I reckon. I dont wish ever to see that.

Pleese dont write again. Not ever. It made him so angry. He took it all out on me and Rosie.

Me I can take a beating fine. But I never knew Pa had that in his nature to hit a woman.

If ever you do write make it only to Jasper. I told Jasper to keep it secret and sneek it to me without Pa finding out. But I worry that Jasper's Pa might tell ours maybe. But if you MUST write then make it only to Jasper.

Pleese thats importent. I dont want Pa killing me and Rosie over some letter. He even hit the drink after your last letter and was waveing his gun around.

But write to Jasper if you must ever write. Only

Jasper. Last time I thaught Pa might shoot me or maybe himself.

There is one other terrible news.

Such bad news Billy. I do not know the way to say it. So I told you all about Pa first.

This other news is maybe worser even. For you it surely is. I am so sorry.

I guess you wonder why I write but Cass dont. Me being not much for letters like you and poor Cass.

I am sorry Billy.

No good way to say it.

They all died. The Macphersons.

A fire. Big one.

All dead in their beds. Few days after you left.

I am so sorry.

Only good thing they didnt suffer none. Smoke got them befor they woke up. One of them left a reading lamp burning and went to sleep and it nocked over onto a bed. That was how it was they reckon.

All dead.

Even Cass.

Also Annie and Jimmy and Lucy and old Tom.

That all upset Pa too. His best frend and his yunger son both dead to him now.

I bet that fool Jimmy done it. Allways readin like you Jimmy was.

I know you planned to marry Cass. But not now Billy. Shes dead and gone with her famly.

Theres nothing here for you now.

I am sorry Billy.

I will allways remember you.

But dont come back.

They sent the Macpherson bodys back East sumwhere for burrial.

Goodbye Billy.

I am sorry Cass is dead.

Horace Ray. Cottonwood Falls.

PS. Dont blame your self Billy. Put it behind you and fight. Even if you was here nothing you could have done about a fire.

Billy's body was numb, his thoughts raced and scrambled as he tried to make sense of it all.

It ain't real. It ain't.

His breath was ragged, his face somehow hot, though the air still felt icy around him. Someone spoke to him ... somewhere, somewhere not here.

"Name?" said the voice. Then louder, "*You there!* Are you still with us?"

Billy Ray looked down at the face behind the desk. He felt somehow out of his body, and looked a moment at his hand. It looked too big, and was wet. No, it was dirt from the post he had leaned on. Dirty and wet.

"Name?" the insistent voice asked again.

Fire, was all Billy thought.

"Fire," he said.

"Fire?" said the mouth in the face down below him, far away down there behind a desk.

"Fire," Billy said once again, his mouth so slack it could

barely give shape to the word. And he looked once again at his hand, this time the back of it.

"I knew a family of Fyres back home in Pittsburgh," said the voice. "Kin of yours?"

"What?" Billy clutched at his chest now as the words cut through him again, and he felt as if he might be sick.

Dead. Cass is dead.

"Not the sharpest saw in the toolshed, are you?" that voice said now, and it sighed. "Fyre with a Y?"

"Why?" said Billy, repeating the sound. Then he said, "Why?" again, but with conviction this time — for it was an angry question he asked of the Lord. But Billy knew, even then, there could never be an answer.

"First name?"

"What?" said Billy, as he slumped against the post again, his arm wrapped around it this time. He was numb all through, could not think, the blood roared in his ears as the heat and the pain of his grief almost overcame him.

"Listen, Country-Boy, I don't have all day, there are others waiting behind you," said the man behind the desk then — and someone behind Billy laughed. "What's your first name?"

"Billy," he said. And with that, quite suddenly, he saw where he was, and remembered just what he was doing. "William," he said, much more firmly. He took a deep breath, let go of the post he was leaned against, and stood up to his full six foot two.

"Next of Kin?"

Billy drew back a moment, his face stricken. "I got no one now."

"I'm very sorry," the man said, and he struck a cruel line on the paper. "Age?"

"Seventeen." It had come out Billy's mouth automatic.

The recruiter feller waved his hand as if to say *stop* — then he leaned forward, placed a single finger to his lips, and smiled. Then he removed the finger and calmly, quietly said, "What's that you say, William? Eight-teen?"

"Eight ... teen," Billy repeated. As another wave of grief washed over him, he barely knew he was there, let alone what the word meant.

"Congratulations, Country-Boy," the man said, pushing a copy of the recruitment notice into Billy's right hand. "Well, go on, you're done here," he added.

"Next?" he said then, looking past Billy. And he waved away the newest recruit to Clark's Brigade of the Missouri State Guard, in service of the Confederate States Army — the eighteen-year-old William Fyre.

CHAPTER 22
THE LOOTING OF BOONVILLE

There were things Billy Ray didn't know of as they went on around him.

To the south of Boonville, Price's rear guard, made up of Marmaduke's and Fagan's men both, fought off the Union Brigade of Federal Brigadier General John B. Sanborn.

While, in the town, what had seemed to Billy like drunken disorder among some of the troops, was evolving into much worse. Problem was, many of Price's men were far from the cream of the crop — no, these were more the dregs of society. Some there by choice, and some not.

A quarter of Price's men were former deserters who'd been forced to return to the Army. Many were unarmed, and had few provisions — and these men took to looting Boonville, the whole town and its surrounds becoming dangerous.

Indeed, it was only Mrs Ward's quick thinking — and her enjoyment of shooting at intruders — that stopped two unarmed looters from stealing Rob's and Billy's horses and gear from the stables.

They were just lucky her hands weren't so steady as they used to be, or she'd have been feeding those two men to her pigs.

That was just some of it though. In the town itself, there was almost a riot, which saw Rob and Daisy unable to get home for a time.

William "Bloody Bill" Anderson and his bushwhackers had come riding into town, whooping and hollering for all they were worth, and even skittled some soldiers, who drew guns and offered to duel with them.

Old Pap had seen the whole thing, and roared loudly at them all to stop. Then he noticed what at first he had not — that Bloody Bill Anderson and his bushwhackers had Union scalps dangling from their horses' bridles.

Appalled by this atrocity, Old Pap outright refused to speak to Anderson, until the scalps were removed and appropriately disposed of. Once they were, he sent Anderson immediately away, with instructions to behave more honorably — and to destroy the North Missouri Railroad. Or rather, the bits of it Anderson had not yet destroyed already. It was the very railroad that Billy had last traveled on.

If General Price had known what Anderson would go then and do, he'd have had the man locked up instead, or perhaps even shot — for Bloody Bill and his men went off on a rampage, not only destroying the railroad, but killing soldiers and civilians alike, and looting as they went.

Even with Bloody Bill gone, the looting in Boonville

was rife by now. Unable to find Billy in all the confusion, Preacher Rob had his work cut out just protecting Daisy as he escorted her home. He had to draw his gun more than once, but he never fired it.

The pair found Billy two hours later, back home at Daisy's, sitting on a low stool in the one empty stable.

"He's in here," Rob called. "You'd better come, Sis."

Billy looked up as they walked in. Looked at their faces. Looked back down at the letter in his hands. It had been crushed and rumpled somehow.

"What's happened, Billy?" said Daisy. "We were worried about you."

He jerked a little when she placed a gentle hand on his back.

"Cass," he said. "Cass."

He looked up into Daisy Hind's eyes, but the sight of her made it worse somehow, so he looked away from her. Looked at Preacher Rob, who looked mighty worried about *something*.

"What's happened, Billy?" Rob said. "Is it the letter? Can you show it to Daisy?"

Billy looked back at Daisy again, and the look in her eyes just about made him cry. He took a deep breath, squared his shoulders. Noticed he was sitting on a milking stool, out in the stables. Couldn't remember coming back here. Couldn't remember much of anything. Only the letter.

"Can I see it, Billy," she said softly, rubbing his back. "Would that be alright?"

He looked down at the letter he clutched in his hands,

then back up at the nice lady. Without speaking, he pushed it into her outstretched hand.

Then she moved away a step or two into the doorway, where there was more light she could read by.

While Daisy read the letter, Preacher Rob got down on his haunches in front of Billy. He squeezed Billy's shoulder — half firm and half gentle — same way Morris did after they just shot the Red Legs.

Somehow, it was a comfort.

It didn't fix the hole that had grown inside him, but regardless, it was a comfort.

But he still didn't feel alive.

They just sort of stayed like that awhile — Billy couldn't really tell for how long, only that it was awhile — and then he noticed some noises, and those noises were Daisy.

Then she was there with him, in front of him, and tears was running all down her face. And she said, "Oh, Billy, Billy, I'm so sorry," then her lady voice broke some, and she was embracing him so tight it hurt him even more in his heart.

That went on awhile too, Daisy just about smothering him, her fingers clutching his hair and her wet tears all on his face and she even was kissing his cheeks and his hair some, and his ears was wet from it all, and she seemed all around him.

Then Preacher Rob said, "I'm so sorry, Billy. So sorry. And I know this can't help, and there's no words that can, but I *do* understand how you feel."

Billy looked up at him, as Daisy released him some —

her arms were still around his neck, but her face was away now — and he tried to speak to Rob, but he couldn't. A strangled little noise almost came out, but it died in his throat, and he felt just a little ashamed, but he didn't much care.

"I'm sorry, Billy," Rob said again. "I won't lie to you. Thing like this never heals, not really. When I lost ... well, never mind, perhaps we'll speak later. Only if you want to." Then he gripped Billy's shoulder again with one hand, and helped Daisy to her feet with the other.

"Come, Billy," said Daisy then, "let's all go inside, I'll make coffee, and we'll all get warm."

He allowed them to help him to his feet, one each side, then pulled his arm free, wiped the tears from his face with his sleeve. He knew those tears weren't all Daisy's, and he felt just a little embarrassed.

"Sorry, Billy," Daisy said then, as they came to the door and Rob opened it. "I got you all wet with my crying. Go clean up if you like."

Billy Ray went and washed his face then, and looked at himself in the mirror.

I'm still me, I guess, by my looks, just not by how I feel. But maybe this all isn't real, and only a nightmare.

He pinched himself hard on his side then, and it hurt, but not so much as it should have.

We'll see if I wake from it, I guess.

But it felt way too big, the hole inside him too great, and he had no faith at all in his chances of ever waking from it.

Maybe it's me dead, he thought then, *rather'n Cass.*

Maybe this is my punishment in Hell. Cass gone, and Pa sayin' I'm dead to him, right now when I need him the most.

He choked down a sob, took a deep breath, stood up tall — and he slapped his own cheek so hard it turned white and then reddened.

"You alright in there, Billy?" Rob called then.

"Yessir, Preacher Rob," he answered. "I'll be there in a moment." Then he looked at that mirror one more time, and said, "Billy, you damn foolish kid, you're dead to me now."

And the face that looked back at him seemed older, harder, so much less forgiving than his own — and that suited Billy just fine.

"War. That's what a man needs."

Even his voice sounded different.

And Billy turned away from that mirror, determined to leave his childish self far behind.

"I hope we leave Boonville soon," he said to Rob when he walked into the parlor. "I can't hardly wait to get amongst them Union skunks."

"Billy..." said Daisy, but the pained plea trailed off into nothing, and she looked to Rob to take over.

"Well, maybe," said Preacher Rob. "Or maybe it'd be better you take a few days, join us later. I can write you where to meet us, and —"

"I joined up to fight," Billy said then, his voice cool and even. "I've no less reason to do so now than before."

"But Billy," said Daisy, "surely you need to—"

"No, Daisy," he said. "Thank you for being so

considerate, but I *know* what I need. You've been so good to me, and I have no way of repaying that. But I need to leave with Preacher Rob and be part of the fight. I'm a soldier now."

And he took the Recruitment Notice from his pocket, and handed it to her.

She looked at it, then looked up at him strangely, then showed it to Rob, who looked at it too.

"What?" Billy said, and he felt suddenly panicked, for he had not yet looked at the notice — and perhaps the fellow had not joined him up after all, and he'd lost that as well. *"What?"*

"William Fyre," said Rob, holding the paper up before him. "You said your name was Ray."

"It is," Billy said. "Show me that." He snatched the paper out of Rob's hand.

Sure enough, it said William Fyre on it.

"Fyre," Billy said.

Then as the other two stared, Billy began to laugh — but the sound was not pleasant, not to anyone.

"William Fyre," he said loudly. "That's who I am alright. Billy Ray is dead, just like everyone he ever knew before he left home. Dead to his father, dead to his brother, dead to poor Cass, Billy's *dead!* William Fyre it is then, rising up from the ashes of who he once was."

And once again Billy laughed, his eyes gone wild inside their sockets. But Rob Brimstone said nothing, for he'd seen it all before, more or less — and in truth, he had lived it himself.

For he too had grieved for the woman he loved, and he

knew that there wasn't much of anything to be done, but for being a friend to Billy now.

From that moment he did what he could, of course, and so did Daisy. But Billy refused to speak of what had happened. Refused to write home. Refused even to acknowledge it, really.

He understood how the mixup had occurred with his name, and saw it as only a good thing. "I'm glad of it," he said. "Best thing could ever have happened. New name, new me."

He cleaned and oiled his guns, even though they didn't need it.

He cleaned his boots, unpacked his gear and had Rob look at it with him — discarded what he didn't need. Repacked it all, unpacked and repacked it again, just for practice. Practiced drawing his sidearm quick too — though he knew he'd never get good as Morris.

He gifted the pack horse to Daisy, despite knowing Price wanted every available horse for his army. "It doesn't go even part way to repaying your kindness, Daisy, but Jack's a fine horse, and might be helpful when you and Mrs Ward need supplies from in town. Not a bad riding horse either. I'd appreciate you taking him, is the truth. We became friends, I guess. Not like me and Jenny, there could never be another Jenny, just like..."

His voice trailed off then, and he couldn't go on. He looked away from Daisy, and wiped his eye with the heel of his hand. That was the closest Billy came to breaking down again that day, but he just sort of smiled and said, "Will you look after Jack for me, Daisy?"

"Of course, Billy," she said, touching his arm. "He'll be right here for you to collect once the war's over with. I've a feeling that won't be long, I really do."

"It's alright, Daisy, you keep him. Chances are, I won't be back." Then he paused a second or two, looked at her stricken face and added, "I just mean I won't come back through this way. Not that ... you know."

But the truth sat right there between them. Billy Ray — or Fyre as he now preferred — had no plan to return from the war. There wasn't nowhere to return *to*.

That was just how he felt.

And while Morris had seemed like a brother to him — and indeed, *all* the Brimstones now treated him like family — he did not feel any depth to all that now. The roots of family run deep, and grow all through time. Morris was nice and all, and there *had* been a great sense of kinship — but once all the fighting was over, Billy would be all alone, with no deep roots to bind him to anyone.

And after forty-eight hours in Boonville, when new recruit Billy Fyre rode out with the rest of Price's Army toward Chouteau Springs, he felt no desire to live, had no sense that his life was worth anything, and no thought to preserve or prolong it no further than the first battle he could get into.

It was not that he consciously thought all these things — he did not. He was simply lacking the normal desires that keep people safe and alive.

Which was partly why Billy did what he did, just three mornings later, in the midst of the Battle of Glasgow.

CHAPTER 23
THE BATTLE OF GLASGOW

Billy's first two days of service went without incident. He did his best to numb himself to his pain, as he and the rest of Price's Army moved slowly east — slower than seemed sensible to Billy.

He heard grumblings about that too. Seemed Old Pap was a whole lot more interested in keeping hold of things his Army had captured — spoils of war — than he was with moving quickly to strike with surprise on his side. And also, most of the 1500 new recruits had no horses, and were unarmed — a rag-tag bunch on foot, no use unless they could get hold of some guns.

The night of the 13th, they camped at Chouteau Springs. It was there that Old Pap received word of 5,000 guns, locked up in a storehouse in Glasgow.

An hour later, just as Preacher Rob told Billy and his other men to go get some sleep, an excited General Clark came to the group and said, "Prepare to travel, Brimstone. Our entire Brigade, and 500 of Jackman's, are to ride north, cross the river at Arrow Rock, and attack Glasgow morning after next."

The morning of the 15th was Billy's first lesson in the hit-and-miss nature of war. It was meant to be a co-ordinated attack, but it never went that way at all.

Glasgow was well protected, but the Confederate Generals, Clark and Shelby, had no shortage of numbers. More important, all their men were experienced fighters — all except Billy anyways.

Just before dawn, General Shelby's artillery opened fire from the west side of the Missouri River. But someone had made a judgment of error, and most of Clark's men — Preacher Rob Brimstone and Billy *"Fyre"* included — had trouble crossing the river. The plan was all shot to bits then, and a new plan made on the run.

Two hours later, Clark's men advanced on Glasgow from several directions. The Union soldiers were outnumbered, but well fortified, and plenty brave along with it.

Billy stuck to Preacher Rob, no matter what, just as he had been told to. Men around him were being shot down, but on they continued regardless, fighting for each yard of ground. To Billy, the killing and wounding seemed to follow no pattern at all. A man might be speaking, mid-sentence, reloading his musket, and a small thud be heard, and all present look to the man's chest where the small thud had come from. A small hole might be seen in his coat — and with his heart pierced, his sentence forever unfinished, another man would fall, left behind.

In the hours that followed, they moved through the

open at times to gain some new position. There were moments when shots flew so close past Billy's head, he felt the rush of the air the bullets displaced.

And he cared not at all — he was numbed from the truth of his life, for he'd given up on it.

Billy, Preacher Rob and six others finally found themselves isolated from the rest of their men. They were at the extreme right of their troops, but caught in a stalemate. If they could get around further to their right, the enemy flank would be vulnerable, and be forced to retreat. But for now, both sides had good protection each from the other, unless someone dared to move.

But moving's easy to think of, less easy to accomplish, times like these.

It was a conundrum alright.

They were tied down here by the enemy, unable to advance or go anywhere useful from the solid stone building they sheltered behind. They had been on foot now three hours, and lost several men in that time. There would be no riding out of here, not unless they won the battle — for Rob and his small elite crew were in the riskiest, most vulnerable position of all Clark's Brigade.

They crouched now, low on their haunches, in a row at the back of that solid stone building, reloading their Colts as they listened to Rob's plan.

"We ain't worth a damn to our friends from here," Preacher Rob told them in a battle-wild voice. "Our job's to get round to the right, attack their flank, drive them back."

"It ain't possible, Sir," said a red-bearded giant called Simpson. He was a battle-scarred veteran, afraid of no man, but he yet had a sense for survival. He spat on the ground and said, "Ain't no way outta here but for backways — not if we wants to be breathin'. They's had time to prepare, and thought they's defenses out good."

Rob half turned on his haunches, his boots squeaking in the dust in a rare quiet moment where not a single gun fired. He pointed toward a log fence, a good way off to their right. It was four feet high, as solid as a house, and had a full water trough behind it. It was all dirt between here and there, not one blade of grass.

"I'll break for that fence over there," said Rob, his eyes wider'n saucers, "while you boys keep firing to give me some cover."

"But Sir," growled Simpson loudly.

Rob ignored him and went on with his plan.

"I might have a shot at them from there. If not, I'll reload, call out 'Now boys,' and sprint to that barn — and I'll sure give 'em plenty from that side with this Henry — enough so you boys can get out and join me. Once we're all there, they can't hold that position, and we'll surely have routed them."

"It's suicide, Captain," Simpson groaned, "and you know it, well as I do. That fence is more'n thirty-five yards away."

"If I don't make it," said Rob, "you're in command, Simpson. And I charge you ongoing with Billy Fyre's care."

"But Sir!"

Preacher Rob was sat on his rump now, and using both his hands to work one of his knees back and forth, for it had been giving him trouble, and he needed it loosened to run.

"If I fail, don't no one else try it. Just wait here until our men prevail some other way, and it's safe to come out and move forward. No sense the rest of you dying."

"But Sir!"

"No, Simpson," said Rob, shaking out his arms a few seconds before picking up his rifle. "It's my fault we're in this predicament, and I'll have no more words about it. That's an order. All of you loaded and ready?"

No one noticed, of course, but Preacher Rob Brimstone wasn't the only man stretching and readying his body all of this time.

"Ready, Sir," came all seven voices. Six had their handguns out, and Billy picked up his Henry.

"I'm goin' on three," said Rob, his eyes filled with the fire and madness of a man making ready to die. "One," he whispered, holding up one finger. "Two," he said, two fingers thrust in front of him. "Thre-aaaarrrggg" he growled, as he crashed down into the dirt.

For at the very moment Preacher Rob coiled his body to leap into action, young Billy Ray — now Private Billy Fyre — used all the strength he possessed to knock his Captain to the ground. Billy sprang then into the open, that awkward-looking but fine supple body sprinting hellfire for leather, the long legs working like pistons, the lean arms pumping the lever of his Henry, the yip-yipping howl of the Rebel yell erupting from his mouth as he flew, flew, flew for the impossible goal of the fence that was so far away, his feet barely skimming the ground, so quick did they move.

The bullets hit dirt only inches away to the front, to the side and behind him, as the battle raged on all around. But

Billy was fast, he was flexible; he was downright and outright elusive; so light on his feet and the thinnest of targets, that maybe, he still had a chance.

And it was mighty fortunate that Billy was *all* of those things — in addition, some might say he was *lucky* as well — for if he weren't every single *one* of those things, *some* of them bullets would surely have hit him, and ended his life then and there, in his very first battle.

When Billy knocked Preacher Rob over, his other six comrades had all been so shocked, they all just turned round and looked — and they didn't give him cover right away.

By the time them boys got their wits back and started firing on the enemy, Billy had halfway gotten to the safety of the fence. He was firing wildly himself as he ran, with no intention of hitting anything — yet somehow, he heard a cry from a feller he'd hit, and he just kept a'runnin' and firin' as fast as he could.

A bullet clipped his boot near his heel, putting him off his stride, and he just about fell to the ground — saved his life, that did, though he never knew it. For as Billy stumbled, a bullet went right through the space where his head woulda been if he hadn't.

He swerved and he ran and he fired that Henry, and another of them bullets went clean through his hat, and parted his hair down the middle. Woulda set the whole schoolyard to laughing if they woulda seen him sport such a style.

But still Billy ran, his blood pumping, his whole world alive with the sound and the feel of it now, as everything around seemed to slow. And so close to that fence now, he twisted, as if dodging the imagined path of a bullet — and Billy dived, somehow flew through the air, and let go of the Henry as he tucked that long body of his in a circle and rolled.

And then he had made it.

Made it!

Face down to begin with, he scrambled, upways and sideways, got his back against those thick logs of that fence. And Billy took a deep breath, looked about him, and decided — for now — he was safe.

But the Henry — *my beautiful Henry* — was eight feet away from the end of the fence he'd taken cover behind.

"Billy?" he thought he heard someone call. But he didn't answer, he was too busy shaking and breathing, now that bit was over. He could even see them Union boys from here, through a little chink in the fence — if he could just get the Henry back, he could set them boys to retreating fifteen to the dozen.

He took a slower, deeper breath, as he pictured his father, then put him and all else from his mind. Ignored the noise of the shooting, as if it wasn't happening at all. He sat with his back to the fence, looked over his arms and his legs for anything missing or hit, but he seemed all intact. Took his Army Colt out then and readied it — just in case. One more deep slow breath, and Billy gathered all of his strength up, put it into his voice and called out, "Sorry 'bout that, Preacher Rob."

The reply came back at him, fast as the report from a rifle. "Ya dang *fool,* Billy. Are you hit?"

CHAPTER 24
SURE GLAD I AIN'T AN INCH
TALLER...

"Don't reckon I'm even scratched," Billy called, wiggling his fingers and toes. He figured Preacher Rob didn't need to hear about his boot, and his newly parted hair didn't probably count. "Be needin' my good gun back though, all I got's this baby Colt, and I ain't much with that, as you know. Little cover'd be helpful."

"Few moments, Billy," called Preacher Rob. And he knew that the men were all reloading — for none of the others had repeaters, and would already have emptied their Colts.

A few of the enemy took random shots at the Henry, but it was in sort of a hollow that had been worn into the dirt by whatever critters had been near this fence through the years. So them fellers soon gave up on that, and saved their bullets for Billy's attempt to retrieve it.

About fifteen seconds later, all hell erupted from where Preacher Rob was with his men. But as many shots as they got off, the enemy got off still more — and it seemed like all them shots was directed right into that space between Billy and his Henry.

Billy sure did love his slouch hat. Wasn't official for Cavalry, but roundabout half the men wore them. By this late point of the war, uniforms seemed like just a suggestion. Even grays and blues could be seen on both sides. Sometimes men got shot by their own fellers, even. Crazy business, war is, that's for sure and for certain.

Pulled his head in right quick, Billy had, when he lost his hat. Shot off hat sounded like a thing from a storybook, one a' them dime novels Billy had read. He'd never thought it much likely — always figured the bullet should just pass on through it, unless it hit bone on its way.

But now it had happened to him — he'd see it plenty more times yet, as the war went on and on, day after day of miserable fighting, of men dying in the mud for reasons most of 'em didn't even clearly understand.

Now, the reason Billy was so attached to that slouch hat, it had been a birthday gift from his Pa. When it got shot off his head, it ended up out in the open where he couldn't retrieve it. Then a few of the Union fellers decided it was a game, and a barrage of shots hit the hat, it getting carried further each time, and he heard them all laughing. One of 'em called out, "Nice hat, Farm Boy," and they all laughed some more.

"Laugh it up," Billy called to 'em. "Might as well enjoy your last five minutes alive."

He noticed a wetness by his ear, touched it with two fingers, and held those fingers up in front of his eyes. It weren't much of anything, but it *was* wet and red. He put back those two fingers, let 'em trace up along the drip trail, and felt the small sting when he got to the source of the seepage. Ran his fingers along it, one end to the other. Wasn't nothin' really, as wounds go — just a scratch along the top of his scalp, where that first bullet parted his hair for him.

Sure glad I ain't an inch taller.

If he'd had a mirror he'd have tried to have a look-see, just in case a middle-part suited him. But once he thought about it, he wouldn't have bothered with a mirror.

No, that ain't for me. I'm a part-your-hair-from-the-left man, not straight down the middle.

He almost laughed at his foolishness then, but got his fool brain back to business with a *Forget about that, Billy, think!*

And think Billy did. Or rather, instead, he remembered. There was this one time when he was little, maybe just six, and Billy was tryin' to mount a horse, over and over — and failing the same way each time.

He was a long ways too short to get on that old gray horse without help — *Charlie it was,* he recalled — and no matter how many times little Billy brought that old horse to the stump, each time he let go of the reins ol' Charlie moved out of reach, just a step, maybe two. But Billy *had to* let go the reins — for they weren't long enough, and he needed his hands to climb up onto the stump, on his way to the heights of that old horse's back.

Horse was between the stump and the fence, so at least

he couldn't go sideways — but that wily old gray just kept moving backward or forward.

Then his Pa's voice had rung out from behind him, and the six year old Billy had flinched some, thinking he was in trouble — for he wasn't strictly *allowed* to mount the horse by himself.

"Your brains been kicked out by that horse, Son?" was what his Pa said.

"No, Pa," little Billy had answered.

"Fell out by 'emselves?"

"No?"

"Shot out then, maybe?"

"No, Pa."

"Maybe try puttin' 'em to use then, son. Brains are for makin' new plans when your first plan don't work."

Seventeen year old Billy thought back now to that long ago moment. The six year old Billy had indeed come up with a new plan. He had gone fetched some rope, wrapped it round Charlie's reins — he couldn't tie knots yet, so wrapping was all he could manage — and then he held onto it tight, as he climbed up the stump. And before he knew it, little Billy had clambered up onto that horse, and then he was riding!

Of course, there *had* been a reason Billy weren't yet allowed to ride Charlie, and it was a good one — Charlie threw him off ten seconds later, and Billy broke his arm when he landed.

He gripped his wrist now absentmindedly, as he remembered it.

But still, there were *two* lessons learned that day. And

he only needed *one* of 'em now. Not the one about the broken arm — just the new plan one.

My brains ain't shot out just yet — so I'll use 'em to think up a new plan.

Them Union fellers was taunting him again, and Preacher Rob and the boys were reloading, so Billy sat there and shut out all the noise best he could, as he tried to think up a plan.

Rope, he thought. *Worked then.*

Now, Billy didn't actually have no rope. But like many a Farm Boy, he never went nowhere without some good strips of rawhide in his pockets — or wrapped around him like a belt, as Sheriff Mike had taught him to do.

He undid the pieces from around him, took out the one from his pocket, and tied them all together. Then he took off his coat, looped it through the bottom two buttonholes and tied it off strong. Then he practiced throwing the coat a few times at a stick — behind the fence, out of sight of them Union fellers.

Took maybe six or seven tries before he got it right. But once he had the distance of the throw properly figured, he took aim, took a deep breath, and threw that coat out past the Henry. Then he jerked it so the barrel got caught in the sleeve, then pulled on the rawhide to gather it all in.

Got it first go!

All hell broke loose again from both sides, but Billy ignored all a' that, his entire concentration focused on what he was doing.

It took all of ten seconds, but slowly and surely, Billy reeled in that Henry like a fish. There was fifteen holes in his jacket by then, and a slug embedded in the rifle stock, but Billy's plan had worked, and the Henry was once again in his hands.

From that moment, things went as well as a man coulda hoped for. He loaded up that repeater, and commenced to firing at them Union fellers so quick, they musta thought they'd all died and was in hell already.

By the time Billy emptied the Henry, six of them fellers was shot, and all the others was runnin' away, fast as their Union legs would carry 'em.

Preacher Rob and the others broke cover and chased them, and gained what had previously seemed their impenetrable spot.

That was the moment that turned the battle — from there, it was pretty much won. Preacher Rob had been right about routing them by taking their flank.

The rest of the Union line crumbled, and within a few minutes, they all retreated up the hill and to safety. The Confederates were all behind cover, but within fifty yards of them then, in front of them *and* to the right.

And Billy got his hat back then too.

There came then a quiet hour, in which the only shots was occasional fire by snipers, whenever heads poked out that shouldn't have. Then the leader of the Union troops, Colonel Chester Harding, sent out a flag, enquiring what terms would be granted if he chose to surrender.

By then General Clark had come along the line to where Preacher Rob and his men were. He looked at Billy quite differently now, than the way he had back in

Boonville — for through his field glasses he had seen what Billy had done, it being strategically important.

"Well done, Fyre," was all he said, and Billy felt a little embarrassed to receive such attention. But he never even had time to answer, for right at that moment the Union man carrying the flag arrived to discuss the surrender.

Brigadier General John Clark Junior was an honorable man, and Billy witnessed that for himself now.

The General allowed that Harding's entire garrison could march out under its colors, the officers being allowed to retain their horses, side-arms and any and all private property. As for the men, they would be allowed their private property only — no arms or horses for them of course, this was *war*. But they would be paroled honorably, and allowed to leave completely unharmed. Furthermore, Clark gave his assurance that all persons and citizens of the town would be respected and unmolested for as long as he stayed in Glasgow.

It was a good thing that Billy saw something honorable right then — for in the weeks that followed, he would see many *less* honorable things. None done by Clark though — he was a proper good man.

John Clark paid tribute to Billy that night, offering a toast to his bravery, and commending Preacher Rob on his wisdom, in recommending the boy.

The brave actions of all these men together had won for Price's Army 1200 badly needed rifles, a few hundred horses, and a large supply of military overcoats — good thing for Billy that last one, for his own coat was shot full of holes.

As for Preacher Rob himself, he waited until they were alone before quietly saying, "Billy, assaulting an officer's a serious offense. Anything to say for yourself?"

"Sorry, Preacher Rob. But you wasn't gonna let me go instead a' you, so I *had* to do it that way. And you still got family to live for. What would Morris have said if I let you get shot? And besides, I'm a *lot* quicker'n you."

Rob Brimstone rubbed his chin a few moments before answering. "Well, next time—"

"How 'bout we agree," Billy jumped in and said, "that we use my speed and suppleness to advantage from now on? I ain't got nothin' to go back to, Sir, and I might as well die for a *reason.*"

"Billy, I promised Mike and Morris I'd protect—"

"Please, Preacher Rob. This is all I got left, don't you see? She's *gone! She ain't never comin' back, just like all these dead fellers around us! And even my Pa don't want me no more!*" He paused half a moment, then his voice came out quieter, more even. "I got no home, nothin' to go back to, dammit all! Don't you get it?"

"But Billy, you gotta listen to sense," said Rob, grasping the boy's wrist now and looking into his eyes.

Billy shrugged him off and broke free. "I don't *want* to live, and I *won't be*. If you don't allow me to do such things as are useful, I'm just gonna do somethin' stupid anyway — maybe even get someone else killed while doin' myself in. Please, Preacher Rob? *Please?* Let *my* death at least be worth *something?*"

Billy's eyes filled with tears as he pleaded with his Captain. Then a single tear ran down his cheek, fell through the air, plopped down into the dirt. And right then, to Preacher Rob Brimstone, that boy looked about twelve years old.

Preacher Rob knew he had no choice, and he sadly relented.

So that was the first of many times Private Billy Fyre risked his life doing what seemed impossible.

For there ain't nothin' in the world like a soldier without somethin' to live for — and since receiving that letter, that was just who Billy had become.

CHAPTER 25
THE TAMING OF MARSHAL CLEM JENKINS

Back in Cottonwood Falls, a whole lot had been happening.

For one thing, Cass had often been feeling unwell. She had drawn right in on herself, and spent much of her time alone in her room. Understandable, given all that had happened. John and Rosie just figured she needed some time to get over what happened, and made allowances for it.

But while Horace stayed on his best behavior at home — and was particularly kind and attentive to Cass when he saw her — he was up to all sorts of no-good-ness elsewhere.

He figured his letter to Billy should be more than enough to stop him from writing, or ever coming home for that matter. Not that Billy making it home was in any way likely — *he's just a fool kid,* Horace figured, who *can't even shoot straight.*

No, Billy's chances of surviving the war were none or a

little bit less. But for Horace's grand plan to work, he could not afford for Billy to write home before he got killed.

Still, Horace knew that, what with Billy being how he was, it was unlikely he'd risk his Pa hurting Horace or Rosie — *he's a noble fool alright* — but he wasn't taking no chances.

First chance Horace got, he went on his own to see Jasper's Pa, Marshal Clem Jenkins.

When he walked through the door into the combined Postal Office and Town Jail, Clem looked up at him, somewhat concerned. "Why alone, Horrie? Somethin' happened to Jasper?"

Natural reaction, that was — for the Strawheads was rarely apart.

For the moment though, Horace put Clem's mind at rest. He stopped just inside the doorway and said, "Jasper's fine, Marshal. At least for now. I gave him a job to tie him up awhile. Because you and me, we needs to talk some in private."

"Private it is then," said Clem. He had seen something strange in Horace's demeanor right off, and he didn't waste no time arguing. "Turn the sign around then, and bolt the door."

Back In 5 Minutes, the sign said. But sometimes it sat like that for awhile as Clem took a snooze in the cells. If it was important, folks'd look through the window, see he was back there and holler.

Horrie turned the sign, bolted the door, then clomped across the boarded floor — spurs jangling as always — and sat down right across from Clem. Didn't take off his hat. No manners, some fellers.

"We got a small problem, Marshal," Horrie said with that smile of his — the one that meant the other feller had the problem, not him.

"We do, do we?" The Marshal shifted in his seat some. He didn't like this. The feel of it was all wrong. "Well, let's have it straight then, no fooling. I can see by your eyes it ain't good."

"You read things good, Mister Jenkins," said Horace, still smiling that smile. "I guess that's why you're the Marshal. Alright, I'll be straight and quick. But before I say what it is, don't get no notions of startin' no foul play on *me*. There's someone else knows the truth on this, and if anything happens to me, they been instructed to tell it — and when they do, you'll go down too, for a cover-up."

Clem Jenkins looked from Horace's eyes to the door then, and back. "What the *hell* are you sayin', Horace Ray?"

"Alright, calm down. You heard me and understood, right? Someone else knows — but they ain't gonna *ever* say nothin'. Not unless I say so, or if I turn up dead."

Clem Jenkins's mouth tightened into a straight line then. "Understood and point taken. Now just spit it out, boy."

"If anyone digs up them graves and checks the MacPhersons, they'll find every one of 'em has bullet holes through their bones." Horace's eyes grew even more cruel then, as he watched the Marshal take in the words.

"You..."

"No, Marshal," said Horace, finally taking his hat off and throwing it down on the desk. Then he leaned back in his chair, and put his feet up on the desk, all over some paperwork, before going on. "I'm the law abiding type, me. Jasper went on before me, remember? Jasper went *alone* to the MacPhersons that night. You and my Pa know the story, and Jasper was there when I told it, and agreed to it all — you're a witness."

"No," said Clem then, and his left hand clawed at his eyes, as if that could change things. "No."

"I'm sorry, Mister Jenkins, I really am. See, my guess is that you filed all that paperwork with the authorities, wrapped it all up nice and proper — and someplace in your report, it tells that Jasper was first on the scene, a half hour at least before me."

The pair sat in silence a minute. That whole time, Clem stared at his desk, or maybe through it, and never looked up. Horace studied him closely — watched the man break, and enjoyed every moment of his torture.

"You were with him, of course," said Clem Jenkins, when he finally spoke again.

"That ain't nohow what matters though, is it? All that matters is us protectin' Jasper. He's my very best friend, and I'd hate to be watchin' him hang." Horace took his feet down off the desk then, stood up and sauntered across to the door, moved the curtain a little to peek out at the street.

"Get back here," Clem said sharply, "and tell me just what it is you want. You didn't tell me all this without reason, what is it you think I can do for you?" Then a look of horror came over him, and he added, "Are there others too?"

"No others, Marshal. Not yet at least. And maybe there won't be, if things all go smooth." Horace let go the curtain and came back and sat on the edge of the desk, showing no regard at all for the paperwork on it. It was deliberate, and both of them knew it.

Horace Ray held all the cards.

"Just spit it out, Horrie. What is it you want?"

Horace picked up a Wanted Poster, studied it a moment, took his time. Then he smiled at the Marshal, watched his face as he let the poster go, let it float to the floor. "Don't want nothin' much *yet,* Marshal. Just wanted you to know is all. And *don't* say nothin' to Jasper. He's *never* to know that you know — you got that?"

"I got it," Clem said, shaking his head at the horror of it all. "Wouldn't know what to say to the boy anyway. My Lord, what would his poor mother think?"

"Luckily she'll never know," Horrie said. "There is just one thing for now ... Postmaster Jenkins." He paused then and let his choice of title sink in. "If that fool young brother a' mine sends a letter, it's to come to me only, y'hear?"

"Oh, I hear you."

"Good. Damn fool's probably already dead. Won't last long off at the war, I shouldn't expect. But he might just send one before he dies, perhaps to my Pa, or to me, or maybe even to Jasper. Whoever it's sent to, it comes to me only, and in private." Horace took a sheet of paper from his pocket then, a note Billy had written to him some time back, and handed it to Clem. "Here's a sample of his fancy handwritin', just in case he sends one to someone else, so you'll recognize that if it happens."

"So that's all then?" Marshal Clem looked almost relieved now, and pushed back his chair and stood up, as if their business had all been concluded.

"Not quite, Marshal," said Horace, staying put where he sat on the desk, and picking up another Wanted Poster. "If Billy *does* happen to come back, you'll be needin' to kill him before he sees Cass or Pa or anyone else."

Clem Jenkins' eyes widened and he smashed a fist down on the desk. "I can't just kill folks for no reason!"

"Quiet there, Marshall," Horace said in an even tone. "You don't want no one hearing now, do you? As for killin' Billy, it's not likely you'll ever need to. War'll do that job for us — it's only a *just-in-case* thing. I trust you'll find a way though, if ever it's needed. Accidental, I expect it'd be, him lookin' just like one a' these fellers on Posters, and seemin' to go for his gun. Besides, it couldn't be Billy, he's already dead. Says so in the letter you'll be handing Pa when next he's in town. The one you'll write out that's like this one — change your handwriting though, and fill in some better details."

While he was speaking, Horace had produced a letter from his pocket, and slowly waved it around in front of the Marshal.

"What in the name of...?" Clem sure looked confused as he took the letter from Horace and studied it.

"Maybe write it out with your left hand or something. Needs to be from somewhere in Missouri, as Billy went off to Boonville. Wherever fits with the news of the fighting round there. The letter's to tell of my dear brother's noble death, you see? *Such* a tragedy, ain't it? You can see now why we don't need *another letter* arriving — or Billy himself, if it came to it."

"Why, Horrie. Why?" Marshal Clem held onto the letter and looked nervously toward the door again — but no one was there.

"Never did like Billy," growled Horace, "him always bein' Pa's favorite. Just ain't nice, playin' favorites, I reckon. Sticks in my craw, that. Figured Billy'd get killed in the war soon enough if I got him there. He was just one part a' the problem though. The *real* problem was women, y'see, Clem?"

"Women?" Clem screwed up his eyes and rubbed his overlarge ears.

"Sure, women. You don't see 'em exactly thick on the ground round here, do ya? And that little skunk Billy had one, and I didn't. I tried to get Annie to like me, a'course — but her damn parents didn't favor me. Reckon they poisoned her against me."

"All this for a woman?"

"Two women, it was meant to be. Jasper needed a wife too. We can't go through life just with each other, now can we? Ain't right. I got a ranch to take over soon, and I need to get on with startin' a family. A whole dynasty, I'm gonna have. You just wait and see, Mister Jenkins."

Marshal Clem walked on over to the cells, still clutching the letter in his hand that Horace had given him.

He banged his head on one of the bars a few times, then stood leaned against it, making a low groaning sound.

Horace finally got up from the edge of the desk, stood and faced Jenkins, picked up his hat and held it in front of his chest. "Careful a' your head there, Marshal, we don't want *you* hurt. Aw, we ain't so bad, me and Jasper. See, Annie weren't meant to be there that night, just the parents and that young skunk Jimmy, and he ain't worth nothin'. With them three outta the way, and Billy gone too, they'd have nothin' left, the two girls, and *have* to marry. I figured I'd have a good shot with Annie then, and Cass would consent to marry Jasper. Once they grieved some a'course, with us bein' attentive and caring the whole time. It all went wrong though, when Annie was there in the house."

"But why? Why?"

"Why? Any fool can see why. Man *needs* a good wife, and a pretty one's even better. Where else was me and Jasper gonna find two such pretty wives? If only Annie hadn't stayed home sick. Well, at least we got to enjoy her — though between you and me, I reckon the mother was better. Anyway, now with things changed, I'm gonna take Cass. We'll get Jasper someone else soon's we can."

The horrified Clem spun about to face Horace. "No more killing!"

"No sir, Mister Jenkins, a'course not. We'll be *real* good boys from now on, you just wait and see." Horace smiled, turned and walked to the door then, looked out the curtain, turned the sign back around. "Well, it sure was nice seein' you, Marshal — we really must chat more often. But always in private, okay? I'll expect a copy a' that there letter in your hand to arrive for Pa soon."

And with that, Horace Ray unbolted the door and walked out into the street. He knew he had made it quite clear — he was boss in this town now.

CHAPTER 26
GRIEF

It was exactly four weeks after Billy left, when Cass's sickness began. It was a Monday.

Just like every other Monday, Cass woke up in Mary Brown's house.

Unlike other Mondays, she felt like she needed a bucket — but it never quite came to that. Still, it was now Thursday, she was due to go home later today to the Ray place, and here she was, sick again. Just as she had been for four mornings straight now.

"I'm sorry, Mary," she said. "I expect it'll be gone by lunch time again. What a strange bug it is. I hope you don't catch it from me."

Mary Brown shook her head slowly, and smiled the smile of the knowing. She had seen such a sickness before — indeed, she had lived it herself, each time she was with child.

"Cass, dear," she said in her old creaky voice, as she sat herself down on the edge of the younger woman's bed.

"You're a precious girl, but not yet wise to the ways of the world."

Mary spoke strangely sometimes, and Cass thought the lovely old woman was preparing to launch into one of her many long stories — which sometimes went somewhere, and sometimes did not.

But Cass was about to get a surprise — or rather, it would be a shock.

"Dear," Mary said, "I know you're a very good girl, and I'd never let anyone judge you harshly. Not if I can do something to help it."

Cass managed a thin smile, and held onto the bucket — it was no time for one of Mary's rambling stories, but she was too polite to say so. *I'm so tired of holding onto this bucket,* she thought. All week she'd held it, two hours each morning, but never yet actually needed it. *Still, if I do, I'd best have it to hand.*

The old woman looked at her kindly. "Cass, whatever is said now, it'll always be a secret between us. No one else can ever know the truth."

"Alright," she managed to say, thinking Mary was going to tell her some secret about her own past.

"Each time I was ever with child, I had a terrible time of it. For just a few weeks, near the start. Sick every mornin' I was — mostly I didn't use the bucket, but sometimes I did." She placed her palm against Cass's brow now, checking there was no fever, as she had at this time every morning — every morning since Monday.

"This same bucket?" Cass asked.

"That's the one," Mary said. "It goes different for some

— but for me, that sickness always came about three or four weeks in."

"Sounds uncomfortable," said Cass, turning to face Mary again.

"Cass, dear," the old woman said, rubbing the girl's shoulders and the top of her back now. "It's four weeks ago Billy left, you'll remember?"

"Yes, of course," Cass answered her, leaning her head against the old woman's shoulder now. She still had not grasped what Mary was saying. "I've counted the days since he left, and I'll keep doing so 'til he returns to me." And she almost retched then, but as usual, nothing quite happened.

"Cass. The night before Billy left, I slept soundly as always. I never heard him arrive, and in the morning when I awoke, you said he'd just got here."

She continued to rub the girl's shoulders, and Cass trembled a little under the old fingers.

"But as I told you already, dear, I've been through the same thing you're going through now — each time *I* was with child."

The back rub continued, and the trembling grew.

"I know Billy stayed here that night, Cass. And also, I know just what happened. I thought I read it in your eyes that very morning — there was more to it than just Billy leaving, and I knew it. Felt it, I suppose. You'd become a woman. Only, Cass — you were a little unlucky, first time. You're with child, dear."

Cass MacPherson had sat there sick and trembling as the truth of it all dawned upon her as Mary Brown spoke. And her first thought was to deny it. But there *was* no denying it. It could not be more obvious — Cass was carrying Billy's baby, that's what this strange feeling was, not an illness at all.

"Oh, Mary," she said, burying her face in the old woman's chest as she started to cry. "What can I do?"

"There there," Mary said, patting Cass's back to comfort her. "Soon as the feeling passes for the day, write to Billy and tell him. Perhaps it's all for the best. I'm sure he'll come right on home the moment he hears."

"Do you think so?"

"I know so," said Mary. "In the meantime, stay in your room in the mornings as much as you can, and try not to let on. No sense giving reason for gossip, you know how some folk can be."

But as it turned out, Cass MacPherson found another good reason to stay hidden away in her room every morning.

Grief.

As if she hadn't had enough grief to deal with already, she was now just hours away from a whole lot more of it.

John Ray rode into town that very Thursday afternoon to collect Cass and bring her on home. He had almost sent Horace instead, for Cass seemed to be warming to him a little, with the kindness he had been showing her.

But he figured he'd put that off until the next week.

Mail always came in on Thursday too, and he hoped for news from Billy. He would have had their letters by now, quite probably. And hopefully had time to write home. John was eager to hear from his son alright.

But John Ray had no way of knowing what Horace had done; no way of knowing what the boy had been up to; no way of knowing that he'd *not* sent the letters he and Rosie and Cass had written to Billy; and finally, no way of knowing that Horace had sent one himself, a letter that was so full of lies it had broken Billy Ray's heart, and set him on a terrible path.

He had no way of knowing, either, that the Marshal, Clem Jenkins, was being blackmailed by Horace. Or that as soon as the mail came in, Marshal Clem had searched the newspaper, found news of the battles at Boonville, Sedalia and Glasgow, then commenced to write out a letter, a whole pack of lies. With Glasgow being the most bloody — the newspaper told of 450 lives lost — naturally, Marshal Clem Jenkins chose that one.

The sample letter Horace had written had Billy dying as a fool and a coward. But blackmailed or not, Clem Jenkins wrote no such thing. Some acts are just too contemptible.

He'd known he must do this to save Jasper's skin — but he would at least afford Billy an honorable death.

At first he had started writing the letter with his left hand, as Horace suggested. But he quickly found it was almost unreadable, and badly tired his hand. So instead, the blackmailed Marshal used his usual right hand — but wrote as small as he was able, as if paper were in short supply. The result was quite unlike his usual handwriting, which was blocky, large and unadorned. So this time he also put large rounded flourishes on each capital letter. It looked strange, but when he put it beside his own writing, no one would have picked it as his.

And the details he gave fit well with the newspaper report.

So when John Ray came in to check the mail, about an hour later, he'd received a letter alright, but it wasn't from Billy — the poor man was so worried, he thanked Clem, went out through the door, and opened it right then and there, outside Marshal Clem Jenkins' Postal Office and Town Jail.

John was worried right off, of course he was. If it had been in Billy's handwriting, he'd have gone to where Cass was before opening it up.

But this — this wasn't good.

If his wits had been with him, he might have sensed the Marshal watching him through the window — but he did not.

John Ray's hand shook as he opened the letter. He sat down on the step, unfolded it with a flick, and commenced then to read.

To Mister John Ray.

It is with deep regret I write to inform you the sad loss of your brave son, Private William Ray. He was one of 132 souls lost to our glorious army this day.

While he had not yet officially joined up, I took it upon myself to write and inform you of his passing. It was quick and merciful.

There is no other way to say this, but it must be said. Large artillery damages men in such ways as to leave nothing behind we can recognize. The parts of William and the men he was with became mixed together and burned some. We buried them under a cottonwood just out of town. I think he would like that.

It is important you know William's sacrifice was not in vain. We won the battle for Glasgow by the valor of such brave souls as his.

My deep sympathy goes to you Sir.
Corporal J. Smith

It was a long time before John Ray moved.

His worst fears had come true. His son, his wonderful son, the one shining light in his life, was gone.

Gone forever.

Dead.

Like so many others.

And while many of those others had mattered to John — for *all* of them mattered to such a man — none ever mattered like this one.

It was as bad as when he'd lost Billy's mother. Perhaps it was worse — for everything John had left of her was *in Billy*. With him gone, he lost all remnants of the woman he had truly loved, as well as his wonderful son.

At least Billy's mother experienced a true and pure love, just as John had with her. And perhaps Billy had too — for a very short time, with young Cass.

Oh no, he thought. *Poor Cass.*

Less than a month after losing her entire family, she would now lose Billy as well.

The thought of telling her was unbearable to him, and John Ray, as tough as he was, felt unable to go on then.

Perhaps I won't tell her at all.

For now.

Just for now.

But he knew how wrong that would be. Knew that he must tell Horace too — for although the boys had their differences, they still were brothers.

John Ray took a deep breath.

Face the day.

Even the very worst day of a life must be faced. And I owe it to Billy to tell Cass the best way I can. To look after her.

Face the day.

John Ray willed his big body to move, placed the letter in his pocket, pushed himself up from that step, and onto his feet. Then he put one foot in front of the other, and kept doing so, way a man must, when he faces the day.

Two minutes later, he stood outside Mary Brown's door. He took a deep breath and knocked upon it three times.

As always, it was Cass who opened the door. Even when Annie had been there, it had always been Cass, so full of life, so full of enthusiasm, always embracing opportunity, lifting everyone's heart.

No wonder he loved her so.

"John," she said with a smile that cut him to the quick. Then, seeing the terrible darkness upon his usually kind, gentle features, the smile fell from her face too. "What is it?"

"Sit down, Cass," he said. "Let's sit down."

For once, old Mary Brown was awake. He had seen her last Sunday in Church, he recalled — but even there she had slept. "Hello, John," she said warmly. She stood and walked toward the kitchen, called, "You must visit with me awhile and have coffee."

"Best we just sit, Mary," he said as he pulled out a chair — *Annie's chair* — and sat himself heavily down. John Ray was so weary, he felt his whole body might fall through the chair, through the floor, through the earth itself, to lie under the ground evermore.

"Sit, Cass," said Mary, as she turned on her heel and returned to sit on her day bed. Her voice was full of the tremor of one who already knows bad news is coming. Then she nodded gravely to John Ray.

"What is it, John?" Cass asked again as she sat. "Not Billy?" she cried. "Please not Billy."

He put his hand on hers, where it rested on the table. "I'm sorry, Cass. I'm so sorry."

Then that big man broke completely, and the young girl broke with him, and together they grieved the life of the man they both loved more than anything else.

Old Mary Brown had seen such grief before — had lived it, along with her husband. It was how she had known which words would come from John's mouth. She had heard the same words from her husband, and not only once.

And as much as she *wanted* to help them — to comfort these two dear people now — she knew there was nothing she could do, not a thing she could say, no way to help besides pouring coffee they would not drink, and cutting up cake they would not eat.

So Mary Brown grieved then too, though she did not intrude. She shed a quiet tear of her own, cut the cake, poured the coffee — and she thought of the baby now growing inside Cass.

Billy's baby.

And she tried to work out what was best for poor Cass to do.

CHAPTER 27
A SECRET AGREEMENT

For the very first time in his life, John Ray had been rendered unable to do as he must do.

He could no longer speak, so complete and full was his grief.

An hour after he walked out of the Marshal's Office, Mary Brown had walked in there, and told Clem Jenkins to come drive John and Cass home to the Ray place.

"The letter was about Billy?" Clem said to old Mary.

"You should have known," she said, looking at him so hard he looked down at his feet.

"I suspected," he mumbled, as he took his rifle from the rack. "Still hoped it'd be something else."

Damn you to hell, Horace Ray, was the words that he thought then.

Clem was not a *bad* man — and right then, he felt like the lowest down skunk of a man ever lived. He was almost overcome with the urge to tell Mary the truth, and to run to her house, to scream out a confession at the top of his lungs.

He knew he should make the truth known to John — and also to poor Cass, who never deserved any of this. She had always been such a sweet girl, always kind, even to Jasper.

But of course, he did not say a word. The Marshal could do no such thing — for that would be as good as putting the noose around the neck of his own son. And although the boy may deserve it — *did* deserve it — his poor mother did not. Problem was, Clem knew it would kill her. Nell Jenkins had problems of the mind — she had tried to end her own life on three occasions already, feeling the weight of the world on her shoulders as she did. Clem had to hide all newspapers from the gentle creature, for the reports of war upset her to the point of ranting and raving. If she found out her own son was a killer, she would never survive the deep shock of it.

And for all his many faults and shortcomings — drinking and gambling and visiting a particular widow in Emporia mostly — Clem Jenkins still loved his wife dearly, and wished to protect her.

Some days Jasper's mother was okay, others she could not remember who Clem even was. Shocks and surprises affected her badly. Their marital relations had suffered — yet still, she was dear to his heart.

As Clem settled/drew up the wagon out front of Mary's home, he readied himself for the deception. On closer consideration, the *last* thing he wanted was his Nell falling down dead.

That Emporia widow would expect me to marry her. And besides, Billy will soon enough be killed in that damned war anyway. They can start getting over it sooner this way.

And so the Marshal said nothing, and eased his own conscience a little. He drove the grieving pair home, and when they arrived, Horace and Jasper were there.

Clem didn't go into the house. Didn't even look at the Strawheads to start with. Not while he was within reach of his rifle. He just played his part, helped John and the girl down from the buckboard. Then as Rosie came out to help, Clem told Horace, "Your Pa's had a letter, bad news. I'm sorry, Horace, it's your brother. Letter says he died in a battle, place called Glasgow. There's a report on the battle in the news here."

And Marshal Clem Jenkins handed Horrie the newspaper, then glanced at his own son — for the briefest of moments, but that's all it took — and he said, "Sorry, Jasper. I know you liked Billy too. You best attend to this horse and wagon, and leave these poor folks to grieve."

Then Clem untied his own horse from the back of the buckboard, climbed into the saddle, and left without another word.

He would go along with being blackmailed — but to him, it was his own son who had died. Jasper was not who he thought, not who he knew. He had seen something in the boy's eyes when they went to the MacPhersons — and he had ignored it, not wanting to believe his own instincts.

But he could ignore it no more. The Strawheads were murderers. Until he saw Jasper here in the flesh now, he had held out some sort of hope that Horace was lying; that the boy had somehow tricked him. But Clem knew it now, surer than eggs. Jasper Jenkins had killed those poor folk — if not alone, then with Horace. He had violated the women too. It was written all over his face, not just guilt, but pride too, and that was the worst of it. And Clem Jenkins was certain — he could never love his son again.

In the house, the women wept and huddled together. Poor Rosie had come to them just two weeks after Billy was born. She had raised him. Had loved him. She was not John Ray's wife, had never been with him in that sense — though she had wondered, when she came there, if that might eventually happen. But that man's love was all for that baby, and the woman who'd died after delivering him into the world.

He had never had room in his heart for another, and was too honorable a man to lead Rosie along.

And yet, she had grown to love him.

She had loved baby Billy from the start, and she had loved John Ray too, all this time, without him knowing. And now, Billy was gone, lost to them all. To Cass too.

Rosie and Cass huddled together, their tears and their broken howls intermingling, a great mess of grief for the life they believed torn asunder.

But John Ray, he did not say a word. He had not said a word since telling poor Cass of the letter.

And now, he could not even speak to his other son.

He handed the letter to Horace, ran his fingers through the boy's hair. Tried to speak but could not. Then he shook his head, wiped the tears from his eyes, and walked, one foot then the other, to his room, where he fell down onto the bed and stayed the next hour.

Horace was the strong one, of course. He acted heartbroken too, but in the way a strong man does, when he must stand up for the family. The way John had done always before, but no longer could.

In the days and weeks that followed, Horace seemed thoughtful, attentive and kind. He took charge of the home as well as the ranch. Whenever John or Rosie or Cass saw him, he turned away from them a little, made a great show of wiping his eyes, then stood up very straight and asked what they needed.

Got it for them too, he did.

Horace was the rock that the family now rested upon. He did not seem indifferent or uncaring — indeed, Horace seemed more decent and loving than he ever had in his life.

He heated the food, made the coffee, even did some of the dishes. The others never suspected how he laughed when he went out on the prairie with Jasper.

In those few days that followed, the good folk of Cottonwood Falls dropped by with food they'd prepared to make grieving somehow a bit easier.

Rosie was in no state to cook much, that was for certain.

Most folk stayed only a few minutes, and did not come in — when invited in, they mostly said they were busy, way folk do at such times.

Families must be left to grieve.

But one who did come inside was old Mary Brown. She came two days later, on the Saturday, and she brought chicken stew. Drove herself there in a borrowed wagon, she did, behind a horse that seemed older than she did. They weren't in no hurry, neither the horse nor the woman.

It was the first time Mary had left the town center in three years.

But instead of dropping off that chicken stew and leaving, Mary asked Rosie to take her to Cass. She knocked on Cass's door and called out to her.

"Cass, dear," she called. "It's Mary."

And the girl let her in.

Mary stayed in the room for an hour. If anyone had listened at the door, they'd have only heard crying, and howling, and other sounds of grief, just the sort of sounds one might suspect.

But there were words spoken in that room that day. Quiet words. Some of them gentle, some of them urgent. Many times the word spoken was *No*.

But by the time Mary left, Cass understood something important, even through the black cloud of her grief.

Mary's words about this had been so strange, the sound of them so utterly impossible, that a cold, almost inhuman laugh had come from Cass's lips, the first time she heard them.

"When Horace offers to marry you, dear, you tell him yes."

The odd little laugh had come out then, so strange to both of their ears, that Mary had looked at the girl in alarm, then quietly said it again, just slightly different.

"Tell him yes, Cass, when he asks." Her kind old eyes looked deeply into Cass's, and she held the young hands in her old ones, rubbing her thumbs over Cass's again and again, in an effort to soothe her. "Marry Horace as soon as you can. He *will* ask you. And the baby — *Billy's baby* — is what matters now. It must have a father."

The thought of protecting the baby shocked Cass right

out of her grief for the moment, and there were no more strange noises. She looked at Mary intently, and gripped the kind old seamstress's hands with her own now, listening to her in silence.

"Horrie will be kind enough, and John is the very best of men, as you know. Live here in this house and raise up your child, just as you would have. And never — *never* — tell Horace or John that the child is Billy's. That secret is ours, and ours only."

And the two women, one young, one old, looked into each other's eyes then, and made a secret agreement.

That secret is ours, and ours only.

CHAPTER 28

A BATTLE BOTH LOST AND WON

It was three days after they got the letter about Billy dying, when Horace first spoke of marriage. The very next day after Mary Brown told Cass to say *yes* to it when he asked.

They were on their way to church when it happened. John was driving the buckboard, and the canvas was in place to protect them all from the elements. Rosie sat up front beside him, and Cass sat down the back by herself, for she felt like being alone.

Understandable.

The tailgate had been removed, and she sat facing rearwards, her legs hanging down, her head lolling around on her shoulders, and her eyes closed. She was resting her eyes, for they were still sore and red from her crying — and her throat was sore from it too.

She was wishing she'd never been born, way folks sometimes do, when grief stacks itself up on grief.

Out of nowhere, more or less, Horace's horse came

a'clopping up to the back of the buckboard. Kind of caught Cass by surprise. He rarely attended church, though he had done this past few weeks — just since Cass had lost her family — but always, whenever he did go, he rode in on his horse by himself, once the others had left. Even when Horace went, Jasper didn't. Seemed like the one time they were ever apart.

"Cass," he said abruptly as he caught up the wagon, and she opened her eyes with a start. He didn't waste a moment, just launched right on into it. "I know how much you loved Billy. And I know you could never feel the same about me. But with him gone, you're my responsibility. He would expect me to marry you, and it's only right that I do."

"You don't have to do that," she said. Her voice came out weak, overwhelmed even, she vaguely noticed.

"It ain't only the *should* of it," Horace answered. "Billy always reckoned things happen for a reason, and I'll honor his beliefs and call that the truth. I *want* to marry you, Cass. I wanted to marry Annie, didn't you know? Broke my heart too, what happened — but I ain't much a' one to show it."

Cass pursed her lips and nodded her head, but didn't speak. Horace seemed genuine at least. But still, she just wished she were dead, wished it weren't real, wished she could turn back a clock and this all not have happened.

"Thing is," Horace was saying, "it's worked out this way for us now, and we just have to go with how the cards fell. Maybe one day you'll learn to love me. I'll always do my best for you, I promise. Say yes, Cass. Please."

It gave Cass no pleasure at all, she felt numb when she

spoke, and it sounded like somebody else — but out came the words.

"Okay, Horrie," she said. "Thank you."

Horace Ray looked at her and nodded his head, as if that was the settling of it. Then he tipped his hat to her, gave his horse a kick and went up along beside the buckboard, up by where his Pa was at the reins.

"In case you didn't hear me back there, I just asked Cass to marry me," he said, as matter-of-fact as if reporting he'd just bought new boots. "She said yes. Do you reckon today or next week?"

John Ray looked almost as if he'd just walked out of the smoke and confusion and quiet of a battleground, a battle both lost and won. He looked at Horace a moment, didn't say anything.

Then Rosie, from beside him, said, "Congratulations, Horrie. Not today, I don't think. No matter the circumstance, a girl deserves time to plan such a day. Next week perhaps?"

"Sure, Rosie," he answered. "Pa? Do we have your blessing or what?"

"Yes, Horrie," he answered, his voice sombre. "Of course you do. You're a good boy. We'll talk to the preacher today, get it planned out. I'll be proud to have Cass in the family, official-like. You honor your brother. I do believe he'd be pleased."

Soon as they got to the church, John had Rosie speak to Cass right away, make sure she wasn't unhappy about it. She didn't *look* happy.

But then, no one expected her to.

It was a wedding borne from circumstances of grief, rather than from love and joy, as she'd always hoped her wedding would be. But everyone had expected Horrie to ask her — it was the right thing to do, and men and women all over the country were marrying for similar reasons.

Cass went and told Mary Brown, first chance she got. The old woman was resting in the shade of a tree — she never entered the church until the last minute, preferring to wait in the garden overlooking the boneyard where her husband was buried. The old seamstress looked relieved, quietly told the girl not to put it off. "Not today though," she said. "That would look strange. But a week at the latest."

In the end, they married three days later, the preacher suggesting the Wednesday.

Mary Brown had told Cass to make sure Horrie consummated the marriage, no matter how much Cass didn't want that to happen. She needn't have bothered saying it — Horace not only expected to exercise the full benefits of marriage available to him, he did so each night, no matter that Cass cried her heart out.

He wasn't surprised the first night, and was even apologetic, almost gentle. But by the third night, he was far from it. And when she cried he got angry, raised his hand as if he would hit her. He stayed his hand that time, but growled unkind words as she cowered, before mumbling something like, "*Sorry.*"

But nothing stopped him doing what he wanted.

Outside of the bedroom, he was all smiles. A devoted husband he seemed, Horace Ray, on the surface.

John insisted that Cass should still stay in town with Mary, Sunday to Thursday as usual, which of course led to an argument. But John Ray was a fierce man when he chose to be, and in the end, Horace backed down. He still had her Thursday, Friday and Saturday nights after all. And besides, he was sick of her crying.

As for Cass herself, she just got on with things. One of the things Billy always loved most about Cass was her toughness — and right now she needed every damn smidgen of it. Despite everything she had been through, all the pain and the loss and the heartbreak, Cass MacPherson soon lifted her head, carried it high, got on with living her life with the cards she'd been dealt.

Three weeks and one day after their marriage, when Horrie came to get into bed, Cass did as Mary Brown told her to. She looked up from under the covers and informed Horrie he was going to be a father.

He looked shocked at first, then he grinned. It was the most genuine smile Cass had ever seen on his long face. Then he stood there wearing that grin, and he said, "Are you sure?"

"Mary says so. I was sick this past few mornings, and she asked if I'd had my ... well, you know ... then she told me all about how sick *she* used to get, whenever she was with child. She's pretty much certain — and now she told me, I fancy I feel somehow different. But in a good way — except for the mornings."

"Well, I guess that's fine news," Horrie said. "Ain't it? I mean, are you happy, Cass?"

"Yes, Horrie," Cass said. "I'm happy. Thank you." And she smiled up at him, and meant it.

Up until then, she had somehow managed to mostly hide her morning sickness from him — not that it was easy — and what he had seen of it, he'd just put down to her grieving.

She had truly been happy when she told him. Scared some that she'd be caught out, that he might somehow guess that the baby was Billy's ... but happy nonetheless, and it showed.

There was good reason for her happiness — Mary Brown had pointed out something to her. That baby growing inside her was Billy's. It was Billy's and Cass's, and nothing could ever change that. And while nothing could bring Billy back, his baby would be the most precious thing Cass would ever know.

"You will love that child beyond measure," was what Mary told her.

"But what about Horrie?" Cass had said.

"He's never to know," Mary had told her again while combing her hair. "You will give him his own children, and he will think of them *all* as his own. It won't make no difference to him, Cass. He's just lucky to have you at all."

"What if the baby looks like Billy?"

"I doubt it will," Mary said hopefully. "Your whole family have light skin and hair, and so does Billy's father. There's less than a quarter chance it'll be at all dark. And Billy's not *that* dark. Besides, babies mostly start out pretty light anyway. It'll be fine, Cass, don't worry yourself over nothing." And if Mary was worried at all, she did not let on.

From that moment forward, Cass's grief began to subside, just a little, here and there. Things were better at home too.

At first, right away, after finding out Cass was with child, Horace had still wanted her to yield to his rights as her husband — but she had explained she was afraid of losing the baby. Said that Mary had warned her against it, and other women had too.

"Well, we don't want that, I guess, do we?" Horace had said. Then he'd added, "I'll be back in a minute, I gotta tell Pa the good news."

John Ray had been spending a lot of time out on that porch, looking off into the distance, into the darkness of night. He felt half swallowed up by it, there was the truth — but he wasn't about to admit it to anyone else.

Horace stepped out the front door, then he turned and closed it behind him. Then he stood there a few moments, watching his father stare off into the distance, before saying, "I'm gonna be a father, Pa."

Until he spoke, John had not seemed even to notice Horace's presence. "That's good news, son," John said, turning around from where he'd been leaning on the railing. "Congratulations. It's a wonderful thing. I hope you'll be as happy as I was when I first saw you." And half a smile came to his face, his eyes went somehow softer, and he shook Horrie's hand.

"Pa ... I was wonderin' somethin'. That old biddy Mary Brown reckons Cass could lose the baby if I keep poking her every night."

John's eyes flared with anger a moment, and his one

hand clenched into a fist, but then he relaxed. "Horrie," he said firmly. "That's no sort of language to use about Mary Brown, let alone saying such words when you speak of your wife. Don't call Mary an old biddy, her age has been hard won, believe me. As for the other, perhaps call it *marital relations* — with me, I mean, if you have to speak of it at all. And never a word about it to anyone else. It's disrespectful, you see? My fault, I guess, for not teaching you."

"Sorry, Pa," he said. "So should I stop makin' her partake of some marital relations or not? Is it true or a lie, is what I mean?"

"Hmmm. It *can* happen alright," John answered, his body tense once again. "And if it does, she'll never get over the loss, and may even become unable to bear you any children at all. You just let her alone 'til a few months after that baby's born."

"A few *months*? Are you loco, Pa? A few *months*? What's the dang use a' bein' married? I can't only poke her but one month a year!"

John Ray grabbed his son by the collar and threw him against the wall so hard the door shook on its hinges. "You listen to me, boy," he said, his voice not at all loud, but low and menacing instead. "There are a great many uses to being married — and marital relations is *one*. Another one is, it learns a man some *respect*. Respect for his wife, respect for his children, respect for the process of building a life for his family."

Horace was shocked at the speed and the strength his father had showed when he threw him against that front wall. "Lemme go, Pa," he growled, but his feet were off the ground, one of his hands was pinned behind his back, and he wasn't quite game to raise his one free hand against his father.

Sort of evened 'em up it did, one of Horrie's hands being pinned.

John Ray held his elder son against the wall by the collar, and he was so close to that boy they was breathing each other's stale air. And the eye he looked into Horrie's with, that eye told a story — a story of what might soon happen, if that boy didn't learn some respect. "Grow up, you damn fool," John said in a voice filled with fire, "and don't touch her. I mean it, don't you *dare* touch her. It's time you became a true man."

Then he let go the collar, let his son's feet down to the boards of the porch. He leaned back to see better, smoothed down the boy's shirt, and grasped Horrie's shoulder a moment — and he looked at him tenderly then, in stark contrast to how he'd just been. "It's time," he said softly. "Be *good,* son. Be *good.*"

And suddenly, it seemed like the strength all left John Ray again. He walked slowly back to his railing, looked out into the night, and it was almost like Horrie had never been there at all.

When John Ray went back to his railing, back to staring out into the darkness, back to the troubles that filled all his thoughts, Horace stood awhile watching him.

Hating him.

Thinking of ways he might kill him.

Then he went back into the house, but he didn't stay there. Instead, he sneaked out the back door, and crept away to the bunkhouse. Weren't nothin' to go back to bed for nohow. He went and woke Jasper. Made him put on his boots and his coat, come outside and tramp through the back forty. And the whole time they tramped, he filled Jasper's ears with plan after plan. Each one a plan for killing his father.

Horace slept in the bunkhouse that night, and the very next day, he carried all Cass's things out of his room, made her move back to Billy's room instead.

He was polite about it, telling her that she was too beautiful for him to keep his hands off of, and that it would be easier this way.

He told his father the same thing.

For now, he was respectful around them all.

He treated everyone fairly, at least on the surface.

But underneath it all, Horace Ray plotted and planned. He *would* kill his father. He *would* take over this ranch, and he *would* expand it into the biggest ranch in all Kansas. He would be rich beyond *anyone's* dreams.

He was Horace Ray — and he would have *everything*.

CHAPTER 29
DEPUTY BILLY FYRE, U.S. MARSHALS

War changes a man, that's for certain. Billy had found that out for himself.

When word came that the fighting was over, Private William Fyre and Captain Robert Brimstone were with General Price down in Mexico.

Price had fled there rather than surrender.

Billy and Rob were more than 1500 miles from home. Not that Billy felt like he had one.

In only a short period of fighting, Billy had experienced many sides of war. Glorious victories at Glasgow, Little Blue River, and Independence too, were soon followed by a series of crushing defeats. At Mine Creek in particular, despite Billy's bravery, he was left feeling even more hollow and broken, as man after man died around him, or had limbs blown off, or died later from their wounds.

But even in the battles they'd won, he had seen good men's lives taken from them. Seen terrible, needless destruction — the futility of it all.

And always, when the fighting was over, he looked around at the dead and the dying and the wounded, and he thought of his father — first the wisdom of the man, then after, the pain of being disowned by him.

For a man of such wisdom to disown me, it must be deserved.

And Cass — well, he thought of her at all sorts of times. Sometimes even in the midst of the battle — and always, always, when he slept.

And her letter, the precious letter she'd given him, he kept over his heart, took it out only rarely, and even then struggled to read it.

For whenever he read Cass's letter, he heard her voice clearly, as if she was with him, as if she might yet be with him again — and his heart broke, over and over. He could never quite understand how he, Billy Ray — Billy Fyre now — had survived all these skirmishes, these battles, all this fire and destruction, all the harm he put himself in the way of. Could not understand either, how it could be, that his beautiful Cass no longer existed — how she'd had her lovely gentle life snuffed out so easily, by a simple and random mistake.

He had never been able to glean even some *hint* of sense in it, felt that there must be nothing worth learning in this whole wide world. And yet, these nine months since he left her in Cottonwood Falls, he had learned much about human nature — both the good and the bad.

Preacher Rob Brimstone was a gift. Billy could never have hoped for such a great man to protect him, to teach him, to befriend him.

The Brimstones, *all* those he'd met, were the best of the best.

Brigadier General Clark too, had proved his immeasurable worth, been a fine example to Billy. The man had held his head up right to the end. He never once faltered in his goodness, honor and decency to all men — not just his own, but the enemy also. By the time the announcement of the end came, he had already gone home.

As had many others.

The only reason they had not gone with Clark, was that General Price had asked Clark to leave them with him. Asked for them by name. It was an honor, in a way, to keep traveling south with the General — and Billy had nowhere else to be. His thirst for war had been not only quenched, it had been drowned forever.

Never again — Pa was right.

As for Preacher Rob, he had taken an oath to protect Billy until the war ended. Man like him takes an oath, he follows it through. War hadn't yet ended, so Rob went with Price too, as requested.

Before he left, General Clark had told them the official end of the war would come very soon, and to think on what they might do when the whole thing was over. "Good men will be needed then, more than ever," he'd told Rob and Billy, as he shook their hands before leaving. "Keep in touch, both of you. It's been an honor."

They had promised to do so, and meant it.

Finally, two months later, another two-hundred miles south, Old Pap proclaimed the words. "It's all over, the war has ended now, men. It's not yet official, but there will be no more fighting. I would have all of you stay, if you wish to. We shall establish a colony here in Carlota where all Confederate men are welcome. For many of you, there is nothing left to return to — your homes and communities destroyed by the Northern Aggression. I offer you here a new life. But your service is ended, and each man may do as he pleases."

Billy had no idea what to do. No life to go back to.

It was a strange hour, a strange day, and became a strange night.

Those who remained were quiet, mostly, at least for awhile. Some packed up their gear and left right away, heading home to see for themselves what remained of the lives they had left. To try to rebuild them, perhaps, with whatever was left of themselves, of their land, of their homes. Other men simply got so drunk they slept in the dirt where they fell.

But Billy, he just sat with Preacher Rob, and the pair stared into a fire, and every so often drank coffee. Real coffee it was, not peanut or chicory.

Coffee.

It was a hot June evening, and the sparks of their campfire flew into the boundless, endless darkness of night, an uncertain future awaiting them.

"You can stay here with Price if you want," Preacher Rob finally said. He poked at the fire with a stick, sending a small shower of sparks up into the smoke haze. "But better you should come with me, visit Morris and Mike. There's a place for us there in Wilmington — both of us, Billy."

"I'd like that, I guess," Billy answered. "I'll think on it. When did you figure on leaving?"

Rob knew what Billy was thinking, what he *wasn't* saying. Wilmington was just 55 miles from Billy's old home.

Preacher Rob poked at the fire again, then threw his stick into the flames. "Might leave in the morning, I reckon. But I'll wait a few days if you like — if you need time to think."

"Might come with you part way and see," Billy answered, still sitting, still staring. But no matter how long he stared, the flames offered no certain answers. "Nothin' much else to do," he finally said.

Several more minutes went by.

Then a man came — a man with a letter. "Are you Captain Brimstone?' he asked. "Captain *Robert* Brimstone?"

"I am," said Preacher Rob, getting to his feet.

The feller handed over the letter, nodded and turned right about, went back to wherever he'd come from.

"Thank you," Rob called after him. The feller raised a hand in acknowledgment, but never turned around.

It had a real official look to it, fancy wax seal and all. Preacher Rob showed it to Billy, who just raised his eyebrows then looked back into the fire.

Rob sat back down, opened the letter and commenced to read it. Looked up at Billy awhile. Then he read it again.

Billy ignored the whole thing, showed less curiosity than a cow would. Wasn't his business, he figured.

Preacher Rob folded the letter, caught Billy's eye, and

made out like he was going to throw it into the fire. And still, Billy never reacted, never said nothin' at all.

So Rob unfolded it and read it again, while Billy ignored him some more. Could have gone on that way all night, if it was left up to Billy to stick his nose in.

Finally Preacher Rob said, "Ain't you even curious?"

"Maybe," said Billy.

"It's from General Clark."

"Well, why didn't you say so?" Billy said, sitting up straight now and craning his neck to look over at it. "Well, go on and tell me, how's he doin'?"

"More about what he wants than how he's doing." Rob handed the letter to Billy then, adding, "He wants *us* to join the United States Marshals Service."

"Is he a part of it?" Billy asked, as he moved side on to the fire so he could see the words properly to read it.

"Nope. But he was asked to recommend some men. Seems some Marshal friends of his want good men from *both* sides — they're sending a clear message that no one's excluded, and the war's *really* over, forever. I got my own thoughts on all that — but you read it and see what *you* reckon."

Billy read the letter. It was a fine letter alright. Every word as noble and true as General Clark was himself. And it was just as Preacher Rob had said — Clark had written Billy's name in there too, and the offer was real.

Thing is, though, thought Billy, *there ain't even no such person as William Fyre.*

He looked up from the letter. Preacher Rob had been watching him intently, and he didn't try to hide it. There was a fire of sorts in his eye. The good sort, not the crazed battle one he sometimes got.

But all Rob Brimstone said was, "Well?"

"I'm seventeen years old." Billy cocked his head sideways, rubbed his chin. "Wait. What month is it?"

"June. Seventh I think." Rob said.

"Not eighteen yet then."

Close to it," said Rob. "See all that in the letter? Two months since Robert E. Lee surrendered. Almost a month since the last of the fighting. Wonder if Old Pap knew, and kept it all from us? Oh well. Trust John Clark to give us the truth of it." He shook his head real slow, but his eyes kept their fire, never left Billy's face, still searching for a hint of his answer to Clark's offer.

"I'm done with war forever," said Billy, "and I say that for certain. There's no good a man can *do* playin' at war. Not really. Now I understand better, seems like both sides was wrong, and both sides was right, just like my Pa said all along. So whatever a man does in war just gets canceled out, stands for nothin' or less. But in peace, a good man's acts of violence might yet do some good." And he looked at his Henry, which was never far away, even now — for this place too, was never entirely peaceful.

Rob rubbed his hands together and nodded over and over as he took in what Billy was saying. "You understand numbers good, my young friend, always did. I reckon what you said's close, but you ain't *quite* right."

"Do tell, O Wise One," said Billy, bowing his head in mock deference to the older man.

"Alright then, I shall," Rob answered in a fancy English

rich-feller voice. But then he went back to his own voice, as he went on. "In war, we *multiply* violence — one act leads to another, we get more and more men involved, end up with life after life all lost or ruined. That's multiplication. The numbers just keep gettin' bigger. But if we become Marshals, and we kill—"

"Always kill?" said Billy, raising his eyebrows.

"No. We either kill," said Rob, "or preferably *otherwise* subdue the fellers doin' the wrongs — so as they can be jailed — and either way, that's more in the nature of *subtraction,* for we're removing wrongdoers from where they keep doing harm. Then we're *actually* gettin' somewhere, and making society better."

Billy grinned a little. "Never knew you was such a good numbers man, Preacher Rob. Missed your callin' maybe. But bein' so good with numbers, answer me this. Can a Deputy Marshal be so young as I am?"

"Well, I guess we could go and find out." Between the new aliveness in Rob's eyes and the firelight reflecting there too, he just about looked like his hair might catch, and burn up what was left of his hat. "Besides, Billy *Fyre,* you're *eighteen*, and have documentation to prove it. A better question might be, *do they allow old farts of thirty-six to be Deputy Marshals?*"

"You are *kind of* old," Billy said. Up until now, he had never had the same kind of banter with Preacher Rob as he'd had with Morris. The war had taken its toll on that relaxed sort of humanity.

As had Billy's personal heartbreak.

But somehow, the war being over, it felt like a new start.

They were like two new people, in some way at least. And while Billy and Rob had both seen things, done things, lived through things they'd never get over, there was something about that new start that they grasped with both hands.

Preacher Rob stood up and stretched. "Got a nice ring to it, don't it?" Then he put on that fancy Englishman voice again and said, *"Dearest citizens, I should like you to meet Deputy Billy Fyre, United States Marshal Service, Child Division. Looks twelve, but insists he is older. Very likely a fibber, going by visual inspection."*

"You best get some sleep, old man," Billy answered with a laugh. "I hear old folks need extra, and we got a long way to travel, so we better start early."

CHAPTER 30
"SHE'S NO WHORE AND YOU KNOW IT..."

While Billy was fighting to keep himself and his comrades alive, his brother Horace had been plotting and planning, working toward having *everything*.

He acted out the part of the best son a father could have, and just about the best husband too. But Jasper and Clem knew the truth.

And Jasper was not just his friend — Jasper was on a promise. He would be Horrie's partner, in all of their future business. Powerful men together, they'd *own* this whole county and more.

"We'll get you a wife soon, Jasper," Horrie would say. "Maybe one a' them pretty Welsh girls down in Emporia. Same way I got Cass, if we have to."

But Jasper wanted to wait awhile. At least, he *said* that. Horace enquired as to whether his Strawhead friend had shied off from killing, if he'd perhaps lost the stomach for it, but Jasper said, "No, it ain't that. Just ain't in a hurry is all." So Horace let it go.

But Horace Ray was like two different people in one. He showed himself calm on the surface — for now — and even Cass was taken in by it.

Then eight months after Horace married Cass, the baby came.

"It's too early," Horace said, when Rosie sent him to fetch the midwife who lived in the town. "Even I know that much."

"Sometimes they come early, it's normal," Rosie told him. "Hurry, quick as you can. See if Mary Brown will come too, but don't let her delay you." Then she'd hurried back to Cass, in Billy's room.

Later that day, when he saw that baby, Horace Ray had his doubts right away.

"They all look red and strange and wrinkled that way when they're born," his father said. "Makes 'em look darker'n they really are, every time. He looks just like you did, I reckon." And he took out the one bottle of good whiskey he kept for very special occasions. He poured them one each, and they drank to the health of the baby.

But it made no difference what anyone said, or what excuses they offered. Time has its way with all things, and a baby's looks ain't excepted from that, no matter how special it is or how much it's loved.

Within a few months, everyone knew it, though not a word was ever spoken in public — that baby grew dark as an Injun. He had black hair, dark eyebrows, and beautiful features. His skin was an in-between color, not like Horace's, or Cass's, or John's either for that matter. It could scarce have been any clearer. That baby belonged to Billy Ray—everyone round the town knew it, but only spoke the words behind closed doors.

Cass kept living in Billy's room. She named the child Tom, for her father. Thomas Ray, he was called.

Before long, Horace ceased to *act* as if nothing was wrong. He became more openly angry, and if any of the family spoke to him, he just stared at them in defiance. He kept going off to Council Grove with Jasper, instead of doing his work.

John did not push back against it, only hoped the boy would come to terms with what happened, settle down and grow up.

John Ray had a ranch to run though, so he hired two brothers from town to help out a few days a week, make up for the shortfall.

Then the day came when John saw Horace fingering his gun as he watched Cass through a window.

The two new fellers, the brothers from town, had gone home for the day. Jasper, Phil and Pete had gone to clean up before dinner, but Horace had gone on alone, made his way toward the house.

John had heard Horace's boots, the thud of them mostly, and the ever present jingling of his spurs, as he walked along the side of the barn. That boy sure loved them spurs.

John wanted to speak to him anyway, so he walked to the doorway. But there was something in Horrie's movement, something John didn't like, so he stayed where he was and he watched the boy a few moments.

Horace Ray stopped then too. He was only twelve feet away, but had not heard or noticed his father. With the sunset glowing brightly behind him, Horace cast a long shadow that filled the whole yard, all the way to the corral.

John looked at where Horace was looking. There, framed by the open curtains in the window, Cass was sat on a chair in Billy's room, feeding the baby. Horace watched her. Held his hand up in front of his eyes, wiggled the fingers. He made of that hand and fingers a gun, and he looked down the sight of it, pointed at Cass. Then that hand went down to the revolver on his right hip.

The hand wrapped itself round that gun, and seemed then almost to caress it.

It was clear to John Ray that something now had to be done.

John stepped out through the doorway of the barn, walked toward his son's back and spoke loud and clear. "Horrie, what the hell are you—"

At the first sound of his Pa's voice behind him, Horace spun around, drew his revolver and pointed it from the hip, like a storybook gunfighter.

Didn't impress John, that sorta thing. All show. "Woah, boy," he said, putting his hand up in front of him. "I know you're not—"

"You know I'm not *what?*" From six feet away, Horace kept the gun pointed in his unarmed father's direction.

So much malice, thought John. *Wherever did I go wrong? Best handle him with care, he's unhinged some.*

"Son," he said, calm as a milkin' cow, "I know you're not happy about all this. But you can still have a good life."

"Can I? And you'd know, I suppose. You married a *whore* too, did you?" And his eyes blazed so bad they looked like they might pop right out of his head.

"Horrie, please," John said. "She didn't tell you, so what? Put yourself in her shoes, she had *nothing*. She's no whore and you know it, show some respect."

"*Respect?*" Horrie growled in a low voice, still pointing the gun at his father.

"Let's be truthful now," John said calmly, "about all this. We've left it too long, but it's time. It's time we discussed it, as *men*." And then John Ray's voice grew more urgent, and his face wore an expression of consequence, of importance, yet somehow too one of compassion. *"Horrie, that's not some stranger's baby, it's your brother's. And you get to raise him! That's Billy's son. Billy's!* Surely *some* part of that makes you happy — at least a little. To not have lost him so completely, to be able to look at that baby and know that—"

"*Shut up,*" Horace Ray said. And he lifted that gun then to eye height, cocked the hammer, and looked down the sights of that Colt, at the head of his father.

CHAPTER 31
ON FOR YOUNG AND OLD

Horace looked down the sights of that gun, and he smiled that smile, the one John had never understood — that cruel smile he'd gotten from his mother. It had never once meant anything good, that damn smile, all these years.

And still, no one noticed the two of them, thirty yards from the house.

As for John, he still watched Horace carefully — but even as unhinged as the boy clearly was, John did not believe for a moment he might pull the trigger. "Please, son. Just tell me what it is you want. If you don't want to be married, we'll fix it. We can arrange that, you know? Right or wrong though, what's happened has happened. We can't *change* it — but we *can* fix it. Whichever way you want."

"What I *want,* is for *you* to admit she's a *whore.*" He smiled that damn smile again, and waved the gun just a little, for his hand was beginning to shake.

Bad sign, thought John. *Some signs really IS worse than others.* But he didn't speak.

"Cass is a damn filthy whore. Go on, Pa," he said quietly. And then, top of his lungs, he yelled, *"Say it."*

That was when Cass turned and looked out the window. She saw John with his hand up, and Horace pointing the gun. And she screamed.

Three things happened right then, pretty much all at once.

First thing, Baby Tom got such a shock he stopped feeding and commenced then to screaming right along with his Ma.

Second thing, Horace Ray got a shock too, and turned his head for a moment toward Cass's screaming.

Third thing — well, it might have been the first, hard to tell, for it happened so quick — John Ray, who knew Cass must eventually notice them and was waiting for this very moment, put his head down and charged forward and knocked that crazed boy to the ground. Somewhere in the middle of all that, the gun had gone off, but John Ray was unharmed, and he beat at his son with his one fist, and wrestled from him the gun, and threw it away some fifteen yards into the dirt.

Horace might have been loco, but that too gives a man a sort of strength he might not ordinarily possess — and the fight was then on for young and old.

Horace had two advantages, of course. He had youth on his side, for a first thing — and twice as many arms, for a second. He was ferocious alright, and for a minute, his dreams of killing his father looked like they might almost come true.

But youth and two arms ain't everything. John Ray had wisdom on his side, and experience too. And more even than those, John was a righteous sort of man, and he was protectin' his kin — Cass, and his grandson, Tom.

He remembered to breathe, and to not lose his calm — and John Ray proceeded to beat the living daylights out of his son.

He beat him with all that he had, which was not just his fist, but his elbow, his head, and a knee — most importantly, John used his brain — and after a minute or two, that damn foolish young man had been beaten near enough senseless, and busted up like a feller who's survived a stampede, but only just barely.

For John made sure not only to beat him, but to put him right out of action, at least for awhile. Horace Ray would piss blood for a week, that much was certain.

Then John stood himself up, brushed the dirt from his clothing, and turned and saw Jasper Jenkins. Jasper had heard the scream too, and come a'running. He had seen most of the fight. Been rooted to the spot as he watched, but never dared make a sound. And Jasper knew — *no matter what Horace said later* — that John Ray had beaten his son fair and square, and had proven himself the better man.

John then cast a fearsome gaze upon Jasper and said, "Bring me your guns, Jasper, now, and don't argue. And every other gun here, Phil's and Pete's both included."

"But, Mist—" Jasper said, and that was as far as he got.

"Do it," came the answer. "Or do I need to deal with you as well?"

He took a step forward, and stared Jasper down then — and the younger man shrank before John Ray's gaze like the coward he so truly was.

"Never mind, I'll see to the guns myself," John told Jasper. "Go get some water and see to your friend. Don't force him to drink though, and don't let him choke on his vomit."

As for Horace, he wasn't moving except for his breathing, and his eyes kept on opening and closing every few seconds as he lay in the dirt.

Then the other two cowhands arrived, as Jasper went to fetch water. First was Pete, just about fully dressed, but half-hopping-half-running, all lopsided on only one boot — then a few moments later came Phil, wearing only his underclothes, and that funny bowler hat he was never seen out of.

John Ray had them gather up every gun on the ranch, all the ammunition as well, and lay it all in the back of the buckboard. He'd have known if they'd left any out, and he made sure to check, just in case.

Horace woke every so often, and Jasper dragged him across to lean him against the barn wall — but he wasn't making no sense, and kept falling asleep again. No one else went near him.

Once they got themselves properly dressed, Pete and Phil brought all the guns, then loaded up all Cass's clothes and things too, as well as John's, in the back of the buckboard. Rosie packed and brought out her own belongings, along with her cooking pots, plates and such from the kitchen.

John told her they weren't coming back, and if there was one thing Rosie knew, it was that he was a man of his word — so she brought along *everything* she wanted, damn that Horace to hell.

Between them all, they didn't miss nothing. Almost forgot the blankets, but Cass went to get the one Mary had knitted for the baby, and remembered. So she asked Pete to go collect them all off of the beds.

John even remembered to collect the few personal things he'd kept over the years — notes from Billy's mother and such, mementoes that meant a lot to him. His mother's gold locket was the only thing of monetary value in it all — and it was more precious to him than all the money in Kansas. He loaded his saddle, his bridle, and a few other things from the barn, including Cass's Pa's broom.

Then he tied his good riding horse behind, and Tom MacPherson's horse too. And finally, he helped Cass and Rosie climb onto the buckboard, ready to leave for town.

He had every cent he owned too — a considerable sum. For the final time, he had accessed its hiding place in a secret compartment he'd built into a cupboard years before. Even Horace had not known of it — although Rosie and Billy both did. From that huge wad of cash, he paid all three men their wages 'til the end of the month, and shook all their hands, thanked them all for their work here.

"Sorry about this, boys," he told them, ignoring the still senseless Horace as he started up groaning and moaning. "You can stay or go as you choose, but *he's* your boss now. You can pick up your guns from in town in two days, once that hothead's had time to think. Not that he'll be able to do much — he'll be sore awhile, but I reckon nothin's broke. If any of you come to town before then, I'll take it as a declaration of war — much as I like and respect you, you wouldn't likely survive it."

"But Boss," said Pete, "we'd *never—*"

"I know *you two* wouldn't," said John, then he turned his gaze on Jasper. "Just makin' it clear to you *all*. Two days from now, Pete and Phil can come get the guns and the buckboard. You can do without both until then, plenty to do near the house without goin' nowhere."

"Yes, Boss," said Pete. And Phil, ever the quiet type, just nodded.

"About ready, Rosie," said John, "don't forget to release the brake this time."

"I remembered," she said. But she and Cass smiled at each other, because both of them knew she forgot the brake every time, and always set the poor horse to straining for nothing.

"One last thing, boys," John told them. "Tell Horace he'll have the lease on this one-sixty now. With his own place, that gives him three-twenty all up. I'll sign the lease on it soon as I can. He'll have the house, the barn, the stock and everything else — and he owes me nothing. By the terms of the lease, if I die, or Cass or little Tom — his lease ends, and he's out on his ear. If all three of us die, ownership of it'll go to a charitable institution. Understood clear?"

Pete and Phil both nodded, definite like, and Jasper, from under his hat, said, "Yessir, Mister Ray."

"He gets full use of the place, in perpetuity, long as me, Cass and Tom are *all* alive, to do whatever he wants with it. I'll word it all clear in the lease. And no need for him to speak to me ever again. So, it's in his interests to leave us all well alone. As for his inheritance, he'll need to keep turning a profit here, make that himself. It's a fine ranch, and already making good money — and all his from now on, rent free. But make sure he knows this next thing, and don't mince the words none."

The look on John Ray's face then would have struck fear into any who saw it. And his words came out slow and deliberate, filled with a deadly menace none present had heard from him before.

"If *ever* he comes near Cass or this baby again — if ever he so much as *looks* at either one of 'em — you tell him, I promise, I *will* kill him."

CHAPTER 32
SOME SPOTS IS BETTER'N
OTHERS...

A man changes a lot in seven years. Some men do anyway. Other men, not so much.

Cottonwood Falls had changed too, in the seven years since Billy left it. Not that he'd ever been back. He knew that the railroad should be there by now — he'd read it in a newspaper Morris had sent him, how the new section from Emporia to Cottonwood Falls was just about done.

Wonder if Pa was right about the path of the Railroad. If he was, Pa and Horrie might even be rich now.

The thought of that made him smile. They were most likely prospering anyway, he figured, for his Pa was a hardworking man with a brain in his skull. And now they could send cattle East by railroad car, they'd be even more prosperous for sure.

Billy's work for the U.S. Marshal Service had been varied alright. In a little over six years, he had been a

Deputy to four different Marshals. Sometimes the Marshals lost their jobs, sometimes they moved on.

But always, whatever happened, both he and Preacher Rob got snapped up by other Marshals right away. Good Deputies weren't easy to find, and they were right up with the best.

Some fellers saw becoming a Deputy as another way of lining their pockets dishonestly, and used their positions in ways more suited to outlaws. Thing was, some of them fellers actually *was* outlaws — or were working their way toward the profession. And for a dishonest Deputy, there was money aplenty to be made.

For the honest ones like Preacher Rob and Billy, the work was more about helping others, and there sure weren't much money to be had from it. If it weren't for the occasional bounty that came their way, they'd barely have enough to survive.

They'd worked together in Missouri awhile, then down in Indian Territory. Billy was still down there now, working out of Fort Smith, Arkansas — but he didn't much like it no more. He plain didn't trust the new Marshal he worked for.

There was a lot of corruption down this way, and more than once, Billy had missed out on being paid bounties he knew he had earned.

Then just two weeks ago he'd brought in and locked up a real bad sorta feller, one he *knew* had raped and murdered at least one Seminole woman, and probably two — and yet, two days later that feller was gone, and Marshal Pitt told Billy it was a case of mistaken identity.

Now, Billy had tracked that feller every step of the way

— from the woman's dead body, to the hideout he caught that lowdown excuse for a man in. Billy knew what Marshal Pitt was saying was hogwash and hokum, and he told him so.

Only *hogwash* and *hokum* weren't *exactly* the words he used in getting his point across.

Billy stared down his boss that day, and, using words he would never have used in front of women or children, told the Marshal that he and the other Deputies could only work effectively here if the Indians trusted them — and they *had* trusted Billy, until then. Trust wasn't so easy to earn — but when that guilty feller was let go, some of that trust was lost, perhaps never to be earned again.

Billy wasn't much of one for bad language, and was surprised at which words came out of his mouth — one of which, he'd never used in his life before.

Didn't make Billy no friends, swearing that way at the Marshal. And if that weren't bad enough, Billy had given him an overly colorful warning, all about what he'd do if it happened again.

The warning itself had to do with a particularly dark place — a place where Billy would stick his revolver. He also assured Marshal Wallace J. Pitt that there wasn't much chance he'd enjoy it.

Pitt hadn't given Billy much useful work since — unless you consider wild goose chases as bein' somehow useful. And what with Deputies only getting paid by what warrants they serve — or outlaws they bring in — he'd made almost no money this two weeks past.

He was starting to suspect that Marshal just wanted

him out of the way, and wasn't game to say so. He figured Pitt was trying to send him broke so he'd quit. But the same thing had happened with another Deputy, and that feller had been found on a lonely trail, a bullet in his head, and no clues as to who might have done it.

He didn't really believe that a Marshal would do that, though that's how some rumors had it — but Billy was being even more careful than usual, especially as he was currently working alone. There was too many places a feller could just disappear, and a shallow grave wasn't ever no part of his plan. At least not since the war ended.

No, Pitt was just starving him out, and he'd probably be better off elsewhere anyway, if he thought about it.

He was riding along on one of them wild goose chases this very minute — he felt pretty sure about that. The Marshal reckoned some fellers who'd robbed a stage down in Texas had been seen by a young Choctaw brave. He had been hunting alone, and them six fellers had roughed him up some and taken his rifle.

There was something about it didn't ring true. A few things really. The whole dang story, most likely. Billy rode out to talk to the young Choctaw as he was told to, but he sure was keeping an eye out. It would be more than a full day to get there, and not much likely he'd find any sign to lead him to the six guilty parties — even if they existed. The sun was getting low in the sky, and the longer he rode, the more he thought about leaving, going somewhere new awhile.

But it sure was beautiful out here, just riding along on

your horse. He was thankful for that. Plenty of time to enjoy being out in the world — and time too to think.

He'd had a recent letter from Preacher Rob, and that had *sure* got him thinking.

It had been two years since they'd seen each other, but they both still wrote on the regular. Billy wrote some to Morris too, although that big-headed, bow-legged, skunk-stink-accusin' insulter was about the worst letter writer in four states. He managed to write Billy once or twice a year though, which was nice — but the pair hadn't seen each other at all since they'd been seventeen.

Morris was doin' real well though. He liked being Sheriff Mike's Deputy, but it was getting a bit quiet now, as the train didn't go through Wilmington, so the town had been shrinking some. Figured he might go somewhere else, maybe join his Pa in Cheyenne. In every letter, he always told Billy that Jenny was real happy. Last letter, he'd said Jenny was no longer quite so afraid of gunfire, and he wondered if maybe she'd gone a bit deaf, but she hadn't. He'd just gotten her a little more used to it in the course of his work. Still wasn't the best though, and in that way could not be relied upon. Aside from that, he never had nothing but praise for the wonderful mare. Maybe even loved her like Billy did, so it seemed.

Never woulda dreamed of insulting her.

But that Morris, he was a wonder, even in letter form, when it came to firing off insults at Billy. Last letter Billy got from him had begun with, *Dear Billy, it's been awhile, but I'm sure you are still a dung eating, wobble bottomed mule face, with breath that smells like what comes from the business end of a sick cow.*

And that was only the start of it.

It sure would be good to see him again.

As for Preacher Rob, his last letter said he quite liked Cheyenne, and might put down roots there, or somewhere nearby anyway. Might even quit Law work soon, try breeding some horses. He was forty-three years old now, and had met some nice women, and figured he might yet find one he'd marry. *"Plenty of choice here,"* he'd said in the letter, *"surprising as that may seem. Widows mostly. Tough and decent, just how I like 'em. Morris's mother was that way. I sure do miss her."*

Billy liked the sound of that. Well, he liked the horse breedin' part. He had nothin' against the marriage part either, long as it was Preacher Rob standing up at the altar, not him.

He was moseying along on ol' Percy — still as reliable as ever, that horse was — just thinking about all these things, and was just about completely decided.

Cheyenne it is.

But no women, he thought then with sadness.

He still had the letter.

Both letters, in fact.

Somehow, he could not throw away the letter from Horace, as much as he wished to. It was the last thing he ever got from home, and as terrible as it was, he could not let it go. He had wondered about that before, and decided that, perhaps, he kept it because the moment he'd read it was the moment his heart broke — and no matter how broken it was, you might need your heart someday. So he kept it.

But he *never* opened it. Not in all the years since the war ended.

Cass's letter though, that was different. He'd take it out every so often, usually in some remote and beautiful place, then carefully unfold it and read it.

This sorta remote and beautiful place, he thought, as he came to a good spot to camp for the night.

But spots are like signs, or they can be.

So some spots *is* better'n others.

And this spot, as it turned out, would be one of the bad ones.

CHAPTER 33
THE OLD UNREST

Billy rode in off the trail. It was a nice little clearing by the stream, a well used spot, and for good reason. Decent sorta hill other side of the creek, but thick enough that no man could get a horse in there, or get through without making noise.

Just the trail to keep watch of really, unless someone came walking up the stream, and that would be noisy too. At least, that is to say, a man with *Billy's* ear would hear it. He'd grown attuned to such noises, learned a lot from Preacher Rob these few years.

It seemed like the best place he'd find to rest for the night. And someone had made a fair sort of fireplace from rocks, making life all the easier.

Billy appreciated *easier* when it presented itself. Things were hard enough most of the time, so he took what small gifts were given him.

He got down off ol' Percy, unsaddled him, let him roam about on his own. He would rub him down some a bit later, didn't need light for that. But for now, he built himself a small fire to heat up some bacon he'd brought along. Eggs he had too, carefully wrapped in his old red bandana, and fresh biscuits. He had a small pot for coffee, and he got that out too, commenced to make up a brew.

Then while he yet had the daylight, he went to his saddlebags, and he carefully took out the letter. He walked across the clearing some, set himself down with his back against a nice rock, with a view of where the trail went by. He'd left the Henry back with the saddle, but he had his six-shooter on him.

Always, he wore that gun now, except while sleeping or bathing, or visiting an accommodating lady. Even then, it was always within his arm's reach. A Deputy can't never be too careful.

He stared at the letter a moment before opening it. So soft and delicate — yet it had survived, while Cass hadn't. She had been soft alright. *So soft.*

But delicate?

Never.

She was always the tougher of us two.

The paper was worn thin by now, had small holes at two places where the folds crossed each other.

The paper wasn't the only thing that was thinning though.

Seemed like her voice got thinner and thinner, each time he read the letter. The very act of opening it up now took all the courage he could muster.

What if her voice wasn't there?

He took a deep breath, faced it front on. Looked at the

words, commenced then to read and to listen — and was relieved beyond measure when he heard her. So faint, but it was Cass's voice alright. He figured one day it would be gone completely — his last tenuous hold on her voice would be gone from his mind.

But still, he could picture her like it was yesterday.

All sorts of memories he had of her, and in every one she was beautiful.

The most beautiful.

He'd been with other women, of course. But only ever those he paid. He very much appreciated what those women did. Some men had no respect for painted ladies, but Billy could not understand that.

To Billy, those women were a wonder.

Despite his deep need, and the way it felt like he was burying his whole life inside them, he was always remarkably gentle and loving toward them — he didn't think he was, but they often told him so, after. He didn't understand how any man could be less than honorable with a woman — any woman.

The wonderful painted ladies always managed to patch up his broken heart somehow. Sort of put his busted pieces back together, just enough so as he could keep going.

And sometimes — not much, but it happened every so often — Billy cried once he was done.

Not one of those women had ever looked down on him for it. They wrapped him up in their arms, held him closer than close, shared the same space with him for those moments. They buried him in their bodies just like he needed, and they gave him the heart to keep going.

They gave him a piece of *their* hearts, was how he figured it — for his own was too broken to work.

They *loved him* somehow — but without expecting it back. Knowing he could never give them anything else besides money, respect, and his honesty.

Yessir, they were a wonder, those women, and he always paid more than he had to.

Wasn't the only time he cried though.

Sometimes too, when he camped all alone, he'd be reading the letter, and tears would run out of his eyes and fall to the ground.

Kerplop they would go, in the dirt.

Just like right now.

He didn't feel none ashamed, but Percy sure looked at him funny. Billy sat here right now with his back against a rock, holding the letter in one hand, and wiping away tears with the other. And he wished he could go and see Jenny — he figured she'd be more forgiving of tears than ol' Percy.

And yet, Billy had never gone back to Wilmington, where he could have visited Jenny, and Morris, and Sheriff Mike and his wife.

It was just too close.

Not too close to here.

Too close for comfort.

The problem wasn't that he felt compelled *not* to go there — the problem was opposite to that.

Always, always, the old unrest filled him, drawing him back to Cottonwood Falls.

More and more every day.

But why? For what? She's gone. And even my Pa don't want me there. Dead to him, I am. And yet...

Billy folded the letter, stood up, and was walking toward the big flat rock his saddlebags were on when he heard it.

Nothing much.

Something.

He didn't know *what* it was, but that sound was somehow unnatural, didn't belong in this wild and natural place.

He was a lot bigger target now than he used to be. Seven years fills a man out. He had grown into them big hands and feet, just like his Pa always said he would. But all that time Billy was growing in muscle, he never forgot to keep working at keeping himself supple.

Some men laughed at his stretches, but he still reckoned they were a wonder.

Billy sprung sideways off of his right leg, and was already quarter way into a roll, when the first bullet rang out. It went through the air he'd just been in, right around chest height it sounded.

No time to think about that though, the feller had a repeater, and the second bullet hit right where his foot had been, when he took off to his right from the end of his roll, and took cover behind that big rock his saddle and bags were sitting on.

Billy's hat had come off in mid-roll, but he sure weren't about to go get it.

"Problem, Friend?" he called out, sliding his revolver

from its holster, but staying down low, every sense alive for a clue.

A third bullet came as an answer, and again, it flew by real close. Right over his head this one went, not far away neither. Feller was a real good shot, whoever he was. That bullet so close over his head, it recalled to his mind the time one parted his hair, his very first battle at Glasgow. Still had the hat, and it still had the hole, but the scratch on his head hadn't stayed long.

This feller was a pretty good shooter, and had him pinned down. Billy wanted the Henry, but he didn't want it so bad he was gonna reach up to get it — he liked having two arms, even though his Pa always managed with one.

What would Pa do right now?

No more bullets came, no sound either. Billy's ears was pretty good, and he had a way of slowing his mind down that helped him hear even better. Or maybe just *sense* sound instead. But there wasn't no sound at all.

Either that feller's some sorta Indian, or he ain't movin' from where he is.

The Colt would just have to do, at least for the moment. Billy closed his eyes, pictured in his mind what was out there. Pictured the space all around him; where the bullets had passed him; built up a picture, a map almost, in his mind.

And the whole time he did it, he breathed.

He could figure, pretty close, where the man was. Most likely had pretty good cover. But he had to keep watching, if he planned on shooting Billy, and no cover's so perfect as all that.

He's patient, I'll give him that much. I'd best give him some reason to change that.

The rock Billy was behind was just about as tall as Morris. Just about, but not quite. About as high as a Henry stood on its end. It was about double that in length.

Good thing he was so supple, he was too tall to crouch behind such a low rock. Most other fellers woulda struggled to crouch, woulda had to sit down. But Billy's knees and ankles and hips were a wonder, all that stretching only serving to make them the stronger.

That feller will expect me to use my right hand, so to shoot from that end of the rock, a'course. My right, his left.

This was the very situation Billy had been training for. Preacher Rob could shoot with both hands, and was always at Billy to learn. But he never tried it until after Preacher Rob left. Figured he'd surprise him with it when next he saw him.

So, Billy had been practicing shooting with his left hand awhile now. He was getting halfway passable at it as well. Slow as one a'them weeks with the two extra Thursdays — but lately, he mostly hit not too far from the target.

He'd been meaning to buy a second Colt too, but never quite got around to it.

Must do that soon. If I survive this, that is. This shooter's more clever'n most.

He left his crouch now though, and sat with his back against the rock down near one end — the end the feller would be expecting him.

He laid the Colt down beside him, untied the bandana

from his throat, picked up a couple of fair sized rocks and wrapped them in the bandana.

Billy always liked red for bandanas, but Preacher Rob taught him that clothing the colors of trees and dirt helped a man to live longer, so the bandana he wore was a sort of dusky green.

He would always keep his old red one though — Cass had gifted it to him for his 16th birthday.

Billy made sure he scraped around a bit, down that end of the rock, but only enough so a real sharp feller'd notice — seeing as that's who he'd decided he was up against. He pushed the very end of that green bandana up above the rock a time or two as well, just enough so the feller might see it, but not enough for him to shoot at.

Then as he got back into his crouch, he called out, "Still there, Friend? Tell ya what, I'm sure gettin' hungry. How 'bout you come in and we'll talk some over the problem?"

He knew there'd be no answer, this feller was too good for that, and he wouldn't move neither. So Billy didn't bother with listening this time, he picked up the Colt in his left hand and held the bandana of rocks in his right, and he moved quick and quiet on his moccasins, straight down the other end.

Then, careful with the trajectory, he threw that rock-filled bandana to his own right, so it flew out aways from the end a' the rock that other feller should be watching.

The bullet shattered the silence, and shattered the damn rocks in the bandana too — and a split half-second later, Deputy U.S. Marshal Billy Fyre stuck his head and a handful of Colt round his end a' that rock, and blasted a hole right into that other feller's shoulder. Followed it up with another that lodged in his chest, took an edge off a lung.

"Dammit, Fyre. Dammit," the man cried.

Well, Billy knew the voice right away.

No wonder he was good. Deputy F.J. Randell. Came here with Marshal Pitt. Always was thick as thieves, them two.

Randell was still alive when Billy got to him, but was hanging to his life by a thread.

Billy asked, "Why?" But he already knew. Snakes can't help but be snakes, and them sorta snakes stuck together. "Don't die, Randell, I'm takin' you in."

But that feller — who could have been a great Deputy, and could have done a lot of good with his skills — he just smiled a weak one and said, "Good luck with that, Kid, I'm done for."

"Admit it, Pitt had you do it. I'll write it, you sign it. It was him got you killed, don't protect him."

But Billy never even had the time to go for pencil and paper.

Randell said, "You bested me, Fyre, so I'll give you this free. I ain't the only one." His breathing was shallow, irregular. For a moment his eyes closed, and Billy thought he was gone. Then he startled back to life, enough to say, "Save yourself, there's too many. Don't go back, you're a ... a dead man. I ... I admired you, Kid." He fought to keep his eyes open, but was losing the battle. "That's why I ... why I..."

Then Deputy F.J. Randell — if the F.J. stood for

anything, Billy never knew what — slipped away to where wrongdoers go once they breathe their last.

And Billy, after taking five minutes to consider his options, buried the man in the medium-shallow grave he had earned for himself for eternity.

He laid out some rocks on the grave in the shape of an F and a J. Figured the man should have something, but it sure was a pity he'd chosen the bad path.

As for saying words over him, Billy sure wasn't no Preacher — he only said, "Well, I guess you sent him into this world, Lord, and now took him back. It's your own business what you do with him now, a'course — but I'd ask you don't send him back here. We got enough badness already out here in the West, and the cities are *worse,* so they reckon. Anyways, Lord, thanks for listenin', if you did."

Then Billy went and found Randell's horse, took off its saddle and bridle so it wouldn't hurt itself, then hit the gelding one on the rump so it'd head South. Fired a couple of shots too, in case it decided to stop.

Some lucky Indian would find that nice horse, and change the brand so it wouldn't be recognized. Wasn't much of a brand, the two bar. Almost asking to be changed.

That all done, Billy Fyre set out to the North — for some hopefully less dangerous place.

For awhile, Marshal Pitt thought Randell and Fyre both dead, and good riddance to the both of 'em, he reckoned. Fyre was trouble, and Randell had of late grown sloppy, and just about outlived his usefulness.

Officially, he sent men to search for them — Marshals

must be *seen* to cross the T's, dot the I's — but he sent those men nowhere near where they could possibly find them. Wallace Pitt was too smart for that. Then he wrote out paperwork stating that both men had deserted him. Wrote that they *"probably bumped into each other while out on their duties, got talking of some opportunity and rode off together."*

All that was certain was that neither of those two *"fine Deputies"* ever went back for their pay.

CHAPTER 34
FRIENDS REUNITED

※

Billy decided it would be foolish to head for Cheyenne any other way but by rail.

That meant riding north to Omaha, but would save him a whole lot a' time. More than this, it meant riding through Wilmington, pretty much.

It would be a fine thing, to see Morris, as well as Sheriff Mike and his lovely wife, Judith. It was about time.

He wrote to both Preacher Rob and Morris, letting them know his intentions — and also in order to give Morris time to decide if he'd come to Cheyenne as well.

So when Billy rode into Wilmington, they already knew he was coming.

It was just after dark when he rode into town, and it was more or less quiet, except the two saloons. Sheriff's Office was shut, so he rode along a bit further, and up a side street, toward Mike and Judith Brimstone's house.

He stepped down from ol' Percy, and hadn't even had time to tie him and the new pack horse, Frank, to the hitching rail, when the door flew open, and a familiar, mellifluous voice said, "Thought I smelled somethin' disagreeable."

Billy looked up at Morris, grinned a wide one and said, "That'd be caused by your nose bein' so dang close to your feet, Shorty."

"Shorty," said Morris with a disbelieving shake of his head. "*Shorty?* Well, that's just disappointing, that is. Almost seven years to come up with something, and that's all you got. Head of solid bone, Jenny reckons. Speakin' a' Jenny, we best take these horses out back, and I'll attend to 'em while you and her get reacquainted."

The two men shook hands before leading a horse each out back to the barn. By the quality of insults they traded on the way, they had both prepared well for this moment.

Billy wondered whether Jenny would even remember him. She was four when last he had seen her, and she was eleven now.

Can horses remember so long?

She nickered softly as he strode into the barn, then looked at him strangely a moment. Perhaps she wondered at the size of him — he had filled out near enough double since last she had seen him, after all.

Well, whatever she thought, she sure seemed to remember him fine.

When Billy went to her she nuzzled into his shoulder and neck, then playfully pushed him away before nuzzling against him again. Even spoke to him some, and Billy fancied he could just about understand what those whinnies and nickers all meant. He reckoned he felt the same way as she did, only she was better at voicing it.

"Turned out Jenny's hearing was fine," Morris said, "but her love for you sure makes me question her sense of smell. We best get Doc Miller to check out her sniffer."

Such banter went on between the pair the rest of the night — and every now and then, when Billy couldn't quite hold his own at the game, Sheriff Mike tipped the scales in his favor.

Turned out Morris had growed some. Two more growth spurts after Billy left had got him all the way to four foot five.

"You got more than half a foot on your Henry now," said Billy.

"Bit like you havin' half a stone on your horse now, Fatboy," came the answer. That Morris sure was hard to beat when it came to the art of friendly banter.

Billy told Judith the stew she'd heated up for him was the best meal he'd eaten since he left there. It wasn't true a'course, but the woman liked to think she was a top notch cook — and a little white lie or two never hurt, Billy reckoned. Not if it made a nice lady happy anyway.

Mike thanked him for telling that little white lie, the very next day over lunch at Catrina's Family Restaurant.

Billy's palate had developed some over the years — partly out of necessity — and he didn't order plain ol' steak, potatoes and beans, like last time he was here. No, this time Mike was surprised to see Billy order enchiladas to start with, and follow it up with a fine chimichanga. It was easy to see how Billy put on all that bulk — it was a veritable mountain of food.

He sure did savor every bite too — because that really *was* the best meal Billy had eaten in all the time since he'd left here.

Billy now understood why Rosie had always cooked all that stuff, and why his Pa relished it so. He couldn't for the life of him figure out why he'd turned his nose up at it all through his younger years, preferring to go hungry than eat it. No accountin' for a kid's taste, he decided. But he sure wished he could try Rosie's cooking again.

That'd really be somethin', that would. Dear ol' Rosie. I miss her a lot.

Nearing the end of the meal, with Billy all full and contented — this time, he did have a belt to loosen, and he surely did so — Mike brought up a most important matter.

They had been so busy catching up the previous night, that they never got around to talking about him going to Cheyenne. And the one time Billy mentioned it to Morris, he'd only said, "Reckon we'll discuss that tomorrow. But I'll warn you right now, they most likely got bathing laws there, SkunkBoy."

But the joking around of last night was all gone now — Sheriff Mike had brought Billy here to eat, but also to bring up a matter Billy might react badly to. Some things are best done in private, but others semi-public, Mike reckoned — and Sheriff Mike Brimstone was nobody's fool, that's for certain, when dealing with delicate matters.

"Morris ain't going to Cheyenne, Billy. Not yet

anyway." He held up a forkful of steak, but his eyes were on Billy's, not the food.

"That's a pity," Billy replied. "I was lookin' forward to spending some time with him. And I thought he was keen to go out there, spend time with his Pa. Especially with Wilmington shrinking some, and him being less needed here."

"More to it than that," said Sheriff Mike. He looked a bit sideways at Billy, pushed some beans round his plate with his fork. It still had the piece of meat on it, but he didn't seem even to notice.

Billy studied Mike's face a moment, frowned, then added, "What am I missing here?" It was unlike Mike Brimstone not to get to the point right away.

"Billy, listen up. New U.S. Marshal asked me for recommendations for men he can trust. Name of Terence Betts. He's been transferred back here from Colorado. Good reputation, good man. Been some bad things going down, and some local Sheriffs and Marshals covering them up maybe." He put down the fork, looked up into Billy's eyes.

Sometimes, even the best of men have trouble breaking what might be bad news; or difficult news; or news that might go either way.

Billy was no Preacher Rob, but he'd sure been learning how to read folks in the time he'd spent with him. He looked back at Mike and said, "Cottonwood Falls?"

Sheriff Mike's eyes were all the answer he needed about that.

"Morris is going," said the Sheriff, "either with or

without you. Marshal Betts was skeptical, even *after* having seen Morris shoot. I told him about you. Told him you were on your way here. He'd heard of you some."

"So Morris only gets the job if I go?" Billy said. Then he looked up and thanked the waitress as she topped up their coffee cups.

After she moved away, Mike went on. "No, Morris is going anyway. Betts hopes you'll go with him, work as a team. If you don't, he'll hire someone else." He was staring at Billy in earnest now, his bushy eyebrows like question marks.

"You don't want Morris's life left to chance," Billy said. "In the hands of some stranger."

"That's the size of it, Billy, I guess," said Mike, glancing up at the door as two newcomers entered. They were kinda big, mean looking types. No guns on 'em though, a'course — not in Wilmington. They watched the pair 'til they sat at an empty table, then Sheriff Mike went on. "I know it ain't easy for you, Billy. And it's fine to say no. Not even asking you, really. Just letting you know, and giving you the chance, just in case you *want* to go."

It had been years since Billy had seen Sheriff Mike and Morris. And yet, he knew they thought of him as more than just a friend. He was fully aware of all they'd done for him. The Brimstones had been there for him, always, since that very first day — accepted him like family, looked after him as one of their own.

Any one of them could have asked him anything, and he'd have said yes. It was a measure of the man that Mike

Brimstone had *not* asked — and Morris would never ask either.

It had to be Billy's choice, not done from a feeling of obligation.

"I'm kind of insulted," said Billy, with a harsh look.

"But I—"

"Insulted you'd think I might say no." He smiled then at his old friend and mentor. "Besides, we both know Morris would only get himself into trouble with *whoever* he works with. Not everyone appreciates his insultin' manner, way I do. When do we leave?"

The relief washed over Mike Brimstone's features. "Thank you, Billy. I know it's no easy thing, for you to go back there. There's a contract to sign at my Office. Short term Deputies, both you and Morris. You can start soon as you're rested, and walk out of the contract whenever you like."

"So, maybe two more nights here, I reckon. I want Percy well rested. What a horse *he* turned out to be! Which reminds me, Mike — thank you for everything you did for me, all those years ago here."

"That's alright, Billy," Mike answered, nodding and murmuring his thanks to the waitress as she put the apple pie on the table. "I saw right off what a good kid you were. Couldn't have you goin' off to war that way, all so green and unprotected. Still can't believe the whole family survived that damn war."

"I still ain't met Devil Joe," said Billy, his eyes all over that pie as he picked up the small pitcher of cream and poured over it. "But from all I heard, it's a good thing I never met him on a battlefield."

"True enough," said Mike. "Though you might be surprised when you finally meet him. Gentlest feller you ever did see. Soft spoken with it. Name was sort of a joke in the family, and it stuck."

Billy noticed that Sheriff Mike had a Smith & Wesson in his holster. "You switched from the Colt too, I see. So quick to load, ain't it?

"True enough. And beautifully made, about as good as guns get."

"It's a wonder," Billy agreed. "What about rifles, Sheriff? You still using the Spencer?"

"Winchester now. Switched the day they arrived. Like a Henry, but with the Henry's main problems sorted. Still not quite the quality of the Spencer, but better all up. You switch to the Winchester too?" He spooned some fresh whipped cream onto his pie and licked the spoon, before smacking his lips in satisfaction.

"Still with the Henry," said Billy, shrugging his shoulders. "I know the Winchester's better, but I guess I'm attached to the Henry. And it's still as good as the day I got it from the gunsmith here in town. I'd hoped its forty-fours would fit the Smith & Wesson, or the other way round, but no such luck. Including the baby twenty-twos for my Sharps derringer, that's a lot of different ammunition to carry."

"He can fix that for you, you know," said Sheriff Mike. "Our gunsmith here. He's a good'un alright. You drop it to him today, he'll convert that Smith & Wesson to take Henry cartridges. Did it for Morris six months back, and never a problem. Better than carting both types of forty-fours about."

"That's sweet music indeed," said Billy, before turning his attention to that mountain of whipped cream.

They bantered about this and that as they ate up their pie and drank down that good coffee, then they wandered on up to the Sheriff's Office. Morris was on duty, just sitting in a chair out front. His Smith & Wesson looked like a cannon compared to his short legs. The Henry resting across his lap didn't help him look no bigger neither. It seemed funny to Billy when he noticed, because he never usually thought of Morris as small.

Sure, they joked some about his small size — but that big-headed, stumpy-legged fast-walker was as big a man as Billy ever knew, in all the ways that mattered.

And if there was to be any trouble when he went back home, a Brimstone was just who he wanted beside him — and this one in particular, for folks tended to underestimate him.

CHAPTER 35
"MAN AT THE POT!"

As Mike and Billy approached the Sheriff's Office, Deputy Morris Brimstone tipped his hat back a little and looked at 'em closer, trying to read their eyes. But neither was an easy man to read, and he soon gave up on that. "In or out?"

"In," Mike and Billy both answered.

"Damn," Morris replied with a broad smile, jumping to his feet and taking off his hat in one motion, quick as always. "Well, maybe I'll be lucky and catch myself a terrible head cold — or I guess I could just wear a clothes peg on my nose, if it comes to it. Wonder if my sniffer might one day get used to skunk-stink. A man can only hope. Best we go inside and look over the paperwork, Pardner."

"You shouldn't jump up quite so fast," Billy said. "One day that Henry'll discharge accidental, and that'll be the end of your plans to have children someday."

They went inside and gathered around the desk. Morris already had the paperwork spread out on it, and he stayed on his feet while the other two sat. Billy groaned and shook his head more than once, as they went through the paperwork with him. It was full of not-so-good news.

As an experienced and clever Deputy Marshal, he had kept his own initial worries, suspicions and hunches away from his mind — right up until he saw the paperwork. But once they got into it, there was no keeping his worries at bay.

It was clear as the nose on Abe Lincoln's face — things weren't right around Cottonwood Falls.

As they went through the list of crimes this past two or three years, the same word kept leaping from the page, filling Billy's chest and gut with the hurt and the pain and the rage — and he was dragged back to the past, seventeen once again.

Fire.

So many fires. Every one accidental — according to the reports — and never deemed any way suspicious.

A few men had been shot dead as well. Seth Hays' ramrod for one, soon after all this started up — he was the second man to die from a bullet, a week after the Council Grove Sheriff.

Never any witnesses. Just a body found in the open — or in the case of the Sheriff, a shallow grave, not too well hidden. Killing was spread through the Falls and Council Grove too, round about evenly.

"The bodies found in the open were deemed to be suicides, including that ramrod," said Morris.

"The Sheriff in the shallow grave sure hadn't buried himself," Sheriff Mike said. "He was the first one shot, the

Council Grove Sheriff. It was credited to some mean lookin' feller who passed through some days earlier, but couldn't be found. Not findin' him checks out fair, the whole town being in disarray with the loss of the Sheriff himself."

"Sheriff Pratt was a decent sorta man, my Pa always reckoned," Billy said with a shake of his head. "My brother never much liked him though. That Sheriff used to watch Horace unfair close, he always reckoned. Always nice to me though. Killer was Mexican, it says here."

"Naturally," said Sheriff Mike. "Less Indians about to pin things on now, so they mostly say it was Mexicans or former slaves to share out the blame."

"Two of the house fires happened not long before all that though," Morris said thoughtfully. "The second was just a few days before the Sheriff was murdered."

"Might be something to that," said Sheriff Mike, leaning back in his chair and patting his belly. "Should not have eaten so much."

Billy frowned, and looked up from the paper he was reading. Wasn't easy, especially when fire was mentioned, but he set his shoulders against it and did his job. "So how did the Marshal Service get involved? Is there something else, or just the possible corruption?"

"Just the corruption," said Morris. "That Seth Hays has been jumping up and down for more than two years. Somebody finally listened."

"Resources are tight," said the Sheriff, "what with everything else going on."

Morris pointed his little fingers at one of the sheets. "You know any of the names, Billy?"

"Oh, I know 'em alright," Billy answered. "This Clem Jenkins, the new County Sheriff in Council Grove — he was Town Marshal of the Falls when I left. Always seemed a fair enough feller — half Town Marshal and half Postal Officer he was then. That was about right for him too, by my reckoning."

Morris's eyes were shining at the prospect of chasing down any wrongdoers. He was keen to get to the bottom of things. "Jenkins a dishonest man, do you think?"

"Wouldn't have thought so," Billy answered, getting up from his desk and walking across toward the coffee pot. "But his son, Jasper, who's Cottonwood Falls Sheriff now — him, I never trusted."

"Man at the pot!" called Mike, just as Billy took a cup from its hook.

He rolled his eyes, grabbed two more cups, then started to pour the first of the three cups of coffee.

"Knew he'd break first," said Morris with a laugh. Then his voice went serious again as he got back to business. "Seems like it's wrapped up in the family maybe. But every report looks watertight. The T's are crossed and the I's are dotted. Every report thorough and done by the book. No clue of wrongdoing at all."

Mike watched Billy pouring the coffee, then turned back to his nephew. "What about the railroad? Big money around railroads — might be something to look at."

"All above board by the looks," Morris answered. "Don't overfill mine, Billy, it takes too long to cool. The railroad people went through, bought up what land they wanted, no one ever argued or fought it. It all just went smooth, far as I can tell from the paperwork."

"Never so much as a rumor here," Mike said thoughtfully. Then he added, "Thanks," as Billy put down their coffees, then blew on his own to cool it some.

"Too hot," Billy said, and put his cup down on the table. "Got a recent map of the Falls? My Pa always reckoned they'd run the railroad through our — through *his* place. The town's the other side of the river though. Just curious if he was right."

Sure enough, there it was on the map. You coulda knocked Billy down with a feather off a half-growed-up owl. Railroad went right along the Southern boundary of his Pa's place.

"That's Pa's place it's on alright," he said.

Sheriff Mike had picked up another map. He looked from it to Billy, then rubbed a thumb and middle finger over his temples, as if trying to recall something gone too long unthought of. "Thought your Pa's name was ... Jim ... John. John it was, yes? Says Horace Ray on here."

Morris looked up from a different map. "You sure, Uncle? Mine says John Ray owns that property, and Horace Ray the adjoining one-sixty."

"We're both right," said Sheriff Mike. "Your map's ownership, mine shows who's in residence. And it's only just a year old. Billy's Pa must still own the place, but his brother — Horace *is* your brother ain't he Billy? — Horace has the lease of their father's place."

Billy let out the breath he'd been holding. "For a

minute there I thought my Pa mighta been planted in the bone orchard," he said.

"He ain't listed as a resident on these maps, in either the Grove or the Falls," said Mike.

"He owns another property too," Morris added, "extra two miles North."

Billy looked at the map and winced. "Cass's Pa's place."

"No one in residence at that one," said Sheriff Mike. "No record of John Ray currently living anywhere in that county. But no record of him dying either, or any sorta trouble. Just looks like he moved away."

"That's a relief to me," said Billy, rubbing at his jaw. He had over a week's growth of beard now, and it was starting to itch. "Can't help but wonder where he's gone though. Can't imagine my Pa up and leavin', not for anything. Then again, I never imagined he woulda dis... well, you know."

"Might be he got real sick, and had to go somewhere for treatment," Morris said. Sheriff Mike looked at him sharply, then Morris added, "Sorry. Insensitive of me, I guess."

"It's alright," said Billy, the steam rising off his coffee as he blew on it again. "We're working — ain't like it's personal. And if I'm gonna be any part of all this, there's a lot I'll need to come to terms with. Does the Marshal ... what's he called, Betts ain't it? Yes? Does Marshal Betts know my original name? Know I grew up there?"

He and Morris had both turned to look at Mike as he asked it.

"He knows," said the Sheriff. "Unofficial, like. When Betts first wrote me to say he was coming here, I sent a wire off to Preacher Rob, find out what he knew of him.

"You got the telegraph here in town now?" Billy asked.

"No, not here," said Mike. "A friend was going to Topeka. Had him send it, and wait for one back. Lot quicker'n writing. Turned out Preacher Rob had some dealings with the Marshal when he came to Cheyenne once. He reckoned Terence Betts to be solid as a brick penitentiary, yet still the sorta man who knows when to turn a blind eye."

"They's the best Marshals there is," Billy said.

Sheriff Mike nodded in agreement, and went on. "So I told him you used to be a Ray, but didn't give no details why. Also told him to keep it under his hat, good and proper. He promised he would. He reckons it gives you an advantage down there anyway."

"Maybe," said Billy. "Maybe not."

"Well, your name's William Fyre, and that's all there is to that — even the Government agrees to it. If they don't, why do they keep employing you under that name? If something goes awry down the Falls, and your real name comes out, you might then have to deal with it. But outside of that, there's no problem."

Mike looked at Billy then, and so did Morris.

"Well, Billy?" said Morris. "It ain't too late to back out. I don't *need* no offsider who stinks worse'n skunk anyway." He smiled a wide one, and drank down his whole cup of coffee in one go before belching so loud it just about shook the bars in the windows.

"What a charmer you are," said Billy. "No wonder you ain't married up yet, Morris Belch Brimstone. It's a mystery how that size of noise comes out such a small size of body."

"My body's normal size, unlike yours, Stretch. So's my head and most other things, before you start up on it. It's only my limbs that never growed proper, that's all. As for marryin' up, I prefer to spread *my* love around." And Morris wiggled his eyebrows some when he said the last bit.

Billy looked from Morris to Mike. "Sounds an unlikely story at best. Any part a' that true, Sheriff?"

"All of it, I reckon," he said. "No idea why, but no shortage of ladies takes a shine to the bad-behaved belcher. Sure ain't on account of his manners."

"It's the voice mostly," Morris said, "or at least that's what they all tell me. But I think some of 'em gets interested in checkin' out the size of my—"

"*That's* more than I wanted to hear," said Billy, real good and loud, and not one moment too soon. "We'll leave here day after tomorrow, once me and Percy's both proper rested. I need to go down there anyway, find out what's happened to my Pa. And besides, we got some red-tail hawks down that way, might think you're a squirrel and eat you. You'll be needin' someone to shoo 'em away, so I reckon I'd best come along."

CHAPTER 36
A PART-YOUR-HAIR-FROM-THE-LEFT MAN

Two days later, Billy Fyre and Morris Brimstone rode slowly out of Wilmington, as the sun painted its first fiery rays of the day atop the horizon.

It would be in the eighties today, and they wanted to keep the horses as fresh as they could. They took along pack horses too, all the better to hide all their weapons. Folk look at you different when they see an arsenal of high quality weapons — and Billy and Morris didn't want folks to think much about 'em at all, if they could help it.

The horses had an easy enough time of it — that whole fifteen mile trip south to Osage City traversed only one uphill of note, and even that not too steep. They arrived there at nine, and used cash dollars to purchase their tickets.

They could have used their U.S. Marshals vouchers, but preferred to keep their identities quiet to begin with. Kept their badges in their pockets as well. They'd produce them at the right moment, was what they'd agreed.

A half hour after arriving in Osage City, they walked their horses up the ramp onto the train and got 'em settled. The 9.45 to Cottonwood Falls pulled out fifteen minutes later, right on time to the minute.

When first they'd commenced making plans, Sheriff Mike had pointed out that Billy should keep his beard going, at least for a short while. "I wouldn't have recognized you, Billy, when you turned up here. I reckon you put on sixty or seventy pounds since last I saw you. You changed a *lot* in seven years. You weren't even shaving yet then, as I remember."

"He's right," Morris had quickly agreed. "Sorry, Billy, but your baby-faced good looks is gone the way of the dodo bird. Looks like all the women'll be for me from now on."

Well, that last wasn't quite true.

Billy knew only too well, how much women liked how he looked — indeed, they liked the look of him so much, that sometimes, he had to get himself out of situations he didn't ask to get into in the first place.

That is to say, any situation where he wasn't paying the woman for her services.

He had a definite rule on that for himself — though a'course, he never *said* that to women. Imagine the trouble that woulda caused. Made it hard sometimes though, to escape one that persisted in pushing their romantic interest upon him.

But Billy sure had changed, that bit could not be argued.

He was now ruggedly handsome — though unlike his Pa, the handsome part was still winning over the rugged part. With 10 days of beard on his face, and that seventy extra pounds of strong muscle — he weighed just on 200 now — most folk would be hard pressed to pick him, seven years on. And Billy intended to keep that advantage as long as he possibly could.

Even so, he figured Horace would pick him right off, no matter how strongly Mike and Morris argued he wouldn't. He would cross that bridge when he came to it — for now, he had a train ride to get through.

It was a wonder, that train. Billy still didn't much like the movement, the way the cars swayed and lurched — but that clackety iron horse sure ate up the miles. It was thirty miles to Emporia, another twenty from there to the Falls — but instead of arriving two days later with half-tired bodies and horses, it was an almost relaxing three hour trip.

Would have been faster still if the train didn't have to stop every ten miles to take on water and wood. Would have been a dang site more relaxing as well, if they rode in the seats like normal passengers.

But they were not normal passengers, far from it. Morris might have considered traveling in comfort, but Billy wanted to stay with the horses, as always — so they rode in one of the many empty stock cars. Those would be full up with beeves when the train was on its way back, a'course.

First thing they did, before Morris even had a chance to fall asleep, was load up every gun they had, including their pocket pistols. Then they hid most of 'em away in their saddlebags and bed rolls, all the better to appear like two more-or-less average fellers when they arrived.

Kept their sidearms out, and the pocket pistols, just in case.

They discussed some loose strategies too. Real loose — for the whole thing could change on the turn of a card. One plan was to find out whatever they could from the locals — but they knew that wouldn't likely amount to too much. Folks have a habit of staying silent when afeared they might be next to die, if they speak up.

The more likely plan was a bold one — get close to Jasper and Clem. And Horace too, if he was involved. The more Billy considered that possibility, the worse of a feeling he got about it all. And if they had to, they'd warn the probable guilty parties that an investigation was in progress. That looked like their best hope, as it might set the guilty into action, trying to cover up whatever they'd done. Then Billy and Morris could follow them, see what it led them to.

Best part of that plan was, if Horace did recognize Billy, brotherly love was a good excuse for Billy to be warning him.

Once they had their loose plans sorta decided, Morris laid back his head and commenced to snooze, leaving Billy alone with his thoughts.

He had plenty to think about too. But mostly, there wasn't nothin' that seemed solid knowledge, and it was all like smoke in the air — at least until they arrived and found out some facts.

He tried to snooze too, but even if he could have

ignored how nervy he was about going home, the swaying motion of the train woulda bothered him too much.

But ol' Morris, he slept like a well fed dog in the sun on a perfect Spring day. Not a care in the world, so it seemed.

Almost two hours into the trip, Billy had a strange moment — just a minute before the train arrived at Emporia. They had slowed for the run in to the station, and Billy had gotten to his feet for a stretch. Between stretches, he was looking out the side of the train at the scenery, through a large gap right at his head height — it had clearly been broken out on purpose by an earlier traveler who wanted a better view of the countryside.

It was green here, and nice, the houses of a different sort than they were in the Falls.

They were mostly from Wales, the folk who had settled Emporia — and although they still built from local materials, their Welsh heritage showed in the style of some of the houses.

The blocks along here were bigger than town blocks and smaller than ranches. Like baby farms, more or less. Maybe just a few acres each. Extra well cared for, most of 'em. Flowers growing in the yards, paint on the barns and the stables even. These little places seemed like a nice compromise, Billy thought — close to your neighbors and the comforts of town, but space to grow a few things, raise a few animals and children, keep a couple of horses in comfort.

Nice sorta place to retire to. Maybe someday, if I live long enough.

As the train came toward one a' them pretty little

places, he saw a small child — couldn't be no more than six — trying to climb onto the back of an old horse from an upside down bucket.

That sure took Billy back — back to a time in his own life, when all he could think about was gettin' on an old horse called Charlie, so he could learn to ride like his big brother. Only difference, the young Billy had a stump to climb up on, whereas this kid had to bring along his own bucket.

But as the train came closer Billy kept watching, and pretty soon he saw the sense in it. *I shoulda thought of that myself. Lot easier to move the bucket than bring back the horse when he moves.*

The kid wore no hat, and had dark hair, cut medium length, parted from the left side.

A part-your-hair-from-the-left man, just like myself, Billy thought. *Hope the little tyke don't go breaking his arm the way I did.*

The kid stopped his strivings for the horse's back a moment, and half turned toward the train, before commencing to wave.

Billy stuck his head and his arm right out through the slats, then raised up his hand as a greeting. He didn't wave, but held that hand still instead, palm out toward that young boy — and when he did, other moments from Billy's childhood came rushing unbidden to his mind.

That old Indian feller who gifted me my first pair of moccasins.

The boy had stopped waving, as such, and held his arm still now, same as Billy — same as that old Indian used to —

and as the train passed, Billy fancied he saw an expression of grave seriousness on that little boy's face.

He wondered a moment whether his own small face had looked that way to the Indian feller, all that long time ago.

Now he and the little boy stayed that way, just watching each other — saluting, if you could call it that — until the train went round the bend, and they lost each other to the distance.

Then Billy, feeling so strange as he was, looked down to see if Morris was watching him — truth was, he expected some sorta friendly jest about what he was doing — but whenever Morris wasn't moving flat out, he was generally resting flat out to make up for it. And right now, he was sleeping so soundly, some folks woulda called the Doc to make sure he weren't dead.

Minute or two later, they pulled into Emporia, and Billy considered stepping down from the train to speak to the stationmaster there — but Morris awoke and engaged him in conversation about what they'd do first when they got to the Falls.

And so, for the moment, any new facts about Emporia stayed unknown to them both.

Place was a lot busier than it used to be, that much was clear — cattle yards aplenty there were. Place looked to be prospering, and Billy was happy for the folks here.

A half-hour later, they stopped at a Wood and Water stop, halfway between the two stations. There was a gentle bend in the track here, so Billy could see the boilerman jerking the spigot to get the water going. Then while the water ran in, the man loaded the wood in by hand. Looked like not much fun at all, loading that cordwood — but that fireman didn't seem to mind none, and had muscles on his muscles to show for all his hard work.

Billy recalled that there used to be just one big family who lived in a log hut right here, but he couldn't see any of 'em about — Welsh folks they were, name of Keir. Sheep men mostly, but they sold a few horses as well. Quality mounts they were too. Billy's Pa bought a horse off the son once, a real nice feller called Andy — the man was called Andy, not the horse.

Well, at least not to start with.

The Horse was called Horse, so all them Keirs reckoned. But he never answered to it, so Billy's Pa started calling him Andy. Funny, he answered to that right away. No accountin' for horses.

The name thing aside, it had been a perfect piece of business, both parties more than happy with the transaction. Horse wasn't young, but a good mover, sound as the day is long, and they had younger ones coming through. John Ray had been on the lookout for just such an animal, something quiet and reliable for Rosie to ride if she wanted to make a quick trip into town. Seemed likely to Billy that his father would have done more business with them this past seven years.

Wonder if Pa still has that ol' gray, he'd be gettin' on some by now.

Billy had done the Keirs a good turn once — on one of his little camping out trips he'd come upon one of their mares almost dead. There was no hope for the mare, but he'd managed to save her newborn foal, and led the gawky thing home to them.

Anyway, all that was back then, and seven years changes things some. There was five other houses here now, and Billy could hear a blacksmith clanging away at his work. Almost a township, it was — train sure did change things.

But just how *much* it had changed things, Billy was quite unprepared for.

CHAPTER 37
ROOMS ~ WHISKEY ~ GIRLS

A half hour after leaving the final jerkwater stop, he knew they were nearing the station of Cottonwood Falls. Woulda known it even with his eyes closed. A man never loses the sense of his home, the feeling he gets in his bones when he gets close.

Billy felt strange about it alright — coming home to this place — and it churned up a whole lot of different feelings inside him.

Seven years.

Almost seven anyway.

If he had not exactly come to terms with all that had happened, he *had* perhaps ground out a way of *being* in the world. Usefulness has a way of holding a man to the ground, of keeping him going, of arguing for the continuation of his life.

For quite some time he had wanted only to die — that was the truth of it. He had not been able to bear the thought of coming back to this place, not once this place became empty. And without Cass, it would *always* be empty.

But Billy had changed over time. He had regrets, but all good men do. He had grown into a man.

There was comfort to be found in his work; in making a difference; in helping to make the world a little safer and better — better for honest folk, anyway.

It was going to hurt, coming home — of that much at least, he was certain. But he knew he could hold his head high, no matter what anyone else thought. He had left this place as Billy Ray, and was coming back as Billy Fyre — but he knew he was more than a name, more than a rumor, more than a reputation.

He knew he was a good man, and here for right reasons. Anyone didn't like it, was welcome to lump it.

Moment the train slowed he sensed it and sprang to his feet. He watched out the right side to catch a glimpse of his childhood home up ahead. He didn't much care about the town, which was two miles off to the left, other side of the river. Trees lining the river would mostly have hid the town anyway.

There was one other place he might have cared to see — or might rather not have, if he thought on it — but there was no chance of seeing the MacPherson place from here anyway, so he didn't have to decide. Billy was sorta glad of that.

Perhaps Morris had sensed his friend's excitement, for instead of sleeping, he was on his feet too, looking out a small gap between the slats as he stood next to Billy.

Morris's lookout was a good few slats below, him being much shorter.

"That your house up on top a' the little hill there, Billy?" said Morris, pointing at a neat, white building. It was yet a half mile ahead of them, and almost a half mile back from the railway track itself.

"That's it alright," Billy answered, choking down the slight bitterness he felt. "You ever see so many cattle, Morris?"

There was longhorns everywhere. Half the place had been fenced into sections, seemed like hundreds of cattle in each, and all of it leading to a loading race down by the railway track, just a short ways before the station.

"Impressive," said Morris.

It wasn't the word Billy had in mind — for there wasn't one tuft of grass within a quarter mile of the train on that side. It was dusty and desolate, a wasteland of beeves, beeves, beeves, and nothing much else — except maybe flies and dung and dust. And maybe more flies.

It surely was *not* an improvement — and he knew his Pa would never have done this. This was all Horace, all greed, with no eye to the future at all.

"It's horrible," said Billy.

"Not so bad as Abilene," Morris replied, screwing his nose up a little. "Ten times what this is, and then some. This *smells* almost as bad though."

Their stock car was quite a ways back from the front of the train, and as it drew closer to stopping, Billy saw what he couldn't before.

He sure did get a shock. Morris, having never been

there before, saw not much unusual about it. He had been to Kansas City, and to Omaha too, both busy places with lots of huge buildings.

But this was Cottonwood Falls, not some big dang city. And what Billy saw seemed all wrong.

The train pulled up next to a small, tidy station. It was new of course, well painted and more-or-less shiny. It was where the railroad ended, for now. Or at least, it was as far as the train itself went. The tracks continued on Westward, as relentless progress would have it.

For the moment, Cottonwood Falls was the end of the line. But the town of Newton awaited, and a whole lotta places between. So an army of men were at work on the railroad — all through the day they worked hard, then they worked just as hard at spending their money at night. Drinking and gambling and whoring, that's where their money went, and most men could spend it just as quick as they earned it.

So, as always, wherever the railroad went, some sort of town would spring up beside it — and this place, of course, was no different.

Not a town here, so much — for the true town of Cottonwood Falls already existed, could be seen in the distance, on the *other* side of the river, two miles to the south, from the *left* side of the train. But here, not fifty yards from where the train sat at the station, in what used to be John Ray's south forty, was a massive, double storied saloon, with a sign, thick black letters on white, that announced:

ROOMS ~ WHISKEY ~ GIRLS
RAYS RESTRAUNT AND GAMBOLING HOUSE

He never could spell, that brother a' mine.

It was huge. And it was ugly. *A blight on the landscape,* those were the words that came to Billy's mind, though he was too shocked to speak them.

And that was only the sign — the building itself was the bigger blight. Red it was, just about the whole thing. *Redder than red.* Billy had never seen *anything* quite so red as that building. Only part of it wasn't red was the trim around the top floor windows — that part was pink. A bright garish pink. Clearly painted that way so folks could make no mistake about what went on behind those top floor windows.

They unloaded their horses and led them toward the huge building. Lively piano music could be heard from inside, along with excited men clapping and cheering. Must have been twenty horses tied to the hitching rails between the station and the saloon — plus others in corrals to one side. Probably more in the big livery out behind the saloon too.

A giant of a man sat in a huge log chair on the porch, right by the main saloon doors. Like a storybook King on a throne he was — except maybe not a human King. Instead, he seemed more like a King of some strange race of ogres, from a book that was made to scare children into staying at home and behaving, lest they get eaten.

He was six foot six if an inch, you could see it even

though he was seated. Giant was hatless, completely bald up on top, but wore a flowing red beard that reached down to his huge rounded belly. He was two fellers wide, two fellers deep, and more than one feller tall. And in his humongous arms he cradled a Winchester repeater.

CHAPTER 38
TINY JONES

"Feller that size, he *must* be from Texas," said Billy, as he sneaked another look at the giant.

"Ate Texas, more like it," Morris whispered. "Looks dumb as a big bag a' rocks, but I reckon not nearly so useful. What a lump."

Billy turned his gaze away from the feller a moment and replied, "Takes all kinds, Morris, as you yourself know. That poor feller must weigh four-hundred pounds, and ride two horses at once."

Morris stifled a laugh, and they watched that huge man a minute as they tied up the horses, then pretended to look through their saddlebags for something while they kept an ear out. He wasn't really four-hundred pounds, but you'd a'got no change from three-thirty. And not all of it was fat, though that was there too.

They watched as the giant nodded at three dandified-lookin' fellers who walked up the wide steps toward the saloon's batwing doors. In a low gravelly voice he told them,

"Deposit ya guns with the nice lady inside the doors. And no trouble — or I deals with it."

Them three fancy fellers set their heads to noddin' most mightily, and the "Yessirs" flowed freely from them as they crept past the giant and entered the place.

To citified folk, there ain't too many things could be scarier than a gigantic simpleton with a Winchester.

Other men from the train went in too and received the same warning — though some folk completely ignored the saloon, and instead climbed into waiting buggies, or up onto buckboards, to be taken into the town proper.

Billy didn't see anyone he knew, but he kept his head down mostly anyway, and by now there was no one else about, except back on the train platform. Some were loading luggage, others farewelling their friends, and as is always the case around trains, a few were just gawkers with nothing better to do.

And a'course, further back down the tracks, there was a whole bunch of men attending to the loading of beeves from the yards up into the stock cars that had just arrived. Hot dusty work that was, and dangerous besides.

Billy and Morris had a quick discussion, and decided it might be better to hide their revolvers in their saddlebags, rather than risk turning them over inside. They were trying not to get noticed, after all, and men who carried only derringers would not seem much threat to anyone.

And perhaps the lady would not even ask for the baby guns.

The big feller was so far still seated, but by the angle of

his huge head, he was plenty interested in whatever Morris and Billy were doing.

Then he looked hard down there at Billy and spoke to him directly. "Problem, Mister?" When he let that voice out to roam free, it was just the right size for the feller, and it sounded like he had dug it up from deep underground in a coal mine.

Not mellifluous, like Morris's voice — more like malicious, or malevolent, or malignant.

Maybe all three.

I gotta stop readin' that dictionary, it's turnin' me strange.

But Billy weren't about to insult the feller's voice, and rile him up for no reason.

"No problem here, Mister," he said instead, touching the brim of his hat in polite acknowledgement of the man. "Just deciding what to bring inside with us. Can't be too careful in a strange town."

"I'm Tiny Jones," said the giant, as he pushed himself up from his chair. It creaked beneath him as his great bulk threatened to snap the arms of it to matchsticks. Then he stood to full height there and said, "You fellers clearly ain't heard a' me. I keep watch on things here, make sure folks behaves. Ya could leave bags a' gold on them horses, right in full view, with a giant sign pointin' it out — and them bags'd be there for ya, still full up when ya return."

He might be some on the simple side, but he clearly had pride in his work, and Billy had a lot of respect for that.

"Good to know you're on the job," Billy said. "It's my gun I worry for mostly. Heard what you said to those entering, and I'll be honest with you — I don't much like to leave my gun with strangers."

"Well," said Tiny Jones, "no one's forcin' ya. Ya can get on them horses and leave if ya want — or ya can deposit ya guns with the lady. Deposit means ya give 'em to her, but ya get 'em back when ya want. My sis teached me that. And that lady at the door, her name's Betty. She's a *real* nice lady, and she won't hurt yer guns none. But if ya worried, best ya leave yer guns here with ya horses, and I'll watch 'em for ya, no problem."

"Right neighborly of you, Jones" said Billy.

"Call me Tiny," said the feller, leaning heavily on the stair rail as he shuffled and heaved his way down the steps. The rail creaked under the weight of him, just as the huge chair had. Six foot six had been a poor estimate, Billy now saw — Tiny Jones was six-ten at least, maybe better, and that Winchester looked like a toy in his massive right fist as he clomped heavily along through the dust toward them. "Folks don't much hang about out here. Makes me nervy when they do. Ain't here to make trouble are ya?"

"No sir, Tiny," said Billy, holding up his hands so the big man could see they were empty. He stepped around Percy and walked slowly toward the feller, stopped a few feet away from him and said, "Just slow makin' up our minds what to do is all. You lived in the area long?"

Tiny Jones seemed happy to be asked, and he even cracked a smile before he answered. "Just about four years, I come to Council Grove with my family. But then my folks died six month back, and me and my sis come down here."

The smile faded from him as he voiced the sad memory. Then he added, "Ya want a room fer you'n yer son?"

Morris hadn't spoken 'til now, and the whole time so far, he'd looked like he might bust out laughing. But he weren't laughing now, as he left his horse behind and fast-walked toward Billy and the giant. Sure could put the licks in, for such a small feller.

"You listen to me, Fatboy," Morris said, repeatedly pointing a finger at the big man as he came forward. "I ain't his son. I'm—"

"*FATBOY?*"

"Leave it, Morris," said Billy, grabbing his shoulder as he went to go past him. "Man was just tryin' to help." But Morris shrugged Billy off, took two more steps, and confronted Tiny Jones from arm's length. Length a' Morris's arm, not the giant's — those was two different lengths to be sure.

"You's one a' them da-warfs, ain't ya?" Tiny said, leaning back some to look down at Morris. "Couldn't see ya clear, back behind yer horse. My 'pologies, Mister, and no disrespect. I know how it is to be different."

"What would you know?" said Morris, craning his neck to look up at the huge man's face, and stabbing a finger toward it. As for Billy, he was just tryin' not to bust out laughing at the sight of Morris threatenin' a feller four times his own size.

"Look," said Tiny, who was clearly becoming confused. "I ain't got all day, ya two want rooms or not? If ya do, ya takes ya horses straight round back to the livery. If ya don't, ya just gets inside and gets drinkin' and gamblin' and whorin', and stops wastin' my time. I had enough now, y'hear me?"

"We hear you," said Billy, gripping Morris's shoulder. "And we don't need no rooms, thank you anyway, Tiny. Much appreciate your help though. My friend's just hungry, you see, and he gets this way when he ain't eaten."

Feeling a pretty good nudge in his ribs then, Morris said, "He's right, Mister Jones, and I'm sorry about how I spoke. Didn't mean nothin' personal. And thanks muchly for your help, it's appreciated. Listen, I'm Morris, and this ugly feller's called William."

"Fair nuff," Tiny Jones said, shaking each of them by the hand in turn. "I gets that way myself when my belly growls. Grub's inside, back room on the right. Don't eat the stew — damn belly cheater keeps toppin' it up with leftovers he scrapes off the plates when folks leaves. Never empties that pot. Could be a month old, some a' that muck. Made me right sick the one time I et it. My sis tole me not to eat it no more."

"Thanks for the tip," Billy said, as all three began to make their way toward the stairs.

"No problem. Just don't tell the boss I said it — I ain't s'posed to say nothin' friendly, or warn folks off a' the food."

"Say, that's Horace Ray you mean, ain't it?" Morris enquired, twirling his hat on a finger, a trick he had lately been practicing, whenever he didn't have his gun to play with. Always some trick or other, that Morris.

"Sure, that's him alright — but ya best call him Mister Ray if ya meets him," Tiny said. He nodded and laughed like a child at Morris's trick. Then, serious again, he added,

"He gets a mite angry if he thinks folks disrespect him. But he ain't so bad — he give me this job on account a' he's gonna marry my sis. Took us in after our place burned, up by the Grove."

Morris and Billy exchanged a swift glance at the mention of fire.

"I'll be sure to treat your boss respectful," Morris said. "And thanks for the tip. Don't suppose you know if his Pa, Mister John Ray, still lives somewhere nearby?"

"Never met *him*," said Tiny. Then he scowled some and said, "Mister Ray don't much like his Pa mentioned. Once seen him shoot a feller's toes off for that. Best ya don't risk it. Ya know Mister Ray'n his Pa?"

"Not exactly," Morris said as they came to the top of the stairs. "My Pa knew Mister Ray's Pa, I believe. When I said I was comin' this way, he asked me to remember him to John Ray if I run into him. That's all. Don't matter none. You know how them ol' fellers is."

"I reckon I do," Tiny said. "Set in their ways, mostly, and always jawin' on about the good ol' days. Well, it was real nice conversin' awhile. Conversin' means talkin', just so's ya know. Folks usually avoids me, I guess. I'll keep an eye on them horses'n guns for ya. No one'll touch 'em, I promise ya — on my sis's life."

"Much appreciated, Tiny," said Morris. "Real nice meetin' ya, my friend. You're an honorable man." Then he and Billy pushed through the doors, and walked into Horace Ray's lair, to find out whatever they could.

CHAPTER 39
"MY FRIEND'S KINDA SIMPLE..."

Natural enough, Billy had experience of saloons and cathouses — they were always the very best places to find information, every lawman knew that — but mostly, those he had known were smaller and quieter than this one.

They stepped through those red batwing doors and, dumbfounded, stopped right in their tracks. That huge room was a wild whirl of color and music and dancing — like some strange country it felt, and the language folks spoke here was money. Even now, in the middle of the day, there must have been sixty men just in this one front room — and every last mother's son of 'em, seemed ready to spend all he had.

An oil-haired, mustachioed feller played a lively tune on a piano, and three women sang as they danced in a line, up one end on a raised stage. They sure could kick up their feet to the music, them three, and the harder the men in the crowd clapped, the higher their legs seemed to go.

There was other women too, even more scantily dressed than the ones on the stage, and that was pretty dang scanty. If it weren't for their lace and their frills, they wouldn't have had nothin' on at all, 'cept for their shoes, which was pointy as some feller's knives. Those not dancin' were delivering drinks to the tables the men watched the entertainment from.

And as is usual for any saloon, there were tables of men whose main interest was the cards they held tightly in front of them, and the money on the tables between them — although here, the card games were more pushed back to the edges of the room, almost like gambling was an afterthought.

You hardly could blame folks for watchin', them girls sure could dance. Woulda been worth watching even if they didn't have all that bare skin of their legs on display.

"Guns please, Gentlemen," said a friendly voice from beside them. "My name's Betty, and I'll keep your hardware safe while you boys enjoy yourselves. House Rules, you see, as printed here on the sign." She reached up and tapped a colorful tin sign that hung above her counter. Then she added, "Welcome to Horace Ray's, the best entertainment in Kansas."

That woman's smile matched her voice, and she was a pretty one too. Dressed real proper though, not scanty like the others, Billy noticed. And she wore a tall hat, the sort he'd only ever seen on English men before — but she was neither English *or* a man. Billy's attention drifted back to looking for Horace, Jasper and Clem.

"Thanks kindly, Ma'am," Morris replied to the lady,

and he smiled a wide one right back, as good as he'd been given. He held his arms out to his sides and said, "But we ain't heeled, Ma'am, as you can see."

That voice a' Morris's sounded even more *mellifluous* than usual, Billy noticed.

The lady leaned over the counter, looked them both up and down. "Derringers from your boots, please." She still wore the smile, but her head tilted slightly, and her eyebrows was raised a little too.

"You got us, Ma'am," Morris said. He took the tiny silver-handled pistol from his left boot and handed it over. His was tiny, a genuine forty-one caliber, single shot Derringer.

"His too," she said. But Billy didn't seem to hear, his attention still off elsewhere in the room.

"My friend's kinda simple," Morris said, taking his hat off and twirling it on his finger as he smiled his best smile at Betty. With his free hand, he nudged Billy in the ribs and said, "William, give her your lady-pistol."

"Sorry," Billy said, and he reached down, took it out from where it was strapped to his ankle, and handed the tiny brass-bodied gun to the lady. As Deputy U.S. Marshals, they could have walked in there armed to the teeth if they wanted — but for now they preferred to keep their badges a secret.

"Thank you," Betty said, placing Billy's much less fancy derringer under the counter with Morris's before handing Morris a ticket with a number on it. "Enjoy yourselves, boys. Food through there on the right, cards and dancing here in the front room. All waitresses and dancers available for private entertaining upstairs by personal arrangement — please be polite and respectful. Behave yourselves, and you're certain to have a good time."

Morris stopped twirling his hat, leaned on Betty's counter and said, "Sure you don't need to search my britches? I might have somethin' else hidden down there, and I'd hate for you to lose your job over it."

"Oh, I don't think so," she said in a lilting sorta voice. She rested her elbows on the counter and her face on her hands then, so her eyes were just inches from Morris's. Fluttered her eyebrows right at him as she added, "I've completed a *thorough* visual search to see what you're packing — and I'm certain you've *nothing* dangerous in there at all."

Morris let his eyes wander down some to her curves, and said, "Ever been wrong, Ma'am? Surprises are my speciality."

"My eyes are up *here*," she said, putting two fingers under Morris's chin and lifting his face up to where he shoulda been looking. "And just to be clear, I'm not a waitress *or* a dancer. I'm the one woman here who's off limits, so don't waste your time."

Then she waggled those two fingers sideways in front of him, a friendly yet very clear warning.

"Yes, Ma'am," said Morris, laughing heartily as he tossed his head back. "Message well noted. But if ever you change your mind, you be sure and let me know. I got a thing for the sassy ones."

"I'll keep it in mind," she said, and waved him away with a smile.

They walked slowly through the room, taking care not to bump into anyone, and made their way through to the restaurant. Remembering Tiny's warning about the cook, they each ordered a well done steak and two eggs, fried.

"Can't go wrong with that," Morris said.

"Didn't see Horace nowhere," said Billy quietly, after the waitress left to tell the grub-slinger their order. "Not Jasper or his father neither."

"Don't mean they ain't here," Morris said. "This place is huge, I never seen so many doors and staircases leadin' off a' one room." It was true, there were two large staircases that met up above, but even those had doors underneath them, leading to who-knew-quite-where.

When a waitress came by with some coffee, Morris asked where one might find the Town Marshall or the County Sheriff.

"Jasper's usually here somewhere," she said. "He's the Marshal. I could ask him to come out and see you if you like. Although..." She paused then a moment, and a dark look clouded her face. "Is it important? He doesn't like being disturbed by trivial matters, you see? He gets ... well, no matter. Is it really important?"

Right then, a real slickly dressed feller stuck his head out into the dining room, from a door marked *PRIVATE*, and wiggled one finger to call that waitress across.

"Don't bother the Marshal for now, Miss," Morris answered. "Is that a private card game in there, where that feller's beckonin' you from?"

The girl smiled tightly and said, "I'm sorry, I can't really say, Sir." She sure seemed anxious to do that feller's bidding though. Just about tripping over herself to get going. "What goes on in other rooms is private, and I'm not allowed to—"

"It's alright," Morris told her, as he watched that fancy feller grow more impatient. "You better go attend to that feller in black. We'll be just fine here. And thank you, Miss."

They watched the waitress hurry across to the man. He looked angry, she looked afraid. Then she squeezed past him into the room. The fancy feller took a hard look at Morris and Billy before following her and closing the door quietly behind himself. They never even heard the latch click.

CHAPTER 40

SICK AS A BARBER'S CAT

"He was heeled," said Morris, "and *well* too. Fancy rigs, both hands."

"Looked somehow familiar," Billy answered. "Seen him on a paper maybe. Ring any bells?"

Another waitress brought their food right then, and they waited in silence until she left, except for thanking her. The door marked *PRIVATE* opened a little again, but just for a few moments — Billy fancied he saw some straw-colored hair, but he knew he might have imagined it. Whoever had opened it stayed back in the shadows, and they quickly closed the door again. He heard the click of the latch this time though — so he knew it was somebody different.

"I ain't seen him on a poster," said Morris. "But he sure has the look of a hired gun."

"You shouldn't have asked so many questions, Morris." Billy cut into his steak, picked up his first forkful and watched it bleed, drip-drip-drip, onto the plate. *Underdone on the inside.* "We agreed to go slow, play it quiet. We might already have their attention."

"Sorry," Morris answered, screwing up his face at his own undercooked meat. "I ain't done this investigatin' sorta work before. Be better if you took the lead — but more risk you'll be recognized then."

The door opened again, and this time the fancy-dressed hired gun came out through it, and walked straight toward them. He was five-eight, weighed maybe one-fifty — and clearly, all of his strengths lay in the speed and accuracy of a lightning quick right hand. That hand hovered over its gun, and the man himself moved like a cat. But his left hand seemed somehow different — it seemed, under Billy's close scrutiny, to belong to a different sorta man altogether. A talker's hand, not a gunman's. The left gun was, perhaps, just for show. Perhaps.

"You handle it," Billy said real quietly, without even moving his lips. And before Morris's eyes, Billy's features went slack, and his eyes dulled — and there was the simpleton Morris sometimes accused Billy of being.

On arrival at their table, Hired Gun ignored the dwarf completely — as so many did — and instead looked at Billy and said, "You're looking for the Marshal, I hear. Or is it a high stakes card game?" Every word he spoke was clipped and perfect, precise. *Annunciated.* "It seems a strange mix of things to be seeking, a Marshal and a big money card game. Perhaps we should speak in private." When Billy didn't answer, and kept staring at his food, the gunman looked down at it too. Then he frowned and shook his head. "What is this you're eating? Raw meat?"

"It's meant to be well done," said Morris. "I was just thinkin' of taking it out to the kitchen and shoving it—"

The man interrupted Morris before he could finish. "Leave it here. We'll get you some real food. We've the best of everything in the back room. Come."

He was unsmiling, unfriendly, and unused to being disobeyed.

With a precise movement of his left hand he indicated which direction they should walk in. Morris stood up, Billy didn't. Instead, he got rid of the piece of underdone meat by wiping his fork on the tablecloth. Then he stabbed a whole fried egg with the fork, and shoveled it into his gob. Sat looking off to the distance after that, his chewing overly noisy, without even closing his mouth.

Wasn't like Billy at all.

"What*ever* is wrong with your friend?" There was mostly menace in the gunfighter's tone, but also a hint of flusteration.

"He's a bit simple," said Morris, real quiet-like, as if confiding a secret. Then louder, he added, "He'll come along once he eats his eggs. Real fond of eggs he is, that's all. Best just to wait, and not rile him. I've seen him eat up to sixteen at a sitting. It's how he grew so big and ugly, I'd wager. Sometimes I can't even get him to eat up his steak, he likes eggs so much."

In truth a'course, Billy was *thinking*. He was buying some time to get things all straight in his head. If, to do so, he had to act like a gump with a fondness for eggs, then that was just how he'd act. He was kinda glad there was only four eggs on the table though, not sixteen.

Feller's armed and dangerous. Educated, but surely no lawman. Working for Horace, most likely — but why? Here in the restaurant, we're more or less safe. Through that door in private...

Billy put the second egg in his pie-hole, looked wide-eyed up at the feller as he noisily chewed. The man wore expensive clothes, soft black linen tailored to fit him, and his fingernails were clean. He moved — and spoke — in a most precise manner.

"William," said Morris in a kind voice. "Shall we go now, talk to this nice feller in that special room there? They might have more eggs."

"Got eggs," said Billy, with half a slack-jawed smile. And he reached across to Morris's plate, picked up one of *his* eggs with his fork, popped it right into his mouth, and commenced to glare at Mister Hired Gun with all the wide-eyed defiance he could muster. Wasn't even chewing now, only glaring.

"Sorry 'bout this," Morris said. "He was gettin' the grumbles up back on the train, so I promised him eggs, y'see? He's usually better behaved."

"Are you a gambler, Sir?" Hired Gun said to Morris.

Billy kept chewing and thinking.

"Yessir," said Morris. "Was hoping to play a little poker. But to tell you the truth, Friend — and please, don't take this personal — I'm less keen now I see some a' the players is heeled, and I ain't afforded the same opportunity. Not my kind of odds, so I think I might pass."

"Last I heard," said Hired Gun with a small laugh, "those little derringers you and your big strong friend carry are not classed as real guns anyway. Still, if that's what you need to feel confident to gamble, you can have them right back." He shook his head, laughed a proud one and said, "Derringers!"

Billy shoved in the final egg, and chewed it a second or two with his mouth still wide open. He smiled up at the feller then — and keeping his stare as vacant as he could manage, and as if he agreed with the sentiment that derringers were indeed funny, Billy half-laughed and half-spat the word — "Derringer."

The pieces of half-chewed up egg flew from his mouth, all over the gunman's pristine linen britches and highly polished black boots.

"Son-of-a..." That feller sure had stopped laughing right then. "I'll have your guns brought," he said, barely able to control his seething anger. His right hand hovered over his own gun, but he turned toward a waitress and crooked a finger of his left hand.

She made her way there double quick, and the gunman spoke to her quietly. He used the short time she was gone to clean some of the egg off his clothes with his kerchief — though he never so much as dabbed at his boots with it.

Looks sick as a barber's cat at the thought of touching anything dirty, Billy noticed.

Then the girl was back, and offering the guns to the gunfighter — but he scowled and waved her away, motioned toward Morris instead. That over-proud gunfighter feller never even looked at the guns, making it clear that such trifles were beneath him — if he had done, he might have thought differently, Billy's being a four shot revolver. It was only the hammer that revolved, but the effect of it was the same — four shots that could be fired quickly, and kill at close enough range.

With a murmur of thanks, Morris took both the tiny pistols, checked they were still loaded, and put them into his pockets.

But even now, as Morris took a step toward the PRIVATE room, Billy stayed stubbornly seated, didn't even acknowledge the others.

That waitress got a real worried look on her face then, and put them shapely bare legs of hers to good use. *Mighta been a long-lost cousin to the Brimstones, way she got them legs pumping* — and in no time flat she'd put distance between herself and whatever might unfold here.

"Let's go," came the low growl. Hired Gun — or *Barber's Cat*, as Billy now thought of him — grabbed two good handfuls of Billy's collar and half-dragged him up onto his feet. Billy more or less let him do it, though he sure didn't help none — and even looked up at him like he was scared. Well, near to scared as he could manage anyway. Billy knew what fear was, a'course — it was a good and necessary thing. Fear had kept him alive, warned him when not to take foolish risks.

Once the young Billy had lost the recklessness of wishing his life would end, he had learned all about fear — and Preacher Rob had taught him to respect it, and learn to let it help him. No, it was not fear that Billy was unused to — but rather the *showing* of it. He had become so adept at hiding it from others, he now found it hard to act out.

And while Billy had been in far worse situations, and

was not afeared now at all, he at least had the sense to be wary.

He might have been playing the gump, but Billy had watched the Barber's Cat feller closely the whole time, and noticed things others wouldn't. He had no doubt the man's right hand was fast as chain lightning — but just as surely, the left hand had some sort of weakness. Billy had felt it when the man gripped his collar and dragged him to his feet.

He had shaken the wrist out right after as well, and winced half a moment as he did so, before pretending nothing was wrong.

Some sort of nerve disorder perhaps.

Whatever the cause, the weakness was there. And it wasn't his only one — that gunfighter feller was prideful. Billy had no doubt that his simpleton act was all that had let him get away with what he'd just done. And ol' Barber's Cat did not like it at all, having to give Billy some leeway on account of his being simple — it had rattled him. He was a man unused to being rattled.

If push came to shove, knowing how to rattle a man might well make the difference in who dies, who lives, and who walks away still in one piece.

As they approached the door marked PRIVATE, Billy and Morris seemed to be at a great disadvantage — yet Billy actually saw things quite different to that. He took a deep breath and stepped through the door, knowing the sharpness of his wits, and Morris's too, would see them through anything that might happen.

At least, that's how he *chose* to see it.

Whatever was there, they would deal with.

As he walked through the door behind Morris, his first thought was that the doorway — and the walls and even the door — were at least a foot thick. *Soundproof.*

And his second thought was that the Strawheads had been eating far too much, and doing far too little.

The Strawhead on the left, with the dark-haired woman behind him, just sat there dull-eyed as ever, and watched Billy and Morris enter from under his hat. But the one on the right nodded at them and — not just proudly but vainly — said, "Boys. I'm Horace Ray ... owner of this fine establishment, and everything else that matters round here. What can I do for you today?"

CHAPTER 41
THE CHUCKLEHEAD ACT

It was a huge room, table in the middle, a couple of huge matching chiffoniers against the side walls. Lots of room to move if you had to. Billy wished he had his derringer, but knowing Morris had two was a comfort — and at least this way he could focus on positioning his strong supple body to take any action he had to.

That huge polished fancy-carved thing of mahogany in the dead center of the room was a dang site bigger and fancier than any card table — and there wasn't no cards on it neither. Not much of anything on it, just expensive whiskey and glasses mostly, and a few crumbs the waitress had missed when she'd taken their plates.

On a shelf of one of the chiffoniers was the fanciest cellarette anyone ever saw. Wasn't just the polished mahogany, it had two foxes carved on it as well.

Whole place smelled like money, and not honest money neither. Billy had been such places before, and had a theory along the lines of *fancier the place, more corrupt the feller.*

Wasn't always true, but it mostly seemed to work out that way.

It occurred to Billy that them two carved foxes might as well have had straw-colored fur painted on 'em.

The Strawheads themselves sat facing the door, and there was one other feller with his back to it, who faced Jasper and Horace. That feller was big in all the wrong places — he craned his neck best he could to look round at them, then shifted sideways in his seat so as to half face everyone present. In addition, two beautiful women, both standing, somewhat well dressed. Not waitresses — these were *kept* women, and the one behind Jasper wore the unmistakeable remains of a recent black eye.

Walls were covered with planks, but underneath that was brick — Billy had noticed that detail as he went through the doorway, for a small unfinished part there showed the inner construction. Clearly, the planks were not decorative, but there to catch any bullets fired within the room.

No chance of a ricochet here — this was a room for meetings, and for killings if the meeting went bad.

Another thing strange — no rifles in the room whatsoever, not even up on the wall.

There was a thick grate up near the ceiling for air, but no windows at all. And another door at the back — just as heavy as the front one. Massive hinges on both doors a'course, four sets on each. Pad bolts on the doors an inch thick, and rammed home into the heaviest door frames anyone ever saw.

Seen banks less heavily fortified.

Billy stood half behind Morris, while behind him, Barber's Cat closed the big heavy door without barely making a sound, then locked it with the big heavy pad bolt.

Morris did the talking again, while Billy went on with his chucklehead act — vacant look on his slackjawed face, scratching at his nose with one finger, looking up at the ceiling a bit, then down at his feet.

He made sure not to look Horrie in the eye, believing that would give up the game for sure.

It weren't easy for Billy to do that. This was his brother in front of him — and after all these long years, his strongest urge was to greet him as family, shake his hand and share stories. And most of all, ask after his Pa.

That was what the seventeen-year-old Billy Ray woulda done — but that green youngster was long gone. And Deputy William Fyre was here to investigate suspects. Until proven otherwise, Horace Ray was one of them, and wouldn't get no special treatment.

He three-parts expected Horrie to suddenly recognize him anyway, and the whole thing turn into a happy family reunion. But Horrie's eyes passed over him as if he was a steer, just one of many, then went back to Morris, who was speaking.

In answer to Horrie's question about what they wanted, Morris stood across the table from him and said, "My friend and me's just passing through, and thought we might find some friendly folk amenable to playin' some cards."

"Well ain't you just somethin'," said Horace, his voice filled with amused disrespect. "Three foot nothin' and too good for the regular folk out there in the dance hall."

"Four foot five," Morris said, wearing the slightest of smiles as his eyes bored into Horace. "But if you think that gives me an unfair advantage at cards — or you're afraid of losin' your women to me — then I'll take my money elsewhere, and wait for your lovely ladies to follow."

Say one thing for Morris — he had an innate ability to cut right at what hurt folks the most. And his own smile grew, as quick as Horace's left him.

Now, Horace Ray wasn't a complete fool. But his strong suit had always been planning and conniving, not witty banter. Never did seem to know when he'd got himself into a battle of wits with a better armed man.

Yessir, Horace shoulda quit while he was behind.

But the fool tried again. He looked at Jasper, then Barber's Cat, then the other man at the table — almost the size of Tiny Jones that feller, but six inches shorter and a lot better dressed — then Horace said, "He's a funny little one, ain't he? Thinks he can take our women *and* our money. Now why would our women chase you, *little* man?"

The women were both standing half-behind the Strawheads now, and waited expectantly for the answer. One looked a little amused, but the other seemed almost unhinged.

Morris took his time — let his gaze roam over the body of Jasper's woman, then Horace's. Jasper's had dark brown hair, but Horace's lady's hair was bright red — same shade as Tiny Jones's beard — she was tall, not so much as her brother, but nudging six foot. Pretty though, *real* pretty, and slender, not bulky like Tiny. Face of an angel, with a cute button nose, and sprinkles of freckles all over. Didn't look much more clever than her brother — but the clueless innocence of her smile had a beauty of its own.

Morris was making it clear that he was enjoying the sight of both women.

"I don't like *him* lookin' at *my* property that way," said Jasper. He had never been very tall, but he looked shorter now than he used to, having gone to fat worse than his father, and his bulging waistcoat was food-stained.

Strawhead's a disgrace to the badge.

"I don't like it none either," said Horace. He freed an arm, wrapped it around the redhead, and made a great show of slapping her behind. Then in a mocking voice, he said, "But what's such a teensy feller gonna do, Jasper? We should feel sorry for him. What could *he* possible give our women that we don't?"

Morris took his time, smiled at each woman in turn, then, staring into the eyes of the redheaded girl, said, "Respect for one — good looks for another. Are those *faces* on your men, ladies? Or did someone drop two pies in a cowchip, scrape it all up, and smear it on the front a' their heads?"

The redhaired girl had to bite her tongue not to laugh, and it didn't help none when Morris wiggled his eyebrows at her.

"Enough now," Horace growled as he jumped to his feet and looked down at Morris. "Enough a' this banter'n'bull. What is it you *really* want here? Why was you askin' the whereabouts a' the Marshal?"

He might have been the shorter in stature, but Morris towered over Horace when it came to plain old levelheaded cleverness. "Shouldn't the Marshal be the one asking that? Or can't he think for himself?"

"That's true," said Jasper now. "As Marshal of Cottonw—"

"Oh, shut yer damn pie-hole," growled Horace. "And you, Shorty, get talkin', hurried-like. Gimme one good reason why I shouldn't have my man Patterson here fill you with lead, and feed you to the pigs."

"But..." the big overfed stranger started to say, then sunk down in his chair best he could.

Patterson, Billy thought. *Barber's Cat goes by Patterson.* He racked his brain a moment, but it still didn't ring any bells.

Morris's quick banter had dazzled Horace so good, the Strawhead didn't have time to think straight. "Well," Morris said then, "for one thing, I've actually come here to help both you *and* the Marshal."

Two funny things about dwarfs: first thing, most women adore them, as long as they don't treat 'em rotten; second thing, most men underestimate dwarfs, think of 'em as odd-looking children or something, and that was always a fool thing to do around Morris. Not one feller in the room — besides Billy — had noticed that Morris's hands were in his waistcoat's oversized pockets, and had been for awhile now.

To them, he was just a funny little feller who stood a bit strangely.

Horace sorta scoffed at the suggestion Morris could help them. "Help *us*? Only help you'll be is pig food, little man." Then his gaze darted to Billy, and he said, "Patterson, shoot the big gump first if he moves. Now, Da-warf — what's yer other good reason I should listen to you?"

"Well," said Morris in his smooth, mellifluous tone, "I got derringers in both pockets, one pointed at you, and one at the Marshal."

Horace roared with laughter at that, and hammered the table a good one with his fist, the force of it knocking over his glass. Whiskey ran off onto the floor as he said, "Betty's the one woman here who refuses to bed the men. Only reason I keep her around is there ain't a man alive can get a gun past her. So that's *two* swacking great lies for such a small man."

"Ah, yes, Boss," said Barber's Cat. He was standing beside Billy now, and his hand hovered over his gun, but he looked none too certain. "I was, ah—"

"What is it, Patterson, dammit?"

"He ... that is, they ... I mean—"

"Spit it out ya damn fool," cried Horace.

Patterson's right hand still hovered, but his left hand was doing almost as much talking as his mouth was, way he waved it about everywhere. "You said to bring them in here whatever way I had to. I couldn't very well drag a dwarf and a simpleton through the restaurant in front of the patrons, now could I?"

"So?"

"So I gave them back their guns, Boss, in order that they would come quietly. They felt insecure, and fair enough too, what they are. Having their guns back was the only way they would agree to come in here. Now don't go losing your temper, Boss, they can't kill us all, and are not at all likely to try."

"Damn fool," Horace growled, shaking his head then taking a better look at the pockets of Morris's waistcoat.

It was Morris who spoke next, and his eyes danced with amusement the whole time he did so. "You see, Patterson, Mister Ray here's a smart man. He knows it makes no difference to *him,* whether I can kill you *all* or not. All that matters to him is ... *he's first.*" Morris laughed before adding, "Correct, Mister Ray?"

"So what is this?" said Horace, holding his hands up in front of him. "A robbery? What?"

"No, not that at all," Morris told him, slowly taking his right hand out of his pocket so they could see that he did indeed have a tiny four-shot Sharps pointed at Horace. "I told you, we've come to help you and Marshal Jenkins here."

"Maybe stop pointing that gun at me," said Horace, "and I might start to believe you."

Billy didn't remember his brother as being so ... smarmy ... not to mention useless, and afraid. As a child, he had looked up to Horrie, the way younger brothers do, without any good reason required. There was something strange in his feeling it — it was like one more part of his old life had been smashed to pieces, and he felt disappointed. Not just in Horace, but in himself. And with a sharp pain, the thought of Cass came to his mind, and he chased all his feelings away.

"Put the gun down, hmmm," Morris said. "Nope. Won't be doing that. Not yet anyway. First, this Patterson behind me hands his guns — backward — to my big simple friend here. If I count to three and he hasn't, I reckon that won't tickle me — but'll tickle my fingers."

"Do it," said Horace.

"Guns first, knives after," said Morris.

Both Jasper and the big overweight stranger had kept their hands on the table since the thing began, and did so still now, as Barber's Cat Patterson handed his guns to Billy then backed away a couple of steps. Billy turned one gun on him and the other on the big round feller.

Given Patterson's earlier reaction about the derringers, Billy knew he wouldn't have one, as a matter of pride. Prideful, he was, that's for sure. Didn't carry a knife either. Man with hands so soft, it was no surprise. He was a specialist.

Morris then had Jasper take out his guns, real slow — he wore two as well, real nice Colts with fancy engraving on their silver handles — and place them on the table, at the end of his reach. His knife too — now *that* was a deadly affair, eight inch blade he unsheathed from a special scabbard built into his boot.

And of course, Horace had one to match, so out it came next.

Strawheads always did do everything together.

All this time, the women hadn't moved, hadn't spoken. The redhead wore a slight smile — seemed to Billy to be mighty impressed by Morris, she did. But that other woman, she only stood behind Jasper, unsmiling, unmoving, like a shell almost, not a whole person.

Finally, Morris told the big round feller to take out his guns real slow, and put down on the table.

"I've only a Philadelphia Deringer myself," he said. He was an Englishman, as it turned out. He had come here on business, got caught up in all this, and was clearly unhappy about it — but not so unhappy as to take a risk by complaining.

He went to place the Deringer on the table, but Morris realized it would be within easy reach of either Jasper or the Englishman himself. So to Jasper's sad woman, Morris said, "You, pretty lady, come round here please, pick it up and take it over to that chiffonier in the corner. Then come back here for the others."

She looked like a deer with a shotgun pointed at it. She stared at Morris a moment, then at Jasper, then finally at Horace. Then, shaking like the final leaf of Fall before it departs life forever, she walked around the table and stood beside the big round feller. She began extending her hand toward his to accept the gun, but stopped mid-reach, turned toward Morris and smiled, her sad eyes melting into his somehow. He nodded to her, just a small one. Then that poor sad-eyed girl turned away from him, reached out for that tiny, pearl-handled, single-shot Deringer — pointed it at Horace, and fired.

CHAPTER 42

A SAD DEATH

It was almost like Horace expected it.

He might have been carrying fifty unnecessary pounds, but he sure lit a shuck when he had to. He took off leftways and backways and downways so fast, that well aimed piece of lead, fired from four feet away, went through the side of his right upper arm instead of his body.

It was a hellabaloo and a conflusteration and a shindy all rolled into one, what happened next. A real bag a' nails, that's what it was.

When the girl aimed the gun, Horace jumped for his life, while the red-haired girl screamed and jumped in the other direction. And Billy cried, "Horrie, look out!"

Gun went off, and in the confusion, Jasper speared forward and grabbed one of his own guns.

It all being so unexpected, Billy and Morris had no idea which way to move, who to cover, or even which way to turn — and in that twinkling of uncertainty, Jasper found the moment he needed.

Two seconds after getting off her own shot, that poor sad-eyed woman had four holes blown in her body — two in her chest and two out her back — as Jasper Jenkins, the very man who should have *protected* her, fired his silver-handled Colt twice. The impact jerked her body sideways, almost knocking Morris off his feet. Billy launched himself forward at Jasper, knocking him to the floor on the other side of the table. The gun flew loose from his hand, clattered across the boards, and came to rest with a clunk against the great heavy rear door.

The shot woman fell forward, face first on the table, and Morris cried, *"Nobody move,"* and covered them all with his guns.

As Jasper tried to get up, Billy's fist crashed into his jaw, the blow so mighty it sent the Strawhead's eyes rolling back in his head, and he slid away into dreamland. Ol' Barber's Cat Patterson froze where he was, his left hand up in front of his face, his right gripping an empty holster, and too far from the action to actually do anything, as he clearly spoke the word, "Unarmed."

And that big round feller, the back of his hands was on the table in front of him, and the palms of his hands had his face in 'em, and he kept saying, "No-no-no-no," as if he could change what had happened, if he just said that word enough times.

As for Horace, he had stayed down once he got to the floor, and now it seemed over he carefully looked up, gripped his shot arm, and said, "Damn her eyes! I told you that woman was loco. Is she dead?"

Things have a way of escalating fast when the

unexpected happens in the West — it had been only six seconds since she fired the gun.

Morris kept his derringers pointed, one right at Horace, the other on Patterson. The redheaded woman stopped screaming, threw herself down in a chair, and sobbed into the palms of her hands.

Billy sprang to his feet and went to the shot woman then. She was sprawled across the table, limbs all askew and dark brown hair every which way. Her right cheek and ear laid flat against the desktop, as she coughed up bright blood and bile on the polished mahogany.

"They murd—" was all she got out, before the coughing took her again.

"Don't try to speak," said Billy, his gump act forgotten. Then he looked at his brother, nodded toward the chiffonier behind him and said, "Water, Horrie. Bring me that water."

"Try anything you're a dead man," Morris said, the four barrels of the tiny Sharps pointed menacingly at Horace Ray's chest.

"Fire," the woman somehow gasped from the midst of her dying. "They—"

"Murderous cow," growled Horace as loud as he could, drowning the voice of the dying woman out.

"Shut your mouth, Horace," said Billy. "One more word, shoot him," he told Morris, then leaned down close to the dying woman and said, "It's alright, Ma'am, we know. Shhhh. I'm a Deputy U.S. Marshal, and I solemnly promise you, Ma'am — the guilty men *will* pay in full for their crimes."

That poor shot-up woman looked into Billy's eyes then, and somehow she managed a tiny hint of a smile — and with a *thank-you* on her lips, she drifted away, left her pain all behind her.

Billy gently closed the dead woman's eyelids, turned to look at Horace — he had never made a move toward bringing the water — and slowly shook his head.

"Best retrieve that Colt," said Morris, nodding toward the back door.

Billy sighed the deep sigh of a man who's seen too many innocents die. Then he walked across, picked the gun up, held it in his hand and studied it a moment.

Then he turned toward his brother, pointed the Colt at him and said, "Why, Horrie?"

"Hey," said Horace Ray as his eyes went wider'n dinner plates, and he put both his hands up in front of him. "You ain't no gump — you're ... you're ... *Billy? Billy Ray?* Billy, is that really you?"

Well, that sure grabbed everyone's attention. Even the *"no-no-no-no"* feller quit his mumblings, went quiet as a mouse in a church around midnight, and looked up at Horace, then Billy.

"Hello, brother," Billy said. But his sharp brain was already partway adding things together, and the word *brother* sure left a sour taste in his mouth. "You got some explainin' to do." And he kept the gun pointed.

"You look so different," Horace said. "Double sized, and so old-lookin' now. But I'd a'knowed that voice anywhere! You saved my life, Billy. If you hadn't cried out your warning, that crazy cow woulda killed me. I'm shot through the arm as it is, but I think it's missed bone." He clamped his left hand back over it, but blood dripped free through the shirt now, and down to the floor.

Jasper began then to stir, looked wild-eyed round the room, then propped himself up against the wall without trying to stand.

"Don't move, and keep your mouth shut," said Morris, pointing the little Sharps at Jasper now instead. There were still three loaded revolvers on the table, and he wasn't about to take chances.

Billy had Barber's Cat Patterson walk over behind the table, and the big round feller as well, so he and Morris could have 'em all in their sight all at once. Made them all stand, spread out across the back wall — all except for the lady. She was allowed to sit. She'd sure stopped her flirting with Morris now — poor girl wore a dark, broken look on her pale freckled face. Her hands shook so much you could hear her fingernails chatter against her teeth, as she tried to chew them.

Then Morris said, "We two are Deputy Marshals, in the employ of Marshal Terence Betts of the United States Marshals Service. He put his left hand gun in his pocket and pulled out his badge and showed it, before throwing it onto the table. "We're here to investigate corruption and cover-ups by the local Marshals and Sheriffs."

Jasper looked like he wished the floor would open right up and swallow him whole. He blinked hard a few times then said, "Horrie? What the blazes is goin' on? Am I dead or what's happened? That big gump feller sounds just like Billy."

"Shut up, Jasper," said Horace. "You got knocked cold in the dustup after that crazy cow a' yours shot me. Quiet down now 'til your wits comes back." Then he turned to Billy and said, "Billy, I cain't hardly believe it's you. It's so good to see you."

"Is it?" Billy tilted his head and looked at his brother sorta sideways. "Is it *really*?"

"Sure it is, Billy. Oh, we gotta get you and Pa together, Billy. He'll be as happy as a dog with two—"

"Where is he? And why'd that woman shoot at you, Horace? You got serious questions to answer."

"Pa's up in Council Grove now," said Horace, wincing a moment from the pain in his arm. "Went down to Texas for awhile, but come back here a few months ago and settled in the Grove. Still got Rosie with him."

Billy couldn't tell if his brother was lying or not. He leaned toward it being a lie, but the maps were just old enough it was possibly true. He stared at his brother's eyes, intent on reading whatever lies they might tell. "Why'd that woman shoot you, Horace?"

"Lost her marbles, I'd reckon. Truth is, the poor thing knew somethin' was up, and it ain't no surprise with what happened. See, her husband died drunk in a fire. She weren't there at the time, and she always figured somethin' about it not right. Sent her plumb loco, it did — always on about it in poor Jasper's ear."

"It's true," Jasper said. "Always on about it. Always, just like Horrie says."

"Calm down, Jasper, and relax, while I explain," Horace said. "Thing is, Billy, we thought nothin' of it at first. But after awhile we put things together — and sure 'nuff, her suspicions was founded."

Billy's eyes never left Horace's, whose own eyes never wavered, never flickered, never looked away once.

"Explain that all clear now, and no obfuscations," Billy said.

"Obsca-*what*-ay-shuns?" said Horace, shaking his head as if to clear it. "I'll tell you it straight as I can, Billy, but it ain't so simple. When we looked back at all that went on — me and Jasper I mean — we seen things wasn't right, not at all. First the fires, well, fires happens sometimes."

"Happens sometimes," said Jasper.

Horace scowled at him and went on. "But then Sheriff Pratt got killed, and Jasper's Pa put his hand up for the job right away, and it all got pushed through so quick — hell, Jasper didn't wanna be Marshal here, but his Pa made him do it."

Billy took a hard look at Jasper. "That true, Jasper?"

"Yessir, Billy," he said. Then he rubbed at his jaw some, and said, "You sure growed up big and strong, Billy. Hit pretty hard too, I can vouch for."

Horace jumped back in quick, saying, "Every time Jasper tries to do any Marshal stuff, his Pa tells him to back off, and let him handle it himself. Clem writes all the reports himself, then has Jasper copy and sign 'em. That's why Jasper's here most a' the time, he ain't really allowed to do nothin' anyway. Clem's up to all sorts, Billy — you better be careful when you go there, he's got some bad deputies too. Billy, I'm losin' a lot a' blood here."

"It ain't much blood, Horrie," said Billy. "You'll live, unlike that poor girl."

"Billy, here's the truth," Horace said then. "Patterson here's a top gunman. We guessed awhile back what Clem was up to, but truth was, we didn't much care — then he started to lean on me here. Demanded a share in the takings. I'd sold all my cattle, put every penny into this place. Borrowed some too, just to open. I only been open four months, Billy, and need to make my money back — but Clem and his deputies are a bad threat to all that. Greedy, you see? So I hired me a top gunfighter for protection — and to maybe do something about all this wrongdoin' too."

It was Morris who spoke. "That true, Patterson? If that's even your real name."

"All true," the Barber's Cat said. For a man with no gun, he sure wore a confident smile. "And *Patterson...*" — he paused then, as if to enjoy the sound of the word — "...is all the name I've ever needed. I'm surprised you've not heard of me — I've killed seven men since the war ended. Then again, they were all in fair fights, where the other drew on me first." His smile grew then, and his narrow eyes twinkled.

Prideful.

CHAPTER 43
THIS PRIDEFUL MAN MEANS TO KILL ME

Yessir, that Patterson feller was prideful — but Deputy Billy Fyre was *not*. He was a man who knew the value of other's opinions, and it was not beneath him to ask for them.

"Hmmm," Billy mused as he rubbed at the new-grown fur on his chin. "Thoughts, Morris?"

"Nice story. But I reckon none a' that explains just *why* that poor girl shot Horace." Morris saw the slightly surprised look that came over Horace, and added, "I'm only short, Strawhead — not stupid."

"Well, that's just it," Horace said, scowling at the dwarf before turning his attention back on Billy. "I ain't stupid neither — but she was. About a week ago we told the crazy cow she was half-right all along. Told her it was Clem and his Deputies — one a' them fellers ended up with her husband's ranch, y'know, it's down between here and Seth Hays' place. Train's gonna run right through it, tracks are already laid."

Billy studied his brother closely and said, "Hays' top man was murdered too."

But Horace didn't miss a beat. "Exactly," he said, "though Clem always insisted the poor man done for himself. I reckon it's all over graze though — there's new fellers come in now, thousands a' cattle all over, too much competition. That's why I got outta cattle and opened this place instead."

"Doesn't hurt, it being right where the trains get loaded," said Morris.

Horace ignored him and went on. "So crazy Emilie here, she mixed it all up, what was said. Loco she was. Kept blamin' *me* for it somehow, and goin' on and on all the time. Seemed to think it was all to do with the railroad — and because my place is where they put the station, it musta been me at fault. We shoulda sent her off to one a' them lunatic asylums right off — she might still be alive if we did."

Questioning Jasper didn't get things no further toward the truth either. Fact was, the thirty-year-old Jasper was no different to the twenty-three-year-old Jasper that Billy had last known — no different to the sixteen-year-old he'd been either, when it came to it. Seemed like no amounts of seven years was ever gonna change him for the better — just like always, he never said an original word, and only backed up whatever Horace had said the minute before.

Like some sorta talking parrot he is. Or maybe a sheep, way he's always followed Horrie around. BAAAAA!!!

The big round feller had nothing much to say about anything at all. Claimed only to be drumming up sales for a new type of barbed fence, and to have no knowledge about any of what was discussed. His story checked out. Had tiny samples of two different fence-rails in his suitcase right there beneath the table. Took 'em out and showed 'em off when asked, and went right into his sales pitch, like as if Billy or Morris might be interested. Nasty spikes in 'em too. Woulda tore the Barber's Cat's soft hands to shreds had he touched one.

As for Tiny Jones's pretty red-haired sister, she was clearly too shocked to speak sense. Bundle a' nerves, was poor Susie. She'd stopped crying mostly, but was in no shape to answer questions. Her pretty eyes had been half-vacant and half-smiling before — but now they just darted about in terror whenever anyone spoke to her. They quickly decided to just let her be.

Better speak to her once she's calmed down though.

"So you survived the war after all," Horace said to Billy, in a mocking sort of tone. "Finally learned to shoot straight, I expect?"

He's fishing. Men don't fish without a good reason.

Billy managed to look a little embarrassed. "War ain't about shooting straight, Horrie," he said. "It's more about staying safe from harm as much as you can."

"So you spent your time running and hiding," said Horace, making his disrespect clear as he shot a glance at Patterson.

"Maybe you would have too," said Billy. "I'm alive, ain't I? And now I have a good job, investigating wrongdoing and writing reports for the Marshal. Just about what Pa always wanted for me, I guess."

In the end, Horace grew weak from the blood loss — so he *reckoned*. He pleaded to be allowed to sit, and to have a doctor brought in to attend to his arm. It was only his left arm anyway. He'd lost blood alright, though not nearly enough to make a man faint — Billy knew plenty about that.

Horace hadn't lost but half a pint. Wasn't even breathing funny or gone the slightest bit pale.

Billy had once seen Preacher Rob lose a quart of blood without even keeling over. Ol' Rob's skin had gone white as the moon, and his breath shortened up some as well — but he'd stayed stood up on his hind legs and held a gun on an outlaw long enough for Billy to arrive and take over.

No, Horace's weakness was an act, and not even a partway convincing one.

Still, the wound would have to be treated, and Billy wanted a doctor to see to Susie anyway — so he sent the big round feller to unlock the door and ask one of the waitresses to fetch in a doctor.

Turned out there was one in the saloon — or rather, he was upstairs, enjoying the company of a lady. He came down with his doctorin' bag, cleaned and bound up Horace's wound — the big Nancy just about squealed the whole time, Billy noted, and kept pulling his arm away and breathing in sharp gasps like it really hurt.

Squirrel piss. Or maybe another act. Likely both.

Eventually, Doc Bennett said, "Mister Ray needs bedrest, and must not move this arm before tomorrow." He'd bound it up good in a sling, tied up tight to Horrie's body.

Then the Doc spoke quietly to Susie Jones a few moments, before turning to Billy, twirling both sides of his impressive mustache, and saying, "She's had a terrible shock, Sir, a most terrible shock indeed. More than a woman can cope with, all this. I'll give her a sedative and send her to bed. A *separate* bed to her husband, mind. They *both* need complete rest. I'm strict on that point, and won't be argued with on it."

Billy was surprised when the doc said *husband*. "Are you married to her, Horrie?" he asked.

"Course not," he said with a smug smile. "Like to keep my options open. I tend to run the fillies ragged inside of a year, mostly."

"Runs the fillies ragged," laughed Jasper. "Rides 'em hard, Horrie does!"

He don't seem too upset, for a feller who just killed a woman he supposedly cared for.

Billy and Morris had to decide what to do, and quick. If Horace was lying about Sheriff Clem Jenkins, he'd given no indication of it.

On the other hand, Jasper had shot his own common-law wife to death, right in front of witnesses — *after* she'd already emptied the Derringer. Coulda been to stop her from talking.

Still, people don't always think straight under duress. And Jasper always was about as slow as a slug on a salt lick.

In the end, Billy and Morris agreed they would travel straight to Council Grove to interview Sheriff Clem Jenkins — taking Jasper and Patterson along with them for backup.

This last part was the bit they were least certain of, but Jasper seemed absolutely convinced of his father's guilt in the matter — and genuinely glad of Billy and Morris's help. He didn't admit he was afraid of facing his father alone, but that was the sense Billy got of it. As for Patterson, he was a hired gun — his eyes gleamed, and his proud head went higher, when Horace asked him to assist.

"My pleasure, Boss," he said. "It's time Clem and his two-bit gunfighters got their comeuppance."

And so, for better or worse, Horace and Susie were taken by the doctor to their rooms, while Jasper and Patterson went off to saddle their horses for the trip to the Grove.

But even as Billy walked out the front to his horses, he could not help feeling a great nagging doubt — there was something he was missing, he was certain.

But I guess we'll see some signs soon, he decided.

He took a deep breath, strapped on his gunbelt, took out his Henry from where it was hidden and placed it in its scabbard.

And Deputy William Fyre was once again ready to face things front on.

It was near twenty minutes before Jasper and Patterson came out the front, ready to go. In that time, Billy and Morris prepared themselves. Morris ate some jerky and an apple, but Billy took only an apple, being mostly full up with eggs. They filled each other in on their thoughts and suspicions, and made *just-in-case* plans for the trip.

They had told Tiny Jones what happened inside, and the huge simple man had been pretty upset — but relieved to hear his sister was okay. "Emilie was sad a long time," he said. "Might be she's more happy now." Then he had gotten Betty to ask someone else to take over his job, and gone off to visit Susie. "Thank you, friends," he said before leaving. "I'll take good care a' yer pack horses 'til ya gets back."

They'd decided to travel light to Council Grove. It'd be faster and easier, and the benefits outweighed the drawbacks. There was always rooms available up in the Grove, although they weren't cheap.

"I don't trust our companions as far as I can throw 'em," said Morris. "And me bein' a dwarf, that ain't far at all."

Billy told Morris about Patterson's weak left hand, and also why he thought of him as the Barber's Cat. "Looked like he was gonna spill his own breakfast when I spat half-chewed-up egg all on him."

"I noticed that too," said Morris, "though not the weak hand. He might be a problem if he wants to be — he has the look — but that Jasper ain't much, I shouldn't reckon."

"Used to be a fair shot with a rifle," Billy said. "But without Horrie nearby to pull his strings, he'll be like a puppet with no one to work it. Don't know if I believe their story though."

"Somethin' didn't ring true? I'm inclined that way myself."

Billy fed the remaining half of his apple to Percy, and stroked his neck a little. "I never rated Clem much, but he weren't the ambitious type neither. Sorta just did enough to get by. Men *can* change, a'course — but to me, ol' Clem's picture don't fit the frame. Well, here they come, be ready for anything."

First thing Billy noticed, was Patterson had put all clean clothes on. Exactly the same as his others, all expensively tailored black linen — but these were all clean and pressed. Clean boots he had on now too, shiny as a pair of new pins. Things gleamed most in the sun though, was them big guns he was so proud of. He still wore 'em low on his hips now, fancy-like — either he'd never learned to wear 'em different while riding, or he didn't anticipate trouble.

Strangest thing of all, neither Patterson or Jasper took rifles. Jasper too dressed in black now, and wore his six-shooters low. Like a short round copy of Patterson, he looked. Maybe half Barber's Cat, half balloon.

But their lack of rifles was strange.

The four trotted their horses out side by side, and only Jasper seemed less than relaxed. It was close to two already, and they had eighteen miles to travel, so they didn't dilly or dally.

To begin with, Barber's Cat Patterson was in a talking mood. He looked at Billy different now, more respectful, and ignored Morris completely.

Billy noted that Patterson positioned himself to the right of Billy, a distinct advantage if he wanted to draw on him. Billy let him do it as a message he wasn't bothered — but only because Morris was on Patterson's right anyway. And Jasper, he rode to Billy's left.

"So, Mister Deputy," said Patterson, pretty soon after they started. "That was some act you pulled back there. I really did believe you were a gump, and your tiny friend a gambler." Just like earlier, each word he spoke was clear and concise, an exercise in precision.

"Maybe I'll go into theatre," said Billy. "Though I fear my acting talent is limited to the one part that suits me." He loosened his grip on the reins, and Percy immediately switched to a canter, a gait he much favored.

The Barber's Cat spurred his horse once, and he and Billy moved ahead of the other two. Even the way the gunfighter sat a horse was precise, definite and practiced.

"Oh, you're no sort of fool whatsoever," Patterson said with a knowing smile, as he caught Billy up. "On the contrary, I believe you to be a very clever man."

This prideful man means to kill me. It wasn't the words, but something in the tone of them that rang all Billy's warning bells. He had learned to trust such slight feelings, and the subtle change in this man was enough to make Billy certain.

"You gettin' to some point, Patterson," said Billy, "or just jawin' on for no reason? Seems like you got *somethin'* to say. So why don't you just pop your corn and come out with it?"

"No, not I," he replied. "Merely getting to know you. I find it helpful, learning all I can about people."

"You mean learning about future victims?" And with the slightest movement of Billy's hands, Percy immediately slowed, putting him a length behind the other horse, and giving Billy the advantage if Patterson went for his gun when Billy slighted him.

Billy's timing was perfect. Percy dropped back a length and veered right, went behind the other horse so fast the expected bullet had no chance.

But instead of reacting how Billy expected, the gunfighter had only laughed, moved to his left and slowed some to allow Billy the advantageous side of the trail.

"Neat trick, Deputy," he said as Billy caught up even again, "but it's not me you need to worry about."

"Just checking," Billy answered.

"I'd have done the same," said Patterson, and there was a note of camaraderie in his voice. "I take it you don't believe your brother. And that worries me, I'll be honest. I expect things will get dangerous in Council Grove. And while it's what I was hired for, I don't fancy going up against Clem Jenkins and his Deputies unless I'm certain of my allies. I need to know I can trust you."

"We're only going there to talk," said Billy. "Ask Clem some questions. If you start something without me, I *will* arrest you. Just saying."

Patterson laughed a hearty one. "I'll just follow your lead, Deputy Ray," he said.

The name sounded strange to his ears, and Billy went to correct him, but stopped himself just in time.

Deputy Fyre I am, not Deputy Ray.

At the moment he thought it, they came over the rise and saw Cass's family's place on their right. Most of the trees were gone. The house had been built a quarter mile back from the road, and a little of the ruin was still standing, he saw now.

And of course, the pain of his loss went right through him, and without even thinking, he'd stopped.

Seven years, a man does some healing — but some things only heal partway. And right now, sitting and looking was all Billy could do.

CHAPTER 44

EVER SEEN A SHEEP RIDE A
HORSE?

❦

Patterson hung back a little, but Billy only half noticed. He got the vague sense the man knew what had happened here, all those long years ago.

Damn Barber's Cat, gloating over me.

Then Morris came up past them both, turned his horse about so he could face them — *all* of them. "That the place, Billy?"

"That's it."

There was an uncomfortable silence. Patterson and Jasper stayed back just a little, out of their way. Then Morris said to Billy, "You wanna go in, take a look?"

But before Billy could answer, Jasper said, "We gotta keep movin'. Horrie said we shouldn't go in there. He wouldn't like it, Billy."

Who could blame Billy for what he did next? Right here was the place all his horrors had come from. That terrible event had ruled his emotions since the moment he found out it happened — and despite all the growing up he'd done since, all the wise decisions he'd made, and the cool, considered thinking he always brought to tight situations, all it took to bring poor Billy halfways undone was to see those charred remains for himself.

From there, the words that the puppet master Horace had put into Jasper's mouth, were enough to push Billy over the edge.

And Billy was not now himself — he suddenly became seventeen again, that same green heartbroken boy who'd been incapable of saying any word but "Fire."

Horace ain't tellin' me what to do.

A shake of the reins was all it took.

Percy, given his head, galloped toward the ruin as if a battle was about to be fought there, and he hoped to get in the middle of it — he was a wonder, that horse, and not just courageous, but willing. And somehow, Percy had sensed here a battle, and forward he charged to take part.

Billy had sensed no such thing. And though some part of his mind noticed the barn, the corral and the outhouse, he had eyes only for the ruin where his dear Cass had surely breathed her last.

Billy's keenness to defy Horace by taking that four-hundred-yard trip was so strong, he never noticed that, as he and Percy took off, Morris cried, "Dang, my horse has a shoe loose," and stepped down from his saddle to the ground.

Patterson's eyes widened then, but he spurred his mount into action and took off after Billy — and Jasper, ever the puppet, the parrot, the sheep, had blindly followed Patterson's lead.

Thing was, Billy was not the only soft, decent man here, not by a long stretch.

Morris too, was a man given to heartfelt feelings of loss. Seeing his own mother killed had not hardened his heart, but rather, had softened it in some way — at least once the initial shock of her murder had passed. Perhaps it helped that he'd taken revenge on the killer.

And perhaps, too, this was the real reason most women loved Morris — he was a hard man, but also a soft one.

But of all the things Morris Brimstone was, he was, above all, a man of strategies and intellect. A dwarf lacks the raw strength of his peers, and so learns early on to employ *all* his senses to advantage.

Morris had *seen* Billy lose his composure and urge Percy forward — he had *heard* the deceitfulness in Jasper's voice — he had *smelled* the eagerness of their two companions — he had *tasted* the fear in his mouth when, too late, he saw trails that led to the barn through the long prairie grass —

And now, having tricked Patterson and Jasper into leaving him behind with nary a backward look, Morris bounced right back into the saddle and urged his wonderful horse on. Horace's men were fifty yards behind Billy, with Morris another fifty yards behind them and gaining — for his horse was fast, and his light weight was barely a burden at all.

As Billy came within a hundred yards of the house,

Jasper, unused to fast riding, could not get his gun out — but Barber's Cat Patterson had no such problems, his right hand reached for his gun, out it came, he lowered it now to look down its sights toward Billy.

Yet in those same few moments, Morris was working at using the *fifth* of his senses — he had *seen, heard, smelled* and *tasted* — and now he *touched* his Smith & Wesson revolver.

And indeed, he didn't just *touch* it, he *filled* his right hand with the cold steel deadliness of it. He pointed it at Barber's Cat Patterson, right as the man lowered his own gun to look down its sights, murder Billy. And before that very clean man in crisp black linen could shoot, Deputy Morris Brimstone fired, and blew a hole through the man's back from forty-five yards, causing the Barber's Cat's shot at Billy to go awry, and the bullet to whistle past his head.

First thing Morris's shot done, it got blood on that *very* particular feller's black shirt and vest — put an unattractive hole in 'em too.

Third thing — *yessir, I know this one's out of order* — all Patterson's clothing got filthy, and even his boots scuffed and scratched, as he fell from his horse to the ground, rolled and flipped in the dirt, like a child's rag doll in the mouth of a bad-behaved dog.

That third thing had happened because — *this is the second thing now* — Morris's bullet lodged in Patterson's spine, severing the cord as it went, so the man lost control of his legs for the rest of his life.

Fourth thing — well, the fourth maybe did him a favor

— the final time the man flipped he landed head first and his neck snapped. And Barber's Cat Patterson — or whatever his real name was — died right there in the dirt with no further ado.

Wasn't the end of it, things was just gettin' started. But the problem sure wasn't Jasper — the Strawhead was still struggling to get out his gun, and what with him leaning all sideways in the attempt, and his mare shying away from the gunfire, she took off real sharp to her left, away from the action.

But them tracks through the grass to the barn Morris noticed, they was a prime sorta clue, and Billy should ought to have seen 'em. As soon as Patterson fell from his horse, two other men stuck their rifles round the corners a' that barn, one aimed at Morris, the other at Billy, and them rifles exploded with flame.

If Billy and Morris was ordinary fellers, they'd have been dead that very next moment — but ordinary fellers they wasn't.

Billy mighta felt seventeen just a moment before — but when two gunshots rang out behind him, he got back his other seven years real fast, and maybe aged an extra one besides. And ol' Percy seemed to read Billy's thoughts afore he even knew he'd had one — that warhorse threw on the brakes half a moment, turned to his left as a bullet zinged through the space they shoulda been in, and accelerated again on a darting diagonal sprint toward the safety of the one good stand of trees still remaining.

The bullets came thick and fast, but the speed and

agility of Percy was somethin' to see — if anyone'd had time to watch it, a'course.

Billy had problems enough just holding on, flattened against Percy's back how he was, and riding him mostly with thoughtful suggestions.

This horse is a wonder, was all he had time to think. And then he was behind the trees, safe as salt meat, and jumping to the ground. "Good boy, Perce, now let's just wait here." Billy patted the gelding just twice, and reached for his trusty Henry.

Besides being underestimated, there's another real advantage for a dwarf in a gunfight. As a target, he's some amount smaller.

Morris's horse was a good one as well — good being not enough word for it really — he was plenty courageous, quite some faster than Percy at sprinting, and every bit as agile too.

Half wind, half twister, he was.

No good at all for long distance, but in moments like this, that horse was as good as they came. That fine little gelding sprinted and ducked and weaved, every bit as good as young Billy Fyre had in his first battle.

Good thing he did too. Them two behind the barn had Winchester repeaters, and must have got off a dozen shots each, before Morris joined Billy behind the trees. Good shots though they were, all them two Winchester fellers hit was a whole lot of air.

As for Jasper, he had his own problems. Right now, it seemed that horse of his weren't much good for nothin' but havin' good looks — appaloosa she was, and Jasper had taken that horse for his own when they burned down Emilie Hill's place after shooting her husband.

Jasper had coveted that horse just as much as he'd coveted Emilie.

Thing was, that horse wasn't quite proper trained up yet. Behaved well enough, was already easy to ride — but Jack Hill was a peaceable feller, hardly never even fired his gun. First gunfire that horse was ever close up to, her owner got shot off her back, and she dragged him a ways, real scared. Didn't learn nothin' from it but more fear. And a'course, she had no fondness for Jasper, on account of him being who'd done that first shooting that scared her.

So with all the extra shootin' that followed Morris's first shot, that pretty appaloosa was almost a mile away, still had the fire in her eyes, the bit in her teeth, and was foaming at the mouth good and proper. Making it only worse still, Barber's Cat Patterson's horse had followed along, and what with it being riderless and hot on her heels, the appaloosa kept bolting — and the truth was, Jasper had never been much of a horseman.

Ever seen a sheep ride a horse? That's about how good the Strawhead was. Though as Billy watched him disappear over the horizon, he couldn't help but notice that Jasper's flailing limbs gave him more the look of a puppet — *maybe one with a few broken strings.*

Billy shook his head slowly and said, "Send us a letter when you get there, Jasper," then turned to face Morris.

"You'd already rushed headlong for it when I noticed the danger, ya tall streak a' foolishness," said Morris.

"Sorry, ya big-gunned, small-fisted ... can't think a' nothin' right now. How 'bout we save the insults for later?"

Morris's smile spread all over his face as he looked up from reloading his six-shooter. "Never was much of a thinker under pressure, was you?"

Billy smiled right back. "That's what your Pa always says."

CHAPTER 45
REMEMBER THE ALAMO!

At least the two friends had made cover — but they were a long way from safety. Real bag of nails, it was.

A pair of bullets hit a tree not far from them, but it didn't rattle them none, they were safe where they were. Then again, so were them two Winchester fellers behind the barn.

"We are Deputy U.S. Marshals," Billy called out, good and loud. "You boys are breaking the law by firing on us. Stop right now, or you are under arrest."

The reply was two hoots of laughter — one low-toned laugh and one high — followed by the gravel-voiced feller calling out, "Don'tcha reckon we knows yer both Deputies? Why else would we be shootin' at ya, ya damn fools?"

"Do you work for Horace Ray?" Billy called.

More hoots of laughter from behind the barn, then the same voice called out, "Nossir, we's workin' fer Colonel

William B Travis. I's Davy Crockett, and this other feller's Jim Bowie. You's maybe heard of us some. Or don'tcha remember the Alamo?"

This was followed by a whole lot more laughter from the both of 'em.

"At least *they* think themselves amusing," said Billy.

"Seems like we got a standoff," said Morris, wasting a bullet just to let them fellers know he still had a keen interest in killing them if they moved — it hit right on the corner of the barn, a little under head height.

"Nice shooting earlier, Morris, thanks kindly," Billy said. "Although I was rather looking forward to using what we knew about Patterson's weak left hand."

"I coulda just let him shoot you in the back if you wanted — I mean, he was lining you up in his sights — but next time, just let me know if you want some feller saved up, and I'll stay my hand."

Billy smiled back at his friend and said, "I'll let you off with it this time, on account of how I'm still alive, and leave the next one to your judgment. Listen, this is only a standoff until more of their men shows up. Might happen, might not. Either that, or someone breaks cover and *makes* somethin' happen."

"Good luck with breaking cover," said Morris, as another bullet hit the same tree, same height as the last two. "These two fellers ain't so funny as they think, but they sure know what Winchesters are for." Then he chuckled a little himself and said, "And if that fool Jasper ever gets his mare back under control, he might yet pick us off from down back by the creek."

Billy looked around, but Jasper was still outta sight. Coulda been miles away, coulda been just over the hill — but that last didn't seem likely. "Are we sure there's only two of 'em here?"

"Only two sets a' tracks through the prairie grass. Two's a safe bet, I reckon."

Billy sighed deeply and looked at the battlefield. The outhouse was the place to be. The shooters had made a strategic error in both of them waiting behind the barn. One should have been behind the outhouse. If Billy or Morris could get there, this whole thing would be over in two shots. The *getting there* was the problem.

He looked at Morris now and said, "If we'd brought a packhorse, we coulda sent it galloping out to draw some fire, and you coulda covered me enough to make it to the outhouse so I'd have a better angle on 'em."

"True," said Morris. "And also, my friend — if we had some bacon, we could have bacon and eggs. If we had some eggs."

"See what you mean. Next time I'm bringin' the pack horse."

"Next time," Morris agreed.

"Pity we ain't in the barn," Billy said, "and them behind the outhouse. There's a tunnel leads from one to the other. Big secret it was — even my Pa never knew of it, and he was Tom's best friend. Me and Cass used to play in it when her Pa weren't around. Was supposed to go to the house too, but things got peaceable round here, and ol' Tom never finished it. I might be too big to fit through now. We coulda come up through it and—"

"More eggs, more bacon," said Morris. "If maybe, perhaps might be useful."

"Sorry," said Billy. "Sometimes helps me to think out loud is all. And that outhouse there is the place we need to get to. No tunnel from here though."

They thought for a bit, but time was a'wastin', and they had to do *something,* but quick. After a minute, Billy suggested a plan — and Morris reckoned that plan sounded a *lot* better than waiting for a bunch of other fellers to turn up and pick 'em off right where they stood.

So they left the horses tied where they were, and went to opposite ends of the stand of trees. There had been no gunfire for awhile.

Then from his end, Billy called out, "Now," and he and Morris both started shootin' up a storm. What a mess of gunsmoke they made.

They each had their Henrys plus a six-shooter — and they had a whole passel of cartridges. Not just on their fancy leather gunbelts, but a bagful around each of their necks too, that had been in their saddlebags.

It was kinda their *thing*. Most serious fellers had taken to wearing the fancy new leather gunbelts, or bandoliers that hung from one shoulder to down near their waists — and one or two a' them full was how many cartridges they carried, plus those in their gun.

Billy had an odd thought then, and it sure made him smile. *That Tiny Jones feller would be a real worry — feller that size wouldn't never run outta cartridges. Glad we made a friend of him. Leastways, I hope we did.*

Now, the more Billy and Morris fired, the more them

other fellers did too. It was something Preacher Rob had first noticed, some years ago, not so long after the war. Men always seemed to catch a gunfire fever of sorts, when the other side fires as if there won't be no tomorrow — almost like they wanna make sure they got the most possible use from their guns, just in case the world ends or somethin'.

It was working a treat, Billy noticed. It was hard to keep track, what with everyone firing at once sometimes — but he knew these other fellers must run out soon, for they were quick loaders, and fast repeat firers too. And every so often Billy and Morris would throw things out through the smoke — branches mostly, or a rock here and there — and the sight of something moving never failed to get "Bowie" and "Crockett" to fire a whole lot more rounds.

They kept this all up for awhile. But after a time, Billy noticed them fellers slowed down a whole lot. They only fired now when something got thrown out through the smoke. Even then just two bullets, most times — just the one each, in unison.

It was what Billy had been waiting on.

He smiled to himself and called out — not too loud, but enough — "Hey Morris, you got some to spare? I got just six cartridges left. Meet you back in the middle."

"Dammit, Billy," cried Morris. "I just used up my—"

"*Shut up,*" Billy screamed loud over the top of him.

But them fellers had heard the whole thing alright, that was for sure and for certain.

After a few moments, Morris called, "I bet they're low too."

And again, Billy yelled at the top of his lungs. "Shut up, Morris ya fool. I got plenty, meet me back in the middle."

"Alright, alright," Morris called, but he stayed right there where he was. It was he who was in the right spot for what was to happen. And being the dwarf, it was he who them two bad fellers was least worried about.

Billy did go back to the middle then, and as he went, he found three good sticks the right size — then soon as he got to the middle, he tied two of 'em together in a cross that fit his hat proper, and the other he tied to 'em to make a body and neck for the hat to stand up on.

Horace's men, by this time, had learned the trick of throwing things out to be fired on, and were no doubt excited to use it themselves. First thing they threw out was a coat — and from the middle where he'd gone, Billy fired two quick shots at it, then yelled, "Dammit."

And Morris didn't fire at all.

Then Billy put on a sorta low urgent voice, like as if he was trying not to be heard, and said things like, *"No, only the two."* And a few moments later, *"It's your fault, Morris, you was meant to bring some spare boxes."* Next was, *"Don't tell me I'm too loud, they can't hear nothin' over there."* Then finally, *"We'll have to try, get the horses."*

Then "Bowie" — or maybe it was "Crockett" — threw out another coat. Billy fired, a'course, just the once, and put a hole through that one as well.

Then that gravel-voiced son-of-a-gun called out in a mocking sorta voice, "You boys ain't short on bullets, are you now? Why don'tcha come on out and we'll give you all you need?"

"Yeah," came the other feller's voice. High as a songbird's that other voice was, though not nearly so pleasant as one. More like a screech it was. Then he added, "Come out'n bend over, I'll put a few right in yer chamber."

Then the pair of them fellers, Screech-Voice High-voice and Gravel-voice Low-Voice, laughed just about fit to bust.

"I got plenty a' cartridges thanks," Billy called, top of his lungs. "And as for puttin' things in my chamber, I reckon whatever you pair a' Marys get up to in private, you shouldn't tell others about."

Then he thrust that stick with his hat on it out through the front of the trees, and them two angrified fellers went to town on it. Shot up a storm they did, before one of 'em — Gravel-voice Low-Voice it was — yelled at the other, "Stop wastin' bullets, ya damn fool, it ain't ought but a hat."

Weren't *much* of a hat no more, Billy noticed. What was left of it had stayed on the sticks, more or less — but he didn't think it much likely to stay up on top of his head again. Most likely drop all the way down to sit on his shoulders. More holes than hat it was now.

Billy waited quietly for the sound he knew was coming. Then he heard it.

It was the sound of four gunshots — all from one place — and somewhere in the middle of all that, the sound of two dying fellers crashing against the barn wall then hitting the dirt. One of 'em groaned some, but not long at all. Too many bullets in 'em, and all four well placed.

By the time Morris and Billy got there, Low-Voice and High-Voice had both breathed their last.

"That's a most unpleasant attitude they ended up in," said Billy. It was impossible to know which voice had belonged to which feller — but one had landed face down on the other, right below that feller's gun belt.

"Maybe they was both called Mary after all," said Morris.

"Nothin' wrong with that, if they were," Billy said, then looked over at Morris's wide eyes. "It ain't my thing, so don't start up about it, Ya Bow-Legged, Squirrel-Sized Fast-Talker. Just sayin', it takes all kinds, and there's worse kinds than that. I met a few real decent ones, that's all."

"Fair enough," Morris said. But he still looked at Billy some sideways.

They went through them two fellers' pockets, found just over forty-six dollars. Morris told Billy to buy himself a new hat with it, and maybe a bath. Weren't all they found — each of them fellers carried a nice Sharps four-shot derringer, same model as Billy's, in special-made shoulder holsters.

"One each, I reckon" said Morris. "I wanted one since I seen yours." They looked well cared for, and freshly loaded as well — but they fired them off and reloaded 'em both, just in case.

"We'll keep the Winchesters too," Morris said awhile later with a grin. "Unless a'course there's bounties on these fellers."

"Morris..."

"What? This job hardly pays enough for all our ammunition. Fair's fair, Billy."

Then, still keeping an eye out for Jasper, they commenced the work of loading up three dead bodies to take back to the Falls — no way Billy was leaving trash like that on Cass's family farm, and insulting her memory.

CHAPTER 46
A TIME TO DIE

Horace Ray had made a mistake. In truth, he had made a great many, starting from long, long ago. But how *he* saw things, he had made just the *one* — that *one* being, he'd allowed his father to get away with holding things over him too long.

He'd begun to think up a plan even before the Doc finished binding his arm. Only part of his plan he *didn't* like, was that he wouldn't get to see Billy killed. But a man had to make *some* sacrifices, after all.

As soon as Horace gave Patterson and Jasper their orders, the other man he'd sent for had arrived at Horace's room to help him prepare. Within a minute of Billy riding away to the doom that awaited him, Horace and Pope climbed onto their horses, and headed for Emporia.

He thought it all through again as they rode — Pope was the quiet type, deadly when it was called for, in it for the money, and no questions asked. Horace would fill him in on the plan when they got closer. It was twenty miles ride, and he might yet adjust his plan — Pope was no fool, but there was no sense in confusing him needlessly.

Horace knew that if John Ray found out about Billy's return, it would change everything. And he must surely find out sooner or later, for Billy was a U.S. Marshal's Deputy — when Billy and the da-warf didn't come back, that U.S. Marshal would send someone else to investigate.

Every bit of the County Sheriff's paperwork about all the murders was rock solid — and the Town Marshal's paperwork too. But even though Billy was dead now, Horace knew he could maybe be caught out and jailed for lying about Billy's death, all those years ago. He wasn't quite so good at covering things up yet back then — and even if they classed it a minor offense, he might get a month in the calaboose.

A month he could do with no problem — even six if it came to that, and it might. Wasn't the time itself, it was what the jail sentence would then cause to happen.

Problem was, John Ray had had the foresight to include an extra clause in the lease he had signed — a clause that stated, **"If Horace Ray is ever sentenced to more than one consecutive night in jail, it brings a lawful end to this lease."**

That damn high-falutin' city lawyer thought that one up, Horace reckoned. John Ray had ridden the sixty miles north to Manhattan, and done the paperwork there, to keep the details away from all locals. The man never thought much of gossipmongers at the best of times — let alone the worst. And he wasn't the type to add fuel to their petty little word-fires.

He was a straight shooter, John Ray, and a straight thinker besides. But only one of his sons had inherited such virtues from him.

If Horace had spent half as much energy on thinking straight as he did on blaming others, he mighta seen things a lot clearer.

If he *had* thought more clearly, Horace might have seen his *real* mistake — he had sorely underestimated not only Billy, but Morris as well. To him, Morris was nothing at all — just a foolish little feller who shoulda been put in a circus for people to gawk at.

And Billy, well, to Horace, Billy was still that same soft kid who could not even shoot straight, and didn't like killing — not even animals. Saw Billy as that very same kid, only bigger now, and with a damn badge in his pocket. If Patterson didn't get him today, the other two would.

The sneaking sort of man, always looking for a dishonest shortcut to riches, misses the point of hard work — hard work, done in good spirit, with a yearning for excellence applied to it, always leads to new skills. Hard-won as those new skills are, they are there for the hardworking man to fall back on, at the moment when he most needs them.

Skills earned this way are their own reward, and withstand the test of time too.

But the schemer, he always needs a new one — for schemes have no solid foundation, and eventually crumble.

Having never worked at increasing his own skills, it

never occurred to Horace Ray what a few months of war plus several years of serving as a Deputy Marshal had done for his brother.

But even being sure Billy would die any minute now — *Patterson could have done it alone, but even if he fails, Spinks and Matich are both dead shots* — Horace knew he still needed insurance, a way of protecting the glorious future he'd planned.

When Pa finds out Billy was alive all this time, then died today on his way to the Grove, he'll know for sure I had a hand in it.

The terms of Horace's lease had tied his hands tight all this time. He could not kill his father or Cass or even Billy's damn child without losing the lease. Could not harm a hair on their heads, much as he wanted to. He had paid for a top lawyer's time, just to be sure there was no loophole.

And it was all tied up tight.

But everything has its season. He had heard those words in one a' those dang fool church sermons — or words close enough anyways. And while he ignored most of what he heard in that church, he took away parts of this one, and kept them close all the time.

The parts that suited his purposes.

Like, *a time to die, that's for Billy today. And a time to pluck what was planted.* He laughed to himself about that one, as he rode along beside Pope, who looked at him funny, but never said a word.

Then Horace laughed once again, even louder, very much enjoying the thought of Billy dying right where the fool believed that Cass had.

He felt a pang of regret then.

Shoulda told Patterson to kill him slow, and tell him Cass is alive, and he has an ugly damn son. I woulda paid to see that.

It had taken Billy's turning up here for Horace to get to the point of forcing the issue, and now he was more or less glad of it. He had partway thought up the plan before, had even scoped his father's place out, just in case he needed to act fast. But now, he was so impressed with his foresight and planning, he almost felt like he should have *thanked* his fool brother for bringing things to a head.

A'course, if he had known of what was happening this moment back at the MacPherson place, Horace Ray might not have felt quite so smug.

Might have hurried along a bit too. But as it was, he and Pope were making good time, and would arrive in Emporia before it got dark, and be ready to take full advantage.

Halfway to Emporia now, the pair rode into the Keir place, and hired themselves some fresh horses for the rest of the trip. Gray ones, he chose. Horace had never owned any gray ones, always disliked 'em, on account a' how much Billy liked 'em when he was little.

But right now, using gray horses suited his purpose. And he offered Andy Keir triple payment, to keep quiet about him having been here.

He could tell Keir disliked him, but business was business, and Horace's money was as good as anyone else's. Or three times as good, on this occasion.

He'll keep his mouth shut. Hell, hardly says two words

at the best a' times. Likely got his own shady business, now I think on it.

Once they returned and swapped back the horses, there would be no proof he and Pope had ever been here — or down in Emporia.

CHAPTER 47
"LUCKY HAT..."

Billy and Morris led a trail of horses behind them, keeping an eye and an ear out for Jasper the whole time. There had been no further sign of the Strawhead, even when Patterson's horse had returned. They were halfway back to Horace's place when they saw a lone rider coming toward them from the Falls.

Well, a rider-and-a-half, more accurate.

Even from a fair ways off, there was no mistaking the hulking great form of Tiny Jones.

"Told you he rides two horses at once," Billy said.

"Reckon twos about right," Morris answered, shaking his head in wonder at the sight that approached them.

They were wary when first they saw him, after what had just happened, of course. But Tiny Jones was approaching with both his hands up and waving — it was done as a greeting, but also to show he had no ill intentions toward them. Can't shoot at no one when you got both hands in the air.

Tiny was six foot ten, and that horse was about right-sized for him. The magnificent beast was about eighteen hands, had feathering that dropped down all round its feet, and each a' them feet was bigger'n dinner plates. Stepped high too, that huge feller. Turned out he was a stallion as well, but a more docile horse had never been sat on.

It occurred to Billy that Tiny must have felt like King of the World up there on that wonderful high-stepping animal. He looked across at Morris, and the wistful look the dwarf wore said more than words ever could. Neither man spoke awhile, just watched horse and rider come closer, enjoying the moment.

The sun shone down on them, the wind played at the huge horse's mane, and at the feathering too — and the whole thing seemed like a dream, or a page from a childhood storybook. It was a dang site more pleasant, looking forward at Tiny and his mount, than it was to look back at the trail of horses that carried the outlaws' dead bodies.

"I see ya didn't need no help after all," Tiny called when he came within distance. Then he reined in his horse and waited for them to arrive.

"I should have known," said Billy. "I'm a fool to have fallen for Horrie's trap. Coulda got me and Morris both killed."

Tiny nodded a greeting to Morris, turned to Billy and said, "My sis took awhile to calm down. And she's some like me — we ain't much clever, ya should ought have guessed that by now. But she reckons yer Mister Ray's brother. That true?" He stared intently at Billy.

"Yes, Tiny," Billy answered earnestly. "I'm sorry we couldn't tell you before, but we didn't know who we could trust."

"Aw, that's alright," Tiny said, glancing back at the row of horses and the bodies they carried. "I never know such myself. 'Til today I thought Mister Ray not a bad sorta feller. Mistakes is made sometimes, it seems, when snakes acts like dogs. If ya get what I mean."

The other two murmured their agreement, then Tiny wheeled that big horse around, and they all got moving toward the Falls again. The three of them rode side by side, with Billy in the middle.

"Did ya kill all four?" Tiny asked.

"Not Jasper," said Billy. "His horse bolted soon as things started. Halfway to Canada, I reckon. Or maybe just Council Grove."

Tiny looked thoughtful a moment. "That was Jack Hill's horse, ya know? Emilie's husband, he was. I was just thinkin'. Might be the horse heard 'bout how Jasper killed poor Emilie."

"That might be the true of it, Tiny," said Billy, nodding at the giant.

"Mister Ray mighta sended Jasper to fetch Jasper's Pa. Sometimes he does that."

"Reckon you might be right on that, Tiny," said Billy. "Jasper never was real brave. He probably figured the two riflemen would kill us anyway. And he sure won't be keen to tell Horrie no different, even *if* he does know what really happened. I seem to remember Jasper always did hide bad news from Horace, rather than get him riled up."

It was Morris who spoke next. "Is your sister alright, Tiny my friend?"

"Not so good, but okay considerin' I guess. She tole me what's what, 'bout what you fellers was sayin'. She always did reckoned poor Emilie loco — all that stuff 'bout her husband bein' murdered'n all. Yell at Marshal Jasper sometimes, she did — *'always prancin' around on my dead husband's horse,'* what she said. Terrible thing for poor Emilie, and she weren't really loco at all then, I guess."

"Terrible thing," Billy said. "And you're right, she wasn't loco at all."

Tiny Jones looked like he just might cry then, and he turned his head a moment, looked at the dead bodies once more before setting his face hard again, and going on. "Sis knows it was true now, she tole me. We jawed on it some, the whole thing. And seems to us — me and Sis — they musta kilt *our* family too, and burned all our farm. We never knowed they done that. Thinked it was a accident."

"I'm very sorry, Tiny," said Billy.

"Me too," said Morris.

"Me three," said Tiny. Then he smiled half a sad one and added, "That's a joke, that me three thing. Even I knows that much. Mister Ray's gone, did y'know? Betty tole me Mister Ray left with Augie Pope right after you did. He's a bad man, Augie Pope. Calls hisself a per-fessional — I reckon that means a bad man. If it don't, they should change it. Anyways, they headed Emporia way."

"Knew Horace was faking, I'm a fool," Billy growled, then he punched his own shoulder so hard he winced. He took a deep breath then and added, "Good work, Tiny, thank you. You're a man to ride the river with, don't ever let no one tell you different. Any ideas about why they'd head out that way?"

"It sure ain't usual," Tiny said, looking down at Billy from way up there on that beautiful high-stepping horse, his huge body framed by a beautiful blue and white sky. "Augie Pope lives down there partly. Halftimes here and half there I reckon. I don't know why."

"But not Horace? He never goes there?"

"I never but once knowed Mister Ray to go down that way. And that one time weren't on horseback. But he mighta gone other times I never knowed about."

Morris hadn't been saying much, but now he broke in with, "On the train was it, Tiny?" He was glad he wasn't too close to the giant — even from the other side of the trail it hurt his neck to look up so far.

"Sure, on the train," Tiny answered. "Just a week after it first come. What a noise! Scared me at first when it come. still prefer ridin' my horse just like this, I don't trust them trains, all that huffin' and puffin' and squealin' all like they's dyin'."

"Billy don't trust 'em either," said Morris, "so you got an agreeable friend there on that. So Horace went on the train down Emporia way?"

"Sure he did. Sis went with him too, and Jasper and Emilie — she sure liked that train. Jawed on about it for a week or more. They dressed all up too, real fine, all four together. Like fancified city folk they were. Never seen 'em look that way since, but they all sure looked fancy that one time."

"Interesting," said Billy, as Percy stepped over a short log that had fallen off the back of someone's wagon onto the trail. "What else, Tiny, think!"

"Well, thing was, when they got off in Emporia, that other bad feller, Pope, was already there to meet 'em. Then they all got on a handcar and went up and down some. Sis telled me all about it next day."

They were almost back to Horace's place now, but Tiny's story had sure piqued Billy's interest. "Let's stop here a bit and work all this out. Up and down where exactly, did they take that handcar? Did she say?"

Tiny took the opportunity to roll a smoke as he talked. Had pretty deft fingers for the size of 'em too. "Just past the station, Sis tole me. They just went a mile or so on the handcar, then stopped and talked awhile, then went back again, real slow like. After that they sended Sis and Emilie to a eatin' place while they went off in a buggy somewhere. Musta been Augie Pope's buggy, I guess."

"Just the men, in a buggy, in their fancy clothes? Hmmm." Billy rubbed at his jaw and said, "That all of it?"

"No, that *ain't* all, now I remember," Tiny said. "She said they went on that handcar a second time. Same trip as before, just a mile or so, then right back. I remember she sayin' she didn't want to go, on account of how it was raining. But Mister Ray bought a humbrella and made 'em all go. He got angry about it, she reckoned. Tole her it was important, and to stop her complainin', or he'd stick that humbrella where the sun don't shine and open it up good and wide. That's why I remembered just now, made me angry that did. I didn't like hearin' all that, but Sis tole me not to say nothin' about it, so I didn't."

"Other side a' the station," said Billy, thoughtful-like. "Just past it." He thought of the small boy trying to get on that gray horse, and while there were some nice little places there, he hadn't noticed nothing worth all that spying and planning to steal it.

There was still no sign of Jasper coming behind them, so they carefully proceeded to Horace's place. Would have avoided it if they could, but there was no other good place to get over the river to the Falls, and they couldn't just leave dead bodies out on the trail. Besides, they needed things from their pack horses. More rimfire cartridges, just for one thing.

They left the bodies with the feller in charge of the livery, though he weren't too happy about it.

"I ain't no damn undertaker," that grimy thin feller grumbled. "What'm I a'sposed to do with three bodies?"

Billy looked at him hard and said, "I *could* get someone else to take care of 'em — but by then there'd be four, if you get what I'm sayin'. See, I'm in just the mood to add to the tally. And your lack of community spirit offends me, now I think some about it."

That scarecrow-thin hostler changed his mind quicker'n a ferret disappears down a rabbit hole. "I'll have someone collect the undertaker from town, Mister Deputy, sir," he said. "And I'll guard these bodies myself in the meantime, real diligent-like."

"Mighty community spirited of you, friend," Billy said,

with a hint of a smile, before flipping the man the two dollars he had in his hand.

They decided to risk going inside to speak to Tiny's sister. Susie was feeling much better — that pretty, over-tall girl sure did seem to like Morris, so Billy left the questions to him and Tiny. She did add one piece of clarity to what her big brother had already said — they was spying on a particular place that day from the handcar, and it was the prettiest of all the places along there. Prettiest she *ever* saw, so she reckoned. Had flowers 'agrowing, chickens a'pecking, an old gray horse a'wandering, and a white painted stable down back near the railroad tracks.

"Foolish men were more interested in the stable than all the pretty parts though," she said.

Morris and Billy looked at each other then, knowing just what the other was thinking. There must be something mighty important down there, for three men to waste a whole day.

They wanted to get going, but delayed awhile in the hope Jasper would return. But still, there was no sign of him. It was a pity — Billy figured that, without the puppet-master around, he might have been easy to break.

Probably halfway to Canada by now, Billy thought with a smile. *She looked to have stamina, that fine appaloosa.* There hadn't been time to laugh back then, but Jasper sure had looked a sight, a'galloping over the horizon, limbs all akimbo as he tried to hold onto that horse.

Billy had brought in a piece of scrap leather, and he put some holes in it with his knife, then used strips of rawhide to fix it to his hat while they talked. There was no shortage of holes in the hat to tie the new scrap to. Didn't look much, but it stayed on top of his head now, just about where it should.

"Lucky hat," he explained when they all looked at him funny. "Gift from my Pa."

Tiny Jones wanted to head to Emporia with them, but they all finally agreed it would be better for him and Susie to hole up somewhere safe.

"We need you to look after Susie," said Morris. "You have to protect her, in case Horace or Jasper or Clem tries to take her."

"I didn't think about that," Tiny answered. "I won't let 'em get near ya, Sis."

Then Billy asked Tiny about some trustworthy folks he remembered, but seven years had changed things a lot, and they'd all moved away. In the end, Billy wrote a note to Seth Hays, and sent Tiny and his sister to wait there until he returned.

"Mister Hays don't like Mister Ray," Tiny said. "Maybe won't like us neither. Might just shoot us instead. His hands don't ever come here."

"Take this," Billy said, and he handed Tiny the note. "This explains that me and Morris are U.S. Deputy Marshals investigating local corruption. He'll take you in, or his men will if Seth isn't there. Now listen, *real important!* When you ride up, keep your hands where they can see 'em, like you done when you rode out to us."

"And Sis too?"

"Pretty ladies too," Morris said with a smile. "Don't forget now, Susie."

"I won't forget," she answered, squeezing Morris's arm as she smiled.

Billy took out his badge, and was going to give it to Tiny Jones to wear when he rode up to the Hays place. But Morris pointed out they would recognize Tiny anyway, and the sight of the badge was more likely to make them think he was pulling a hornswoggle.

Billy saw he was right, and handed the badge to Morris instead. "Here, take this for me, will you? If we separate somewhere, I'd rather not have it on me. Me and your Pa used to do it sometimes — when we didn't want folks to know we were Deputies."

Morris put it in his pocket, and they all went out to their horses. Tiny and Susie headed west to the Hays ranch, while Morris and Billy went east to Emporia.

It had already been a long day — and would soon turn into a long night. A night when people would die...

CHAPTER 48
A DAILY RITUAL

It was late afternoon, and John Ray felt somehow uneasy. It was unusual for him these days, for he had settled into a comfortable life in Emporia, which was, if not entirely blissful, at least happy, and somewhat fulfilling.

When he left the run of the Falls and the Grove to Horace six years back, he'd at first planned on leaving the area completely — *perhaps further West,* he'd thought at the time.

But the thought of leaving didn't sit right. It wasn't the being near Horace — if he never saw him again it'd be too soon. There was something wrong with that boy — but John wasn't afraid of him either. The terms of the lease had made certain Horace would leave Cass and young Tom alone.

John had no desire to run into him though.

After they'd spent a few days in town with Mary Brown, the wise old seamstress spoke to him in private. "I know a thing or two about loss, John. And I'll give you this one for free — if you run off out West, you'll be miserable, and come back inside of a year. For now — and for awhile yet, maybe always — Billy's spirit will seem to be *here*. Or at least *hereabouts*. That boy put his mark on this county and those either side of it. Settle somewhere out of Horace's way ... but let yourself settle awhile."

She was wise, that old woman, he knew it — and he felt the rightness of her words the moment she spoke them.

He had always liked Emporia, and liked how it was, for the most part, a pretty dry sorta town. It wasn't that whiskey went *completely* unappreciated down there — but a lot of the Welsh folk did not drink at all. It looked a good place for a child to grow. Billy would have liked the idea of his son growing up strong and straight there.

John looked around thereabouts, and bought himself one of the closest one-sixties to the town. It wasn't exactly cheap, but not too costly either, for it was a little away from the river. He looked at the lay of the land, took in all possibilities, and decided it was the place he wanted to be. Way John figured it, this was the way the railroad would come, if it ever did.

The family who owned the place wanted out quickly, and not too many folks had much money, the war having taken so much from people, even out here. And so, John Ray made a fair offer, and it was accepted.

The place already had two comfortable homes, about fifty yards apart at the western end of the property — the closest part of it to town.

It turned out John Ray had been right about the

railroad, both here *and* in Cottonwood Falls. And while Horace had used that little windfall to build a massive saloon, and turn their ranch into a wasteland where cattle waited to be loaded onto trains, here John Ray did something different.

Something *better*.

He made it a place where families could grow, without *too much* hard work and sacrifice.

He sold parts of his one-sixty off in small portions, some ten acres, some five. The value of land here had gone through the roof, once folks found out the railroad was coming. The railroad tried to buy it all out from under him, of course, before making it known they'd be coming this way. But John stuck to his guns, refused to sell. In the end, it wasn't worth it to the railroad to fight him, or to route the tracks some other way.

But instead of selling each place for a high price, John sold each small plot on easy terms to folks who seemed like good people. Took less in some cases than seemed sensible. The sort of riches John Ray sought was not silver dollars or gold dust — it was *community*.

He sold off twenty small places to families who wanted space to move, somewhere they could grow a little food, perhaps raise a couple of horses, raise poultry or pigs, keep a milking cow — and those families not only found affordable land here, but together, they each added something of value, helped build up a real community.

He even built a schoolhouse on a two acre portion, and soon, young Tom would go there too, along with those older children already attending.

Cass and little Tom had both thrived here, which was what mattered most in the world to him now. The girl had become even more like a daughter to him, and his grandson was more of a blessing than he ever imagined he could be.

Rosie too, had been happy. She was a beautiful soul, she truly was. John knew how she still felt, and sometimes wished he could give the lovely woman what she wanted. But when they lost Billy, any chance of that had gone too. John had only enough left inside him, to give love to Tom, and to Cass. But the little boy had redefined everyone's roles, and though Rosie had never had children, she was just as surely Tom's Grandma as Cass was his mother.

And happily — though quite unexpectedly — old Mary Brown had come to Emporia too. She'd moved into the other small house, right next to the main one. Even more unexpected, old Mary seemed to get a second wind. Seven years ago, she had spent more than half the day sleeping, as well as the nights — these days she still liked an afternoon nap, but in her role as Tom's Great Grandma, Mary too had thrived.

She still had a *little* to teach Cass, although not very often. Cass sewed all sorts of things — even moccasins, bandoliers and gunbelts — and though she worked only from home, she had built a reputation as the best seamstress and leathergoods maker in four counties. Indeed, folks came from miles around to buy what she made.

Life, for them all, was comfortable, rewarding, and mostly predictable. It was better than John would ever have imagined it could be again. For him, the loss of Billy was just like the loss of Billy's mother — not something that would *ever* stop hurting, but a thing he somehow accepted. In time, it had melted itself into a gentler, almost loving, sort of pain.

Six years ago, John Ray had wiped back his huge manly tears, taken deep breaths, and set his shoulders against that new load in his life. He had moved forward, made the best of what he'd been given.

What else can you do?

He watched now as little Tom rushed out the back door to play again. There was still an hour 'til sunset, and that little boy's love for horses was just about the same as his daddy's.

John often sat Tom in front of him and rode about on his own horse, and the little feller sure loved it. When no women were around, they would canter, and the child would laugh at the top of his lungs. Sometimes, he put the boy on ol' Andy's back and led him around, Tom pretending he was riding him on his own. But that boy was determined to be all growed up, to ride that ol' gray by himself, with no one there to help him.

If only Billy could have seen him. 'He's a wonder' — that's what he'd have said.

Little Tom, of course, *thought* he was getting away with something. But everyone knew just what the little boy was up to.

He would chase the hens home to their henhouse — that was his number one chore — then he would play with the dog awhile.

Then — once he thought no one was watching — he'd

pick up his bucket, sneak away down the back to old Andy's paddock, and try to climb up and ride him.

This evening, just like most others, Mary was home at her own place, Rosie was cooking something that smelled good, and Cass was sewing in the front room. She was expecting someone to come by and pick up an order.

John sat on the back veranda, watched little Tom and the dog round up the chickens to put them away. It was about the only work that dog did. John had wanted a watchdog, but the little brown bundle had been offered to them, and he'd grown up soft, roly-poly, and a whole lotta fun for a child — dog was no good for anything else, but that didn't matter.

John watched them now, that boy and his dog. The dog barely had sense in its head, but it was as gentle as any dog could be. The dog too watched the boy, and his eyes were so loving, John wondered how foolish some folks were, them folks who say dogs got no souls.

Oh, that boy though.

He was such a little *man,* same way Billy had been at that age — he looked so serious as he upturned his bucket, climbed on it, and closed the latch to the henhouse. Then, as always, he checked it — same way Billy used to do — before turning toward the veranda to make sure John saw he had finished.

John Ray nodded at the little boy, called out, "Best get that dog to run about some before you come in, Tom, he's gettin' too fat."

Then he picked up his newspaper, stuck his head inside it, and pretended he was no longer watching.

It was a daily ritual now.

There was no real reason for John to feel on edge. Truth was, it was a feeling that came to him every so often, and usually never bore fruit. Less and less lately though. He always wondered though, when it came over him, if maybe somewhere, someone he knew was in danger. And his thoughts went to Billy, though he knew, of course, that was plain foolish.

But a man like John Ray, who lives with the ghosts of wars past, is naturally sometimes thrust into such feelings, and lives with the ghost of wars present — and maybe wars future as well. At least, that's what John put it down to. It was better than just being on edge, and all for no reason.

He truly is a wonder, that little boy, he thought, as he watched him from the corner of his eye, having angled the newspaper down just slightly to do so.

That old horse was so gentle, John knew Tom was safe, even if he *did* manage to climb up onto his back. He was waiting for the day when it happened — wouldn't be much longer now. John just hoped the horse would move forward once Tom finally mounted him — the little boy deserved a reward for all his persistence.

"*Well done,*" was what he would say to him, when he *eventually* looked up, casual-like, and saw it. Just as he had when Billy did the same thing — *oh, my little Billy. He sure was proud of that broken arm.*

John heard the knock at the door, but even uneasy like he was, he didn't move none.

Cass's client is all. Stay, watch the boy.

He heard Cass call out to Rosie that she'd get the door

herself, heard the footsteps on the floorboards, imagined the girl opening the door.

Sure has grown into her life well, though it could not be easy.

Then he heard the beginnings of a ruckus, and Cass crying, *"You can't come in here, no, No, NO,"* then the heavy front door slamming shut. **"John,"** she cried out in alarm. ***"JOHN!"***

John Ray was up and outta that chair and on his way in a second. He picked up his Colt from its shelf right over the door frame — just inside the back door it was — and he charged through the house, into the front room past Cass, who was backing toward him, away from *someone,* and shaking.

And there, right there in his house — John Ray could barely believe it — was Horace, his back against the closed front door, his hands in the air, and unarmed.

"Hello, Pa," Horace said. "I'm unarmed, don't want no trouble, just come here to talk, and that's all."

CHAPTER 49
"YOU AIN'T MY SON..."

"You got no call to be here, Horace Ray," said John. And while he did not point the gun at him, it felt alive in his hand, as his every sense warned him, something about this ain't right.

"I know that, Pa, and I'm sorry. It's just, I needed to talk with you. Important-like. To do with our lease, and the railroad, and some worries I have now."

He'd spoken slowly and surely. It would have been calming, if John didn't know what Horace was like. But his speech didn't give the whole story. There was something in the arrogant look of the boy — he was hardly a boy now, but a thirty-year-old man — that set John's senses to jangling, worse every second.

Not armed, but dangerous yet.

"Ain't you gonna say nothin', Pa? I come all this way, and it's been a long time. I thought maybe we could all get along now."

John noticed now, Horrie's shirt had a small patch of

blood showing through near the shoulder, and he could see it had been bound. "You been stabbed or shot?" Then, remembering Cass behind him, he said, "Go bring the young'un in, Cass. He's still out back with the horse."

"Just a minute please, Cass," said Horace, and she halted mid-stride, turned to look at him, clearly unhappy. "What I got to say concerns you as well, Cass. And your place. Your ol' Pa's place down at the Falls I mean, a'course. Not this one here. This one's real nice. I heard you was all here. A feller's been wanting to buy—"

"None of it's for sale," said John. "Don't worry, Cass, go get the boy in."

Horace smiled. It was that muck-eating smile, and it wasn't never good news. It was cold, unfriendly, and said he knew something you didn't — and that things would get worse before long.

Some things don't change, not in six years, not in sixty. That terrible smile of Horrie's was one a' them sorta things.

Soon as Cass left them, John Ray, his legs wide apart, his head high, and the gun still filling his hand, said, "You got no call to come here, boy. You know that. If you think we got business to discuss, you send a letter, y'hear me? Now get out, and don't never come back."

"Pa," Horace said, and his voice had an edge to it now. "Maybe thirty seconds from now, you'll be havin' a great urge to shoot me. That'd be a *real* bad idea. If you do, the meanest sumbitch I ever met will do something that'll haunt you the rest a' your miserable life." His smile had grown as he spoke, and his eyes had an eagerness in them, a fire almost, as his gaze bored into his father's. Horace sure was fascinated by other folks' suffering, going by how he looked.

"What the dickens are you talkin' about, boy? Spit it out."

"He won't just kill him easy, if it comes to it," said Horrie, clearly savoring every word. "If I ain't at the meeting place on time, and all in one piece..." — *He stopped a few moments then, let it hang in the air there between them* — "...that horrible, terrible feller, he'll start loppin' off fingers to start with, then other things too, one each hour." Horace Ray shook then like it sent a chill through him, and added, "*Such* a bad man."

John raised the pistol now, pointed it at his son, and his eyes showed a curious mixture of anger and bewilderment.

"Calm down, Pa," Horace said, as relaxed as an old lady knitting. "It's all gonna be simple and easy. I got simple terms, and they leaves you all still protected, just like the terms you made back six years ago, but with only one difference. You just sign my own place over to me, Pa, and instead a' me leasing it, I *own* it. Cass's place too, her Pa's I mean, I want that one as well, just for luck. Then you and Cass get the boy back, and all in one piece." Then he set his face hard, and cold as a gun, he added, "If you're quick."

John Ray heard Cass scream then. And if he had been slow to *begin* understanding, his quick mind made up for it now.

He cocked that Colt and pointed it at Horrie's head, but the boy only smiled the wider.

"Pa, please," he said, and a small laugh escaped him.

"We both know you ain't gonna do it. I'll wait here while you go calm her down, then we can talk turkey. Won't take but a day of your time, and you'll have the boy back safe and sound — then we'll all be assured of our futures, and put this behind us."

John shook his head at the horror of it all, looked at Horace and wondered just how he had ever become how he was. "You ain't my son," he said. "Don't you move from that spot."

John rushed out the back. Rosie was already out there, her head darting this way and that, as she made her way down to Cass.

And Cass, poor Cass, who had already been through so much, stood in the middle of that back paddock, Tom's little hat in one hand, and his bucket in the other. "Where is he, John? It was Horrie, wasn't it? Give me that gun, let me kill him," she cried. The tears streamed down her face, and the slump of her shoulders as she stood there, told a story all their own.

She'll break now, if she don't get him back.

"It'll be alright, Cass," said John, his voice strong, yet full of love too. "They *won't* harm him. I only have to sign over the places at Cottonwood Falls. Don't worry, girl, that's all he wants. They *won't* harm him, I promise."

"But where *is* he?" Cass cried, flinging her arms about, and balling her hands into fists, again and again, as she looked every which way.

"No way of knowing just yet," John said calmly. "But I *promise* you, Cass, I *promise*. They have no intention of harming him, they just want the two places signed over. I'll give him what he wants, it doesn't matter none to me anyway. Just be good, wait for me here, do just as Rosie and Mary tell you."

"Alright," she said, with one last look back at the rail tracks, then along them, once in each direction. And she looked so small now, so broken, it near busted John's heart.

Then he turned to Rosie and said, "Take her to Mary's, and don't any of you leave there until I return. Tell no one. I'll go with Horace, and I'll bring our little boy back. I'll be gone a day, two at most. I *promise,* it'll all be okay."

CHAPTER 50
HARMONY

By the time Billy and Morris reached the halfway point of the twenty-mile trip to Emporia — which is to say, they had just reached Andy Keir's place — Horace and John Ray were just leaving Emporia, headed toward them.

Horrie had been in no hurry to get going, even though the darkness was almost upon them. He had sat himself down in John's parlor and explained the new terms. Made sure his father understood there would still be a clause that protected him and Cass and the little boy from Horace in the future.

"I'm not a monster, Pa," he had said, between slugs of whiskey from his hip flask. "I just need to be assured of my future. So if any of you die within thirty days of the property transfer, I lose it. Gives you a month to sell up here and move someplace else if you want — then you'll never have to see me again."

John had wanted to ride his own horse, but Horace insisted he ride a gray he'd brought along for him.

"Surprised you've got grays," John said as he mounted up, out front of his house. "You always hated them."

"Rented," said Horace. "Let's just say I'm in disguise. Could not have been me here, could it? Everyone knows I'd never ride some filthy gray."

John squinted at the brand on the horse then, in the failing light. "Keir's," he said, and they got going then. "Surprised he'd even rent to *you*."

At that moment, ten miles west, Morris and Billy rode up to the old Keir place. Good and loud, Billy called out, "Hello the house."

It was Andy himself who came out, a scattergun in his right hand. He looked at them, somewhat wary, and said, "I don't rent horses to strangers, if that's what you're after."

Billy looked down from Percy's back and said, "That's alright, Andy, we don't need horses. Permission to step down a minute?"

Andy peered at him in the twilight and said, "Do I know you?"

"Sure you do," Billy said. "Or you did. I'm John Ray's son, Billy."

"Billy Ray died in the war. And he was thinner than skin on a custard."

"I sure do feel alive," Billy said. "Though I will agree, I packed a few pounds on."

Morris grinned and said, "Fat as two pigs, ain't he just?"

Andy still looked mighty skeptical, so Billy said, "Andy, remember when I saved that foal a' yours? Its mother had died, you remember? Also, my Pa bought that old horse off a' you, and it never answered to Horse, so he changed it to Andy, and it took to the name right away."

"Billy! It is you, I can't scarce believe you're alive. Well, ain't this a day? First your brother, then you. Only, why aren't you traveling *with* him? You can step down, a'course you can — and your friend too. Come in and have coffee, the both of you. Have you eaten? I'll let my wife know—"

"It's fine, Andy," said Billy, smiling as he stepped down. "Coffee'd be nice though, and something good for the horses. Truth is, we're Deputy Marshals, and we're trailing Horace. How long since he came through?"

Morris showed him both badges, just to make sure he knew it was true.

Andy went on to explain they were too far behind Horace and Pope to easily catch them, and how Horace had paid triple not to tell anyone they'd been here. "I don't tell anyone anything, he should have known that. But you being Marshals, that's different. Triple payment or not, I owe nothing to Horace. Ain't afraid of him either, way most folks round these parts are."

They stayed only long enough to water their horses, drink their coffee, and find out that Horace and Pope were now on gray horses with the AK brand, and had *said* they'd be back with them tonight. Andy fed Billy's and Morris's horses a high energy meal as well — a slurry with apple, carrot, sugar beets, best quality hay and a little molasses.

Knows what he's doing, Andy Keir.

Morris suggested they stay right where they were and wait for Horace, but Billy decided it wasn't worth the risk.

"Just because he *says* he's coming back tonight don't make it the truth. Even more so with Horace than others. But if he *does*, Andy, don't say we were here. He had fellers ambush us today, you see? Most likely thinks we're both dead, and I'd prefer to keep it that way."

"I won't say a word," Andy said. " Wouldn't have anyway. Just watch out for that Pope, he's a dangerous man. I mean, *real* dangerous. I know you *think* you know what I mean, but..."

He left it hang in the air, and his silence got the message through better.

Billy put his foot in the stirrup, but instead of mounting, he turned to Andy and said, "I know he didn't *say*, but I'd value your thoughts on it, Andy, on *why* Horace was going this way?"

"I don't know, Billy, but I'd worry for your Pa."

"Horace told me Pa lives in Council Grove now."

"Then he lied to you, Billy — and I'm sorry to say it. But I reckon you know I'd only ever tell you the truth, if I spoke up at all." He was a quiet one, Andy, never wanting to overstep other folks' boundaries, always kept himself to himself. He seemed almost embarrassed now, to be saying all this. "They moved to Emporia, about a year after you left for the war, guess it was. Moved there to get away from Horrie."

"Sure?"

"Sure. And lived nowhere else, only Emporia. They been down there ever since then, so we don't see much of your Pa. Once a year maybe, and I've never seen your brother all this time, not 'til today. But ... well, Billy, truth is, I *never* much trusted your brother."

"Seems your instincts were good, Andy," Billy said, stroking the impatient Percy's neck some to calm him.

"You'll have to take care in the dark, but you should get there quick, Billy. Too many people have died around here already from strange goings on. And now I know Horace tried to have you killed ... well, I'd be worried for your family."

Natural enough, Billy assumed that when Andy said *family,* he just meant Pa and Rosie. He knew how Andy was, and didn't push things no further. If he had, it might have changed how things went. But instead, Billy and Morris climbed into their saddles, ready to ride.

"Where's Pa's place, Andy?"

"Half mile or so past the railway station," Andy said. Whole time he spoke, he sorta gave directions with his hands, like as if he was moulding the thing out of clay. "Backs onto the tracks, but the road to his front door veers left just after the station itself. White painted gates it has, gravel driveway, and a sign on the gate, neat black letters. I think they named the place *Harmony,* something like that. Anyway, nice white-painted house with lots of flowers out front. You can't miss it, Billy."

They thanked the Welshman, mounted up and rode up the drive. As they turned right, out onto the trail that led to Emporia, Andy called after them, "Just watch out for Pope, I heard he can be sneaky."

They wanted to hurry along some then, but couldn't go

too quick, on account of poor light. No moon at all, not much in the way of stars either.

"Might get some rain like you predicted," said Morris, a minute or so down the trail. "I done a rain dance earlier, hopin' it might wash the stink off a' you, ya Long Blubbery Streak a' Deer's Droppings."

Billy didn't bite though, worried about his Pa as he was, and they rode along in silence awhile, keeping a lookout for anyone coming toward them.

They hadn't left Andy's ten minutes when they saw a buggy coming toward them. Wasn't completely unusual, it being not long after dark. Billy just figured it most likely someone from the tiny new township where Andy lived. Buggy was drawn by two bays, both with white blazes, but there wasn't enough light to make out a brand.

Morris and Billy went off the trail — both on the same side, so as not to seem threatening, and kept their hands on their reins. They waited there a few moments, watched the driver as he went by. Morris stayed silent, but Billy said, "Howdy, friend, might get some rain."

That driver looked a hard man, and he nodded a greeting from under his hat without smiling or speaking, never taking his eye off the pair. He drove only with his left hand, and likely held a pistol in his right — though it couldn't be seen, for he had a light blanket over it.

Well, all that was understandable, after dark, on a lonely trail, alone. Man'd be a fool *not to* have a hand on his gun, with two riders approaching at night.

It was a fancy buggy, but they couldn't see if anyone was inside, on account of its curtains being drawn.

If they *had* been able to see in there, they'd have noticed a very small boy, with dark hair parted on the left, and a scarf tied tight round his mouth so he couldn't make noise. His hands was tied together by rope, and he was lashed down to the seat so he couldn't move none.

That little boy's name was Tom Ray, and he was afraid.

CHAPTER 51
A LONE RIDER

Billy and Morris kept going. It was a dark night, and for awhile it seemed like they'd make it to Emporia without seeing anyone else.

Then Billy sensed someone approaching.

He had a sort of theory about that — believed that men who rely on heightened senses to stay alive, somehow *feel* someone coming before they hear it or see it.

"Someone coming," he said to Morris. "I got an odd feeling, let's get off the trail and watch."

Morris didn't argue. He was a Brimstone. He'd grown up among men who were not only accustomed themselves to such feelings, but also all sorts of suspicions and rituals that had to be followed by the rest of their kin without argument.

He just shrugged his shoulders and rode down to the river behind Billy. They got behind some trees there, dismounted, and watched.

Sure enough, within a minute, two men came, riding

grays. Billy and Morris looked at each other excitedly — surely, this must be Horace and Pope.

They weren't speaking, and it was too dark to see anything but their outlines as they came closer. But the truth of it washed over Billy like a waterfall — one was Horace alright, the way he sat his horse was prideful, but somehow sneaky too. Like a snake who's busy pretending he ain't gonna strike.

But the other man, he sat a horse another way altogether. He had pride too, but of a different sort entirely. This was a man who would take a deep breath, face his problems front on, stand by his principles to the end — no matter what that virtuous stance cost him.

And clearly, one thing it had cost him, was his right arm.

"It's Pa," Billy whispered.

But Morris only nodded, put a finger to his lips, and they watched the two men ride on past.

Now, that particular part of the trail runs close to the Cottonwood River — close enough for the water to drown out low sounds, anyway.

Billy and Morris, being down by the river, knew they'd have to wait a bit longer, once they could no longer hear the clip-clopping of hooves. But no sooner than the clip-clop sound stopped up ahead, than another started up again from behind.

"Shhhh," Morris whispered. "One rider."

They watched from their vantage point as the lone rider came. Billy's first thought was, *It's a woman.*

But no woman would be out alone on this trail, it was

just a small man, that was all. Not small like Morris — but maybe only a foot taller. Halfway between his height and Billy's. Feller had a slight build though, not chunky like Morris.

The rider's head craned to the side some, looking and listening for whoever it was up ahead. Then the horse stopped and stood, and the rider leaned forward again, cocked an ear, waited perhaps thirty seconds, before moving forward.

Clearly, this one was following the others, and didn't want them to know it.

They both studied the figure, at least as well as they could in the available light. Wrapped up tight in a coat against the rising wind, and the rain it threatened to bring. Hat worn pulled down low on the head, and a bandana worn across the face — maybe a red one, Billy fancied, though really it was too dark to tell.

They waited until the sound of that horse's hooves was gone, then it was Billy who spoke.

"Thoughts?"

"Not sure, Billy." You knew things was serious whenever Morris just called Billy *Billy,* rather than *Stinkin Streak a' Pumpwater,* or some such. "Clearly, the lone rider's following, and don't want to lose 'em. Pope maybe?"

"Maybe," said Billy, slowly stroking Percy's neck, which always sorta helped him think clearer. "But surely *he'd* know just where they're going. He'd either hang further back or stay with them. Don't make no sense to be Pope."

"Well," Morris said, "I don't like it. Them slight fellers are always good with guns."

"Bit like you," Billy smiled.

"I ain't slight," Morris said, patting his belly, then his muscular chest. "But same principle. Lotta big fellers learn to get by with fists — but us smaller ones, that don't mostly work. What was he? Maybe five-three and one-thirty? I don't like it. Don't like it none at all. Feller like that, he's a danger."

They quickly discussed it, and agreed the best plan would be to hang back, not get seen, and when they got to Andy Keir's, he would fill them in on who was who.

They rode along quietly, sticking to the treed side of the trail so they'd blend in on those occasions they might be sighted by the rider in front.

When almost back to Andy Keir's place, they woulda ran slap bang into the rider in front, if they hadn't been so experienced. Sure enough, that rider knew where the first pair would be stopping, had stopped at the edge of the trail. Waited awhile for Horace and John Ray to go into Andy's, unsaddle their horses and mount up again.

Didn't smoke either, Billy noticed.

Then after maybe ten minutes, whoever it was started up again. Just rode quietly past the Keir's little township, keeping their head down.

Billy and Morris knew they had to be quick. Didn't even need to get out a, *"Hello the house,"* though, for Andy was waiting for them as they rode up, with two buckets of his good slurry.

"It was your Pa came with Horace," he said, taking

charge of the horses before the Marshals even dismounted. "Did you see it was him, Billy? Your Pa acted some strange. Pretended like he never hardly knew me."

Morris stepped down, took hold of one of Andy's buckets to help do the feeding, did not interrupt.

Billy stepped down then too. "What about the third rider, Andy?"

"A deer with no eyes."

"What?"

"Sorry, Billy," said Andy. "It's part of a joke we use in these parts now. No eye-deer — no idea, you get it?" Andy waved it away with his free hand. "Sorry, no time for that now, I'll tell you it later. Point is, I don't know *who* that was, no idea whatsoever. Thought it was you at long distance, almost came out from the shadows to hail you. Wrong size and shape altogether though. Mighta been a woman, my first thought — but a woman wouldn't be out. No woman I ever heard of."

Billy knew they had to get going. They could not afford to get far behind — it was bad enough having another rider between them and the others. "Wasn't Pope then? You'd know him, yes?"

"Pope's about normal size. Maybe five-nine, medium build. That buggy come through, not long after you left here — couldn't get a good look, but that mighta been Pope. I heard he had a carryall down in Emporia, but I've never seen it. They say his is nice. This one was, as you musta seen for yourself. But I can't say for sure. You know me, Billy — I keep my beak out of other folks' business, less said the better."

"We always liked that about you," said Billy, then he looked at the sky. "Best get our slickers on I guess."

By the time they got their rain slickers on, the horses had finished their slurry. They allowed them a slurp at some water and got back on the trail, just as it started to rain. It was coming down steady, but at least it wasn't too heavy. Not yet anyway. Took about a minute before the heavy part came.

"I gotta get this hat sewed up proper," said Billy, another two minutes later. He took the lucky hat off a moment and wiped away some of the water off from above his left ear before putting it back on.

"Looks like Deputy Tall Streak a' Stenchwater's sprung hisself a leak," said Morris with a lopsided grin.

Then they went quiet again and kept most a' their eyes and their ears out for those up ahead.

CHAPTER 52
"LISTEN, IF THIS ALL GOES CATAWAMPOUS…"

The rain mighta been unpleasant — more so for Billy with his half-patched hat — but it sure made it easier to track all those they was following.

When they came to the edge of the ranch Billy grew up on — right before the cattle yards started — they came to a halt, looked ahead, to the side, and behind them.

"At least the rain's over," said Morris.

"Over's a strong sorta word," Billy answered. "Enjoy a dry few minutes, my friend. It'll start back up soon, this is Cottonwood Falls."

Morris groaned, but said nothing.

Billy smiled to himself, took out his pocket-watch, lit a match so he could read it. "Almost eleven," he said. "Light the lamp, Morris."

They had not risked the lamp until now, but here, so close to town, they would not seem suspicious, even if those they were following looked back and saw it.

It had been a real downpour alright, just as Billy had predicted early that day. Morris lit the oil lamp, and didn't even need to step down to study the tracks. To be fair, he wasn't all that far above them.

"Buggy turned in right here," Morris said. "Maybe an hour ago, that was. Then later, the two horses followed it in without stopping. But the single horse stopped a bit, moved around willy-nilly, like the rider spent a minute deciding, before following the others." He waved his hand all around, pointing out all the tracks from the single horse.

"So maybe the single rider's acting alone, and considering other options."

"Reckon so," Morris said. "He thought about whether to follow this way or not. The others all chose without thinking about it at all."

"Makes sense they'd go in here," Billy explained to his friend. "This little side-trail runs behind all the one-sixties that front the trail to Council Grove. Goes all the way up to the MacPherson place. It's outta sight of them other places though, on account a' the trees that line Fox Creek. Creek's wide most places, but narrow at the MacPherson's — my Pa and ol' Tom built a bridge there, just enough for one horse, for when the creek's up. But normal times, like now, you can drive across with a buggy if you're any good."

"Creek won't be up, all this rain?"

"Takes a day or two of this to much raise it."

"You know the creek well, Billy — and this path?"

"Me and ... well, you know." Right now, how Billy felt, he could not say her name. "We used to ride out that way a lot. From her place, I mean. Lotta wide open space out behind there."

Morris looked at his friend. Billy's wet hair clung to his collar, and the fur on his face glistened like it was covered in shiny-black oil. Looked like a rat three-parts drowned, he did — but it was no time for jokes. Instead, Morris said, "You think that's where they're all headed then? Where we was before? Maybe to that barn?"

"Noplace else I can think of," said Billy. "They ain't at Pa's old house here — if they were, there'd be lights. Just wish I knew what was going on. Andy reckons my Pa ain't spoke with Horrie in years. Must be somethin' big for Horrie to go down and get him. And whatever it is, it's me turnin' up here that's set it in motion."

"Billy," said Morris now, earnest-like. "Thing is, Horace very likely thinks we're dead. *And* he thinks that's where it happened. Might even think our bodies are there. *What if it's that?* Now think, Billy — *why* would Horace go get your Pa, and bring him to see your dead body?"

Billy looked at the side-trail, then back to the trail ahead. A few cattle bawled in the pens by the railroad, and the stink assailed their nostrils. "I see where you're goin' with it, Morris. And Horrie always was one to play to the gallery. Might be he's got some story for how it happened — some story that might make him look good to Pa, get back in his good books. It's a sticky one alright."

"Well, we can't just stay here," Morris said, screwing his nose up. "Seems this hundred-odd acres a' cowchips smells worse with the wet, if it's possible. I say we just follow the trail, tie the horses up when we get close, then sneak up and see what's goin' on."

"At least visibility's poor."

"Billy, listen. Hear me out. This is what I'm thinking. Unless Jasper *did* sneak back and see us after — *and* own up to the failure — then Horace believes we're both dead. He didn't go any further than here, so he won't know what happened. My experience, most folks tend to underestimate dead men."

Billy nodded his agreement. "We could go swap horses and clothes with them two dead Winchester fellers," he said, his eyes dancing at the thought of the trick. "I always did like a good hornswoggle if it saves bloodshed. And it might just get us in close before Horrie and his men know it's us. Close enough to arrest 'em, and maybe not have to shoot it out."

Morris frowned at him, shook his head real slow and said, "Except them fellers was High-Voice and Low-Voice — and us two is more like Tall-Ass and Short-Ass, remember? They'd pick us a mile away."

There was good things about Morris being a dwarf, but this wasn't one of 'em. Too easily recognized, even at a distance. At night. In disguise.

"Never quite thought it right through," said Billy. "Alright, let's just do it your way and see. But whatever happens, don't shoot my Pa. I'd bet Kansas to a penny he ain't done nothin' wrong. And maybe — *maybe* — the lone rider's on *his* side. Or, maybe *not*. But most likely, anyone else there's guilty as sin."

Finally, they blew out the lamp, and took the side-trail.

The tracks were all there, good and clear. As they rode out there that two miles, the rain started up steady again, just as Billy had predicted, so the pair rode in silence. Billy spent the time thinking about what Morris had said — *Horace probably does believe we're both dead* — and people tend to underestimate dead men.

Billy called a halt and dismounted, then walked down nearby the creek, where he knew of a gap he could look through — sure enough, he saw a dim light coming from ol' Tom MacPherson's barn. He further considered the plan he'd been making, thought of the lay of the land, knew he had the resources.

I sure do love a good wrinkle, and I think it can work.

Billy laughed to himself as he scrambled back up the slope, then he climbed up on Percy's back, leaned across and said, "Hey, Morris, you ever see a dead man stand up and fire a Henry?"

"Not me," the dwarf answered. "And this ain't no time for ghost stories, Billy, I'm plenty enough spooked already."

"Well, it's you that gave me the idea, and I reckon you might just enjoy it," said Billy. Then he told his friend the plan he'd thought up as they'd been riding along.

Morris whistled through his teeth when he heard it. "Deputy Billy Hornswoggle," he said, "that's as cunning as a fox with four aces hid under his tail fur. Remind me never to play cards against you for money."

"Cunning might not be enough, Morris. I'd feel better about it if we knew who the lone rider was. Err on the side of caution — but don't get killed neither. And whatever happens, don't shoot my Pa. If in doubt, aim for the straw colored hair. Their hats'll be off to dry out from the rain."

"What if Horace somehow knows you ain't dead?"

"He almost certainly don't know," said Billy. "But even if he does, the trick'll still be a diversion — just won't work quite so long is all. We'll cross that bridge when we get there."

"Or swim the floodwaters, more like it," said Morris. "Wish this dang rain'd stop again."

Three-hundred yards further on, almost to the bridge, they heard a noise and saw movement up ahead, and both of them went for their guns — didn't fire, but they were both ready to.

Turned out it was only a horse — the lone rider had tied up his horse here, just off the trail, thirty yards past the bridge.

And nearby to that — better hidden — were the other two horses and the buggy. Pope had placed it well, for despite its size, it could not be seen from the trail until they were almost upon it.

They were wary a'course, and Morris was spooked some — but he got down with the lantern and checked out the tracks, before walking back to where Billy stood by the horses.

"His feet are tiny," he half-whispered. "I don't like this at all. If small size makes men grow up dangerous, this feller's deadly as a whole nest a' snakes in your underwear. Got on moccasins, too, but don't walk like no Indian I ever tracked. Too even-footed, not enough on his toes. I don't like this, Billy."

"That all you got?"

"No. The other one, Pope. His feet ain't big, but he's heavy. Heavier than you maybe. Ain't like Andy said — so maybe it ain't Pope at all, might be someone different."

"Tie the horses just here," Billy said, pointing to a spot near enough to the others they wouldn't call out to each other, but not too close either. Then he took the lamp and checked out the tracks for himself. Morris was right — that little feller was tiny, and weighed maybe less than they'd earlier thought.

"Might be a kid, fourteen or fifteen," Billy said, real quiet. "Well, I guess we just stick to the plan. Remember, only shoot yellow hair."

"What about the big feller?"

Billy studied the other tracks, looked up and grinned at his friend. "It's Pope alright. But he's carrying something. Something heavy. I'll show you how to read it in the tracks one day when we got time. Preacher Rob taught it to me — surprised he never taught you."

"I didn't always listen, like most kids. I don't like this, Billy. How do we know for sure who to shoot, if one of 'em might be innocent?"

Billy rubbed his chin before going on. "Andy said Pope's hair's brown for a start. We'll know him alright — he'll be the sneaky one tryin' to kill us. Listen, if this all goes catawampous, Morris, I just want you to know—"

"That you'll have a bath before comin' to my funeral? Good to know, Deputy Stenchwater. Maybe wash your hair with some soap while you're at it."

"See you when the mud dries," said Billy. He blew out

the lamplight, and they let their eyes adjust to the more complete darkness.

Then they quietly crossed the little bridge over the creek, before heading in different directions, quiet-footed as they sliced through the night, each to his appointed part of the plan.

CHAPTER 53
THE TUNNEL

All the years since her family had died here, Cass had never set foot on the place — and it had taken all the courage she could muster to ride through the night, follow the tracks made by John's and Horace's horses, and also the buggy her son must have been in.

She had no idea what she'd do — but she knew Horace too well to believe he'd keep to his word.

My son's life is at stake.

John Ray was a wonderful man, but no great shakes as a liar. As hard as he'd tried to reassure her, she knew young Tom was in danger.

She had seen light coming from the barn, left her horse the other side of Fox Creek, right near the two harnessed to the buggy. Then she'd crept as low as she could to the outhouse. She could only just hear the voices from inside the barn — the voices were raised in argument, but she could not make out what they were saying. And ever so carefully, quietly, she scraped off the dirt, lifted the board, and silently climbed down the ladder.

Her feet, through her moccasins, felt almost bare — she could feel the shape of the rungs on the ladder. The ladder made by her father. Her hands wrapped around the rungs too, then she was fully inside, feet flat on the floor. She pulled the board above her head into place, turned around in the now complete darkness, reached for the lamp on its shelf — *it was there*. And beside it, too, the matches inside the jar.

Just like old times.

Not quite. There's no Billy this time.

She unscrewed the lid, said a quick prayer and the quietest possible *"Thank you"* to her father, and she hopefully struck the first match. *It caught!*

Cass lit the lamp and it took. It sputtered and fizzed, the oil having congealed some with the years — but it was working, for now. Ahead of her was a tunnel.

Slow and deliberate, Cass crawled along the tunnel, hands and knees in the damp dirt, quiet as she could manage. She moved the oil lamp before her, a foot-and-a-half at a time, and made as little noise as she could.

She'd forgotten how tight the tunnel was. It would have bothered her more if she hadn't been in here so many times as a child. But the dank smell of it didn't trouble her at all — indeed, it somehow felt welcoming, a part of her childhood returned to her.

When her Pa built this tunnel, he had made sure it was vented, both inside the barn and the outhouse. False walls in both hid the vents, but there was one drawback to the venting — it allowed sound through.

As she came closer to the barn she began to hear the men inside. Not clear words, but sounds floated to her sharp ears. Cass knew they'd hear her too, if she wasn't careful. She came to the end of the tunnel, where it widened, and placed the lamp on its shelf. She took a good grip on a carefully placed timber handle. Slowly, carefully, she turned. Closed her eyes as she let her right foot find the step down below her, then allowed her left foot to join it. She let go the handle, stood to full height now, stretched herself out some and listened.

Her own breathing sounded too loud — but she knew from experience it wasn't really the case.

Two voices, a back and forth argument. John was angry, as expected — and Horace was arrogant as always.

"That wasn't the deal," said John. "I've signed over the ranch, this place too. That's all you need — now stick to your word for once, boy."

"You'll sign," said Horace. "Tell you what, I'll give you five minutes. If you ain't signed your Emporia place over by then, the little boy loses a finger."

Cass made an involuntary noise, her hand flew to her mouth, and she gripped her face tight in her anguish.

She heard Jasper's voice then, close by. "What was that?"

"Shut your pie-hole, Jasper," Horace snapped. "Go outside and check, ya damn fool, if ya think you heard somethin'. It'll only be Spinks and Matich. They was meant to wait here for me after doin' their job, but the fools musta gone and got drunk. Clem, you go with him, but leave that paperwork here, I don't want it wet."

Cass knew this was her chance. As she listened to — and felt — the dull thud of the Jenkins men's boots on the dirt floor, she took out the tiny derringer pistol John had taught her to use years before. She knew it was no good at distance, but from where she'd appear — halfway down the barn on the left — she knew that Horace wouldn't be much more than five yards away. She had practiced before at that distance, and done pretty well.

The barn was a pretty good size, but she'd spent enough time in here with Billy, listening to their two fathers, to know where the voices were coming from. Men tended to gather certain places, do things a particular way — they'd be standing or sitting about, leaning their backs against the posts of the hay loft.

She wished Tom would speak or make some noise, for she needed to know where he was before she could shoot. But it was so late, he must surely be sleeping by now.

"How do I know you won't kill us anyway," she heard John Ray say then. "Way you keep going back on your word, I'll need more assurance than these papers. You might yet falsify them."

Damn Horace, he'll kill them both for sure, he's a liar.

Thing was, Cass had figured all along that it must have been Jasper who'd brought her son here — it never occurred to her that there might be someone else. So knowing Jasper and Clem had stepped out the door, she planned to shoot Horace, then deal with the other two as they came running, for they were clearly in on the kidnapping.

Cass raised up the derringer, took a deep breath, ready to shoot. She pressed her right foot down onto the lever that opened the hatch — and it stayed right where it was, nothing happened.

She tried again, both her feet now, to get that lever to move under her weight — but again, nothing happened at all.

Stuck from the years, or maybe too much weight on top.

She remembered now, there was one time when it had taken her own weight and Billy's together to open it.

"No one out there," Clem said as the footsteps thudded back into the barn.

"No one at all," Jasper added, helpful as ever.

Then Horace said, "Clem, go outside, keep an eye out just in case. I'll call you back in when I need you."

She heard the big man's steps — loud at first, then quieter until they were gone.

Cass tried to think fast, to think clear.

I'll have to come in frontways, kill them all best I can. If I can get past Clem first.

But even as she thought it, she knew she would die in the attempt. But if it saved little Tom, her death would be worth it.

No one's chopping my little boy's fingers.

And quiet as a man whose foot just paused over a rattler, Cass climbed up again, picked up her lamp, placed it into the tunnel in front of her, and crawled back along to the outhouse.

CHAPTER 54
WHY DO THEY ALWAYS WEAR BLACK?

When Billy left Morris behind him, he was careful, optimistic — and pretty soon, partway miserable.

First thing tomorrow, I'm buying myself a new hat.

Billy had never been one to waste money, and his sewing skills were better than average — but if his patching job this time had been any worse, he might well have ended up drowned.

Hat must have holes in the holes.

Lucky for him the rain had eased again, and it was almost stopped now. And at least there wasn't no lightning to give him away if anyone looked out there, once he got in position. No lightning yet anyway.

He crept along in the dark, staying downwind from the horses, so they wouldn't notice him there, and maybe warn Horace and the others.

Left their horses outside in the rain. Pa would not have liked that, it's Horrie who's got the control here. Four horses this side — but who? — John, Horace, Jasper, and probably Clem.

He knew Horrie wouldn't pay attention to whinnying horses, but this other man, Pope, was an unknown quantity.

Boneyards are chock-full of fellers who once underestimated the unknown.

Until he found out otherwise, Billy would credit Pope with every imaginable skill.

Minimize risk, that's what Pa always told me. Deep breaths, Pa, whatever's happening. I'm on my way.

Billy had a fair way to go. His plan relied on the light being low. That low light had its advantages as well as its drawbacks. And though the years had filled his mind with many new things, he found that he still knew every inch of this land. Could have closed both his eyes and got to where he was going.

At least the rain's stopped again.

The open barn doors meant that Horace believed his men had killed Morris and Billy.

That helped plenty, made Billy happy as a frog in a pond.

He had finished his initial preparations, and was two-hundred yards from the barn doors when he made his way across to where he could look through them, and took out his little spyglass.

But when Billy put his eye to that spyglass, everything changed.

A child. A child with his mouth all tied shut, standing at the edge of the hayloft. THAT's the load Pope was carrying.

For a moment, it made no sense at all. Not the fact that

the child was there — clearly, the child had been used as some sort of bait to lure John Ray. No, it wasn't that — the thing that made no sense was the bright yellow bandana tied over the little one's mouth.

Completely unnecessary, out here so far from everything else.

Then he saw Horace. That arrogant way he still stood. Even with the spyglass, Billy could not make out facial features at this distance — it wasn't a powerful one, but was compact and light — but even without being able to see it, Billy knew beyond a doubt that his brother was wearing *that* smile. The one that never meant anything good. The child's mouth was tied shut so that Horrie could show he was boss — that he, Horace Damn Ray, was the one with the power.

Billy studied them all through the spyglass, tried to read the whole situation, work out how it might fit with his plan.

To the left, halfway down, stood two men. Jasper was the further away, his short rounded stature and shock of blond hair all too obvious. And beside him, closer, was almost certainly Clem. Both men leaned against the workbench, just a few feet from where Morris waited down in the tunnel — right by where Morris would open the hatch a few minutes from now.

Then suddenly Clem and Jasper were looking around, and both of them walked to the doors. They seemed wary as they readied their guns, walked out into the darkness. Billy didn't move, stayed alert — but the pair walked back inside within less than a minute, and both seemed more relaxed. Then, as if he'd changed his mind, one of them turned and walked out, back into the darkness again — but this time, his shoulders wasn't so bunched, and his gun stayed pointed at the ground.

Definitely Clem. Ten pounds heavier now, but I'd know him anywhere. Pear shaped, and a real lazy mover — like half of him wants to stay behind where he was.

It wasn't a good thing. Clem was outside now. If the cloud cover broke, or if lightning lit the sky even a little, Clem would see Billy was here. He'd have to move even slower than he'd planned.

Unable to see where Clem was, he kept his ears open, and set his gaze back on the barn.

Between middle and right — half-facing Jasper, half-facing the hayloft — were Horace and Pa. Horace, half-obscured, leaned against the barn's stable-rail, while John stood up straight, true as ever. That fine man was laying down the law about something, pointing a finger at Horace as he spoke.

He won't take his eye off that little boy, not even when he seems to.

And right in the middle, further away, but right at the edge of the hayloft, the small boy — he was perhaps only six — was being held standing by a man from behind.

Pope.
The unknown quantity.
And in black, of course.
Why do they always wear black?

Billy thought of the irony of it — for right now, he wore

black himself. If he'd had his Pa's Spencer with him, Billy could have killed Jasper from where he now stood.

That's what a fool would have done — but Billy was patient, he knew he must stick to the plan.

It would serve no purpose firing yet — their positions were wrong, and Morris wouldn't get a clear shot. Horrie was more or less behind John, and Pope held the child as cover in front of his body.

Pope's a Just-In-Case man, aware of the open barn doors, the outside chance of a shot in the dark. That's why he's stood behind the child. Clever.

Didn't matter. Shooting into the barn from long distance was never part of the plan. And now there was a child involved — a child Morris could not know was there — Billy had to be even more patient, work out his angles, take his time.

Still, he was confident. He held a fully loaded Henry in his hand, and that was enough. Morris had both of their pistols, and three derringers as well, for if things went sideways — each of them were Sharps with four shots ready to go.

It's more bullets than Morris will need.

Billy kept watching through the spyglass, his ears straining for a clue to Clem's whereabouts. Sometimes he heard the man's steps. Every so often, he saw him go through the patch of light in front of the barn. Whenever Billy thought it was safe he inched forward, crawling on the wet ground.

He was still worried about the lone rider — where was he now? *Is he watching Clem? Has he seen me?*

There was nothing Billy could do about that, except for be ready to adapt if the lone rider changed things.

Morris would be lying in wait now, Billy knew that for certain and sure. He'd be *ready*.

They were outnumbered alright, but only by four to two, probably — five to two at the worst — and Billy had learned that it doesn't take *much* to tip the scales back in your favor.

Buy a second or two here, practice some sleight of hand there — like magician's tricks, but with guns.

Billy was mighty thankful for having learned from the Brimstones — wasn't a one of 'em hadn't surprised some seamstress or other with the creativity of their requests for a strangely placed pocket, just for one thing. It was like they all tried to outdo each other with the best trick. But these days, Billy's mind even came up with tricks of his own. Like this one right now. Even Morris had been impressed by it, and that took some doing.

Hopefully Clem would go back inside, for the plan couldn't work if he didn't. He probably would before long. Ol' Clem never much liked discomfort, and it wasn't much of a night.

Biggest problem is Pope.

Pope was an unknown quantity, but Billy could not see a rifle within the man's reach. Indeed, he could not see a rifle *anywhere*.

Not even Clem has one.

He had seen this before — gangs of men who relied exclusively on their sidearms. Usually — it held true in this case — such men wore fancy rigs, and the guns themselves leaned to showy as well. Etched silver handles, or pearl. Such men often showed off with fancy gun-tricks as well, at least most of that type did.

Morris seemed like an exception — he knew all the tricks, and was good at them too. But he mostly just did them in private, and not to show off to strangers. No, Morris was different.

Mostly, that other sorta man overrates his ability. And usually, only one of their whole gang can shoot worth a squirt.

Clem was never much good, and wasn't the sort to improve himself. Jasper's shooting today had been sloppy, and even that from a short distance. And when things started up, John would take care of Horace somehow for sure, no matter the personal cost.

Pope. Only problem is Pope.

Lying on the damp ground, Billy's eye went often to the spyglass, to watch the men in the barn. If they saw him, the plan would all change. But so far they had not — and closer he went, inch by inch, through the dark of the night.

But still, there was a long way to go. And *anything* could happen.

CHAPTER 55
"WHY DO PEOPLE KEEP SAYIN' THAT?"

When Morris and Billy parted, Morris knew he had plenty of time. He kept *very* quiet, of course. And while he had lots of experience with his Uncle Mike, he did not have the wide knowledge Billy did.

Thing was, Morris had gotten away with a lot these few years, and was prone to take risks Billy wouldn't have. But Morris Brimstone *was* worried about the lone rider.

Why is he here? Whereabouts?

So instead of going *straight* across to the outhouse, he took a risk that wasn't part of the plan, and would have curled Billy's hair if he knew. But when Morris got something in his head, he just had to do it, so he did a little scouting of his own first. Gun in hand, a'course, he wasn't a fool. He even crept up close to the barn — close enough to hear voices, but they were too muffled to make out what was being said.

Finally, he made his way to the outhouse to do just what he was told to.

Well, Morris's timing wasn't great, but it coulda been worse.

He was not a nervy man, by disposition. But the lone rider's presence — wherever, *whoever* that lone rider was — had set his nerves all a'jangle.

So when he sneaked into that old outhouse, knelt down in the doorway and felt around in front of him for the edge of the board he must open, Morris's mind was running just about twenty-four to the dozen.

He thought he could smell a lamp burning for a moment — but he quickly decided it was only a lingering smell, from the one he and Billy had just used. Still, smells are powerful things, and that one set Morris on edge even worse than before.

He did not need any surprises, and he reached down now, and found the edge of the board. *Good.* It was right where Billy said it would be.

But right then, lickety split, that dang board rose up, a dull light escaped from the gap that it made, and a hat — a hat that must be on a head — rose up through the opening.

Scared the living persnickety out of Morris, all that did.

His body snapped to attention, but his feet didn't move. Woulda flew straight up in the air, if'n he had the power of flight.

He knew he had to act fast. Thing was, whoever that head belonged to, now had a clear view of Morris's boots. That sorta thing makes folk nervous — then bullets start flyin' around, before anyone knows what was who.

"Make a sound or move a muscle, and I'll blow your head right off your shoulders," said Morris, quiet as he could manage, while still making sure he was heard.

The hat didn't move, the head didn't speak.

Morris drew his six-gun and cocked it, pushed the barrel down through the hat so it rested hard against head — just to show he was serious — and he said, "Best put your guns up here first, I don't like surprises."

"I don't have a gun," said the voice that belonged to the head that was under the hat — and he could not believe what he'd heard.

A woman!

"Ma'am," he said. "I am Deputy Morris Brimstone, of the U.S. Marshals Service, and I *do not* ... like surprises. Put out your guns, and be quick. I *know* you got some."

"Please don't shoot me," she whispered, and she sure talked fast. "Are you really a Marshal? Please be telling the truth. My boy ... my little boy. They've kidnapped him, he's in the barn."

"Ma'am, your guns," he said again, his voice quiet yet urgent.

A delicate hand — it was shaking a little — came up beside the head, and placed a single-shot Philadelphia Deringer down on the floor. In the pale lamplight he saw it, and found it surprising. It was medium sized for a Deringer, three inch barrel and all — but somewhat unusually, it had a *rear* sight as well as a front one.

Never seen that before.

He picked it up with his left hand, and moved back half a step. "That *all* your guns, Ma'am?"

"Please," she whispered. "What if they hear us? Time's wasting, they'll chop off his fingers."

The voice struck all the right notes — either she was a very fine actor, or it was the truth.

"Climb out," Morris said. "But if I see a gun, or a closed hand that might have one in it, I'll shoot first and ask questions later."

It wasn't *much* light coming up through the hole, but enough for Morris to see by. The woman climbed out, got to her feet, and looked ... straight ahead first, and then down.

Morris was used to it, people's surprise at his height. "Yes, Ma'am, I'm a dwarf," he said. "And yes, I'm *really* a Deputy. That outta the way, down to business. Who are you and how did you know about this tun—"

"Quiet," she whispered urgently, grabbing his shirt to pull him further inside so she could close the outhouse door. "I grew up here, I'm Cass MacPherson, and—"

"Ma'am, you're a liar," said Morris, pressing a Smith and Wesson barrel hard against the woman's ribs. "Cass died. Who are you really?"

It was roomy, as outhouses went, but such rooms are not made for two people — not even those designed for access to underground tunnels — and the pair were breathing each other's air, they were so close together.

"Listen you fool," she said, getting her face down even closer to his. "If you really are a Marshal, you need to help me."

"I'm trying to, Ma'am. And I'm a Deputy, not a Marshal."

"Well *why* are you here anyway? Come to think of it, how did *you* know about this tunnel? *Well?*"

"My partner Billy told me — he's a Deputy too, and he's Horace Ray's brother. We've come—"

"Ha," she said, almost too loud. Then in a whisper, "Now who's lying? Billy Ray's dead!"

Morris shook his head as he said, "Why do people keep sayin' that?"

"Because it's true. I should know, we were going to marry. You're not a Marshal at all are you?"

"You're right, Ma'am, I'm not, I'm a Deputy." And he undid his slicker a little, pointed out the badge on his chest.

Her voice rose then as she lost her control some. "You could've stolen that badge. Why, you're probably working for Horace! Oh my boy, my poor little boy!"

It was hard to sound exasperated *and* stay quiet, but Morris managed it well. "Ma'am, I'm mostly polite with the ladies. Pride myself on it, in fact. But please — shut your mouth now and listen. This *is* my badge. I *am* a Deputy Marshal. I *have* come here to arrest Horace Ray, and Jasper Jenkins as well."

"Jasper's in there," she said, "and his father Clem too, I heard them. Please hurry then, if it's true, if you're really a Deputy."

"What about Pope?"

"Don't know any Pope," Cass whispered. "It's just those three and John. And my Tommy must be asleep, I couldn't hear him."

"Lady, listen," said Morris, holstering his gun now. "Me and my partner made a plan, and I need to stick to it and get in there *now*. As for *you*, you're a bad complication. I need to go along this tunnel and get to the barn — for your own safety, I'll need to tie you up here and gag you quiet until this is over."

"It won't open, I already tried."

"What won't?"

"The lever is stuck. I was gonna shoot Jasper with my Deringer, but I couldn't open the hatch."

Morris forced out a breath. "Dang it. I mean ... sorry 'bout that, Ma'am, I don't usually—"

"*I don't care!*" she whispered. And if a whisper could be fierce, hers was. "Please, there's no time, we'll both go. There's too much weight on the hatch, or maybe the lever's stuck. But the two of us *will* be able to open it. Then we can *both* shoot."

"Ma'am..."

She knelt down, lifted the board again, sat and swung her feet over the edge. Then she looked up at him and said, "We can't talk down there, they'll hear us. I'll go first. At the other end, I'll place your feet where they have to go, so you don't make a noise. But *don't* speak." Morris could see the gleam of her eyes as she looked up at him and said, "Please."

Morris considered giving up on the plan, going quickly now to find Billy. But that had its own set of problems.

"Alright then, but wait," he said to the girl, and she did. "You don't do *anything* except help with the lever. It may take awhile, but we wait for the signal, and *do not* ruin the plan. That's what's most important. It's a good plan, but you can't interfere with it, or it won't work. Promise me."

"Alright, I promise."

"I'll give you your gun back, in case something happens to me. But don't come up shooting — me and Billy will have that all covered. If you shoot, you might hit your son — me and Billy *won't* do that, I promise. Wait — has your gun been fired and reloaded today?"

"Of course," she said, "Right before I set out. And you might be surprised at how straight it shoots for a Deringer. John had it modified some, and taught me to use it."

"Alright then," said Morris. "You'll keep your gun hidden, and only use it as a surprise if our plan goes wrong, and me and Billy are already dead. But be *patient*. You got one shot, and you'll get but one chance, pick your moment. You understand?"

"I understand. Patience. Pick my moment."

"Promise me you won't fire when I do, but stay down and wait until later."

"Again, I promise," she said. "But one thing — whoever this Billy of *yours* is, he's *not* Billy Ray. We'll argue *that one* out later. Let's go save my boy. And don't shoot John either. You do know—"

"I know not to hurt John," said Morris. "So does Billy." He took off his rain slicker, folded it in half, draped it over the seat, then put his hat on top of it.

"Don't leave those there," said Cass, "bring them into the tunnel. Just in case someone comes in here."

That impressed Morris.

Then Cass climbed down into the tunnel, and reached for the lamp once again.

CHAPTER 56
HALF A TOE

Morris and Cass had been in place two minutes, and she looked downright itchy to move — Morris sure hoped Billy would start the party soon. He stayed cool though, and that seemed to reassure Cass.

If she really is Cass, he thought, as he listened to the voices inside.

John was still refusing to sign, and was demanding to go with Clem to the Grove. Wanted to lodge all the papers himself, make sure there weren't any tricks.

That was when it all went to Hell.

Horace was angry, and they heard him clearly when he growled, "Enough! Pope, it's time. Take off the damn kid's little finger."

Whether or not Pope would have done it, Cass and Morris didn't wait to find out.

Together they jumped on the lever, and Morris yelled,

"Drop your guns, you're under arrest," as Cass flew outta that tunnel like she'd been fired from a cannon.

"*Tommy,*" she screamed as she scrabbled forward from under the work bench.

Morris summed up the room, had no clear shot at anyone but Jasper — who was turning toward him and drawing his Colt — but as Morris went to shoot Jasper in the chest, Cass's scrambling foot hit his arm, and his shot went awry.

Instead of a forty-four in the chest, Jasper got it much lower. His foot was in the air as he turned, and the bullet tore the edge off his boot. But not just the boot — half a toe came away with the leather. As the remains of the toe flew across the barn, Jasper squealed in pain, fired a wild shot that went between Cass and Morris, tripped over his own legs and fell.

Soon as the whole thing unfolded, Pope had jumped backward, over the hay to take cover. When he did though, the sleepy little Tom lost his balance, toppled forward right off a' that hayloft. The six-year-old plummeted head first toward the dirt floor, where his neck would surely be broken — but ol' John Ray's gaze had never left his grandson.

As the boy plunged toward certain death, John leaped forward, his one arm outstretched, scooped the boy in close to his body, and rolled. Rolled right in *under* the hayloft, and threw himself *over* the child to protect him from bullets.

As Cass tried to cross the room to her son — *too late,* she had thought — Horace had been on her in a second.

Horace pulled Cass up by the hair, held his gun to her head. And at Morris, he yelled, "Put down your guns, Runt, real slow."

"I got a bead on the dwarf's little face," said Pope, from somewhere behind all that hay.

Morris knew that his cards looked bad for the moment — but he knew he still had an Ace, for Billy was somewhere outside.

Best I stay alive long enough to help him.

He laid down his Colt, put up his hands, said, "Yessir, Mister Ray, you're the boss."

"My damn foot," Jasper cried as he scrambled to his knees. "Damn da-warf, I'm gonna *kill* you now!" And with a trembling hand, he picked up the gun he had dropped.

But Horace, loud and clear, yelled, *"NO, JASPER. No."*

"But—"

"Leave him, Jasper, or I'll shoot you myself," Horace growled. "I need to talk to our tiny friend first — maybe *then* you can kill him. For now, you keep my Pa covered, make sure he stays where he is. Dammit, where's Clem?" He shook Cass violently then to stop all her struggling, and pressed the barrel of his gun against her cheek.

Clem called out to them then from the darkness. "All under control in there? What's goin' on?" He had never been the bravest of men, and running toward gunfire had never been part of his make-up.

"I'm shot, Pa," Jasper called out to the darkness. "Damn da-warf popped up out of a hole in the floor and he shot me! It hurts, Pa, it hurts real bad."

"It's only your foot, you big Mary," yelled

Morris. **"I'm a U.S. Deputy Marshal, throw down your guns, you're all under arrest."**

"That's rich," said Horace. "You with no guns, and me ready to splatter this damn whore's brains all over you. Jasper, drag the runt up outta there. And Pope — you kill him if he tries anything."

"Don't struggle, Cass," said John Ray, low, calm, and urgent. "I've got Tom, it's okay."

She did as John said, and went still.

Jasper squealed from the pain when he bent down, and Morris, a touch loud, said, "He's useless, I'm climbing out on my own." Then *real* loud, **"Don't shoot the girl or the child, and don't shoot me. Alright?"**

Horace said, "Alright. And shut up all your noise."

Morris sorta cocked an ear sideways at Horace and, not quite so loud as before, said, "WHAT? Damn ringin' in my ears from the echo a' the shots in the tunnel."

And Pope said, "One wrong move, little man, you'll be nothing but guts and red paint all over that floor."

Then Morris climbed out, slow and careful, kept his hands where they could see 'em, and got to his feet. His ears were fine, a'course — he just needed Billy to know what was happening inside.

"Clem," Horace yelled, "get in here, ya damn fool."

"No," said Pope firmly, coming out from behind the hay. "Tell Clem to wait a minute first, then I'll swap with him. I wanna make sure no one else is out there myself."

Jasper just whimpered some in the background, while Horace called, "Wait out there a minute, Clem."

Pope came down the ladder — facing forward, with his gun still in hand — and walked over to Morris, gun pointed. "I'd bet a dollar you got a palm pistol, little man," he said.

"You're right, Pope, he had derringers today," said Horace. *"Two* in his pocket, the little sneak."

"Yessir, it's true," said Morris to Pope, like he was embarrassed. Then a little sadly — pathetically almost — he added, "Just, please don't kill me, Mister. Not easy, life as a dwarf, but I do hope to live awhile longer. I'm happy for you to search me."

Morris had looked into Pope's eyes as he spoke, tried to engage his attention — for right now, the arrangement of the men in the room was his best chance to kill them all with his lightning fast movement.

If he could get Pope's concentration to lapse for a moment, two or three men would be dead in the seconds that followed. He had done it before — most men underestimate a dwarf.

But Pope made no such mistake, kept his already cocked gun trained on Morris while he took the derringers, one at a time, and transferred them to his own pocket. Then the man took out something else — it was Billy's badge.

Pope stepped away, outside Morris's reach, before glancing down at the badge on Morris's chest. His gun was pointed right at it. He looked into the dwarf's eyes now, fingered the *other* badge in his hand. "Two badges? You're barely big enough just for one. Always carry a spare?"

"Course not," said Morris, his voice already loud, and it kept getting louder by the moment. "I took it off Billy after that damn piece of excrement there had him murdered." He was *really* making a noise by the time he shouted, **"You FOUR will hang, for the murder of Billy Ray here today—"**

"Shut up," Horace growled.

"What are you talking about?" said John Ray, turning to look at the dwarf. "Billy's been dead for years. Died in the war."

Morris looked at John sideways and said, "Why do people keep sayin' that?"

"What the hell's axe-cromit?" Jasper finally managed to say.

"Ex-cre-ment," said Morris, pulling a screwy face at the Strawhead. "It's what *you* see when you look in a mirror."

"Shut up," growled Horace again, waving his gun at Morris.

"I killed your filthy sharpshooters though," Morris said with a taunting smile, *"and* your useless gunfighter, Patterson."

"I. Said. Shut. Up." Horace's voice sure was growling by now. "Pope, next person speaks, splatter his brains on the—"

"Hey," said Jasper, "you said *I* could shoot the little—"

"You shut up too," Horace said, roughhousing Cass some, for she was trying to get her hands free. *"Enough,"* he screamed into her ear. "Jasper, give Pope your handcuffs."

Pope backed away from Morris, keeping him covered, and took the cuffs from Jasper without looking at him. Horace ordered Morris to be cuffed, and John tied up too.

But Pope did it the opposite way — he tied Morris tight to the workbench, then had John come away from little Tom and be cuffed to the workbench, a few feet from Morris.

Pope was no fool. He'd tied Morris tight, and given him no chance to do anything about it.

Dang, Morris thought, helpless now. *If only he'd cuffed me instead, I coulda still used my hidden derringer.* Thing was, Morris had spent many a lonely hour by himself at the Wilmington Sheriff's Office, with nothing better to do than work out how to escape from cuffs — and he had learned how to do so, just in case. And the whole point of taking *three* derringers was so he could give up the first two, and then seem unarmed. It was rare for any man to carry two — three was completely unheard of.

So much for the old saying about the best laid plans of mice and men — should have had dwarves added to it.

Pope brought Tommy out now from under the hayloft. He looked afraid, but when John told him to be a good boy, he let go John's hand and went along with Pope bravely. Went quietly too, even though John had untied the gag from the little boy's mouth, first chance he got.

Horace pushed the distraught Cass across to Jasper and said, "Here, she's finally yours."

Jasper put his fancy Colt away in its holster. "About time," he said gleefully. Seemed he'd forgot all about his shot foot as he spun Cass around and grabbed two good-sized handfuls of her. "Hope you're as good as your Ma and your sister was, night we killed 'em."

"*WHAT? You...?*" Cass's words became an anguished

scream, but it was cut short as Jasper punched her hard in the belly and knocked the wind out of her.

"Me and Horrie both," Jasper said, and he sounded proud of it.

As for Horace, he didn't say a word, only smiled that smile of his and took in the show.

Jasper pulled the back of Cass hard against him, and held her by places he shouldn't ought to have touched as she struggled. Leered mightily at her too, as he breathed his foul breath all over one side of her face. More she struggled, worse he got. Then he punched her hard in the ear, and poor Cass went limp, and quiet except for her sobbing.

Finally, Pope handed the child over to his boss. Horace reached out and took little Tommy's right hand with his left, and said, "Alright Pope, you can go swap with Clem now."

And right then, once more, things changed.

CHAPTER 57
"HE'S GOOD THAT DWARF — REAL GOOD"

Billy's progress had been slow, but it was all in the right direction, and patience was a thing he'd learned well. He was still a hundred-and-thirty yards from the barn doors when Clem swapped over with Pope.

Billy knew *some* of what had happened inside — Morris had been plenty loud, so Billy knew for sure just who he was up against.

He knew Jasper had been shot in the foot — but that also meant no one else was injured, he felt pretty certain. And most likely, Morris would be tied up tight, and he'd have to do the whole thing himself.

He thought of his Pa, took a real deep breath, and waited for the cards to fall his way.

At one point, right after the shots, Billy had thought Clem was going in — but then he had stopped, gone back into the shadows, stayed outside.

He'd stayed near the barn though, from then on.

Feeling safe at this distance, Billy had used that time to pour the fuel from his lamp onto the bandanas and kerchiefs. The smell was strong, but Clem would never notice from there, as a light wind was blowing crossways.

Finally, it seemed like Clem would go in — but the moment he went to the door, Pope swapped over with him, and came out. And Billy was still too far away to be sure of killing the man. This wasn't going well, not at all.

Pope was sneaky by reputation. He hadn't wasted a single moment in the light out front of the barn. Straight to the right side he'd gone. He could have gone any direction from there.

Billy waited, ears open. He stayed where he was. Stretched his fingers and toes, and his neck. Sniffed at the wind for a hint of where Pope was.

Nothing much else he could do.

He knew his moment must come.

They could not stay here forever.

Pope would check all about the barn, then go back in. Or, if the man was *really* good, he'd find Billy, then try to kill him.

But this past few years, Billy had always been better than any man who tried it. He would smell them, hear them, sense these men some other way. He lay in wait now, waited for the mistake Pope would make.

And then a sound came — but it wasn't what Billy expected.

Pope's voice was low, and came from the darkness, perhaps thirty yards to the left, at the edge of the tree line.

"Not planning on killing you, Billy Ray, so don't make me do it. But you best listen up."

Billy flattened himself against the ground, did not move, barely breathed, only listened.

"Don't try to kill me, young Billy, I've got good cover. Your brother believed the dwarf, and now thinks you're dead. He's good that dwarf — real good — even I almost believed him. I'll be leaving directly. Only came this way to make sure you don't try to follow. And because, maybe I *want* you to win. This time anyways."

Interesting, Billy thought. *But if he's so sneaky...*

"I want you to know," Pope said then, "I never signed on for all this. That brother a' yours, he's loco. If I'd known ... well, let's just say, I'm a professional. He *said* I was to grab the child and bring him here, then your father would sign over what Horace was rightfully owed. And he *promised me,* the child would not be harmed, no matter what. Now he's in there talking of chopping off fingers, and he *means* it. I believe Horace Ray is completely unhinged — and that you'll need to kill him to save those people inside."

Billy listened to his heart, the blood as it pounded in his ears, and he listened to *all* of his senses.

This Pope is telling the truth.

"Billy Ray — I don't know *what* you're planning to do with that coal oil — smell of that's how I found you, a'course. But if you're planning a fire be careful, there's a woman and child in there." He paused a few seconds then added, "Good luck to you, Billy Ray. I'd stay and help you — but like I said, I'm a professional. I could hang for my part in what's happened, if something goes wrong. Jasper's useless, Clem too I reckon. Horace has hold of the child now. Your father and the dwarf are tied up out of your way. Woman's loose, but Jasper's hands are full of her. Forget about me, you got enough to do."

Maybe Pope was part Indian, Billy decided. He sure didn't make any noise, except when he wanted to.

Billy stayed right where he was, didn't move, just in case.

Hope he don't steal Percy, he thought. *And I hope he don't make a ruckus.*

A minute or so later, he heard the faint sounds of two horses and that nice buggy leaving, as slow and quiet as could be. He felt a grudging respect for Pope now. A bad man, perhaps, but surely not one of the worst.

Surprised he'd take it so slow — but I guess he knows this'll take awhile. Considerate too, to leave quietly, give me a chance.

Then Billy got on with things, quick as he could. And he launched right on into his plan.

He moved quickly now, stopped eighty yards from the barn doors.

Took the bent stick he'd already sharpened, and started digging the hole. Quickly he twisted and turned it, using the bend as a handle, until the thin hole was ten inches deep. Didn't take long, the wet ground made digging easy.

It was still *awfully* dark. The rain was pretty much gone, but the wind was beginning to blow a clear space in the sky to the South.

Billy stayed low, tied the coal-oiled pieces of cloth to

the sticks he had earlier lashed together with rawhide — then he lifted the whole arrangement, and plunged the bottom of it into the hole he'd dug.

And it stood!

"Do your job well, Billy Fire," he said to it under his breath. Then he struck the match, lit each piece of cloth lickety split, and up it all went into flames.

The effigy of Billy was burning, and the real Billy ran helter skelter, forty yards to his left, out of its circle of light. Felt good to run too, it did. From this angle he could not see far into the barn, but he wouldn't shoot anyone inside if a bullet went stray.

Then Billy raised up his Henry, aimed at the doorway and called — in the loudest, deepest, *eeriest* voice he could manage — **"I amm the ghost of Billy RAYYY. Horace, WHYYY did you KILL MEEeeee?"**

CHAPTER 58
"BREATHE..."

Inside the barn, it was Morris who noticed the flames first. To be fair, he had known they'd come, he just didn't know *when*.

Morris counted to two in his head, then said, "What's Pope doin' out there?"

Every face turned toward the doors, then focused on fire.

It was impressive alright, Billy's effigy. Better than Morris expected. The head even looked sorta round. And then came the voice — well, wasn't *that* somethin', the voice.

"I amm the ghost of Billy RAYYY. Horace, WHYYY did you KILL MEEeeee?"

Just about scared the life outta Morris, and he'd been expectin' it.

"What the Hell," Horace cried. "What the..."

Jasper shrank away from the ghostly apparition, struck

entirely senseless in his horror. Only Clem kept his wits, or something close to it.

Clem drew both his pistols, walked to the door, stared out into the night, open-mouthed.

A half-sliver of a quarter-instant later, several things happened at once.

One of 'em was, Billy fired.

But Billy was *not* the only one to take advantage of the diversion. Turned out Cass *had* listened to Morris *a little*.

And this — *this* — was her moment.

Second-last thing went through Jasper's brain was: *"Ghosts are real?"*

Last thing went through Jasper's brain was the bullet Cass fired from her Philadelphia Deringer. Up through his chin, through his brain, and out the top of his head it went, taking fragments of skull and gray matter with it — some of which rained down on Horace.

Horace leaped forward and punched her before she could move, as Jasper's legs crumpled beneath him, and he fell face first to the floor. He was already dead when he got there.

Same time as all that was happening, two cracks of a Henry were heard, and Clem fell to the ground — not a leg to stand on, as the saying goes — for one bullet went into his left thigh, the other his right.

To Clem's credit, he didn't squeal at all — in fact, those inside all assumed he was dead, he lay there so quiet and still.

Billy had heard the bullet fired inside. He hoped for the best and headed for the barn, keeping his rifle on Clem, who still held one of his guns — though the other had clattered away, well out of his reach.

"I'll kill the kid if anyone moves," Horace cried. Sure, he had a tight hold on Tommy, in front of his body — but his gun was pointed at Cass, who cowered on the floor beside Jasper's carcass, her arms up in front of her face. Then Horace backed away, put the child between himself and the doors, the aim of his Colt going from Cass to the doors, then switching from one to the other again, second by second by second.

"Stay down now, Cass," said John Ray very calmly. "Don't you move."

Billy came close to the barn, still off to the left side, where no one from inside could see him. He still had the Henry pointed at Clem, and the older man sorta smiled a weak one. He pushed away his remaining gun, looked up and whispered, "Jasper's dead, Billy. And I guess you got Pope somehow too. Leaves only Horace, but he's got the child. I'm sorry, I've been a weak man. He's loco, Billy, you'll have to kill him. Be careful."

Billy looked through the crack between the left side door and the frame. Saw the whole situation: John and Morris tied up; the woman on the floor to the left; Jasper dead there beside her; Horace in the middle, backing away toward the posts that held up the hayloft. He was using the child as a shield.

Sudden-like, Horace's gun came up, Billy jumped back as it exploded, and the wood of the door splintered away as the forty-four found it, right by where Billy's head had been.

Nothin' wrong with his speed or his eyesight.

"Let the child go," Billy called, and he jumped to his left, as Horace wasted a second bullet.

"You're supposed to be *dead*," the insane Horace cried.

Billy jumped again as he answered, "Why do people keep sayin' that?"

It worked — Horace wasted bullet number three.

He has a second gun on the left, but he'll have to let go of the child if he's to reach it. If he starts thinking straight, he'll get back behind one a' them posts.

Billy knew he had to act fast, the child could get hurt.

"It's me you want, Horrie," he said, and he jumped to his right, but no bullet came.

He's getting sharper now, not wasting his bullets.

"Let the child go," Billy called, "and you and me can shoot it out fair."

"I ain't stupid," growled Horace. "This kid's all I got, and every one of us knows it. I'm walkin' outta here, Billy, with this child in front a' me. Lay down your guns, let me go, and I promise I won't harm the kid." Then Horrie smiled that smile of his, and he added, *"Your kid."*

A numbness went through Billy then, and a single word fell from his lips. "What?"

"Oh, it's true," called Horace, and he laughed like a maniac now. "Tell him, Cass." Then he laughed again before adding, "Oh yeah, Billy, I forgot to tell you today — your darling Cass didn't die in that fire after all. Sorry, musta slipped my mind at the time."

It was Cass who spoke next. "Billy? It really is you? No, that can't..." And her shocked voice trailed off to nothing.

"Weren't expectin' that, were ya, Pa?" Horace laughed. "He was meant to be dead when you got here to see him, but same ol' Billy, still causin' me trouble like always."

"Stay calm, Billy, let your brother leave, it's alright," said John clearly. He must have been shocked to learn Billy was alive, but he sure didn't show it, or allow it to muddy his thinking.

"Come on, Pa," cried Horace. "Let's be *honest* with Billy at least, he's come a long way to see us. Go on, tell him the truth! Tell your *precious* son how I tricked him, and married his girl. Oh, I *enjoyed her,* Billy, I surely did."

"Don't let him get to you, Billy," called his Pa. "Breathe."

And Billy did as he was told.

"Do we have an agreement?" said Horace. "Billy? This is how it goes, good and simple. I walk outta here with your son, and if you follow, I put a bullet through his damn head."

"Noooo," cried Cass — but that brave little boy only looked to his Grandpa, watched the man shake his head slowly. And the child didn't move, didn't struggle, and made no sound at all.

Then Billy stepped round the corner and faced Horace front on, pointing the Henry at his brother's head.

Horace Ray shrank away a little, but he had his back hard against a post. He held the child off the ground now in front of him, as cover for most of his torso. His Colt was cocked ready to fire, and pointed at the head of the child.

Billy's Henry, too, had been readied, and his finger pressed against the hard steel of the trigger. "Seems we got a standoff, Horrie. First thing, you're under arrest. Second thing, if you don't let that little boy go, I *will* put a bullet through your brain."

"Ha," said Horace, "that's funny, little brother. You never could shoot straight at the best a' times. How you gonna do it now, with your son's life at stake?"

"Don't shoot, Billy, please," cried Cass. "He's right, you never could shoot straight."

It was all he could do not to look at her.

Cass. After all this time. Alive. With a son.

But his eyes never left Horace's.

"They're right, son," said John. "Maybe you'd get him, but he'd get off his shot, shoot your son. He's your *son,* Billy. You can't risk it. Let Horrie walk out the door, leave little Tom in whatever town he comes to, and we'll go pick him up there. You'll do that, Horrie, won't you? Promise me."

"Sure I will," Horace said. "Let me go, don't follow, and I'll drop him somewhere and send word. Just let me leave."

Billy *knew* men by now. He *saw* it in Horace's eyes, *heard* it all through his voice — Horace Ray was lying through his teeth.

But Billy said, "Okay, Horrie. I'm laying down the gun, then I'll walk to my left, to where Pa is, and let you walk out. You can blockade the barn doors once you're out, that'll keep us locked in here an hour at least. Agreed?"

"Sure thing, Billy."

Billy leaned subtly forward, saw Horace move slightly backward — he was right up against the pole now, and it *might* slow his movement.

Billy looked into Horace's eyes, slowed down his

breathing, shut out all other movement and sound. "Ready, Horrie?"

"Do it," said Horace.

Billy's supple body bent at the knees, and his left hand came off the Henry, as he lowered it toward the floor with his right. Slowly, so slowly, he lowered the rifle, a foot from the floor; now six inches; now three; now it touched.

And Horace, seeing the moment he'd longed for, turned the Colt toward Billy and fired — into blank air, as Billy leaped away to his left, *landed-aimed-fired* the Henry, in less time than a star takes to twinkle.

And that was how Billy Ray — Billy Fyre now — killed his twenty-first man. With a very deliberate shot that went right where he aimed it. Right through the brain pan of a filthy, murdering, raping, torturing, kidnapping, lying, false-letter-writing, useless, lowdown piece of excrement.

Horace Ray slid down the pole to the floor, in the very same spot he had raped Cass's sister seven years ago, before putting a bullet through poor Annie's brain. He had an amazed sort of look in his eyes — and a real neat hole right between 'em. Then the light went out of those eyes forever.

Finally, justice had come to Cottonwood Falls.

The war Horace Ray started so long ago had finally come to an end.

Billy looked down at little Tom, noticed he was a *part-your-hair-from-the-left man*. And he said, "It's alright now, don't be afeared. Go along to your mother, Son."

CHAPTER 59
JUSTICE

There was a whole lot of emotions let loose in that barn then — and for the rest of the night. They stayed there until morning, for everyone was exhausted. And that tiredness was not only physical.

When, finally, the danger was gone, and Billy was able to look at Cass — *dear, dear Cass, still alive* — he was overcome with emotion.

So beautiful.

He watched her draw the child to her body, watched the tears fall down over her face as she kissed the small boy, hugging the breath almost out of him — but that little boy didn't complain.

And Billy, he just about broke then. A great wracking sob escaped him, and he fell to his knees, laid down his rifle and watched them. Tears streamed from his eyes, and dripped down onto the dirt floor.

Neither Morris nor John said a word. There would be

time. Even Clem had painfully dragged himself about so he could witness the reunion.

"Tommy," Cass finally said, letting go the tight grip on her son, and turning him round to face Billy, so they both could look up at him. "Don't be afraid. That man there is your father. He's Billy. You've heard about Billy."

And her mouth lost its shape as the tears flowed free from her again.

Little Tom looked over at Billy and smiled a shy one. Then in a brave little voice he said, "My own Pa?"

"Yes, Son," said Billy. And the thrill of the very words filled him. He was a hard man filled up with softness, and his love made a great lump inside him.

Cass and Tommy came to him then, swept him up in their embrace — and somehow, to Billy, it felt like the sky did, on the very best nights of his life, before he went away.

For some reason — just for a moment — Billy pictured that old Indian, the one who gave him his first moccasins, and taught him to track.

Somehow, somewhere deep inside him, perhaps Billy had known all along that Cass and the child were here. He *felt* that now. The push and the pull of it, always driving him forward, the inexorable pull toward home and family and truth.

And revenge too perhaps — or if not that, then *justice* at least. Yes, justice, that was more what it was. For *justice* had to be done, so that Billy and Cass might be healed, and others as well.

And now it *was* done, he was Billy again, plain ol' Billy — not a Fyre or even a Ray, just a man who stood for what all good men sometimes must. For *goodness* and *truth* and *rightness* are what men live and die for, and that's what this was.

And it all tumbled over him, through him, the sure beauty of this moment, as he looked in his dear Cass's eyes, then in his son's too.

"He's *your son*," said Cass.

Billy only said, "Thank you." Then he kissed her, just for a moment, the feeling of it almost more than he thought he could bear.

Cass's lips on his own, after all these long empty years.

Then Morris sorta coughed, turned his head, and looked up at John. And in his most mellifluous voice, he said, "Hello, Mister Ray, I'm Morris Brimstone. Heard a lot about you from Deputy Stench-Clothes over there. If he ever bothers to untie us, I'd like to shake you by the hand, Sir."

Billy looked around at his Pa then, and the man was looking right at him, same way he always had, solid. But John didn't say a word, only looked at his son, calm and true as ever, then he nodded just slightly.

Billy caressed Cass's cheek and then Tom's, before going to his Pa, placing his hands on his shoulders, and saying, "Thank you, Pa. A lotta the lessons you taught me kept me alive. Oh, and I brought your Spencer back, but it's down with my pack horse, and I'm sorry for stealin' it. I left it with Morris's Uncle Mike, and he kept it singin' all a' these years for me, so as I could maybe bring it back to you, and—"

"Billy," said John. "Shut up and untie us, will you?"

Then he sniffed a little and added, "Y'know, Morris here's right, you *do* kinda stink."

And the lot of 'em broke up with laughter.

As Cass helped Billy get them untied, he told them all what Pope had said, and why he had left how he had. The others brought Clem inside and made him comfortable while Morris went off to the creek to get water so they could brew up some coffee. Then he went back and brought the horses across, unsaddled and attended to them.

No matter what else has happened, you need to look after your horses, they sure can't do it themselves.

Clem had been lucky alright. At that distance, Billy could without doubt have killed him — but even now, Billy knew the value of a life, and did not take killing lightly. Even shooting his legs though, there was a chance he could have hit the man's femoral artery, but he didn't. Both bullets passed mostly through muscle — County Sheriff Clem Jenkins would heal, and live to stand trial for his part in concealing the Strawheads' bad actions.

They all managed at least a *little* sleep that night.

Although little Tom, once that was all over, slept like a bear does through Winter.

"He's a wonder," said Billy, every time he looked over and watched Tom's little chest rise and fall in time with his breathing.

John sealed Clem's wounds by pouring black powder into them and lighting it up — he bit down hard on a piece of leather as John did it, so as not to wake Tom with his screams. And after, even Clem slept, the pain having finally exhausted him.

As for Morris, that man's ability to go from fast-moving to fully asleep was an absolute wonder. He nodded off within a minute of laying his head on the straw.

Finally, only Billy, Cass and John were awake. They sat around a corner of the hayloft, leaned against two of the walls, feet stretched out in front of them, weary yet unable to sleep. Against a side wall sat John, looking at the others, catty-corner to his left. It made a pretty picture, Cass's head rested on Billy's shoulder, her left hand in his right.

"Pa," said Billy. "D'you think I might keep it for now? The name, Fyre, I mean. If you took it even slight disrespectful, I'd change it back in a heartbeat — but it surely ain't about that. You know that, Pa. You're the best and greatest man I—"

"It's alright, Billy," said John, wearing a wise sorta smile as he raised his hand. "I understand."

"It's just, I'm kinda used to it now, Pa, *and* it's the name I get paid under — well, it's quite a story, how I got the name. But truth is, that ain't the main reason. I feel like that's who I *am* now — I feel like I *am* Billy Fyre."

"Aw, son," said John. "You keep that name, and wear it proudly, you earned it. You were forged in fire, Billy. We all were, I guess — but you and Cass most of all. Keep that name. Why, I'm half inclined to join you in it."

"Thanks, Pa," said Billy. "I knew you'd understand. I will keep it — long as Cass doesn't mind, a'course. I mean, I'm hoping she'll marry me now, so..."

"Of course I will," Cass said, and her eyes sure adored him as she said it. Then she punched him lightly on the arm and added, "But I *expect* to be asked *much* more nicely before I'll say yes for certain."

"I'll think up somethin' special," said Billy, the grin just about splitting his face. "Cass Fyre. *Tom* Fyre. Real nice ring to it, don't you think, Pa?"

"Tom's been called Tom Ray," she reminded them, looking down at the sleeping child.

Then John said, "You know, I reckon Ray would make a fine *middle* name for the boy. Up to you two, a'course."

"I like that a lot," said Billy.

"So do I," said Cass.

"Thomas Ray Fyre," said John with a deliberate nod. "Tommy Fyre. It suits him down to his moccasins."

"And I'll be William Ray Fyre," said Billy. "Us Fyres'll be fancy as the Brimstones, what with havin' so many names. And if you decide to join us, Pa, you'd be John Ray Fyre — and that'd sure be somethin' too. I know you was jokin' about that, but it sure would be fine if you did."

"I'll think some on it," said John.

"New start," said Cass, "for us all. But I think we should get an hour's sleep. It's a new day tomorrow."

CHAPTER 60
TWO RED BANDANAS

※

The previous day, the sun had dawned red as fire on Cottonwood Falls — but today it shone pink, peach and orange, a blanketing glow of soft warmth for them all, and it truly felt like a comfort. It was as if the rain and the wind had washed the place clean, and the whole group felt hopeful, content, as they commenced the ride back to town.

The dead were draped over their horses, and trailed behind where they could be safely ignored. The Strawheads would never again intrude on the lives they had set out to ruin.

John led the way, as it should be. Clem rode a half length behind him, in pain, but he never complained — he knew he deserved what had happened; knew he could never be a Lawman again; knew he had done the wrong thing from the very beginning. But when he told John *why* he didn't tell, kind ol' John Ray at least partway understood.

"Man has to protect his wife," he said to Clem. "And Nell was a fine woman, despite her affliction. Pity so many others had to suffer in the meantime. How will she cope when she hears?"

"Mercifully, she's too far gone to understand," Clem answered. "Barely knows who I am now. Doc wanted to put her in one a' them places, but I chose to keep her home, look after her myself. The widow Driscoll moved over from Emporia to help with her a few months back."

John heard a touch of guilt in Clem's voice when he mentioned the widow. But it was none of his business, so he waved his hand across the sky and said, "Beautiful morning alright." Then he kept looking forward as he rode.

A few yards behind them, Billy rode Percy, but he did not ride alone — his little passenger Tommy was seated in front of him. Billy had let the boy take the reins. Percy had had enough excitement for a month or two, and as long as no one started shooting, he'd be happy to go along quietly. And it sure did tickle Tommy to be the one riding.

Beside Billy, to his left, was his Cass.

She's a wonder. More beautiful than ever. Got a lot to make up to her alright. All these lost years, I'm a long way behind.

He would show her the letter tonight, tell her how the precious letter she wrote had kept him alive — and perhaps, if he was lucky, she might read it to him out loud. Finally, her voice would be strong again in his ears.

"That faded bandana you're wearing," Cass said then. "Surely it's not the same one I gave you—"

"For my sixteenth birthday." Billy touched a corner of it and smiled at her. "A'course it is."

"It's better looked after than that hat I gave him," John called over his shoulder.

They could see only his back, but they knew he was smiling. And Billy had already decided he didn't need a new hat after all — Cass had offered to properly repair it, make it good as new.

Better than new, it'll be.

To Cass's left now, rode Morris.

My dear friend, Morris — he always felt like a brother. But a true one.

A true one.

Cass asked Morris if he was married, and he was explaining how it wouldn't be fair to all the women who wanted him.

"No," he said with a smile, "all I can do is offer each of them a share. Still, they seem to always accept it. Might go visit Susie Jones later. That's six foot of beautiful woman who can't wait to see me, and I tell you, the feeling's mutual."

Cass laughed that wonderful laugh of hers. Billy had sure missed that laugh, and it thrilled him, filled him with joy. Then she turned to Billy and said, "Is this friend of yours telling the truth?"

"It's all true," Billy answered, a protective hand around Tommy as they rode. "You better watch out for that Morris, Cass. Why, he even stole Jenny from me. Has her livin' the high life in a fancy stable in Wilmington, where he visits her every so often and brings her nice presents."

"Oh, that's wonderful," said Cass. "I was afraid to ask about Jenny."

"She'll make a perfect horse for Master Tom," Morris said, winking at the wide-eyed little boy. "She'll miss me, a'course. But I reckon she might like Tom even better, him being such a fine horseman."

Little Tom's smile spread just about right off of his face then. "Me? My own horse? Oh, thank you, Uncle Morris."

"Long as you look after her proper," said Morris, "she's yours, Tom."

"I will, oh, I will." Then the little boy set a most serious look upon his face and asked, "Uncle Morris, is Jenny the best because she likes us small fellers?"

"Tom!" cried Cass from between them. "You mustn't say..." Then she turned the other way to face Morris and said, "I'm so sorry, Morris, he—"

"It's alright," said the smiling Morris. "He doesn't know."

"But we *are* small," Tom protested, before enthusiastically adding, "When we grow up we'll be big though, won't we, Uncle Morris?"

"Oh dear," said Cass, shaking her head and covering her eyes with one hand.

"I reckon you'll grow up just as big as your Pa, little Tom," Morris said with a laugh. "Big and strong like him and your Grandpa."

"And you will too, won't you?" Tom asked him. "We're brothers, ain't we, we both will!"

Morris's eyes went wider'n dinner plates, his jaw fell

open as he turned to face Billy, and for once in his life he was speechless.

As for Billy himself, he could barely contain his amusement. But he only said, "We'll discuss all that later, Tom, I reckon. Maybe when we're all not so tired. You just be sure to make your Uncle Morris proud, by lookin' after Jenny real good."

"I *promise* I will," the little boy said, and he smiled a wide one at Morris, who smiled right back.

Cass mouthed an apology to Morris, then looked around at Billy again. "Exactly why *did* you leave Jenny behind? I can scarcely believe such a thing."

"She was afraid of gunfire."

"Seems very *sensible* of her," said Cass, giving a little wave to the excited Tommy.

"And *this* here wonder of a horse," Billy said as he stroked Percy's neck, "ain't afraid of nothin' that moves through the air, on the ground *or* in water. Even *wanted* to come to the war, so he reckoned. So, I named him after my fast-movin' friend here, and we went off together to fight."

Cass gave him a strange little look, like she didn't believe him. "Your horse is called Morris then, is he?"

"No, not that," said Billy, winking at Morris before looking back to Cass. "See, them Brimstones that unleashed Morris on all womankind, they ain't like us regular folk, not at all."

She laughed again, said, "How so?"

"Well," Billy told her, with a perfectly straight face, "the Brimstones all has middle names, and nicknames, and family names, and all sorts." Then he covered Tom's ears and — quieter on a couple of the words — said, "So this horse's full name is Bandy Big-Head Sawed-Off Stink-Fart The Second. But mostly I just call him Percy."

"Oh, you," she cried.

"Percy's my middle name," Morris explained. "But Deputy Stretched-Out Streak a' Squirts here, he's been all fixated on me since the very first moment he met me. Can't blame him I guess. Keeps tryin' to be as much like me as he can, you see? So stealin' my middle name for his horse musta seemed like a good place to start."

Billy let go his son's ears then and pointed a ways up ahead, where a lone rider crested the hill at a leisurely pace. "Eyes up, Tom," he said. "That there's our friend." Riding toward them, both his hands raised in greeting, was the unmistakeable form of Tiny Jones on his Clydesdale.

The sun and a few puffs of wind were doing their best to make horse and rider look even more special than ever.

Tom drew in a sharp breath. "Is he a King, Pa?"

"Might be some day," said Billy. "But for now, he's a Prince among men."

"Do Princes wear crowns, Pa, like Kings do? Does he have one on under his hat? Is that really a horse that he's riding? How come it's so big? And why is the hair on its legs all long like that? And why does—"

"Woah, son," said Billy — and Percy stopped right where he was, thinking Billy meant him, so the others all stopped too, even John and Clem. "You sure do ask lotsa questions, Tom. I reckon that was maybe too many to ask all at once."

"Ma says askin' questions is how to learn things. But

Grandpa told me we learn best from watching, so I always make sure to do both. You can ask *us* questions too, Pa. If you want to learn things, I mean. It's *much* quicker'n watchin', you know."

"Alright then," said Billy, looking from Tom to Cass beside him, then to Morris, then John and Clem, and finally back to Tom. "What's your favorite color then, Tom?"

"Red, a'course. I got a red bandana from Ma for my birthday, I wear it most days."

"Just like mine," Billy answered, looking adoringly at Cass, whose eyes adored him right back as he touched his own bandana. "See, your Ma gave me this one."

"Yours is *pink,* Pa. The Lewis twins is both girls, and that's *their* favorite color — and they're *girls,* Pa!"

"It's red," said Billy.

"If you say so," said Tom, "but it sure looks pink to me, and I reckon them two girls'd like it, that's all I'm sayin'."

"It's red," Billy cried as the others all laughed it up. "It's just faded some is all. Alright now, let's see, another question — what's your favorite food then?"

"That's easy," said Tom, turning his head to grin cheekily up at his Pa. "Pie, a'course! And BlackBilly pie's my favoritest pie, same as yours."

"Black...?"

"Rosie changed the name of it, Son," John told him, "in honor of some young fool who run off to the war. Maybe she missed you or somethin', I never asked her. Anyway, lucky for all of us, her blackberry pie still tastes just as good as it always did."

"Is she well?" Billy asked. "I missed her so much."

"She's my Granny," Tom said.

Billy's eager eyes darted to his Pa's — but John Ray answered the silent question by knitting his brows and shaking his head momentarily.

"Any more questions, Pa?" said Tom. "Your friend the Prince is almost here, and I got some questions for him, so you best hurry up if you got some."

Billy looked up ahead, saw Tiny Jones was just fifty yards away now. "I only got one question, Tom, but this one's important."

"It's not about you wantin' Jenny back, is it?"

"No, Tom, she's your horse forever. But I ... I wondered if you might allow me to go to church with you this comin' Sunday, and see if the Preacher there wouldn't mind marrying me and your Ma up all proper-like, so as I can come home and live with you always and forever? That be alright with you?"

Billy was shaking a little as he turned to his left then, looked into Cass's soft eyes, and she took his hand as she smiled.

"I don't know," said Tom. "You won't eat my share a' the BlackBilly pie will you? Rosie told me you could eat a whole pie all to yourself, even when you was little."

"Rosie'll cook *twice* as much pie, if I come home to live, and we'll *both* get extra," Billy told him, running his free hand through his son's hair.

"That's settled then," said Tom. "You can get hitched together on Sunday, long as we get two pies."

CHAPTER 61

HOME FIRES BURNIN'

As the biggity Tiny Jones arrived on his swacking great horse, the little boy who would soon become Tommy Ray Fyre turned toward him, stuck out his jaw and said, "My Pa says you're a Prince. You got a crown on under that hat? How come you're so big? Is that really a horse? I got my own horse, her name's Jenny. You want we should go for a ride together sometime? Do you go to church? You can come see my Pa get hitched up to my Ma if you want. Why is your beard that bright color? Red's my favorite color, what's yours? My Pa says he likes red too, but I think he likes pink best. Don't tell folks about that one, I reckon, I think pink's really for girls. Hey, can you even talk? You sure don't say much, do you?"

"It's alright, Tiny," said Billy to the massive, wide-eyed, conflusterated feller, and playfully squeezed his son's cheeks together to stop him from speaking. "This here is my son, his name's Tom. When he asks too many questions at once, just don't answer at all, that's what I do."

"Howdy, Tom," said the deep-voiced giant with a friendly nod of his humongous red-bearded head. "My name's Tiny Jones."

"Tiny? But ... but ... but you ain't..."

Finally, little Tom was lost for words. He just sat quiet then on Percy's back, and looked up at the smiling face of the giant in wonder.

"Tiny, this is Cass," Billy said. "And that there's my Pa, John Ray. You know Morris and Clem already. Cass ... Pa — I'd like you to meet our very good friend, Tiny Jones. He helped us bring the wrongdoers to justice."

John reached across, shook Tiny's hand, and Cass gave him a smile and a wave.

"Joe Gray come to Seth Hays' ranch and telled us what happened," said Tiny, glancing past them to the dead bodies on the horses behind them. Then he looked at Clem Jenkins and added, "I see you got shot up some too, Sheriff Clem. You gettin' in trouble off Billy and Morris?"

"I done wrong, Tiny," Clem admitted, "and I'll be gettin' locked up awhile for it. I'm glad it's all over though. I want you to know, I never had no part in what happened to your parents. It was them Strawheads done that, no one else. And I'm glad of what happened to Horace and Jasper. I'm only sorry I couldn't stop them."

"Alright," said Tiny, nodding slowly.

It was Morris who spoke next, and he sounded some disappointed. "Susie didn't come with you, my friend?"

"Aw, that Sis a' mine," Tiny said. "I'd die of the oldtimer disease if I waited for her. Said she wants to look nice for *you*, she did. Musta tried on every dress she owns a-hundred-eight times. I cain't count but to ten though, I gots to be honest. She be still home tryin' dresses 'til Sunday, I reckon."

"Look," cried little Tom then, as he pointed in wonder at the rider cresting the hill. "Is that a Queen or a Princess, Pa?"

Sure enough, there she was, and a beautiful sight she made too. Susie Jones, urging her gray to a canter. She wore a long flowing white dress that flew out to the sides and behind her, and the sun shone through it in places, as her blazing red hair bounced around, first to one side then the other — for she was not only hatless, her thick and magnificent hair wasn't tied. And the lovely young woman was waving excitedly to Morris, who sure looked happier now.

"Wonders be," Tiny said. "Is that even a dress, or her underthings?"

"Well, indeed," the sparkle-eyed Morris said, with a slight incline of his head. "That bein' a possibility, maybe best we keep such a sight from the gaze of the child. I'd best go along to Susie, escort her back home to get proper dressed."

"So selfless, Uncle Morris," said Cass, and her eyes twinkled too.

"That's me alright, selfless," he answered with a wink. "Besides which, there's things me and Susie would like to discuss, that ain't for young ears to hear. Now Tommy, you look after your parents for me, I gotta go help a nice lady to make her life happy."

In the years that would follow, those were words young Tommy would hear a great many times.

As Morris urged his horse to a gallop to go join Susie, the others got moving again at a comfortable walk. This time Billy took Percy's reins, for Tom was mightily busy, having started up with his questions again.

"Is Uncle Morris gonna marry that fine pretty lady when he grows up?"

"He *is* grown up, Tom," said Cass.

"Then why's he so little and squashed, Ma?"

"*Tom!* You can't *say* that, don't ever say that again."

"But he *is.*" Then he turned around, looked up at Billy and asked him, "And is he my brother or not?"

"He's your Uncle Morris," said Billy, as he tried not to laugh. "Now, he can't be your brother when he's your Uncle, can he?"

"Well, what *is* a Uncle then, Pa? I never had one before."

"I had a Uncle," Tiny Jones told him. "He was my Pa's brother, that's what a Uncle is, Tom."

"That's the truth of it, Tom," said John Ray. "You listen to Tiny, he knows."

"Alright then," said little Tom thoughtfully. "Then if he's my Uncle, that means Uncle Morris is Pa's brother. Right, Pa? Except no, I *know* that ain't right, is it, Ma? On account of you told me that other bad man was Pa's brother, the feller he killed in the barn, bang with the rifle when he jumped and he spun and he tumbled. So what is it really? Which one's your brother, Pa, really?"

Billy looked at Cass first, and then to his own Pa, for

help, but none was forthcoming. She raised her eyebrows, John shrugged his shoulders, Clem looked away, and Tiny Jones pulled a strange face as he tried to work it out. "Be quiet a minute while I think up how best to explain it, Son," Billy said.

They all of them rode along in silence awhile then, enjoying the beautiful morning, the sun, the clear skies, and the happy sound of the birds. And finally, as they crested the hill, saw the town of Cottonwood Falls in the distance, and the Cottonwood River and the railway there in between, Billy finally spoke.

"Tom," he began. "There's all sorts of brotherhoods, different sorts of brothers folk has. That bad man had the same Pa as me, so yes, he *was* my brother. And mostly, brothers of that sort, they care for each other, and love each other all their whole lives. But that one, he had somethin' wrong with him — somethin' wrong in his head, and he done some terrible things, and he didn't have love for no one, only himself."

"He wanted to hurt me. And he tried to shoot you. I sure don't want no brother."

"It's not that simple," Billy explained as they rode down the hill. "He was a bad man, Tom. But if you have a brother one day soon, he won't be like that. Your brother'll be more like Morris, I reckon."

"So Uncle Morris *is* your brother then, too?"

"Uncle Morris is my best friend. We got different parents, but he's more of a brother to me than that bad feller *ever* was. We got a *real* brotherhood, you see? And whatever happens, forever and ever, Morris will always be there for me — and me for him too. And because you're my son, Morris will always look after *you,* and protect you, even lay down his life for you if it ever comes to it — and I'd do the same for *his* family. You see what I'm sayin' now, Tom?"

The child looked to his left at his mother, then at John Ray, then he turned and looked up at Billy again. "You're sayin' he's part of our family, same way you are, and Ma is, and Grandpa, and Rosie and Mary as well, and Charlie the horse, and maybe Jenny if she's so special as you say she is."

Billy's eyebrows raised, quizzical-like. "Mary?"

"Yes, Pa, Mary. She's my great Grandma, you know. But I'm not so sure she's no greater than Rosie, who's only my Grandma not great, exceptin' she is, and they both are."

"Mary *Brown?*"

"She lives with us down in Emporia, Billy," said Cass. "We've a lot to catch up on, haven't we?"

Billy's grin just about split his face then. "Mary Brown," he said. "She's a wonder that woman. What is she, a hundred years old now?"

"Don't you *dare* say that to her," said Cass. "She's not even ninety — still teaches me something new about sewing most weeks."

"Love," said Tom then. Just that one word, nothing else. And his face looked so wise, and his nod so deliberate, he might well have been forty years old.

"What about love?" Billy asked him.

"That's what brothers is, a'course, Pa. That's why Uncle Morris is my Uncle, because you love him. So he's your family. Family's just who you love — right, Pa?"

Billy looked around him — at his beautiful son, his wonderful Pa, and at his darling Cass, right beside him, where she belonged.

Home, he thought then. *I made it home.*

And his eyes filled with tears — but luckily, his son didn't see them.

For Tom was looking ahead once again, facing the future, way he'd been taught to do. "Mister Tiny," the little boy said. "Do you reckon I could ride that big horse a' yours one day? But I reckon you shouldn't ride Jenny, I think she's too small, and you might squish her down, then she'll look like Uncle Morris. Can a horse look like that, with squished legs, but its head still be handsome? And do you reckon Uncle Morris will marry your sister? Him bein' a grownup and all, I guess he might want to, she looks real pretty. If he doesn't marry up with her, do you reckon she might marry *me* when I get a bit older? Then we could be brothers as well, Mister Tiny, and that'd be fine, don't you think? You should talk more I reckon, you got a good big voice, and I like how it sounds. You think maybe one day I might grow a red beard like yours?"

Tom asked the questions, and Tiny Jones did his best to answer one every so often. The others rode along thinking, enjoying the moment, as the great and glorious sun warmed their jubilant faces.

And indeed, Billy saw it was true, what his wise son had said — family *is* who you love. Later, there would be more reunions, more tears, and some massive great helpings of BlackBilly pie. And on Sunday, there would be a wedding, and Morris would stand at Billy's side then — just as he would through the years, through whatever would come.

But for now, we must leave the Fyres and the Brimstones, though we surely have not heard the last of them. There will be many more stories — adventures, a better way to put it.

Because the Fyres — and the Brimstones as well — stand for goodness and justice and truth. And that's what the stories worth telling are always about.

THE END

ALSO BY J.V. JAMES

THE DERRINGER

If seven-year-old Roy Stone had done what his Ma told him to, he'd never have known the truth of what happened at all.

He'd never have seen the double-cross, never have witnessed the murders, never seen the killer's blowed-apart finger. But the poor kid saw the whole rotten thing, and watched his mother die on the floor.

"I'm going to kill you," little Roy cried at the killer – but Big Jim only laughed with contempt.

But that little boy meant what he said – and what's more, he believed it.

He would grow up and kill that big man. That was all that now mattered.

Available as an eBook and paperback.

WOLF TOWN

Cleve Lawson is a man for minding his business. But when he witnesses a stranger murdered by road agents, then the outlaws kill his best friend, Cleve decides it's high time he stuck his nose in where it don't belong.

As if all that ain't problems enough, he meets a tough yet beautiful woman who takes a shine to him – and a feller with fists of iron who takes unkindly to that.

Throw in a murderous road agent gone loco, an unfaithful dog, a wise-cracking Sheriff, and a range war between sheep and cattle men, and Cleve's got more troubles than an unarmed man in the middle of a gunfight.

Available as an eBook and paperback.

Made in the USA
Coppell, TX
13 February 2023

12774047R00288